SEX,
THE NETWORK NEWS

Paul inched closer to Everly and their lips finally met, at first tentative, gentle, as if they were delicately exploring each other's soul.

It felt so right to be with him here. She could feel herself relaxing, responding to the seductive pull of being kissed by someone who seemed to genuinely care about her. She didn't feel he was rushing her. He seemed to be saying with each exquisite kiss that there was plenty of time, that infinite pleasure could be gleaned from this simple yet passionate act.

What had begun as a faint stirring of emotions avalanched into a sudden rush of feelings. Everly stopped herself and pulled back. Not now, she thought, not now.

"What's wrong?" Paul said. "Is this news producer watching the clock?"

"You're right. I have a meeting to get to."

Paul took her left hand and glanced at her watch. "We have almost a whole hour," he said. "An eternity." He moved toward her again, and she pushed him away.

"What?" he said, clearly annoyed.

"I . . . you don't really know me that well. There's so much you don't—"

He touched her lips . . .

Berkley Books by Hilary S. Kayle

WINNERS & LOVERS
PLAYERS

PLAYERS

HILARY S. KAYLE

BERKLEY BOOKS, NEW YORK

This book is a work of fiction. Names
characters, places and incidents are either the
product of the author's imagination or are used
fictitiously. Any resemblance to actual events
or locales or persons, living or dead, is entirely coincidental.

PLAYERS

A Berkley Book / published by arrangement with
the author

PRINTING HISTORY
Berkley edition / July 1991

For information address: The Berkley Publishing Group,
200 Madison Avenue, New York, New York 10016.

ISBN: 0-425-12818-0

A BERKLEY BOOK ® TM 757,375
Berkley Books are published by The Berkley Publishing Group,
200 Madison Avenue, New York, New York 10016.
The name "Berkley" and the "B" logo
are trademarks belonging to Berkley Publishing Corporation.

PRINTED IN THE UNITED STATES OF AMERICA

10 9 8 7 6 5 4 3 2 1

This book is dedicated to
a special group of friends:

Amy Adelman
Nancy Cohen
Lianne Sorkin Fisher
Julia Fraser
Ann Kolbell
Karen Novakoff

They mean more to me
than they'll ever know.

ACKNOWLEDGMENTS

There are a number of people I'd like to thank for bringing *Players* to life. Stephen M. Pollan has long been a "Rock of Gibraltar" for me and his support was particularly significant when I started writing this book. Dan Cohen, my Lancaster friend, was also invaluable during the early stages of *Players* and I am grateful for his help and friendship, and for all of those wonderful late night phone conversations.

I also want to thank my editor, Hillary Cige (who fought the urge to put an extra "l" in my name), for her guidance and support.

My parents, sister, and brother-in-law have always been important anchors for me, but I want to especially acknowledge Emily, Risa, and Scott Posner, my nieces and nephew—not only because I promised them I would, but because they are constant reminders of what is truly important in life.

And finally, special thanks to my friends and colleagues at the *Today* show, where I spent ten of my twelve years at NBC. Even though I left several years ago, "30 Rock" will always seem like home.

ONE

Rrrrring. Rrrrring.

Everly Dalton opened one eye. 5:07 A.M. Oh, God, she thought, grabbing the phone. Who died?

"Hello?" she said.

"What the hell are the Harcrests doing on *Good Morning America*? "

It was Nigel Elliot, her executive producer.

"That's impossible," she answered, trying to be cogent. She was so terrified when she recognized his voice that it took considerable effort to concentrate.

"Jacobson said they were still in mourning—that they wouldn't do any interviews," she continued, determined to sound nonchalant. She was anything *but*. She'd only been on the staff of *Morning* for four months, and the last thing she needed was to be the cause of a major foul-up.

Jacobson was the bureau chief in Frankfurt. The Harcrests had the unfortunate distinction of being the only Ameri with relatives on a Japanese passenger plane that ha mistakenly shot down by the German Air Force. "He said they turned down everyone," she added.

"I don't give a fuck what was said!"

Nigel was such a sweetheart when he got upset, Everly thought.

"The satellite from Europe is up and ABC's got first crack," he continued. "The Harcrests are sitting there getting miked up. That's not exactly what I would call 'mourning.' "

"What would you like me to do about it *now*?" Everly dreaded his answer, but what else could she say? Their show went on the air in less than two hours.

"Get your ass in here, call Jacobson, and *get those people*!"

Before she could say another syllable, Nigel hung up.

Whoever said the Brits were proper and polite had obviously never met Nigel Elliot, master of television news, idiosyncratic wunderkind of America's fourth network—the Empire Broadcasting Corporation—and Everly's boss, executive producer of EBC's highly successful news program, *Morning*.

She scurried out of bed and ran into the bathroom, wondering whether she should bother to wash her hair. No, not enough time. She flipped on the bathroom light with half-closed eyes, trying to blunt the sudden shock of brightness.

Everly Dalton, what have you gotten yourself into, she asked, squinting at the disheveled figure in the mirror.

Exactly what you wanted, she answered.

She often had these internal dialogues. As long as she didn't start talking to herself out loud, she figured she still had her sanity.

Supposedly.

Sanity . . .

It might seem to be an ironic contradiction, but that's what had brought her to New York City six months ago. Coming to the Big Apple and working in television news was supposed to be the solution to all of her problems. A career that puts you on call twenty-four hours a day couldn't leave much time for anything else—at least that's what she'd originally assumed.

She was dead wrong.

Everly threw off her nightgown, pulled her hair up into a shower cap, and stepped into the shower. She tried to ignore the oncoming headache, but she couldn't disregard the sudden undercurrent of panic that threatened to overwhelm her.

Crises never used to effect her this way. On the contrary, she used to welcome them. Give her a problem, a deadline, and she'd beat it.

She wondered when she would get that back—that strong sense of confidence and solidity on which she'd always counted. Most of that was gone now.

Thanks to Jared Kammer.

Jared Kammer, the man she was supposed to marry.

A steady stream of hot water engulfed her body, and her thoughts were diverted by the comforting warmth, but only momentarily.

Jared's face came to mind, like some hovering ghost searching for a place to haunt: the unruly dark brown hair, parted on the side in a vague attempt to bring order where there was none; his blue eyes, made larger by black-rimmed glasses, like strong magnets you could not elude; and the thin-lipped smile, almost a smirk, with the hint of a dimple near his right cheek.

She forced herself to block him from her thoughts.

Was this a sample of what the rest of her life was going to be like in this crazy town—madly racing from one crisis to the next, while at the same time trying to keep her botched personal life from undermining her career?

That had already happened once.

Once was plenty.

She remembered how she used to think about this city before she got here. It had beckoned like a precious jewel, full of intrigue and possibility. New York held such promise. It seemed to be the one place where she could make phenomenal strides in her career and definitively turn her back on the past.

She was half-right.

No matter where you are, the past never seems to disappear entirely—not even in this supercharged town.

Still, New York City was the only place where she had a chance to really make it big and prove something to the people she'd left back home. Where else was she going to become a star on a network news show?

She was working behind the scenes now, and though being a segment producer on *Morning* was no small accomplishment, it was merely the next tier of an elaborate career plan that would bring her fame and clout. The objective was to go from a network news production staff position to an on-air job. This was not an idle pipe dream. Barbara Walters had done it; so would she.

And with a name like Everly Dalton, she was destined to become famous. The name had a special rhythm to it and it was unusual—at least that's what she'd been told all her life, and not just by her parents, but by cousins, aunts and uncles, friends, even people she'd just barely met.

She wouldn't want to let anyone down.

Everly knew she was just ripe to be discovered. She was thirty-two years old and had been in the business for ten years; she had the right looks—five-foot-seven, long brown hair with blond highlights (one often has to help Mother Nature along)—and she had a distinctive speaking voice.

She'd never given her vocal abilities much thought until a journalism professor of hers had pulled her aside after class one day in college.

"You're going to be a star," he said. "Now I don't say that to many of my students, but you have real potential to make it on the air. You've got the looks, you're smart, and you especially have the voice for it, which is unusual for women. You don't sound as if you're ten years old, and you also don't sound as if you're lying in bed wearing a black negligee."

He had a fertile imagination.

"And you don't even have to change your name," he added.

Everly was also aware of her "terrific eyes." Men always made a comment about them. It was uncanny. Even Jared had said he loved looking into her eyes.

Damn him.

With almost no exception, any man she'd ever gone out with, was, at some point, compelled to say a variation of "Did anyone ever tell you what incredible eyes you have?"

How were you supposed to respond to a question like that?

Of course, right now her eyes were bloodshot—not a pretty sight. Most of the time they were blue, but they did occasionally change colors—gray, green, hazel—cat's eyes.

But Everly wasn't catlike. Even though she took great pride in that, part of her acknowledged that this could be a major weakness. She had never clawed her way to the top; she wasn't sly or devious. People always told her they knew precisely what she was thinking simply by looking into those "terrific" eyes of hers.

She'd have to work on that.

Everly hopped out of the shower, wrapped a towel around herself, and ran a brush through her slightly damp hair. Some star, she thought, looking briefly at the foggy image in the mirror.

There was no time to waste. All her marvelous plans for the future were totally worthless if she didn't get those darned Harcrests on the air.

She raced to her closet and pulled out a pair of jeans and a sweater. The bedroom clock said 5:30.

An hour and a half to air.

She must have been somewhat demented to be fantasizing about all of her convoluted career plans *now*. But, then again, one had to be a little crazy to survive in this business.

Clearly that was one of the job prerequisites when she'd been hired at *Morning* in the first place.

Everly was a veritable fashion plate that day. It was critical not to look like some unsophisticated hick from the Midwest. She was a firm believer in that fashion tidbit "Dress for where you want to be." The designer suit she wore had cost a month's salary. It was the most expensive thing she owned—teal-blue raw silk with matching bag and shoes.

She sat on the edge of her seat in the reception area, trying very hard not to get wrinkled. Or look desperate.

"Everly Dalton?"

Everly nodded at the young receptionist.

"Neat name. Is it real?"

"Far as I know," Everly said, trying to be cordial. The receptionist looked barely post-adolescent, yet here she was with a full-time job at a major network. Everly couldn't help but assume that either she was related to someone important or she was putting out.

Cynical?

No kidding. But Everly knew only too well about the "casting couch" and nepotism. Just five months ago, almost to the day, she had been about to move from a midday news anchor job to hosting her own local talk show when Jared Kammer pulled his great disappearing act. He'd been her station manager for a year, and after a ten-month courtship, they were going to get married. A job offer for him with one of the networks in Chicago temporarily delayed the nuptials, or so she thought. The idea of a long-distance marriage didn't thrill her, but she was willing to give it a chance after he got settled.

He got settled, all right—with the daughter of the network's chairman of the board. His future was assured.

And so was Everly's . . .

She then went through the most humiliating and painful time in her life. It was bad enough returning the gifts and canceling the wedding and honeymoon plans. When she couldn't even get out of bed in the morning, she knew that she'd fallen pretty low.

A few good friends, particularly one who happened to be a social worker, helped her regain some semblance of a balanced existence, as did her determination that Jared wasn't going to destroy the rest of her life. Unfortunately, she'd had to put her career on hold. The station did what it could at first, but she had to forgo the talk show job. She wasn't ready for that kind of showcase under the circumstances, and they went ahead with a replacement.

That was hard. Everly promised herself she would never let anything like that happen again. Once she was feeling better, it was clear that she had to get out of there—fast.

New York, with its prestige and glamour, was the answer.

Of course, getting a break in this town was almost impossible. Everly tried everything—contacts, friends of friends, contacts of friends, letters, cold calls. What she really wanted was to get on the staff of a network show. Then she could work up to getting back on the air. She knew she needed time to regain her confidence before facing a camera again. Trying to do that in front of millions of viewers didn't seem to be the right approach.

She'd already done the local reporter stint in the boonies—being at the mercy of some hack news director assigning her to the disaster of the day, having to stick a microphone in the face of the sobbing mother whose kid had just fallen off a fire escape. Everly had also co-hosted several two-bit talk shows with boring guests and silly program themes. There would be no more of that.

This time, she'd gather her strength in a different way—working behind the scenes. She'd find out who to align herself with and who to avoid. She'd learn who the real decision makers were, make the right connections, and then debut "in the big leagues."

Everly had scrupulously analyzed the network talk shows and decided that *Morning* was her best bet. *Today* and *Good Morning America* were still king, but *Morning* occasionally gave them the ol' run for their money. She didn't want to go near *This Morning*. CBS's attempts to crack the A.M. market were the kiss of death for most on-air folks. Just ask Phyllis George. Or Mariette Hartley. Or Kathleen Sullivan.

For weeks Everly had been trying to get an appointment with Nigel Elliot, and he'd finally agreed to meet her.

The badgering had paid off.

It wasn't quite clear whether or not he actually had a job opening, but Everly leapt at the chance to meet this legend of broadcast television. She had to make him hire her. Of all the producers in town, he was the most eccentric, and therefore the most likely to give her a shot at eventually getting back on the air—provided she paid the right dues.

Meeting him certainly couldn't hurt.

The receptionist pointed vaguely behind her. "Last office on the right," she said. "Jenny Spiegel will show you in."

Jenny, Everly knew, was Nigel's secretary, though she had made it quite clear when they first spoke several weeks ago that she was his "senior production assistant."

Right.

And Everly was the Pope.

Jenny Spiegel turned out to be another young thing—early twenties, Everly guessed—casually dressed in jeans and a gold-studded black sweatshirt. She sat at a desk near what Everly assumed was Nigel's office.

Jenny was meticulously filing away at her nails as if she were performing brain surgery, so it was a few moments before she acknowledged Everly's presence.

Some production assistant.

"Yes?" She peered at Everly over a pair of tortoiseshell glasses, which had slipped toward the end of her nose. A tidy ruby-lipped smirk was plastered across her heavily made-up face.

"I'm Everly Dalton. I have an appointment with Mr.—*Ack!!*"

A cold spray of liquid shot out of nowhere and left a trail of water stains on Everly's precious silk jacket. "What the—"

"Send 'er in!" yelled a voice from the inner office.

"He's all yours," Jenny said. "Don't worry, it's just a water gun. He does that with everybody."

Does he pay for dry cleaning, too, Everly wondered, stepping tentatively through the doorway.

She almost took a double take. It was hard to believe that this was the office of one of the top television executives in the country, let alone the man who held the answer to all her problems in his hands.

Four televisions on the wall in back of her were silently spewing out the fare of the day. Two large upholstered sofas dominated the room, and they were swarming with all kinds of stuffed animals—teddy bears, rabbits, cats, dogs, sea creatures, and a frighteningly realistic gorilla.

Wooden duck decoys and piggy banks of varying sizes adorned the bookcases that lined the walls—there were few books to be seen—and half of Nigel's desk was covered with an array of plastic windup toys. Haphazard piles of paper took up the rest of the desk space, save a small corner for the phone console and a notepad. A miniature basketball hoop had been installed on one of the nearby light fixtures, and a well-used dart board, adorned with a photograph of Harvey Markfield, the president of EBC News, was poised behind Nigel Elliot's head.

The whole effect was that of a two-year-old's abandoned playpen.

Nigel was leaning back with his feet on the desk, both hands clasped, combat style, on a garish pink water gun. He was aiming at the television sets behind her.

Everly fought the impulse to duck.

"Blasted game shows," Nigel said, a thin stream of water passing over her right shoulder.

"Are you sure this is a good time?" Everly asked. She didn't want to compete with some ridiculous water game during one of the most critical interviews in her life.

"Absolutely!" he said. "Sorry." He put the gun down, placed his feet on the floor, and stood up to shake her hand.

He was much taller than Everly had expected, and not particularly attractive. His features were bland: shoulder-length, stringy, dirty-blond hair that clung to a receding hairline; pale, clammy-looking skin; nondescript lips that were barely discernible from the flesh around them; a small, slightly hooked nose; and hooded gray eyes that drooped owl-like behind old-fashioned aviator glasses.

His homeliness made him seem approachable. Something inside Everly relaxed.

A good sign.

"Been in the States so long, I've nearly lost all my manners," he said. "Bloody hell actually living in this maddening city, but it's worth it, I suppose. Nigel Elliot." He put out his hand.

"Everly Dalton."

"Yes," he said. "Lovely name."

It never fails, Everly thought.

He smiled and gestured for her to sit down in one of the two leather chairs across from his desk.

"So, how can we make it better?" he asked, sitting down.

"What?"

"My show—*Morning*. You *do* watch the damn thing."

"Well, of course, but I—"

"Then what would you do to make it better?"

For a moment Everly fantasized about telling him to put her on the air, that *that* would solve all of his problems, but those kinds of balls she didn't have.

And she also knew she wasn't ready—not yet, at least.

"You think it can be improved?" she asked.

"Now, now, dear. If I wanted bullshit, I would have handed you a shovel." Nigel gave her an angelic smile.

"So, you really want my opinion?" Everly asked, stalling for time. Her interview preparation was all for naught. She'd planned to regale him with clever stories about her years with local television in the sticks. This question took her by surprise.

Everly subsequently learned that it was one of Nigel's favorite interviewing ploys. In truth, he rarely gave a damn about the answer—it was more for effect.

It worked.

"I guess I'd make a change with some of the talent," she said. Might as well plant a seed in the right area—she didn't have anything to lose at the moment. Perhaps he genuinely wanted a fresh approach.

"Anyone in particular?" He leaned back, a rather suggestive lear insinuating itself on his malleable features.

Everly took the plunge. "Yes. You should get rid of Morganna Stewart," she said confidently. "All she really has going for her is the family name. Just because her brother is a U.S. senator doesn't mean she's a great consumer reporter." She wanted to show that she'd done her homework.

"Yes, well, I'm afraid you're not the only one to say that. Of course she's been such a fixture around this network. This was the last place they could dump her," Nigel said. He put his feet back up on the desk and clasped his hands behind his head.

"So, what would you do with our lovely Morganna—kick her out or just shove her to the side?"

"I can't imagine what else she'd be good at doing . . . unless—"

The phone rang. Nigel waited a few seconds and Jenny buzzed him. He flipped an intercom button on the phone console, an undeniably eager look on his face. "Yes?"

"Phil Goodwin from the *Post*."

"I'll take it," he said, his voice full of glee. He glanced at Everly. "This will just take a moment," he said. "I *always* have time for the press. They can be incredibly royal pains, but it helps if you know how to use them. It's especially good to have them owe you."

She nodded in agreement. Though she didn't exactly welcome the interruption, it would give her some time to come up with a few ideas about improving *Morning*. It would also be a good opportunity to watch Nigel Elliot in action. His relationship with the media was legendary. Whenever the press needed a juicy quote about any aspect of the television news business, they automatically called Nigel. He always made good copy.

She just might learn something.

"So, Phil, what's the word? . . . You're kidding! No, I hadn't heard that." He looked at Everly and winked, clearly enjoying the fact that he knew some bit of gossip that she didn't.

"Oh?" he continued. "I see . . . Well that's quite extraordinary . . . That, too? You must be joking! Look, if they think a new set is going to get them ratings, they're living in dreamland. It's just an excuse. They're stuck with the talent they have and they've got an executive producer who doesn't know shit about television."

Remarkable how a British accent can make even expletives sound refined, Everly thought.

"Can you quote me? Phil, what a question! Of course, anytime." He hung up the phone.

"Now, where were we?" he asked.

Everly had hoped he would share a hot tidbit or two with her, but that apparently was not on his agenda.

"I was talking about talent—"

"Oh, yes—Morganna Stewart," he said. "Interesting that you should mention her, rather prescient of you, actually."

"What do you mean?"

"Just stay tuned, Everly, my dear, stay tuned." He smiled conspiratorially at her.

For a moment, Everly was panic stricken. What if he wanted *her* to take Morganna's place? It wasn't the right time. As it was, she thought it would be tough enough explaining why someone with her on-air experience would want to change gears in the middle of a promising career.

She kept her mouth shut.

Nigel shuffled through the piles of material on his desk and extracted a single piece of paper. "I see from your résumé that you've done a lot of on-camera work."

Here it comes, she thought. She nodded her head. "Yes, and—"

"And some field work—camera crews, editing, writing and whatnot?"

"Well, actually, I—"

"Good," he said. He opened a desk drawer and pulled out some darts.

"Do you play?" he asked.

"Not really," Everly said.

"Give it a go." He handed her a dart.

What kind of an interview was this? Of course it was better than a casting couch. She aimed at Harvey Markfield's nose and said a quick prayer before releasing the dart.

Bull's-eye.

She was as astonished as Nigel.

"Bravo!" he said. "Now you're not pulling my leg here, are you—about not playing much? Come now, confess to Uncle Nigel."

Everly laughed, pretending it was all a big joke. Was he for real? She wasn't about to call him Uncle Nigel.

"Here you go—have another pop," he said.

Once again Everly took aim. Please, God, don't let me down, she thought. If everything came down to this one lousy dart, she *had* to win. She wasn't asking for much—what was one more measly bull's-eye in the general scheme of things? She'd been through such horrendous times. It wasn't as if she was asking for something frivolous, like a Corvette.

Everly threw again.

Her prayers were answered.

Maybe she should have asked for a Porsche.

"Good God, woman! You're a natural!" Nigel said. "You're hired!"

"What? You're kidding!"

"Of course I'm kidding," he said, smirking.

What a strange man, Everly thought.

"Had you going for a minute, eh?" Nigel said as he put the darts away. "Actually, there are a few more things I'd like to ask you."

"All right." But it wasn't all right. She felt mildly nauseated but hid behind a brave smile.

"What do you think of Lester Kay? What is his reputation like 'out there'?"

That threw her. Lester was *Morning*'s book critic. He was on the air several times a week. Sometimes he interviewed authors or simply reviewed books. Other times he did stories about the publishing industry. He was a well-respected writer of several books on the English language, and he'd been in the broadcast business for years—all of which made the question seem rather suspect.

Only later would Everly understand the significance of Nigel's inquiry. But at the time, all she knew was that

Lester was the venerable "gray eminence" on the program, professorial but avuncular, quite capable of reaching the masses with his friendly manner. She even envied his on-air style.

"I think he's good—"

"Compelling?"

"Certainly interesting, but—"

"Yes, but does he draw you in?" Nigel leaned forward, as if the future of his very livelihood depended on her answer.

"Well, I can't say he forces me to change the channel."

"Ah, I see . . ." Nigel paused a moment, quietly scrutinizing her from behind his large glasses. "Could you write for him?"

"I thought he wrote all of his own material."

"Of course you did, darling, and he often does. But do you think you could write for him—if you *had* to, if he absolutely *needed* you."

"Certainly," Everly replied. She was ecstatic, but she tried to sound detached and professional. "It would take a bit of time to write for his ear, but I know I could do it."

She hoped she didn't sound as if she were pleading.

"Good answer," Nigel said, a broad grin creasing his features. "Now, let me ask you this: how is your vocabulary?"

"Fine," she said, immediately feeling tongue-tied. She knew Lester Kay was a fanatic about correct language use.

"Um . . . let's see now . . . define 'propaganda.' " Nigel relaxed in his chair, clearly satisfied with the little challenge he'd tossed her way.

"Right. 'Propaganda.' " Everly closed her eyes and thought a moment. The muses were with her. Almost immediately she answered, "Dogmatic treatment of political ideology."

She stared at Nigel boldly. If that answer didn't get her the job, nothing would.

"Excellent," he said. "Quite impressive! Welcome aboard—and this time I mean it."

He stood up and they shook hands.

Everly didn't know what job she'd just accepted, what the salary was, the benefits—she knew nothing. But it didn't matter. What she'd gotten was a second chance.

"Plan A" was in effect.

Best of all, as she grasped Nigel's hand, she had a sudden premonition that Jared Kammer was going to strongly regret the day their paths had ever crossed.

It was just the beginning.

Two

6:04 A.M.

Everly sat in the back deck of the control room trying to place another call to Germany.

Every studio control room has its own particular personality. Before going on the air, *Morning*'s control room was like a holy sanctuary. It was quiet, not brightly lit, its front wall a mass of television monitors and technical light panels glowing like a forest of votive candles. Something about the semidark atmosphere made people talk in hushed tones—until they went on the air, that is. Then it was a real sideshow.

This morning, something was different. Tension added a definite layer of panic to the normally subdued atmosphere. People were frantically scurrying around, trying to do their jobs even though the first half hour of the show was still one big question mark.

Everyone was depending on Everly for the answer.

It took an enormous amount of concentration and effort to keep calm. High stress was definitely not Everly's favorite mode of operation.

"Yes, operator . . . I'm calling from EBC News in New York and it's a news emergency," she said.

"I'm sorry. The overseas lines are tied up—"

"But this is an *emergency*! Please," Everly added, "my job's kind of on the line here." This was not an exaggeration. If she didn't get the Harcrests, unemployment was a plausible alternative. She knew Nigel didn't take well to losing a big story. It was easy to envision his firing her on the spot along with the entire Frankfurt bureau.

"I'll see what I can do. I'll call you back as soon as I get through to the connection."

"Thanks, operator."

There was nothing else to do but wait and hope the phone would ring any minute.

Everly hated having to depend on other people. At a small local station, you had fewer staff members and therefore did a lot of things yourself. At the networks everyone was slotted into a very specific job function—bureau chief, executive producer, researcher, associate producer, writer—which meant spending too much time waiting for someone to take care of his or her responsibilities before you could take control of any given situation.

If Ed Jacobson had done his job properly, she wouldn't have gotten into this mess.

And time was running out.

Everly glanced up at the television monitors on the wall—anything for a diversion. The show's co-hosts, Glen Korbett and Corah Washington, were on the set in the studio. Everly couldn't deny the growing sense of envy she felt as she watched them.

Glen had certainly paid his dues, though his thick black hair and blue-eyed boyish looks belied his years in the business. A field reporter from the Southwest who had chucked a career as a college professor, he'd worked his way up to increasingly larger markets and, after a stint at the State Department in Washington, had come up to New York four years ago to host *Morning*. A lone anchor didn't seem to hold onto much of an audience, however, and the subsequent decline in ratings brought his co-host, Corah Washington, to the show two years later.

Her background was quite another story.

In the late seventies and early eighties, she was one of the highest paid black models in the business. Just as she was hitting her photogenic peak, she became a television actress. After a short-lived career starring in a nighttime soap opera, Corah was hired by EBC's news president, Harvey Markfield. It had created quite a stir—an actress co-hosting a news program, and a *black* actress as well—another first for a network morning news show. The salespeople assumed *Morning* would lose massive affiliate stations when she came on board, but they were wrong.

Corah and Glen had an uneasy alliance. Though they rarely socialized outside of the office, they were well aware of their professional interdependence—they had terrific chemistry on the air together.

As Everly watched them on the monitors, she was amused to observe their profoundly different off-camera approaches to their jobs.

Ever the newsman, the impeccably dressed Glen Korbett was going through his morning paper ritual: combing through *the New York Times*, *the Daily News*, and the *Washington Post* He kept nervously checking his watch for the time, even though there was a huge studio clock in front of him. Everly was sure he was wondering who the hell his interview guest would be at the top of the show.

Corah, on the other hand, still cognizant of her *Ebony* cover girl and actress days, was simply primping in front of the cameras.

Her hair was arranged in a profusion of dark curls wildly framing her face. Her skin, the color of roasted almonds, was contoured professionally with a deep rust blush, and her exotic dark brown eyes were rimmed with a smudge of kohl blue. She wore a black-and-gold suit that epitomized the understated elegance unique to outrageously expensive custom-designed clothing.

Corah was one of that elite group of stunning women who knew they were constantly being looked at. It was expected.

Her every movement was controlled and languid. As she studied herself from different angles in a hand-held compact, one couldn't help but think of a preening lioness.

As the minutes dragged by, Everly was keenly aware of the absence of the usual morning chatter. The silence around her only emphasized the undercurrent of tension in the room. They'd be on the air in less than an hour, and they still weren't sure of the show's rundown.

Out of the corner of her eye, she noticed Nigel, who was a few seats away, glaring over at her—waiting for some kind of answer. But there was nothing she could do until she heard from one of the overseas operators.

Everly had already tried to get through to Jacobson, but he was absent from EBC's setup in Berlin and was nowhere to be found. The only thing she could do was try to reach the Harcrests directly herself.

Fortunately, their news desk had all of the important phone numbers for everyone temporarily stationed in Berlin for this story, including a special office that Air Japan had set up. The airline, in a wise public relations move, had arranged to bring the families of those who had been killed to Berlin for a special memorial service.

A surprising number of countries besides Japan had been represented on the flight—Korea, Australia, Canada, France, Switzerland, the Philippines, England . . . but only one American family: one of the Harcrest's sons and his wife, who were traveling with their two-year-old son. It was a heartbreaking story, and as is ever the case with an increasingly voyeuristic country, the entire nation wanted to see the grieving parents.

Everly had assumed that at this point, if Air Japan couldn't connect her to the Harcrests, no one could.

Although all four networks had flown in special reporters several days ago, *Morning* had no specific presence there. Adding to the frustration was that fact that it was rare for their evening news program, *Evening News Worldwide*, even to think of booking anyone for *Morning*, let alone condescend to cooperate with their getting guests. One had to resort to all kinds of convoluted machinations to get EBC's news bureau chiefs to pay any attention to the morning show. And half the time, that didn't do much good either.

A morning show was often treated as if it were the bastard child of the news division.

Everly's phone rang. She jumped.

"EBC News, *Morning*," she said.

"Good morning, *Morning*!" a male voice bellowed.

She hated when the EBC operators tried to be cute.

"This is your overseas operator," he continued. "I have your call to Berlin on the line. Is this Miss Dalton?"

"Yes, I'll take it."

"Go ahead."

"*Moshi, moshi?*" a distant voice said.

Oh, Lord. She had never even *thought* about the language difference.

Everly pressed on. "I'm calling from the United States—New York! I'm an American. Do you speak English?"

Silence.

Where the hell was she going to find a Japanese interpreter at this hour?

She heard what sounded like a rush of Japanese, and then someone else took the receiver.

Thank God.

"This is Mr. Yasuda. Can I help you?" a clipped male voice said.

"Yes, please. I would be most honored." Somewhere in Everly's foggy memory she recalled that honor was important to the Japanese. She knew she couldn't treat the man on the other end of the phone as if he were just another sleazy PR guy. This was quite different—she was a Western woman and there were major cultural leaps to be traversed in a short amount of time.

"This is Miss Dalton. I'm calling from the United States, from the Empire Broadcasting Company, a very large television company in New York," she said distinctly.

"Ah, yes," he said. "American television."

"Yes, and it would be of enormous help to us if you would grant me some assistance in reaching the American family that you have been most generous to."

Everly couldn't believe the verbal gymnastics she was resorting to here, but her instincts told her that this was the best way to proceed. "Everyone is so very concerned about this tragedy, Mr. Yasuda. We want to give the American public a chance to grieve with this family. It would mean so much to us."

"I understand," he said.

Silence.

"And since we are going to go on the air very shortly, I would like to contact them as soon as possible," she continued. Everly felt like a babbling idiot. It was all she could do to keep from screaming at the dear man.

"Ah yes. You want Harcrests?" he asked, miraculously.

"I would be most grateful."

"Not possible," he said.

"What do you mean?" She heard the panic in her voice and tried to calm down. "You must know how to get a message to them—you are arranging everything for them."

"But you not first. Other lady call few days ago, other network. She explain no one else must bother Harcrest family. She set them up in her hotel. She take care of them. You understand?"

Only too well. Everly had heard plenty of stories about how certain network news bookers had the money to spirit away important guests with first class plane tickets and stash them in hotels to keep them out of reach of the competition. Reading about it when you're in Indianapolis, however, was quite different from actually having to deal with it.

"But we are not bothering them, Mr. Yasuda, I assure you," Everly said. "We have very important people here who want to interview them for the American public. One person alone cannot handle a family's grief," she added, improvising madly. "The more people that the Harcrests can talk to, the better they will feel about losing their children and their only grandson. Surely you can understand that."

"Yes, I understand, but this lady very insistent."

"Who was this lady?" Everly was going to have to go directly to the competition—not a pleasant prospect. It was hard to keep the exasperation from her voice.

"Let me check. Moment, please."

Everly vowed to personally strangle whoever had caused this mess.

Otherwise, she'd hire her.

"I have name," Mr. Yasuda said. "Miss Nancy Pollan."

What incredible luck. This was the very same *Good Morning America* producer who'd spoken at a dinner several years ago in Indianapolis, whom Everly had subsequently kept in touch with. With coincidences like this, Everly couldn't help but believe that there must be a God somewhere.

"That's good news, Mr. Yasuda. Nancy Pollan is a *very* close friend of mine," she lied. "Isn't she at the Hilton there?"

"No, not Hilton. Berlin Grand Hotel."

Her fudging had worked. "Of course, the Berlin Grand Hotel. Do you have that number?"

"Yes, I give to you. 045-973. Miss Pollan in room 1012."

She wanted to kiss him.

"You have been most helpful, Mr. Yasuda. I'm sure Nancy will thank you herself."

"Thank you, Miss Dalton."

The line went dead. Everly clicked the phone and got the operator again.

"It's Miss Dalton in the 5K control room. Can we get another call to Berlin?"

"Hang on. I think we can get right through," a woman said. Once in a while she recognized an operator's disembodied voice. But not this time.

"What's the number?" the operator asked.

"045-973," Everly said.

"Yes. It's ringing, go ahead."

"Ya?" a man said abruptly.

"Berlin Grand Hotel?"

"Ya?"

"Room 1012, please."

"One moment, *bitte*." Everly could hear the phone ringing as the hotel switchboard operator put her through.

"ABC News," a tense male voice said.

Bless you, she thought. "Nancy Pollan, please. It's urgent."

"Who is this?"

"Just tell her it's Everly Dalton," she said, praying that whoever she was talking to wouldn't recognize her name as being one of the "enemy's."

"We're about to do an interview, lady. We're doing a pretape."

"It's an emergency. I'll be quick."

No response.

Everly's headache rematerialized. She hoped she wouldn't get disconnected.

"Everly? How'd you find me? What's up?" a woman said.

"Nancy?"

"Yes. Look, I'm under the gun here. What do you want?"

"I'll save the long story. I need a favor. When you're finished with the Harcrests, do you think you could ask them to stay for an interview with Glen? Our tech people will be over there any minute and we'd like to hook up with them. I know how hard you've worked on this and you've done a terrific job, so I hope you don't mind if—"

"Are you kidding?" Nancy sounded incredulous. Everly wasn't too surprised. "Since when does *GMA* help the competition? Give me a break, Everly! This is the hottest story of the week, and we've got an *exclusive*."

"You've got them first. What more do you want?"

"You want a list? Look, I gotta go, they're signaling from New York."

"Nancy, please, I'm begging!"

"When does Nigel Elliot ever cooperate with *us*? You know, I'm a little sick of picking up the paper and reading about what a waste he thinks our program is. We still beat you guys almost every week."

Everly lowered her voice. "Look, most of what he says is just to get his name in the paper. And this isn't Nigel talking—it's *me*. I *need* this, Nancy. I swear. Our bureau chief screwed up and I'm getting the heat. Please, I'll even make Nigel wait until seven-fifteen to take the feed. This way we can't scoop you, or run it at the same time."

"You're going to owe me for this, Everly. And I mean big."

"Fine, anything you want—it's yours." Everly didn't want to think about the day Nancy would want her payoff—no doubt it would be something major—but she couldn't worry about that now.

"All right," Nancy said. "I'll work it out. But your tech people better haul ass. Gotta run."

She hung up.

Everly could breath now. Making the technical arrangements for this interview was nothing compared to what she'd just been through.

She smiled at Nigel. "All set," she announced. "*Morning* triumphs."

"Marvelous! *When* exactly do we triumph?"

"Nigel, *Good Morning America* had an exclusive. The Air Japan people wouldn't help me, and *GMA* didn't want to give the Harcrests to us at all. We'll have to put them on at seven-fifteen."

"We'll look like assholes!" He slammed his hand down on the table and looked up at the satellite monitor. The Harcrests were talking, but no one could hear what they were saying. "If they're pretaping now, why can't we get them at seven? This is *live* television, in case you've forgotten, young lady. The Harcrest story should open our show! Why do we have to wait?"

Everly forced herself to sound firm.

"Because for some odd reason in this wonderfully amicable world of television news, they don't trust us," she said. "We've got to take what we can get, Nigel, which is a hell of a lot better than nothing."

If this was how he was handling a lousy fifteen minute delay, she could imagine what he'd think about her having made a trade-off.

"Those bloody bastards!" Nigel hissed. "Fine, we'll take it. But don't think I'll forget this," he said, his voice thick with acrimony.

When it came to Nigel's getting revenge, Everly would

never want to be on the receiving end. Up until this point she never had been.

If anything, she'd hoped she'd learned a few lessons.

"Nice job, Everly. You certainly saved the show."

Lester Kay was grabbing some coffee in the greenroom. He looked around the dimly lit room, noted that they were alone, and sat down next to her.

The greenroom was where *Morning* guests stayed until they went on the air. Staff members also came in to grab a doughnut and some coffee, or to escape the control room. It could be a real treat to drop by, because you never knew who would show up—that morning's newspaper headline, the latest overnight star, or the inventor of the next pet rock.

No matter how long Everly had been in the business, she never became jaded about how television brought you into close contact with people that most folks would kill to meet.

Of course there *were* times when you were thrown together with people you had no particular desire to meet at all.

An especially memorable morning for Everly was when they had a woman wrestler on the show. The guest must have weighed at least two hundred pounds. Half of her face was painted with a silver-and-blue flame design; she was clad in a silver lamé leotard, black leather boots, and arm bands studded with silver cleats; and she wore a blue helmet adorned with black ostrich feathers. There were a couple of staffers in the room at the time and a few guests.

Everyone was trying very hard not to stare at the wrestler. They ignored her, pretending she was perfectly normal and that there was nothing the least bit unusual about her appearance.

They all could have won Academy Awards.

Another morning, Glen Korbett came in and began pontificating about the origin of greenrooms. It amused Everly that he occasionally felt compelled to show off his doctorate in English Literature. So there he was, holding court, blathering on about how the greenroom was borrowed from the theatrical tradition.

"Oh, yes, it goes way back," he said, his mellifluous voice rich with authority. "Why, at least as far back as the 1700's, theaters in England had greenrooms for actors to wait in when they were offstage." He made quite a big deal about how they were actually painted green because it was considered a relaxing color.

Some up-and-coming comic was in the room at the time. He was a young kid—kind of scrappy-looking in oversized gray pleated pants and a bright pink man-tailored shirt. He was hunched in a corner, probably trying to get his nerve up before his first network appearance. He knew a good opening when he saw one, so he started ribbing Glen about the precise shade of green that was used.

"Green? What kind of green, man?" he asked in a whiny voice. "I mean, hey, you got mucus green, hospital green, camouflage green. Did they have camouflage green back then? Or maybe it was mint green, or kelly green or hunter green!"

The group that happened to be listening in wasn't sure whether or not they were supposed to applaud when the comedian was finished. Glen did not especially like sharing the spotlight, but luckily there wasn't enough time to worry about it, because the floor manager came running in to hustle them into the studio so their segment wouldn't be late.

There was a palpable undercurrent of hostility between them when they went on the air.

Morning's greenroom was furnished like most others—a makeshift living room with a somewhat battered couch, two Naugahyde chairs, a television monitor hooked into the studio feed, and a coffee table covered with the day's papers and two boxes of doughnuts. A long table against the back wall held a large coffee urn and a pot with boiled water in it.

Every television show had its own particular set of renowned behind-the-scenes characters. For *Morning*, it was the woman who prepared the coffee, Maria Hernandez. She was a somewhat eccentric, petite middle-aged woman who was as much a fixture in the greenroom as the furniture.

She'd come to New York over twenty-five years ago from Puerto Rico and had lucked into a cushy union job making coffee and taking care of the greenroom attached to Studio 5K, which was *Morning*'s home.

" 'Allo, Ever*lee*," she would say in a shrill voice when Everly came in in the mornings. Maria would flash a toothy grin and put her hands on her tiny hips, checking Everly up and down. "You losin' weight or somethin'?"

She never failed to say that to all of the women on the staff. In her eyes, they were always getting thinner and the men were always gaining weight.

Everly watched Lester now as he delicately lifted a glazed doughnut from the box and took a healthy bite out of it. She was puzzled by the compliment he had given her because his segment that day had been bumped for the Harcrest story.

"You serious?" she said. "I know how hard you worked on that writer's block piece."

"After fifteen years, I'm supremely aware of what the priorities are around here. I'll just use it tomorrow." He patted her knee lightly with his free hand.

Lester was one of those people who required physical contact whenever he was around the opposite sex. At first, Everly had found this little habit unnerving. They had worked together fairly regularly when she first joined the staff, so it was something she had had to deal with early on. But she soon realized he was harmless—at least with her.

"I'm just sorry that Ed Jacobson and I got our signals crossed," Everly said. "It was not a happy moment when Nigel woke me up this morning."

"I can think of better ways to start one's day," Lester said, a broad smile enlivening his jowly face.

"Can't we all?"

The phone interrupted their conversation.

"Greenroom," Everly said.

"Is Everly Dalton there?"

It was a woman's voice. Everly could barely hear her through the scratchy static.

"This is she!" she shouted.

"It's Nancy Pollan. Can you hear me? We have a horrible connection."

"Yes; I can hear you." Great, Everly thought. "Hang on a sec." She looked at Lester. "Listen, I have to take this call. It's from overseas and I need some privacy. Do you mind?"

He looked a little hurt, but he grabbed another doughnut and closed the door as he left.

"I'm back, Nancy," Everly said. "How'd you find me here? Our operators aren't that good at tracking people down."

"I figured you'd be in the greenroom since the show isn't off the air yet. As you know—just ask Mr. Yasuda—I always get my man."

"Right."

Everly was grateful Nancy hadn't called her in the control room. She didn't need Nigel getting suspicious. But she wondered why Nancy was calling her *now*.

"Thanks again for the Harcrests. The spot really went well for us," Everly said. "Glen did a terrific job. How did your guys do?"

"I'm sure we'll get some good press, and some good ratings."

Everly could imagine the gloating smirk on Nancy's face as she spoke.

"Listen—about the payback, I was serious, you know," Nancy continued.

Everly knew damn well she was serious. Who did Nancy think she was dealing with? She tried not to sound offended.

"No kidding. I told you I would owe you. I meant it," Everly said.

"We'll talk about it when I get back. I'll think of something."

"Don't lose sleep over it."

Nancy laughed. "Yeah, yeah. With all the craziness over here trying to pin down the story, and then dealing with the time difference all week, sleep is one thing I'm not going to lose any more of now that this is over."

"We'll get together when you're back in the States,"

Everly said, unable to hide the resignation in her voice.

"You bet," Nancy said. "Can you get your operator on the line? I gotta get switched back to *GMA*."

"No problem," Everly said, as she clicked the receiver for the operator to come on and transfer her call.

No problem at all, Everly thought.

For now.

THREE

Whoever said we live in a dog-eat-dog world must have worked in television news, Everly surmised, as she thought about what she'd been through that morning. But this certainly wasn't the first time she'd felt frustrated by the extremely competitive nature of the TV news industry.

Cutthroat rivalry may thrive in other professions, but the intensity of live television combined with the up-to-the-last-minute deadlines of the news business produced an especially ruthless horde of self-preservationists.

Add to this pleasant circumstance Nigel Elliot's penchant for fueling any antagonism that existed at *Morning*, and one had a clear idea of what the atmosphere around there was akin to: a combat zone.

Just take Rolodexes, Everly thought. Every office had them. In television news, where timing was everything, they were especially crucial—particularly when you had a precious commodity like unlisted phone numbers. Making that first call—to a source, a contact, a potential guest—before anyone else, could make all the difference in an industry that was supposed to be on top of the headlines.

Although Everly's Rolodex had always been important to her, it was merely one of many business tools. But in her current job, one could live or die by your Rolodex.

Around *Morning*, where Everly was one of fifteen segment producers, it amazed her that people actually *hid* phone numbers. One of her colleagues even insisted he had no Rolodex—it was all "in his head," or he "looked it up somewhere."

Bullshit.

He had a secret file-card box of contacts locked in his desk.

She'd seen it.

People must have thought there was something terribly wrong with her because as soon as she got an important number, she actually "shared the wealth."

Her reasons were twofold: the venerable "you scratch my back, I'll scratch yours" approach (which sometimes worked) and the practical consideration that she just didn't want the full responsibility of being the only person on the staff of *Morning* who could find Jimmy Carter or Jackie Onassis at any hour of the day. That kind of exclusivity she didn't need.

Then again, she did have another motive for being so forthcoming. It couldn't *hurt* to be good to your co-workers. One had to be exceedingly careful about burning bridges in television, because this year's researcher might be next year's executive producer.

In television news, you never knew for sure which end was up.

Everly was headed toward her office when she heard a familiar deep voice.

"Hey, Everly, how's my favorite renegade?"

Hank Forrest, *Morning*'s senior editor, motioned for her to come into his office.

"Quite a coup you pulled this morning," he continued, absentmindedly fingering his beard. "You could say I was surprised when I saw Mr. and Mrs. Harcrest, instead of that flack from the American Medical Association, chatting with our venerable host. It always throws me when my precious prose gets thrown down the toilet, even when it's for a worthy cause."

"It was nothing personal, Hank," Every said. "For some strange reason, Nigel thought we should include the top story of the week on our show today."

Hank had the thankless task of writing what was called "the continuity" between segments—telling what was coming up or recapping the story that had just aired. He also wrote the first interview of the day. He couldn't do his job until the whole show was in place, so he worked long hours. And because this was the news business with co-hosts and producers who had minds of their own, much of what Hank wrote was misused, or not used at all.

It was no wonder that he was the most cynical person Everly had ever met. And though she and Hank had become almost legendary around the news division for their clever verbal sparring, she was one of the few who knew that underneath all his wicked wit and sarcasm, there was a sweetness about him. He had such a compelling mixture of traits, she sometimes wondered what it would be like if they ever had a romance. She sensed they both feared that it would ruin their friendship.

Perhaps they were right.

"You'd think this was a news show we actually had here," he said.

"You're supposed to know the ropes by now. You've been here for twelve years."

"Don't remind me. Why do you think I have all this gray hair?"

Everly had to laugh at that. In contrast to his dark beard, Hank's entire head was covered with thick gray hair.

"How did you know I had anything to do with the Harcrests?" she asked.

"Nigel gives credit where it's due. That's one thing I'll give him."

Hank had a love-hate relationship with their boss. Everly suspected he'd feel that way about anyone in charge. There was something of the rebel in Hank, yet he knew how to play by the rules. And no matter what the circumstances, he was always low-key.

Physically, there was an oversized teddy bear quality about him that was very comforting. He was a large man, but his genuine warmth tempered his great bulk. Hank was one of the few people Everly had met in this city who instantly made her feel welcome. From the moment they first shook hands, she knew she could trust him.

She debated telling him about Nancy Pollan.

"What exactly did Nigel say?" she asked.

"After the usual tirade about our miserable foreign bureaus, he said that if it hadn't been for you we would have missed the story entirely. I just wish he'd come up with some new adjectives for the overseas gang. 'Inept' and 'incompetent' are getting a bit old."

"Why don't we make a list? I'm sure he'd use it," she said.

"Right. The first thing he'd do is change it. And then he'd want to know why we expended so much energy on it instead of on our *real* work."

"We could say we wanted to provide him with a much needed service."

"Spunky enthusiasm only goes so far, Ms. Dalton."

"I'll make a note of that, Mr. Forrest."

"But there's something much more important we've got to discuss." He avoided her glance and Everly instantly assumed something bad was coming. He'd probably been told to find out what she had *really* done to get the Harcrests. Maybe it wasn't such a smart idea to tell him the truth. She was certain he could hear her heart beating.

"I hope you don't mind my asking this," he said. He looked very serious.

She'd been working there only four months—and it was all about to disappear . . .

"Do you think I should shave my beard?" he asked in earnest.

Talk about surprise.

And relief.

"Are you serious?" Everly asked. "Why would you want to do a thing like that? I think it's sexy."

"That's what I figured. I mean, I do have the reputation of supreme stud around here."

"That's not saying much," Everly said.

"You should try me sometime—but you'll have to get in line."

"Dream on, buddy. But for what it's worth, don't shave. It gives you character."

When she'd first been introduced to Hank, he kept pointing out that he was the only man on staff with a full beard. He wore it as if it were some great badge of masculinity. "I'm the only *real* man around here, the only one who can even *grow* a beard!" he'd say frequently. "Most of the guys in this place are just pussy willows!"

It made you wonder about how men think.

"Well, I was just testing you, Everly," he said, suddenly sounding shy. "You see, I had this date last night and it kind of threw me."

"Oh? What did she do?" She leaned in and whispered, half-kidding, "Should I close the door?" They didn't discuss their personal lives that often. She knew Hank had been divorced twice and that he wasn't seeing anyone special, and he knew about her debacle with Jared Kammer. For the most part, however, when they didn't talk about work, they gossiped about people in the industry. It was safe.

But this was different.

"No, don't bother with the door," he said. "That would only start rumors about *us* . . . Of course, maybe that wouldn't be such a bad idea." He smiled at Everly slyly, and for a split second she couldn't tell whether or not he was joking. Hank was not an easy man to read.

What man was.

"So what, exactly, did she say?" she asked.

"Just some damn thing about how I was hiding behind my beard." He looked down and started toying with a magnetic sculpture on his desk.

"That's not terribly original, Hank. You've heard that line before."

"I know. And this was just our first date. Brother." He shook his head. "Fifty-one and I'm still dating."

"How'd you meet this woman?" she asked.

"In the subway, believe it or not. *She* actually picked *me* up. Nice, for a change. So we ended up having dinner."

"And that's when she got on your case about the beard?"

"Yeah, for a while." He seemed upset. "It was funny at first, then it got to be a real pain. I should have hired her instead of taken her out to dinner. She would've fit right in with all the complainers around here."

"Did she just break up with someone?"

He looked at her suspiciously. "Yes, as a matter of fact. Do you know this Bernice Moran?"

"Hank, haven't you learned? I may only be thirty-two, but I do know a few things. When people break up after being together a long time, or when they get divorced, they're kind of 'mentally ill' for a year or so—"

"Isn't that a bit dramatic?"

"It's the truth. They can't help it. Splitting up is a major trauma, no matter whose idea it is. So the next person who crosses their path usually ends up getting all the hostility that was meant for the absent partner. People don't even realize they're doing it. So if this lady just broke up with someone—be careful."

"How long has it been for you?" he asked, his voice turning soft.

"Almost a year," she said, envisioning Jared's smirking face. She suddenly felt very sad. "How about you?"

"Marianne and I split . . . oh, three years ago, there about," he said. "I sure do pick 'em."

"Well, just watch what you get into," Everly said. She was half talking to herself.

"You know, you could be right about that 'mentally ill' business," Hank said. "I can't believe I got so worked up about her. Hell, who knows if I'll even see this chicklette again."

"Chicklette? You really have a terrific attitude toward women," she said, shaking her head.

"Hey, I married two of 'em. What more do you want?"

He leaned back and put his hands behind his head, exposing his wide girth.

"Well, we better get back to work," Everly said. "And I think that for now, you should keep your beard. It's part of your charm."

"I'll take that as a compliment," Hank said. But he looked oddly vulnerable when he spoke and Everly had a sudden visceral urge to give him a hug. In fact, she was vaguely aroused.

It had been a long time since she'd had any physical contact with a man, much less felt attracted to one. She'd known for a long time that there was something definitely appealing about Hank, but this strong feeling of physical attraction startled her because she'd never truly wanted to think about him in that context before.

"Take it anyway you like," she said quietly, trying not to sound flip. Their eyes locked for a moment and Everly felt an inexplicable connection to him. It was hard to look away, but she did what she knew was best for both of them at the time.

She got up, turned around, and walked out of his office.

"How long have you been waiting?" Everly asked.

"It's been almost eight months. The drugs have bought me time, though. The doctors think I can hold out for at least a year."

Everly was on the phone, in the middle of a pre-interview—her favorite part of the job—looking for guests for the show. It was also a convenient diversion from what had transpired between Hank and her earlier in the day. She didn't want to deal with that.

Work was her great escape.

Kathleen Limona was twenty-nine. She was married and had two young children, ages three and six. And she was dying. She'd contracted a debilitating heart/lung disease soon after her last pregnancy. Without a transplant, she would die.

Talking to her was not easy for Everly. She always wanted to know what drove people, what kept them going. That's why she was a good reporter and a good interviewer. But dealing with someone who was seriously ill was difficult because of the pain and emotion you encountered. You had to steel yourself if you wanted to get a story. It was part of the job.

Everly had found Kathleen through a magazine article—one of the many sources for *Morning*'s program suggestions. She was the third person to be pre-interviewed, and after a few minutes, Everly knew she was going to be the main focus of the story.

"Do you jump every time the phone rings? I think I'd be a basket case," Everly said.

"Sometimes . . . it depends. When we first came out here I assumed that every call would be the hospital telling me that they'd found a donor. You can't imagine how tense it was around here then, but after a while, you just try to be as normal as possible. I always have my beeper with me, no matter what.

"We actually had a false alarm a few months ago. Some teenager had been in a motorcycle accident—the majority of the donors out here are motorcycle accident victims—anyway, he was brain dead, and his parents finally agreed to donate the organs in his body that were still in one piece. We raced over there for tests as soon as we got the call, but it turned out that his heart and lungs were too big for me. Someone else in the program—a young man in his twenties, in fact—was a more compatible recipient, so that was that . . ."

Her voice trailed off.

Everly had spoken earlier to one of Kathleen's doctors at Stanford University Hospital. They had one of the top heart and heart/lung transplant programs in the country. There was no reason to discuss the reality of her chances for survival. The problem was finding donors before it was too late. She was sure Kathleen knew all of this as well as she did, but Everly sensed that this was a woman who sincerely believed she would beat the odds.

"He's doing fine now," Kathleen added. "It just wasn't meant to be for me, I guess."

She stopped talking.

Everly didn't want to keep pressing her for details, but that's what she was getting paid for. "What's it like to be competing with other people in the program for hearts?" she asked.

"It's not quite like that. We're all different body and blood types. They're very careful about that sort of thing when they select you for the program to begin with. All I know is, when it's my turn, I'll be ready."

Everly wondered how many people died while waiting for a donor, but she obviously wasn't going to ask that question.

"Well, Kathleen, as I mentioned earlier, I've spoken to a number of people this morning. As far as I'm concerned, you're it. We want to tell *your* story.

"Logistically, we'd come out there with a camera crew—two people besides myself—tape you and your family, and interview you with your husband. Your kids are kind of young, but we'd like to interview them, too, if that's okay. We'd also talk with your doctors to round out the story. What do you think?"

"That's fine," she said. "The more we can do to tell people about donating organs, the better. It's strange, before all this happened, I was a pretty private person. That all changed when I came out here. I'm not sure why. It was a good experience to be interviewed for that magazine article. I want to believe that it will make a difference. And I'd be happy to help you in whatever way I can."

Even after being in this business for ten years, Everly was constantly amazed how private individuals were so willing to open up their lives to total strangers. They were not only opening up to her—the whole idea was that what they said and did was going to be seen and heard by millions. Most folks were ready to plunge into that kind of vulnerable situation without giving it much thought.

Everly was not sure she'd so easily welcome the intrusion, no matter how worthy the cause.

"Great," Everly said. "I have to work out the details, but if I can get a crew soon, we'll fly out there sometime near the end of next week. We'd probably want to spend at least half a day with you, if that's all right."

"You'll bring me luck," Kathleen said. "Maybe we'll get the call when you're out here."

"That would be perfect," Everly said. "I'll see if I can get your doctors to arrange it."

Kathleen laughed and said good-bye.

Everly hung up and glanced at her notes. Now *that* would be great television.

She couldn't believe she'd just thought that.

Nigel's partiality for sensationalism was seeping into her psyche. She was more excited about a possible boost to their ratings than the fact that this was someone's *life* she was talking about.

No doubt about it, something about this business was a little warped.

Getting decent camera crews for *Morning* was always a real tap dance, Everly thought. It was absurd. The best of the bunch automatically got assigned to the network's evening news program. No matter that *Morning* used nearly five times more airtime, they always got the short end of the stick.

She was not going to let that happen this time.

The Limona story needed special attention—a crew who was creative, sensitive, and good with kids. Everly didn't want some rough, potbellied, sloppy grunts hauling equipment around the Limonas' living room, scaring off their kids. Only a handful of EBC's many crews would be right for this story. But they were so popular it was hard to get them.

Phoenix King was EBC's main man on the crew assignment desk. He was a pasty-looking man in his thirties with close-cropped brown hair and a bad complexion.

I'd kill my parents, too, if they'd given me a name like "Phoenix," she thought. "Everly" might be different, but it didn't have the proclivity to encourage obnoxious comments the way a name like "Phoenix" did.

She sympathized with him, and was probably the only

person at EBC who had never made a crack about his name. She also made a point of walking her crew request forms over to him in person. Phoenix's life at EBC was spent glued to a telephone and an intercom. It was amazing how far a little human contact could go under those circumstances.

"How 'bout a kiss, Phoenix?" Everly said, walking over to his desk and throwing him a Hershey kiss.

"Everly! My ray of sunshine!" He unwrapped the candy and popped it into his mouth. The phone console at his desk was ringing madly. "Do you believe this place?" he asked, gesturing toward the many flashing lights. "You'd think I was running a telethon."

"You mean you're *not*?"

"Ah, Everly, you never let me down. News desk!" he said, pressing down one of the buttons. "Are you kidding? It's lunch hour and there's no way in hell we can get a crew up to the Bronx in time! Trust me—there'll be another fire tomorrow. I promise. I'll set it myself." He pressed another button and winked at her. "News desk!"

Everly shook her head. Her job was fairly hectic, and when she got on the air it wouldn't get any better, but compared with all of the various positions available in network news, she thought Phoenix had the worst of it. At least when she got an assignment, there was occasionally some flexibility in the deadline—from "I need this yesterday!" to "Check this out, but take your time."

Phoenix never had that kind of luxury.

He put the receiver down. The phone was actually quiet for a few seconds. "So, tell me," he said. "What tricks do we have up our sleeve today?"

"Got a good one—it's out on the Coast, too."

"Oh, God!" Phoenix said. "Don't rub it in. The only time I get to travel is for the political conventions. And then it's to real glamorous places like Atlanta and Miami Beach—in the summer!"

"It's better than no travel at all," Everly said.

"Maybe, but I don't exactly have a choice . . . News desk!"

She knew the silence wouldn't last.

"You just finished the fashion shoot with Crane? Great. Did you have lunch?"

EBC was a union shop, which was another new thing for Everly. A crew had to be "lunched" between assignments or you could get into big trouble with the union and with individual crew members. The horror stories about out-of-focus shots and lost soundbites should have been enough to reform any field producer.

It wasn't.

"Okay, fine—grab a hot dog," Phoenix said. "But get back here as soon as you can. We're a little shorthanded."

Everly knew that was probably not true. Phoenix had developed a reputation for keeping too many crews around in the afternoon—just waiting for that late-breaking story.

Yet, in an industry rooted in the CYA (Cover Your Ass) principle, she had to admit she couldn't fault him.

"News desk!" He shrugged his shoulders apologetically. He was hopelessly wedded to the ringing phones. "Just in?" he asked. "Hang on."

He pushed a switch on the intercom, which hooked him up with the union "ready room" over in Long Island City, where crews and couriers waited for last-minute assignments.

"Okay, guys," he said. "We've got a load of equipment coming in from the economic summit in Geneva. By the time you get to JFK, it will have cleared customs. Adelman, you and Schlitt take the van and head out there. It's Swiss Air flight 30, weigh bill number H2352-4812-76. Got that?"

"Got it," a voice piped back.

Phoenix got back on the phone. "Adelman and Schlitt are on the way . . . no problem." He hung up and looked at Everly.

"Trust me," he said. "I didn't plan it to be so crazy right now. Lunch hours are usually not so bad. Must be a conspiracy."

Again the phone rang.

"News desk!"

Everly raised her eyes to the ceiling. Would she ever get her crew order in? Maybe she should just leave the paperwork with him.

"What?" Phoenix looked at her, horrified. "Are you sure? I don't believe it—Tina Greene is dead!"

Everly was stunned. Tina Greene was *the* legendary comedienne of their times. She and her husband had created a successful at-home radio show that was turned into one of the leading television sitcoms of the fifties. Although now well into her seventies, she was one of the spunkiest women alive. And the country *loved* her. Tina Greene had been such an integral part of television for so long—what with syndication and five successful series—it was hard to imagine that she was really gone. It was almost as if you'd just lost a precious member of your family.

More important, though, everyone in the broadcast world would have to scramble to get something on the air about Tina's life and death. Everly could imagine the chaos back in the *Morning* offices. Phoenix was one of the best sources for breaking stories, but something of this magnitude had surely made the rounds of the building. She knew the race was on—the search for clips from Tina's shows and from past interviews with the grande dame and her family, the hunt for details about her life, for exclusive photographs of moments never captured on tape or film, calls to her "nearest and dearest" to comment—preferably live—on this most tragic event.

Knowing that the other networks were hustling for the exact same thing did not make the job any easier.

Everly literally sprinted away from Phoenix's desk. It would be a great time to score some points with her boss. The more ammunition she could stock up on before Nancy Pollan called in her debt, the better. She never even bothered with the crew order. She ran down the hall with Nigel's succinct news philosophy emblazoned across her mind:

"First things first."

Four

"Tina Greene is dead! Tina Greene is dead!"

Everly could hear Nigel's ringing proclamation from down the hall. As she approached the front entrance to *Morning*'s office, she saw something rather curious: Victoria Lenox quietly slipping out of a side door.

Everly was dumbfounded.

Victoria was the segment producer assigned exclusively to entertainment stories. If anyone would be given primary responsibility for the Greene obit, Victoria was it. Obviously, she was sneaking away to avoid what everyone knew would be an horrendous job. Someone would have to go through massive archival footage, put something especially meaningful and poignant together, book guests for a live segment, and then prepare a script with questions for Glen or Corah.

But dear old Victoria Lenox was bailing out. She obviously had no idea that anyone could see her sneaking down the hall. Everly could have stopped Victoria if she'd been quicker, but she didn't always have the quickest reflexes for such things. However, she did have a good memory. She was sure she'd be able to use this charming scenario to her advantage at an appropriate time.

Everly opened the front door. Nigel was holding a pow-wow in the reception area; he had summoned the troops to outline strategy.

A cursory glance around the room revealed no sign of Hank Forrest. Everly was both relieved and disappointed. She wondered why he wasn't there, but knew this wasn't the time to give his absence too much thought.

It was no surprise to see Kerri Marks, their special projects coordinator, at Nigel's side, looking typically haughty as she surveyed what Everly was sure Kerri considered the gathering plebeians. Kerri was one of those despicable women who were gorgeous, cunning, and masters at manipulating men—though Everly liked to assume that Nigel had her number. She wasn't especially bright, and it was no secret that she'd risen through the ranks in a supine position. So much for the women's movement . . . *Plus ça change* and all that.

In addition to her other so-called attributes, Kerri was a master at looking busy, and Everly had to admit that occasionally—in a crunch—she delivered.

God knew how . . .

Sure enough, Nigel declared that thanks to Kerri, they'd gotten an exclusive with Tina Greene's son and daughter. Everly could have smashed Kerri's smug face when Nigel made the announcement, but then she probably would've broken a finger or two on her capped teeth—certainly not worth it.

"Where's Victoria?" Nigel asked.

"Probably at a screening," someone said.

Screening, my ass, Everly thought. She saw no point in contradicting that assumption. The only thing that mattered was that Victoria Lenox was not there to help out. Someone else would have to run the gauntlet.

"We've got to get the top guests for the show tomorrow," Reggie Graham said. He was one of a handful of associate producers who worked for *Morning*. He pulled at his lower lip nervously.

Such a lovely habit, Everly thought. And he probably assumed that he'd just said something terribly profound.

Fat chance.

Reggie had the intelligence of an oven mitt, and an equal sense of style. But Nigel liked to surround himself with obedient troops, and Reggie was great at following orders.

"If you're in a crunch, I can always call Jack Preston," Beryl Sharpes said, her voice a shade timid. Beryl didn't often take center stage at such meetings. She was the show's book coordinator and the main force behind Lester Kay.

She had also become Everly's closest friend.

"Who the hell is that?" Nigel asked.

"He's coming out with a major book about Tina Greene in a few months, and I'm sure I can convince him to come on tomorrow," Beryl said, sounding more confident. "Of course we'll probably have to promise him another segment when the book is actually published." She brushed aside a stray lock of blond hair that had fallen out of the loosely gathered ponytail at the nape of her neck.

Beryl was never one for making fashion statements.

"Does he have any good dirt?" Nigel had a wicked gleam in his eye.

"He must—it's unauthorized," Beryl said. "Besides, he'd be better than no one at all. And he's a *great* storyteller." She glanced at Everly, who gave her a look of reassurance.

"Keep him on hold," Nigel said. "Let's see what else we can come up with."

"I'll handle the Greene kids," Kerri purred, delicately gesturing at herself with an elegant manicured hand. Her trendy, close-cropped, jet black hair looked almost blue in the harsh light of the front office. "But we need a good tape piece, that's the most important thing." She glanced slowly around the room, as if *she* were going to make the assignment decision.

Of *course* that's what we need, Everly thought. Everyone knew that, but that was the hardest thing to put together, especially with such short notice. She took a deep breath.

This was clearly her opportunity for Brownie points.

"I'll do it," Everly said. The Limona story could wait another day or two. And it was nice to think that this would put Nigel even more solidly in her court.

"Great, Everly," Nigel said. "We'll get you editing time—use the special effects room—anything you need."

She had no other plans that evening, anyway, so what the hell?

After the meeting, Everly walked down "writer's row," as the staff had affectionately dubbed their office area, wondering how the hell Kerri had gotten Tina Greene's children so quickly—an exclusive, yet. The other networks must have been furious at them. Although Tina Greene had captivated audiences for generations with her humor and strong family values, it had been a surprise to the public when her children grew up and went off in rather different directions.

Leslie was a former cocaine addict who was "born again;" her brother, Maxim, was a soap opera star who occasionally played third-tier heavies in B movies. Considering the significance of their mother's death, their exclusive appearance on *Morning* was certainly a major coup. What kind of tricks had Kerri pulled?

Then Everly remembered. The Greenes were represented by Seth White, a hotshot agent at ICM. Seth and Kerri had been an item several months ago.

It all made sense.

The sacrifices one "stoops to" for the ol' career . . .

She started looking through some reference books for facts about the Greenes. Why didn't they keep obit files the way newspapers did? Maybe Victoria Lenox had some material already compiled. Everly vaguely recalled a staff meeting where Nigel had instructed Victoria to start such files, complete with tape numbers, articles—everything you could possibly need to do a comprehensive death story.

Everly suddenly felt sad.

It was still hard to imagine that Tina Greene was really dead. This was a woman whose whole life had been played out in the public eye. She had brought her family into all of her many projects and was that rare person who had successfully combined her personal life with her career.

And now it was all over.

Everly headed over to Victoria's cluttered office and began searching through the piles on her desk and shelves.

Beryl suddenly burst in. "I thought you'd be in here. I have some catalogue copy and a few pre-publication book reviews on the Jack Preston book about Tina. I thought you could use this stuff."

"Great! I'm hoping to find some material in here. Did you book him?"

"He wants to come over *now* and produce the show—can you imagine?" She laughed and sat on the corner of Victoria's small couch. Beryl was petite and full of energy. It was always great to have her around.

"What did you tell him?"

"I told him that if he set one foot near the control room, I'd shoot him personally." Beryl flashed an innocent smile.

"You didn't! Good for you!"

"Well, not exactly. Actually, he's coming over this afternoon to give us some still pictures from his book. But I told him that after he gave us the photos, he'd have to clear out. Can you imagine him giving Nigel his two cents?"

"We could charge admission," Everly said, rummaging through Victoria's files. "I can *definitely* use those pictures. Could you have one of the researchers put them on adda so I can edit them into my piece?"

Adda was the electronic slide transfer process used in television graphics. Everly had no idea how it was done—it was all magic to her.

"I'll take care of it," Beryl said. "Let me know if you need anything else. And good luck tonight." She got up from the couch and was almost out of the door.

"Hey, Beryl," Everly called. Her friend turned around, her lively gray eyes marked with surprise. "I really appreciate this."

"Don't be ridiculous," Beryl said. "What are friends for?"

"Not a heck of a lot of those around *this* place," Everly said.

"Don't be so cynical. And get to work!"

She left, and Everly continued searching for material.

Suddenly, her heart stopped. There it was—a file labeled "Tina Greene." Terrific! This would save her hours of work. She opened it up.

And cried.

There was information in there all right—but it was all written in hieroglyphics. Victoria was a former secretary who'd mastered Pitman shorthand. She was neurotically protective of her work, and all the goddamned notes were in shorthand.

Everly needed a translator.

And some aspirin.

When Nigel had first hired her, she kept hearing about the great "team spirit" on *Morning*. What a joke. Out of an editorial staff of fifty, she trusted only two people: Beryl and Hank. Even then, she was beating the odds.

And Beryl thought she was too cynical.

Anyone who said television was a "fabulous" industry to work in had obviously never tried it.

Corah Washington was poring over the script Everly had written. It was five-thirty in the morning, and they were in an editing room down the hall from the *Morning* studio. Glen Korbett would have winged it and read the copy as it aired. Corah didn't take those kinds of chances—which bothered Everly because she couldn't stop thinking about how *she'd* do it. She had to keep reminding herself about the world Corah had come from. That was the difference between an experienced journalist and a former actress and model. Risk taking was not on Corah's résumé.

"Could we change this part?" Corah asked, pointing to a section on Tina's relationship with her husband.

"Of course we can," Everly said, restraining herself. She'd been gritting her teeth for a half hour, making infinitesimal changes to please the queen. Each time, Everly had to patiently explain that the words were matched with specific pictures that were already laid down on tape, so it couldn't be altered *too* much.

Corah wasn't always a prima donna, but some gland of hers must have reacted to the pressure that morning, and she made Everly feel as if she were supposed to be groveling at the cohost's feet.

Corah probably would have loved that.

"What's the problem?" Everly asked.

"I don't know," Corah answered. "It just sounds a little sappy. Fix it."

Everly wanted to kill her. She'd been working on the damn thing all through the night, no thanks to the elusive Lenox file, though Jenny Spiegel, Nigel's "senior production assistant," had deciphered some of the Pitman hieroglyphics for her.

Then it occurred to Everly that the *real* problem had nothing to do with the voice-over piece that she and Corah were working on. No, that wasn't it. Corah was furious because Glen had won the premier Greene piece of the day—interviewing Leslie and Maxim. She had been smart enough not to confront Nigel when he handed her the revised rundown of the day's show. Glen Korbett was the only member of the staff who had the balls to cross him—and those were such rare occasions, they hardly counted. So this whole scenario over the script was really just a matter of letting off a little steam.

The truth was that the "talent," as they dubbed the on-air folks, rarely complained about the scripts she wrote—at least they hadn't yet. She had a good ear and knew how to write for them. Each had their own style: Corah, flowing and descriptive; Glen, more staccato and to the point. Even Lester, with his requisite puns and double entendres, liked most of what she wrote for him.

Once she'd worked at *Morning* for a few weeks, she'd been able to create custom-made scripts for whoever was voicing something. Of course, Everly hungered for the day when she'd be writing copy for herself and for no one else . . .

So, in fact, Corah had no real reason to complain about the script; she was simply venting her frustrations on Everly.

Just what she needed.

"Okay," Everly said. "Give me a minute."

She took the copy and changed a few words, trying not to cut too much, because every line was closely timed to exactly match the tape she'd painstakingly edited.

"How's this?"

"That fast?" Corah asked. She eyed Everly suspiciously.

Amazing, Everly thought. Here was one of the most renowned former models in the country, one of a handful of black actresses who'd successfully starred in a prime time soap opera, and yet she apparently was insecure around someone with good writing skills.

Corah then glanced over the script, smiled, and read aloud:

" 'Tina Greene never let anything get in the way of her relationship with her husband, Gregory. When he was stricken with leukemia, all production stopped on her series until his condition stabilized, even though he had been out of the performing scene for years. "Gregory is my life," she said. "It's that simple." Audiences have known for years about their mutual love and respect.' Much better," Corah said. "Can I have a look at the tape? I bet it's good."

"If there's time," Everly said. "Better get into the recording booth so that we can lay this down."

Normally, Everly recorded a soundtrack separately and played around with it to match the edited videotape. There wasn't time for that kind of production work this morning, and when she'd put the piece together, she knew Corah wasn't going to come in too much earlier than she had to for any extra work. For all her inexperience with television news, however, Corah was a real pro at recording and timing, and usually got everything on the first take. She was one of the few people Everly had ever worked with who, when you said "give me ten seconds on that" or "we need to fill for fifteen," would be right on the money—to the second.

That was no small gift.

"How we doing in here? This is not a bloody women's convention, you know!" Nigel roared into the edit room.

"Almost done, Nigel," Everly said.

"This is a very moving piece," Corah said.

"That's why I gave it to *you*, my dear," Nigel said in a cajoling tone. "Consider it a gift. Glen would indubitably murder the damn thing. Of course, he is very good, but let's face it, Corah —there are certain things only *you* can handle."

He gave her an obsequious smile.

"Why, thank you, Nigel. I appreciate that."

Everly wondered if Corah truly believed him. Nigel had such a skill for delicately playing his cohosts against each other. In their own right, they each wielded considerable power. Together, Corah Washington and Glen Korbett could be formidable opponents. Nigel was too shrewd for that, however. He was a believer in the venerable "divide and conquer" philosophy.

"Now, Everly, I do want a quick 'look-see' before we go to air. The piece is scheduled for the premier spot—it's going to open the show," Nigel said.

Everly nodded her head, mildly stunned. This would be a first for her—producing the major tape piece of the day. She couldn't help but feel a little proud. This segment was going to get more mileage for her than she'd realized—if it was good.

"Come back in about fifteen minutes," she said. "It should be ready to roll then."

"Excellent." He turned sharply and left.

"You know, he *does* have a point," Corah said, lowering her voice conspiratorially.

"What do you mean?" Everly was all innocence.

"Well, Glen is just a newsman," Corah said, with more than just a hint of disdain. "This obit requires feeling and emotion. That's exactly why I'm so good for this show."

"Absolutely right," Everly said. "Better get in the record booth so we can get this down."

Corah flashed a brilliant smile—the first one of the morning.

Everly had to hand it to Nigel. When it came to manipulation, no one had him beat, Kerri Marks included.

Nigel was the absolute master.

"Okay, Johnny, get a two-shot of Leslie and Maxim," Mel Stone said. Mel was *Morning*'s director. He was talented, but a little crazy. "You believe the getup on that dame? Take one."

Everly was sitting in the control room in the back deck with all of the editorial people. Cups of coffee, napkins, and an array of flaccid pastries were scattered across the counter. Sitting next to her was Leon Posner, their penny-pinching production manager; next was associate producer Reggie Graham; and brooding on his control room "throne" was Nigel Elliot.

The technical staff, including "crazy" Mel, sat at a long deck in front of them.

The atmosphere in the control room was usually relaxed, though there were occasional moments of panic when there were technical snafus.

Nigel had a reputation for throwing things while the show was on the air—the nature of the day's broadcast determining the size and type of projectile. At the very least, he crumpled up and discarded the day's script, wadding up each separate page into a little ball and periodically throwing them at various members of the front deck.

It had to be a little distracting.

After one particularly vituperative morning, when Nigel literally ripped a telephone from the back console and threw it through a panel on the front deck, Mel came in the next day with individualized crash helmets for all of his crew.

Even Nigel took the hint after that.

"Tight shot on Glen, Camera Two. Balance it, for God's sake!" Mel shook his head. "Leon, where the hell did we get this rope-a-dope?"

"From *Evening News Worldwide*," Leon said, sounding half-asleep. No matter what time of day it was, Leon always sounded as if he'd just gotten out of bed. The accumulation of many years assigned to a morning news show could do that.

"Figures," Nigel said. "They can afford to have bloody fools in their studio. When is Ted back from vacation?"

" 'Nother week," Leon said.

"By then maybe this clown will learn how to do camera," Mel said.

"Keep it down now," Nigel said. "I want to *hear* this damn thing."

"Again, I want to thank you both for being here," Glen said.

His boyish face was most disarming. Thick black hair parted neatly on the side framed a smooth-complexioned, perpetually tanned face—it was mostly makeup—with wide, twinkley blue eyes, a slightly pug nose, and full sensual lips.

Although married, Glen was a lady's man and made no attempt to hide his girlfriend, Yvonne, from the staff. With all the things in the gossip columns, this was one juicy item that mysteriously had never made it into print. That was a real puzzler to Everly.

"We wanted to come on," Leslie said. "Television was Mother's real home. It's where she'd want us to be today, I'm sure of it."

Leslie Greene was dressed in a simple but rich-looking long-sleeved black dress, a slim silver cross dangling from her neck. Her bright orangey red hair was pulled back tightly into a severe bun at the nape of her neck. Though in her early thirties, she looked rather matronly. She could have just come from a convent.

"Mom was a very special lady," Maxim said. "Of course, Dad was special, too."

Maxim was the shorter and younger of the two. Rumor had it that he wore lifts, which didn't seem to do much good. He was wearing a black European-cut suit, an off-white shirt, and a dark gray tie—appropriately subdued, right out of central casting.

"Was there ever a time you wished your folks were around more?" Glen asked.

Everly knew Glen would go for controversy right up front.

Leslie looked upset.

"What do you mean?" she asked.

"When you were young. Your mother was the first woman in history ever to go on camera while she was pregnant. You and your brother were TV stars practically from the womb."

No one ever said that Glen Korbett had the best taste in the world.

"It was very exciting," Maxim said. "We never felt self-conscious in front of the cameras. We were with our parents all the time when we were young—on the show."

"But wasn't it hard to be a kid—have a real childhood and be a television star at the same time?"

"Not at all," Maxim said.

"That's not exactly true," Leslie said.

Everly could see Maxim on a separate screen giving his sister a worried glance.

"Johnny—two shot!" Mel screamed.

"Take it!" Nigel yelled.

"What do you mean, Leslie?" Glen asked, leaning over and touching her knee slightly. Everly knew he was warming her up for the kill.

"Watch it now, Leslie," Maxim said, clearly agitated.

"Get a tight shot of him, dammit!" Nigel roared.

"I'm directing!" Mel yelled back. "Close up on Maxim, Camera Two!"

"You're under a lot of strain, Leslie. We *both* are," Maxim said.

"I think we have to be honest," she said.

"Camera Three, zoom in on Leslie," Mel hissed into his headset.

Leslie's frank, slightly reddened eyes loomed large on the screen.

"Honesty is always very important," Glen said gravely, offscreen.

"There's something I think you all should know about Mother," Leslie said, looking directly into the camera.

"Leslie, don't," Maxim pleaded.

She ignored him.

"For thirty-three years, I've been quiet. Now's the time for truth. The good Lord believes in truth. It's our strength, our survival."

"Oh, God, Leslie," Maxim moaned.

"This is fantastic!" Nigel exclaimed. "Look at the other networks. They must be drooling over this!"

Everly glanced quickly at the tiny monitors on a shelf to their left—silent flickering images of the *Today* show, *Good Morning America*, and *This Morning*. A senator, two baseball players, and a one-time movie star plugging a cookbook. No contest here. If America was switching channels—an integral part of watching television—there was no question as to where their dials would remain.

"All of you know Tina Greene as the great actress—the comedienne extraordinaire," Leslie continued. "Master of slapstick and timing. She was a devoted wife and mother. But sometimes, she wasn't such a *great* mother."

"Leslie, please! She's barely been gone twenty-four hours!" Maxim said.

"It's all right, Maxim," she said quietly. "The Lord knows all and forgives." She looked back into the camera. "Our mother had one great weakness. She hid it as best as she could, but her family and friends knew the truth. And now you will, too."

The control room was dead quiet. Leslie had inherited some of her mother's gifts. Her performance was absolutely riveting.

"Mother had a drug and alcohol problem, and it caused her to do some horrible things."

"Oh, God," Maxim groaned.

"Especially to Maxim," she added.

"What exactly do you mean?" Glen asked, carefully egging her on.

"Sex," Leslie proclaimed.

"Incest?" Glen asked. Even he looked incredulous.

"God no!" Maxim said. "You've got it all wrong."

"This is fabulous!" Nigel said.

Fabulous? Everly felt sick. What were her children doing? What were they talking about? Did they realize they were destroying the reputation of a legend?

Yet as painful as it was to hear all of this, she had to admit that she was as transfixed as everyone else.

"Please explain," Glen said.

"Leslie, how could you do this?" Maxim asked weakly.

"Tell them the truth, Maxim," she intoned.

Maxim looked helplessly at Glen.

"It's all right," Glen said. "Do what feels comfortable."

"We gotta go to commercial soon," Ed Brown, the assistant director, piped up.

"Screw the commercials," Nigel declared.

"But then we'll owe them free give-backs," Leon said, clearly horrified.

This was truly a red letter day. He sounded wide awake now.

"I don't give a bloody hell about that!" Nigel roared.

"We'll have to override the network computers," Leon said, panic creeping into his voice.

"Do it!"

Leon picked up the phone and got Broadcast Operations Control on the line.

". . . so Mother had these . . . I guess you'd call them . . . 'down' periods," Maxim said. "To get out of her bad mood, she'd have parties. 'Little parties,' she'd say." He shook his head.

"In the beginning, she'd send me out of the house on those afternoons," Leslie said, her voice thick with resentment. "Lord knows how many times she had them while I away was at boarding school."

"What happened at these parties?" Glen asked.

When the on-air camera switched to Leslie, Everly could see Corry Haggerty, their floor manager, run up to Glen and tell him that they were giving him the rest of the show for the segment. Everly was selfishly pleased that her obit segment had opened the program. She was sure it never would have seen the light of day if they'd saved it for the end. This interview was too controversial to limit it to the amount of time it had been given on the original rundown, though they sure as hell couldn't go past 9:00. It was only 8:50—

plenty of time left for the whole confession.

Maxim squirmed a bit in his chair. Everly knew Nigel was delighted that they'd captured his discomfort on national television. It *was* good television, but that sure as hell didn't make it ethical.

"Explain, Maxim," Leslie said. "Or do you want me to?"

"It didn't happen that much," Maxim began.

"I'm warning you—the *truth*," Leslie said.

Her brother glared at her.

"What exactly was it?" Glen asked, sitting on the edge of his seat.

They all were. They had all become voyeurs.

"I guess it started when I was about fourteen. I was never really a big guy—it used to bug Mom. She couldn't understand how I could be so short. She took it as a personal affront. It was kind of crazy. Somehow she got it in her head that it had to do with glands and hormones. So she decided that if some of her lady friends . . . uh . . . if they . . . showed me 'the ways of the world,' that I'd . . . grow."

"So they seduced you?"

"I guess you could call it that. I didn't really understand what was happening at first. I was a little afraid, then I didn't mind, but—"

"You hated it!" Leslie said. "You couldn't wait to get away from them. Tell the truth."

"All right, dammit! Yes, I hated it! But what was I supposed to do? I put up with it as long as I had to and then I got the hell out."

"That's when you dropped out of high school and went to Europe?" Glen asked.

"Five minutes," Ed Brown yelled.

"Show him five, Corry," Mel said. "He better wrap up this soap opera."

"Marvelous," Nigel intoned. "Perfectly marvelous!"

"That's right. The only way to say 'no' to Tina Greene was to disappear," Maxim said bitterly.

"It drove me crazy when I found out about it. That's why *I* had so much trouble," Leslie said, similarly disgusted. "But then I forgave her, as we all must."

"You still sound angry," Glen said.

"Everything's been kept inside me for so long, it's hard to be merciful," Leslie said, trying to regain her composure.

"How often did she have these parties?"

"Whenever she felt like it," Maxim said. "I don't know—sometimes once a month, sometimes once a week, sometimes months would go by."

"What about your father?"

"He pretended it wasn't happening," Leslie scoffed.

"Wasn't he there?"

"No, he'd always manage to get out of the house before it happened," Maxim said.

"He didn't know anything about it?"

"Well, he *pretended* not to, but right before he died—" Maxim stopped, his voice suddenly cracked.

"Yes?" Glen didn't want to stop the momentum.

"He . . . he said he was sorry. It was the last thing he said to me," Maxim said.

"We had to forgive him," Leslie said. "No one could control Mother—no one."

"So how do you both *really* feel today?"

"I'm glad it's all over," Leslie said.

"Justified," Maxim said.

"May she rest in peace," Leslie added.

"Ten seconds!" Ed yelled into his headset. "Close it!"

"Well, Leslie, Maxim, I want to thank you both for being here today." Then Glen turned to a different camera. "And for all of us at *Morning*, thanks for joining us. See you all tomorrow."

"Fade to black," Mel said.

Suddenly all the phones were lit up. The EBC switchboard operators were probably having mild heart attacks.

"5K control," Leon said. "What?" He put his hand over the mouthpiece of the phone. "Nigel, it's the *Times*—they want to speak to Maxim."

"Tell them to call back in an hour. Maybe we can have a press conference in the greenroom," Nigel said.

"5K here." It was Reggie's line. He looked panicked as

he listened. He looked over to Nigel and whispered, "It's Barbara Walters's office. They want the Greene kids for a prime time special."

"Tell 'em to call their agent," Nigel snarled.

He wasn't going to make life easier for another network if he could help it—no matter who was calling.

"This is fantastic," he continued. "A legend shattered on EBC's *Morning*. We'll be all over the bloody media for this!"

He was right. So what if Tina Greene's image had been ruined. So what if they'd just opened Pandora's box? Maxim and Leslie would be hounded by the press until the whole story came out.

And it was all thanks to *Morning*. It was truly a scoop for them. They were going to make headlines. Inevitably, this would boost ratings. For Nigel, that was all that mattered.

As for Everly, she wanted to throw up. How could this story make her feel good? Even though this was the stuff that made for award-winning journalism, she could take no pleasure from destroying someone's reputation. So what if it got ratings?

This was one aspect of the business she despised. It upset her that people sometimes blamed *her* rather than her industry for some of the consequences of their stories. She could imagine what her friends outside of the media business would say to her now.

The whole world had thought Tina Greene was one of the most marvelous human beings on earth.

Not anymore.

How many others had fooled them? What other lurid or shocking stories were out there? Everly was sure no one had an accurate idea of what kind of price *really* was paid for success and fame.

Of course when the time came for her, it would be different. She'd keep a balance. She had to believe that.

"Everly, are you dreaming, or what?" Leon gave her a strange look.

"I've practically been up for two day's straight, Leon,"

Everly snapped. "What's the problem?"

"Didn't you hear me? I said this call's for you—Nancy Pollan."

"What the hell does *she* want?" Nigel asked.

He knew exactly what she wanted.

"I'll handle it," Everly said.

Famous last words.

FIVE

"What in the bloody hell do you think this is?" Nigel screamed, thrashing around his office and flailing his arms dramatically, punctuating his tirade.

He stopped pacing for a moment as the group watched him silently. Hank Forrest, looking rather glum, sat next to Everly in the matching leather chair in front of Nigel's desk. Reggie Graham lurked behind them, trying to be as unobtrusive as possible.

Nigel had brought in two key staff people to witness the slaughter of Everly Dalton.

Their boss suddenly whipped around and walked toward his closed office door, shaking his head. Then he abruptly turned and walked back behind his desk, punching the air with his right fist. "Never in all my years in this damned crazy business, *never* have we ever, ever, *ever* done anything like this!" He shook his head violently.

If Everly hadn't known better, she would have had him committed.

He suddenly came from behind his desk and thrust his

face close to hers. He smelled of coffee and cigarettes. A small trail of doughnut sugar on his navy tie made him seem a little less formidable, but not much. Everly was terrified. And speechless.

"What do you think we're running here, Everly?" he whispered, and then yelled, "*Some damned booking agency?*"

"Look, Nigel," she said, with as much confidence as she could muster under the circumstances, "I've told you again and again—we couldn't get the Harcrests yesterday without Nancy's help." Her voice was subdued and sounded oddly childlike. It was as if someone else were speaking. She had to force herself to continue despite a strange sense of detachment. "They were in her hotel, for God's sakes! So I made a deal—I told her I owed her one. What happened today was the payback. She wanted Leslie and Maxim, and I arranged for them to go over to *Good Morning America* after she called."

The more Everly talked, the better she felt. It was all very logical. Couldn't Nigel see that? "She probably could have gotten them through their agent. I don't see what the big deal is. It's not like I did something they wouldn't have eventually done on their own."

"We don't help the competition!" Nigel roared.

"Especially *Good Morning America*." Reggie added his two cents. He hovered behind Hank, ever the eager vulture.

Everly never expected Reggie to defend her. She looked at him now—the "good little soldier," his proud chin thrust forward, his auburn hair neatly parted, his vapid brown eyes absorbing Nigel's every move. He wasn't terribly bright, and Everly was sure that if he wasn't so damned good looking as well as a successful political animal, he wouldn't be where he was today. It was infuriating.

Hank must have read her mind, because he flashed her a look of warning. Everly ignored Reggie's outburst and continued to plead her case.

"But, Nigel, Nancy helped *us*. And we had Leslie and Maxim first. We were the ones to break the story on Tina Greene."

"I know those bastards over there better than you do," Nigel said. "They'll probably give them a five-part series and blow the whole story all over town."

"How much more can there be?" Hank asked, clearly exasperated.

They all looked at him, surprised at his jumping into this mess. It was the first time he'd spoken since he'd joined the hastily called meeting.

"Look, Everly made a deal—so what?" he continued. "We got the Harcrests yesterday; we were first with the Greenes today. Glen's interview will be all over the local news shows. *Entertainment Tonight* will probably pick it up. I'll even give them the footage myself."

"I thought you hated that show," Reggie snapped.

"What does that have to do with anything? I hate *most* television, but they have good ratings and it'll be good for us," Hank said. "By tomorrow morning, the 'shocking Tina Greene story' will be old news, and we'll be on the prowl for some other great sensational story to capture the headlines."

"You do have a point," Nigel said, choosing to ignore Hank's sarcasm. He walked over to the television monitors, his back to the group. "You know, I've fired people for less than this." He turned around abruptly and approached Everly again. "But you *are* relatively new, and this is the first time you've ever mucked up like this. It better not happen again, though, or you'll be out the door. Do you understand?"

"I understand."

Everly sounded like a scared four-year-old.

"From now on, any booking you do that entails anything out of the ordinary—you go immediately to Reggie, or me."

Everly could imagine Reggie puffing out his feathers on *that* one, so she avoided looking at him. "*We'll* decide if any deals are going to be made," Nigel continued. "Consider yourself on probation—for the next two months. *No more bloody screw-ups!*"

He resumed the nervous pacing. No one said a word. Nigel finally stopped walking and stared at her. "Got that?"

Everly felt as if she were supposed to salute.

"Yes," she said.

"That's it then. Back to work."

Hank caught her eye as she left and winked, but Everly didn't know how to respond. All she knew was that she was about to cry and she had to get out of there fast.

She closed Nigel's door behind her and ignored Jenny Spiegel's inquisitive look.

She felt awful.

True, she still had her job, but any points she may have earned over the past two days had been totally obliterated.

So much for great plans.

"The whole Tina Greene situation was such a disaster," Everly said, playing with one of the pop-up books on Beryl's desk. "I almost got fired!"

She was hiding in her friend's office. Everly didn't want to face the rest of the staff. She was sure they'd all heard about the dressing down she'd gotten several hours ago. Bad news travels fast. Most of her colleagues were probably happy about it, except maybe Hank.

"Be real, Everly," Beryl said. "Nigel wouldn't go to that kind of extreme." Beryl was rearranging the publishing catalogues on her desk for the umpteenth time. "He may have a crazy reputation—well deserved, of course—but he does have a good heart. I bet that one of these days he'll admit he was wrong to come down on you so hard."

"Hell will freeze over first."

"Oh, come on. He can really be a neat guy," Beryl said with a genuine smile.

Everly looked at her and wondered how this innocent who used words like "neat" and "be real," and who had such utter faith in people, managed to survive in this city, let alone this profession.

"It's not only that. It doesn't help matters knowing that *Morning* helped destroy Tina Greene's reputation. She was an icon. Everyone *worshipped* her. And now I feel like I put a bullet to her head myself."

"Everly, you're not being fair. Those headlines—well, it's not like this revelation about her was your fault. If *we* hadn't interviewed her kids, someone else would have. Leslie Greene was pretty determined to get that story out. Don't forget that."

"Your Jack Preston didn't even know about those little parties of hers. And he's the king of sleaze!"

"So what? Honestly, you're taking this too seriously." Beryl shook her head slowly. "It's only a job."

There was something devious in Beryl's expression. She knew how important this job was to Everly.

"Right," Everly said. "Maybe if I'd met someone like Stephen I'd have a different perspective."

Beryl had been dating Stephen Skriloff, a public relations account exec, for several months, and it looked as if they were getting serious. "In fact, I'd probably be out somewhere making babies and baking bread," she added.

"I doubt it," Beryl said. "And anyway, men aren't the answer to all the world's problems."

"They only cause them."

"That's not fair. There are a few good men out there."

"Where? Under a rock?"

"You shouldn't be so bitter all the time," Beryl said quietly.

It wasn't that Everly was so bitter; she was afraid. She decided to tell Beryl about her newly discovered feelings for Hank. The way he'd acted in Nigel's office today had intensified her feelings for him. "Well, actually, there *might* be someone . . ."

"Have you been keeping secrets?" Beryl asked, with great animation. "Or hiding some mystery guy from me?"

"Just slow down a minute. I don't even know if this is going anywhere . . . but . . ."

"Who is it? What does he do? I want to meet him!" Her excitement was infectious.

"You've got to swear not to tell anyone . . . and we haven't really gone out or anything, but . . . it's Hank."

Beryl's eyes widened in surprise. "*Our* Hank? Hank Forrest?"

Everly felt embarrassed. "Yes. It's hard to explain. We've been friends for a while, but there's something special between us, at least there seems to be. Good Lord! I sound like a babbling fool."

"Well, what *exactly* is going on?"

"Nothing yet. There's this . . . attraction. We haven't acted on it, but I think it's mutual."

Beryl looked at her with such intensity that Everly had to laugh.

"Hey, Beryl—this is not Romeo and Juliet here. I don't even know where it'll go."

"I'll keep my fingers crossed. I've always thought Hank was kind of cute."

"For some reason, he seems to be especially appealing right now."

"Maybe you should tell him that you want to take a vacation with him or something—you know, get away from the office and the city—and be together without all the hassles."

"Just like that?" That seemed like an utter impossibility. "Not now. I don't want to be pushy, and anyway, I'm going out to the Coast to do that Kathleen Limona story, and then I'll be on call to rush back there when she gets her transplant."

"*If*," Beryl said, with emphasis.

Everly looked at her and acknowledged that she may have already become a little too involved with Kathleen's situation, even though she'd just "discovered" her yesterday. She knew she was already as concerned as Kathleen's family about the transplant.

"Maybe Hank could go out to the Coast with you," Beryl said.

"No. That wouldn't work. I don't want the rest of the world knowing about us. Remember—not a word about this to anyone."

Beryl put her right hand over her heart. "I promise," she said solemnly.

"You must have been a girl scout in your youth."

"Weren't we all?" she asked.

"I guess. Well, I'll take you at your word. There really is something sweet about Hank, though," Everly admitted. "And he even stuck his neck out for me in Nigel's office today—which is a hell of a lot more than Reggie would ever do."

Beryl suddenly looked upset.

"What did I say?"

"It's nothing—tell me more about Hank." Beryl looked down and nervously fingered what appeared to be an antique necklace. Everly envied the fact that her friend was the type of person who went into a flea market, spent twenty dollars, and walked out with a handful of exotic objets d'art.

"Come on. You're hiding something from me," Everly said.

"It's about Reggie."

"What about him? Is he trying to steal coffee table books again?"

"No, not that. Honestly, Everly. I wouldn't care about something as silly as that."

"I'm sorry. Go ahead."

"He's been bothering me about going to Atlanta. Part of the show is coming out of there next month, and Lester had me line up some interviews with Southern writers. Reggie wants me on location a week ahead of time."

"So what's wrong with that?" Evelry asked. "I think that's terrific. Don't you want to do more on this show than hold Lester Kay's hand?"

"But it's the *way* Reggie says things," Beryl said. "He keeps talking about all these great night spots he wants to show me. It's creepy. What should I do?"

"Well, I could kick him in the balls for you—that would put him out of commission fast."

"Great. That and what happened today would do wonders for your career, too. Be real, Everly."

"I seem to be doing such a good job of that."

Beryl shook her head and sighed.

Then Everly had an idea. "Hey, why don't you start bragging more about Stephen—especially to Jenny Speigel. She's the office gossip. It's bound to get back to Reggie."

"I don't know if that would stop him. It might even make him more interested."

"You might be right. I only hope his wife gets as much action as he does. What does he need you for, anyway? No offense, but doesn't he have something going with that blond who keeps coming around the office? You know the one I mean—that PR lady who is suddenly booking a lot of her clients on our show?"

"Maybe she can't go to Atlanta."

"That's it!" Everly said.

"What?"

"Tell Reggie you're glad about going there earlier because you just found out that your boyfriend has a business trip to Atlanta at the same time. There's nothing he can do about *that*, even if it's not true. Just stay in your room at night and order room service. He's not about to check up on you in your room under *those* circumstances. I don't think he's *that* stupid."

"That's a neat idea! I think you've really come up with something." Beryl rewarded her with one of her terrific smiles.

"Come on, aren't I always right?" Everly enjoyed teasing her friend.

"You know, if you're this way now, you're going to be insufferable when you go on the air." Beryl shook her head in mock despair.

"Well, you just stick around and make sure it doesn't all go to my head," Everly said.

"Deal," she responded. "It's a tailor-made job."

Everly was glad they were able to kid around now. It distracted her from obsessing over what appeared to be her botched career.

She just hoped the Leslie and Maxim Greene situation hadn't totally blown her chances for success.

"You've *got* to be kidding!"

"What's the big deal?" Kerri Marks leaned in Everly's doorway, a bored look giving her sharp features a wash of disdain.

It was a few days after the scene in Nigel's office, and Everly was sure Kerri was scheming to make her look bad.

"You want me to find a divorced family—a husband, second wife, *and* the ex-wife who lost custody—who will go on camera and talk about it? With the kids, too?"

Everly squelched the urge to tell her that jumping through fire-ringed hoops was not in her repertoire.

She looked at Kerri, neatly attired in an expensive-looking gray linen suit, a flowing, multicolored silk scarf tied just so around her slim, long neck.

Everly wanted to strangle her with it.

"I thought you had a knack with that sort of thing," Kerri said.

If Kerri thought she was going to fall for her flattery, she was more of a fool than Everly had imagined. But politics were politics.

And someday she might need her.

"What's my deadline?"

"No rush. Nigel wants it for a series we're doing on the family in two months."

"The November sweeps," Everly said.

"Yes."

"Okay. I'll get to it when I get back from California."

"A trip to the Coast?" She edged into Everly's office. Was Miss Special Projects actually going to bless Everly's domain with her presence? "I thought we were having budget problems—no more boondoggles. Does Nigel know about this?"

Great. Kerri was jealous.

"This is *not* a boondoggle," Everly said smoothly. "And we always have a budget for *certain* things. I have a terrific story lined up, and yes—Nigel knows. He's thrilled, in fact."

Everly was sure Kerri, like most of the staff, had assumed that the Greene mess meant no more perks for her—such as travel. She was delighted to prove her wrong.

"Some celebrity?" Kerri asked.

"No, human interest, but it's a hot one." She was *not* going to tell her about the Limona story.

One of the great ironies about being in the communications business was that in many cases, the left hand had absolutely no idea what the right hand was doing. Nigel preferred it that way, which often made Everly wonder how they actually got on the air.

Since this segment was one she had come up with, there was no particular reason for Kerri to know anything about the organ donation spot, and she wasn't going to help her out. Let her learn about it after it was shot, edited, and aired . . . or when it was nominated for an Emmy.

"How long will you be gone?" Kerri asked.

"Just a few days. Listen, I'd love to chat more, Kerri, but I'm headed for the Coast tomorrow, and I have a spot for tomorrow's show," Everly lied. She knew Kerri would believe her. Even if she looked at tomorrow's rundown and checked writer assignments, it wouldn't matter. The show's "routine," as the daily segment-by-segment rundown was called, was changed so often, it was hardly ever accurate. In fact, certain members of the staff had a private pool going. The person who guessed the exact number of shows in a month where the schedule set the prior morning at eleven o'clock actually matched the *Morning* show that aired the next day got a modest pot of money.

So far, there had been no winners.

Kerri gave her an envious look from her heavily made-up green eyes.

How appropriate.

"Well, this 'new family relationships' story is yours now," she said, handing Everly a folder. "Alison is your researcher on this, so maybe she can help you round up a family."

Right. If you believe in tooth fairies.

"Fine," Everly said. "It'll be my first priority when I get back from the West Coast."

Everly watched Kerri's tall, graceful figure turn and waltz out of her office. She'd been given a killer assignment and one of the worst researchers on the staff to "help" her with it. Everly wouldn't have been surprised if Kerri and Reggie had purposely conspired against her.

Nothing like teamwork in network news.

EBC's commissary was one of the few places in the building that had no telephones. The food was legendarily bad—even the salad bar was pathetic, with its days-old offerings of wilted vegetables and sad-looking condiments, but the place was open twenty-four hours a day and it offered a convenient escape from the office.

Everly sometimes hid there when she needed what she called "a mental health break." Tea was one thing even the commissary couldn't ruin.

She was thinking about the trip to California tomorrow morning when suddenly she felt a presence next to her.

It was Hank. Everly hadn't seen him since Nigel's tirade. She hoped she wasn't going to say anything stupid.

"Mind some company?" Hank asked.

"In this case, it's welcome," Everly said, feeling a little awkward.

"I understand you're off on another great journey. How long will it be this time?" he asked, as he started to play with the packs of sugar on the cafeteria table.

"Not too long—three days, tops," Everly said. "You know, I want to thank you for sticking up for me in Nigel's office the other day," she continued, giving herself an opening to mention her new feelings toward him. She wondered if he could sense her nervousness.

"Forget it. You'd do the same for me." He avoided looking at her.

"I hope I would—"

"Tell you what, there's something you *can* do. Bring me back a souvenir!" he said, his pale blue eyes crinkling merrily.

He'd broken the mood. Everly could only go along with it.

"What do you have in mind?" She asked. "Not one of those typical California blond bombshells, I hope."

"Everly, give me some credit."

"I am," she said.

"I want you to bring something back for me that you can only get in California."

"What's that?"

"See's Chocolate."

There was such an intense look in his eyes, she couldn't help but laugh. "You're serious?"

"Absolutely. It's the best domestic chocolate that's made."

"I note your qualification there."

"Well, you know I have a fondness for Swiss chocolate."

"And German chocolate and Dutch chocolate and—"

"Enough!" he said, patting his stomach. "Just try it when you're out there. You'll see what I mean."

"I believe you. How much should I get?"

He was like a child who was going to get a favorite toy. There was such a look of anticipation in his face. It made him seem even more appealing.

"A couple two-pound boxes? Assorted dark and milk chocolate? And don't worry—I'll pay you for it," he said.

"Forget it. Is it expensive?"

"Not too bad. I told you—I'll pay you back."

"I know," Everly said. "All right, it's a deal. What I do for you . . ." She gave his arm an affectionate squeeze. It felt nice to touch him.

Why were they wasting all this time talking about chocolate?

"I'm worth it," he said.

"I know. And in case I forget that, you'll be the first to remind me."

"Hey, you know as well as I do that you have to toot your own horn in this rotten business." He looked at his watch. "Gotta run. I'm meeting Bernice at my apartment."

Everly pretended to be cheerful. "Another rendezvous with the mysterious subway girl?" she asked. She tried to ignore the sting of jealousy that flared in her mind.

"She's taking a class in massage. Guess who the lucky guinea pig is?"

"Just memorize what she does to you. Then one of these

days, you can give me a free sample," Everly said, as breezily as she could manage.

"If you're lucky," he said, as he got up and came over to get her chair.

"If *you're* lucky," she countered. "Wish me bon voyage. God! I still have to pack."

"The joys of being on the road. I miss those days. Doing this job doesn't give me much opportunity to travel. And when I do, the only thing I end up seeing is the hotel room."

"Would you rather be back in the trenches?" she asked.

"No. Don't remind me. I get paid more than you guys do, and I probably work half as hard," he said.

"I wouldn't say that."

"Whatever. I better run. I'll see you when you get back. Don't forget that chocolate now. You wouldn't want to deprive me of one of life's great pleasures."

Everly smiled, but said nothing.

She felt miserable.

Hank walked quickly out of the commissary, and she self-consciously procrastinated as she gathered her belongings.

If he was trying to get her jealous, he'd succeeded. The thought of going home to her empty apartment seemed worse than usual.

What if there had been no Bernice? Obviously Hank wasn't getting married to her tomorrow, but she was clearly going to be in his life for a while. If he'd never met her, what would Everly have done tonight—invited herself back to his place?

She tried to be honest with herself. Maybe his sudden appeal had more to do with his interest in this new woman than with something more substantial between them.

It was all so confusing.

Everly was getting a headache just thinking about it.

SIX

Everly dropped her bag off in the living room, noting one forlorn blinking light on her answering machine.

The way things had been going for her these days, she assumed that whoever it was had probably hung up.

She pressed the playback button and waited for the tape to rewind as she sat on the couch and riffled through the mail. Someone had apparently left a long message. The tape finally clicked on.

Everly almost went into shock.

Jared Kammer's unmistakable voice filled the room.

"Hi, Everly. I know it's been about a year, and I'm probably the last person you wanted to hear from, but I'm being transferred to New York and I wanted you to hear it straight from me before you read about it in the trades. Pam will be moving, too, of course, but not until sometime in June. Anyway, I just thought I'd call and tell you about it myself. If you'll see me, I'll be in town in a few days and I'd like to take you out for dinner—any four star restaurant of your choice.

"Next time I hope I can talk to *you* and not your machine. What the hell did we ever do without them, right? Till next time."

Everly's heart was pounding so loudly she almost expected a neighbor to knock on her door to see if she was all right.

"Till next time." That's how Jared had always ended their phone conversations. It was as if nothing had changed. Everly walked over to the machine and replayed the message.

No, she hadn't imagined it. Jared was moving to New York.

And she'd thought she'd escaped.

She didn't want to think. What the hell was she supposed to do? She couldn't call anyone back in Indianapolis. All they'd do was worry.

She decided to call Beryl.

Her hands were shaking badly, and the damned touch tone phone was so sensitive to the slightest pressure, she had to redial her friend's number three times before she finally got through.

"Hello?"

Thank God Beryl was home.

"It's Everly. Hope I'm not interrupting anything, but you wouldn't believe what I just came home to—"

"Are you all right? You sound awful! Do you want me to come over?"

"No, I'll be okay. But listen to this." She pushed the rewind button on the answering machine and, when it stopped, held the phone receiver close to the tiny speaker and pressed the playback switch.

Once again, Jared's distinct voice invaded her apartment.

Everly's hand trembled slightly when she put the phone back to her mouth. "That was the man I almost married," she said.

"Gosh, Everly. This is the last thing you need now. No wonder you sound strange."

"I haven't heard that voice in a year and I can't believe how he still gets to me."

"What are you going to do?"

"For starters, I'm going to California tomorrow. As for Jared, there's not much I can do. I'll just have to see what happens when he calls again."

"You're sure he will?"

"Only if he needs something. I just have to figure out what the hell he wants after all this time."

"Maybe he just wants to see you," Beryl said.

Sometimes her friend's naïveté was annoying.

"Not Jared," Everly said. "It couldn't be that simple. I've learned that lesson. No, it's more than that. Maybe he needs a way to get to Corah or Glen. Or Nigel. Who knows?"

"But if he's married to the daughter of a network chairman—"

"We'll just have to wait and see what he comes up with," Everly said. It was hard not to sound bitter.

"I'm really sorry," Beryl said. "I don't know what else to say."

"Well, thank God I'm going out of town for a few days."

"I'll come over if you need company."

"No—I feel better now. I'll be fine."

"Call me if you change your mind," Beryl said.

"Thanks. You're a good friend."

Everly put down the phone and walked to her bedroom. Jared Kammer was actually moving to New York. Of all the places to choose . . . Well, there was nothing she could do about it now. She had too much to take care of for the California shoot.

Maybe she could pretend that she had something on the Coast to look forward to.

"I think we should save the kids for last," Kirk said, chewing on a toothpick.

"That's gotta be tough," Eddie, his partner, added.

Everly's cameraman, Kirk Peterson, and Eddie Lister, his soundman, and she were seated at the bar at a Holiday Inn in Stanford, California. They were having a nightcap, discussing the Limona shoot.

Everly had only arrived a few hours earlier, and the crew

had just come in from the bureau in L.A. Phoenix King had come through for her and gotten her one of the crews she'd requested.

She was trying very hard to stay awake so that she'd go to bed at a reasonable time locally and not wake up at four o'clock in the morning thinking it was really seven.

"I happen to be pretty good with kids," Kirk said. "As well as a few other things," he added, pointedly looking Everly over.

Was he for real? He certainly was living up to his reputation, Everly thought. Quite a few crewmen—and not just at EBC—had reputations for being real Casanovas. When you have a job that takes you all over the country and all over the world, you could easily get into the pickup routine—current health considerations not withstanding.

Kirk Peterson was one of those perennial sun-drenched blond "hunks" who belonged on either a surfboard or a set of snow skis. He even wore the requisite opaque sunglasses, tight jeans, and well-worn cowboy boots.

Of course Everly had to admit that she would have been insulted if he hadn't come on to her.

But she wasn't going to take the bait.

"Well, we have a real sensitive story here. That's why I asked for you guys," she said.

Eddie took another gulp of beer. "Must be real tough for that mother," he said. "Bad enough bein' so sick—but seein' those kids, wonderin' how long she'll be around to see 'em grow—can't imagine it m'self."

Eddie was a transplanted Southerner who'd gone to school in California and ended up joining EBC's L.A. bureau at a time when Kirk coincidentally needed a soundman. Eddie had worked in recording studios but had gotten bored with the sedentary life. In television, he'd gone to the other extreme. His background made him a natural for the job.

His tall lanky frame, dark curly hair, and somewhat slow-paced, serious demeanor offered considerable contrast to his bolder companion.

This was going to be a good shoot.

"I bet you've seen a lot of tough stories," Everly said.

"Yeah," Eddie said. "A couple years ago we did a story for *Evenin' News Worldwide*. It was for a 'Close-Up' segment—a place in Tiburon, California—the Center for Attitudinal Healin'. It was amazin' stuff. They have special treatment programs for kids with cancer. They get their regular medication, but they do all kinds of weird stuff, too—havin' 'em draw pictures and teachin' 'em how to relax."

"I could never forget that one," Kirk said. "What a heartbreaker. Little kids so ill. They learn to draw pictures of their cancer germs. Then they draw the germs being destroyed. It was fascinating stuff using mind-over-matter techniques."

So, the body actually had a heart and brain to go with it.

"I think I've heard about that place," Everly said.

"In a lot of cases the mind can really make a difference," Kirk continued. "Kind of unreal. I don't know if I go for all that hocus pocus, but it seemed to work with those kids."

"You shoulda seen some of those pictures they drew!" Eddie said. He turned suddenly as he saw Kirk reach for a cigarette. "Are you nuts?" he said to his partner. "Here we are talkin' 'bout kids with cancer and you grab a damn cigarette! I thought you were gonna quit."

"Some things are hard to give up," Kirk said, flashing a suggestive smile Everly's way.

She couldn't help but laugh at how obvious he was. Still, there was something attractive about him.

"You could do it if you *wanted* to," she said. "Surely you have *some* willpower."

"Not enough," he said. "There are just certain things I won't do without."

"Ha!" Eddie said. "You sure as hell are lucky you don't have a weight problem. With your willpower, you'd probably weigh a couple hunnerd pounds if you did."

"You could stand to gain a few," Kirk said. He turned to Everly. "We really have to work on fattening him up, Everly. You know when Eddie over here turns sideways, you can barely—"

"—see him," she said, laughing as she finished his sentence. "Is this how you guys are going to be getting along tomorrow? I didn't think I came all the way from New York to be a referee."

"No," Kirk said. "You came out for another reason—a far better mission." He leaned in closer to her.

Everly automatically inched away. He's *got* to be kidding. "Oh?" she asked. "And what is that—to teach you a few things?"

Everly could fight fire with fire.

"Oh, great," Eddie said, oblivious to the moves his partner was making, or at least pretending to be. "Don't tell me you're another one of these hotshot New Yorkers who think they're the only ones who know shit about field producin'. If I gotta dime for every producer's ass I've saved, I'd be sittin' on a beach somewheres in the Bahamas sippin' a frozen daiquiri instead of haulin' twenty pounds of equipment around every day. I didn't think you were one of those types."

"I'm not!" That's all she needed—a bad "rep" with the field crews. Everly hoped he was just teasing her. "Who at EBC gives you a hard time?"

"Oh, so you want some gossip?" Kirk asked. "No names, Eddie. Our lips are sealed." He gave her a sly look. "There's nothing you could say or do that will get this information out of us."

"Come on," Eddie said. "What's the big deal? Hell—it's no secret who the biggest assholes at EBC are."

"How long is the list?" Everly asked.

"Long enough," Kirk said.

"Any *Morning* folks on it?"

"Just a few," Eddie said. "Most of you guys are pretty good. You take time to shoot somethin' and you use most of what you shoot. 'Course your Rutie Proctor is another story." He winced at the thought of her. " 'Member when we shot that fashion story in Tokyo? Fourteen tapes, *fourteen*, and she never even *finished* the damn piece! It was bad enough havin' to spend five days with her. And for what?"

"At least we ate at nice places," Kirk said.

"Yeah," Eddie said. "Hell, if she were a stingy broad, no one would work with her. 'Course I really hate it when we have to do 'quick and dirty' shoots for *Evenin' News Worldwide*. Just pluggin' into an audio board isn't why I'm in this here business."

"That's why we're looking forward to *this* shoot," Kirk said. "We can get a chance to be a little creative."

"Well, if you think of anything I can do to make this story better, don't hesitate to say something," Everly said. "I specifically requested you guys because I've heard you're good. I'm glad I'm finally getting to work with you."

"Thanks," Eddie said. "We heard about you, too."

Everly wanted details. She wouldn't have been surprised if one of her colleagues like Kerri Marks or Rutie Proctor had sullied her name. "Like what?"

"We don't want to give you a swollen head," Kirk said.

"Right," Eddie said, joining in the fun. "We got enough egos to deal with at EBC."

"But what did you hear?"

"Good stuff," Eddie said. "Honest. Right, Kirk?"

"You could call it that. Yes, you certainly could call it that." He smiled at her.

Everly started to feel better. "So what exactly did you hear?"

"You know we're just teasin,' " Eddie said, a worried look on his face.

"You *do* have a reputation though," Kirk said.

What about yours, she thought. "I bet I do," she said.

"Nothin' to worry about—it's all good," Eddie said, trying to reassure her.

"I still want to know what it is."

"Not a word, Eddie," Kirk said.

"But that's not fair!" Everly said.

"Who ever said life was fair?" Kirk asked.

He moved closer to her and flashed another smile. He had the sexiest blue eyes she'd ever seen. He took a final swallow of his drink and looked right into her eyes as he licked his lips.

An involuntary chill made Everly shudder.

This assignment was going to be more of a challenge than she had imagined.

"These are all my pills and vitamins," Kathleen said, pointing to an astonishing array of bottles on the kitchen counter, filled with multicolored capsules, tablets, and pills.

Even the sight of all that medicine couldn't convince Everly that Kathleen had a major health problem. She was such a lively woman. Her trim size and hairstyle—dark brown in a pixie cut—made her look like a young healthy teenager.

Kathleen was giving them a preliminary tour of the apartment, and she'd just finished explaining that she was on so many different kinds of medication, she had to have an intricate checklist tailored for each time during the day when she took medicine.

Everly made a note to make sure that Kirk got a close-up of all the bottles.

"Did the hospital prescribe the vitamins?" she asked.

"Not exactly. But Dr. Norman knows what I'm taking. He said that the vitamins can't hurt. I believe they'll help."

"Sometimes, just believing makes it work," Bill Limona said, putting an arm around his wife. Bill was much taller than Kathleen. An affable chap, he was slightly overweight, had thick, sandy-colored hair, warm brown eyes, and a smile that went right to your heart.

"Why don't we go in the living room and get started?" Everly said. She was always careful about not talking much before a taping. Too many times the best material was said off camera, so she kept conversations short before the tape started to roll.

"Where do you want to set up?" she asked Kirk.

"That end of the couch is fine," he said, pointing to the far corner, away from the window. She probably would've chosen the same spot, but she always left that decision up to the cameraman. He knew more about light and camera angles then she did. That's what he was paid for.

"Mommy, what's that?" Wendy, the Limona's three-year-old daughter, pointed to Eddie's tape machine. Her long blond hair was pulled back into a tight, beribboned ponytail. She was adorable.

Eddie had just pinned tiny microphones to Kathleen's bright green sweater and Bill's jacket lapel and was hooking the wires to his machine. He smiled shyly back at Wendy.

"Is it okay for the kids to be here?" Kathleen asked.

"Of course," Everly said. "As long as they're quiet. It's good if they get used to us now."

"Would you like to hear how your mommy sounds through this?" Eddie asked, holding the headset out to Wendy. She toddled over, and he gently placed the equipment over her ears.

"I'd like to look through the camera," Jonathan said. He was the Limona's six-year-old son; tortoiseshell glasses emphasized his serious expression. He had his mother's fine dark looks.

"Okay," Kirk said. "You can help me set it up on the tripod."

Jonathan's eyes widened.

It was refreshing to see kids get excited about the things adults took for granted. On first impression, these kids didn't seem spoiled.

Everly hated to think about what lay ahead of them.

In a few moments, after checking out the equipment, the kids sat off to the side on the carpet, out of camera range. The interview started.

Everly sat in a chair placed kitty-corner to the Limonas. Kirk was right next to her, and Eddie was behind him, checking sound levels as the interview progressed, and keeping an eye on the time. Field cassettes were twenty minutes in length, and you didn't want to miss something good just because you'd run out of tape. Everly had heard that Eddie Lister was a real pro; time was one thing she wouldn't have to be concerned with.

She had enough to worry about.

Even though she was edited out of the interviews she conducted for *Morning*, she always got a high before the questioning began. Nothing could beat shaping an interview, being in control, knowing that you alone could get something special out of someone.

"Bill, we'll start with you," Everly said. "Now remember—the final piece won't include my questions, so try to answer in complete sentences. If I say, for example, 'How do you earn a living?' answer by saying something like, 'The way I earn a living is such-and-such,' instead of just saying 'scientific research,' okay?"

"Sure, I understand," Bill said. "Are you going to make me a TV star?"

"If you want me to," Everly said.

"You better not," Kathleen said. "We have *enough* things to deal with."

Though she was smiling, Everly knew she was only half kidding.

"Are we ready?" she asked Kirk and Eddie.

"Looking good," Kirk said, squinting into his viewfinder.

"It's a go for me," Eddie said.

Everly turned to Bill. "What did you do in Southfield before you came here?" she asked.

Her opening questions were generally for background purposes and fairly benign in content. It took a while for most people to warm up to a videotaped interview, so she saved the more involved issues for later on.

"I had my own research company when we lived in Southfield."

Good, she thought, a complete, articulate answer. He caught on quickly.

"The city government has a pretty open-minded policy towards getting small businesses to locate there, and we got a grant from them," he continued. "We had a group of eight people—three research scientists, some computer specialists, and a scattering of office personnel."

"What were you working on?"

"Our research focused on hardening of the arteries. We were experimenting with a new procedure that would be an alternative to major surgery. We were developing a special device that could widen arteries clogged with the buildup of plaque, fatty deposits, and cholesterol."

"Is the business still functioning?"

"The business is in the hands of my partner. I was lucky to be teamed up with someone I could trust. We've been out here such a long time—never thought we'd be here so long, but you do what you have to do." He looked nervously at Kathleen for a moment. She gave him an encouraging smile.

Everly knew Kirk was capturing every nuance between the two of them.

"How do you pass the time here?"

"Our lives are very different here in California. We don't have any family out here—it's just us. In a way it's nice just to be with the kids and with Kathleen full-time. There's a lot to do—get Jonathan ready for school, take care of Wendy, worry about meals, make sure Kathleen takes her medicine. We go to the hospital every week for her checkups. I don't have a regular job, if that's what you mean."

"Tell me how you manage financially," Everly said, glancing down briefly at her page of questions, to make sure she wasn't missing anything.

"Most of Kathleen's bills are covered by insurance, so we're lucky there. Right now, we're living on our savings. We have a house back in Southfield. It's just waiting for us all to return. We're renting here—got a fairly decent deal. We're lucky the kids are at an age when they can still share a room, so this two-bedroom apartment suits our needs. If I'd known we were going to be out here so long, though, I would have rented out our house back in Michigan. But I guess it's all meant for the best."

"What do you miss most about back home?"

He paused a moment and looked down at his folded hands. "I just want Kathleen to get better," he said. "This . . . this problem came up right after Wendy was born. Before that, our lives were so different. I mean, the focus of everything we do here is Kathleen and her health. It's tough on a family, very tough."

He turned and put an arm around his wife. "But we're all here together," he said. "And we're going to see this through."

It sounded as if he were giving himself, as well as everyone else, a familiar pep talk.

"And she's going to get a donor and we're going to lick this," he added solemnly.

Everly turned to Kathleen.

"What is it like for you to be here?"

"It's hard to describe what I'm going through now," she said quietly. "I really feel so much better, because of the medication I'm on. I'm not nearly as tired as I used to be, and we can get out and do things. But it's always hanging over my head that this isn't going to last forever—that I'm waiting for a major operation, a *difficult* operation. And even though Stanford University Hospital has an impressive success rate with heart/lung transplants, it's still a relatively difficult procedure." She stopped and caught Bill's eye. "And there's no guarantee that it'll work," she added.

"It'll work," Bill said firmly. "It's got to work."

"It must be kind of isolating to be here, away from your family and friends for so long. How do you handle that?"

"Both of us grew up near Detroit and our families have taken turns coming out here to visit," Kathleen said. "They usually stay in a motel nearby for a week or two. A few of my friends have come out here."

"We had a big party for Kathleen's twenty-ninth birthday about four months ago," Bill said. "It was a real surprise."

"That was such a shock!" Kathleen said. "Bill said that he wanted to take me out to a special restaurant, but he wouldn't tell me which one. He said he wanted to surprise me. When my birthday finally came, he was so insistent about my being on time for the reservation—I couldn't understand why he was so concerned. He's usually so easygoing about those kinds of things." She reached up and gave a quick squeeze to the hand around her shoulder.

"Anyway, we finally get to this restaurant," she continued, "and the maître d' made a big fuss about our having a special table. He brought us all the way through the restaurant back to a private room. We walked in, and there were six couples from home—our closest friends, and both our parents." Kathleen laughed. "They didn't yell 'surprise' because they were afraid they were going to give me a heart attack! Can you imagine? But it was wonderful—really wonderful."

"Do you have pictures?" Everly asked. They would be perfect for some before/after comparisons in the final piece that she was going to put together.

"Better than that," Bill said. "I rented a video camera, and we have most of it on tape."

"Great," Everly said. "Can we borrow it? I'll make a copy of it when I get back to New York and get it right back to you."

"That would be fine," Kathleen said, looking to her husband for reassurance.

"No problem," he said.

It was clear that they had a close relationship, so Everly decided to ask a more personal question. "How has this whole experience affected your marriage?"

Bill answered immediately. "When I married Kathleen, I felt so lucky, because I knew I was going to spend the rest of my life with this very special lady. Maybe this sounds trite and silly, but each day with her is even more precious now."

Everly could tell that he was trying very hard not to cry.

Kathleen looked at him. "I never thought I could grow to love someone more each day. But it's true. We've been through some very tough things. But when I got so ill, that was the worst. There were times when I could hardly breathe. It was awful. And then having to drop everything and move here—of course it was exciting to be chosen for this program—still, the change hasn't been easy. If I hadn't married a man like Bill, I don't know how I could have managed."

"But doesn't every marriage have its rough points?" Everly asked. It's what she believed, or professed to. They clearly had a close relationship; she so envied them, she didn't want to acknowledge that they had something she couldn't imagine having in her own life. "In any normal relationship, you can't help but get upset with each other once in a while. Do you feel guilty if you get angry about something? You're all so confined here—don't you ever get on each other's nerves?"

Bill looked at her, somewhat surprised at the question. Everly was sure he hadn't realized until now the full extent of what he'd gotten himself into when Kathleen agreed to this interview.

"There's something that I don't think you really understand," he said earnestly. "There just isn't *time* for that sort of thing. Sure, you get a little testy, but really, for the most part it's not like a normal relationship. It's not normal at all. I mean look at us. We have two beautiful children—and they're just *kids*! And Kathleen, not even thirty yet—to be going through such a thing. We've been married only seven years. No, there's just no time for anger."

Most times when Everly interviewed a couple that claimed to be so lovey-dovey, the cynic in her expected the hollering to start as soon as she and the crew were out the door. But the Limonas were different. She truly ached for them.

And she believed every word they said.

"Those kids were really cute," Eddie said.

They were having after-dinner drinks at the bar in their hotel. It had been a very full day and they all were tired.

"That little girl is going to be a knockout someday," Kirk said.

"Is that all you can think about?" Everly asked.

"Oh, I think about other things," he said, giving her a knowing look.

Everly almost followed his lead, but then decided to change the subject. "That was a good idea you had about having the kids go to play in the playground."

"I have lots of good ideas," Kirk said.

She looked at Eddie. "Is he like this all the time?"

"Pretty much," Eddie said. "Depends on who he's with, I guess."

"You mean if it's jailbait or not," Everly said.

"Touché," Kirk said, giving her a wink.

"Well, I don't know about you guys, but I'm going to call it a night," Eddie said, getting up from the table.

Everly had already signed for the meal. "You're going to leave me alone with this guy?" she said.

"You can handle him," Eddie said. "He's just an ol' stiff."

"Thanks a lot, good buddy," Kirk said. "I don't need enemies with friends like you."

"Always happy to oblige," he said.

"Actually, I'm tired, too. Jet lag strikes again," Everly said.

"Fine," Kirk said. "Let's all go to bed."

"We are," she said. "Only not the way you'd like."

The three of them got up from the table and walked out into the corridor that connected the restaurant to the hotel.

Eddie came to his room first. "G'night, you guys. What time we meetin' for breakfast?"

"We're not due over at the hospital until eleven," Everly said. "We should probably shoot exteriors before that. How about if we just meet in the lobby ready to go at nine-thirty?"

"Okay with me," Eddie said.

"Me, too," Kirk said.

He and Everly continued to walk down the hall. Her room was around the corner.

"So what do you think?" she asked.

"Of what?"

"Are you coming in or what?"

Maybe it wasn't the smartest thing to do, but after spending the day with the Limonas, her confusion with Hank, and the call from Jared, Everly didn't want to be alone tonight. She needed to make some kind of connection with a man, however fleeting or superficial. And besides feeling needy, she was curious.

When it came to men, Everly was probably one of the last women on earth brought up the old-fashioned way. But ever since she'd been introduced to the quaint notion that you were supposed to sleep with only one man your whole life, she'd been incredibly obsessed with every attractive man she'd ever met—not that she always acted on it. But you could say that when times were safer, she'd had her share of intimate experiences.

Meeting Jared had put an end to that—as had these notoriously unsafe times. Ironically, it was partially because of Jared that she was about to take this next step.

Even when she was monogamous, though, she never lost her curiosity about men. Or her needs. She was intrigued by this quintessential stud who typified the kind of guy who had been totally out of her league when she was growing up. Surely wherever Kirk Peterson went through life, he had always been part of the "in" crowd, the elite ones who were popular and never seemed to worry about their social lives. Everly had always been part of a different circle . . .

Yet tonight he was hers for the taking.

She knew her sudden acquiescence would completely throw him.

"Well aren't *you* the foxy one," he said. "I had no idea—"

"Let's keep it that way. No one has any idea. I don't usually do this sort of thing."

"How 'bout my place?" he said.

"Nope. It's here or nothing."

"Let me just get a few things. I'll be right back—promise!"

Before Everly could say another word, or change her mind, he ran down the hall to his room.

She wondered what he was going to get. She also wondered whether this was the wisest thing to do under the circumstances.

But sometimes you do crazy things . . .

If only she could get the Limonas out of her mind. How she envied them. Kathleen was *dying*, but look what she had, what they'd built.

If she could have, Everly would have traded places in a second.

SEVEN

Twelve months without sex.

Everly had chosen Kirk Peterson almost as an afterthought—a man she barely knew—to break her record of celibacy. But in a perverse way, it actually made sense. She would have been more scared to sleep with someone who had any significance in her life. *That* she wasn't ready for—especially after getting Jared's call. She just wanted to connect physically with someone, to have incredible, intense sex and no responsibility.

It was obvious that Kirk wanted the same thing; her decision was an appropriate one.

She walked into the bathroom and rummaged through her makeup kit in search of the diaphragm and pack of condoms she'd thrown in there under the pretense of being "prepared" for absolutely anything. She'd had a premonition that she was going to have a sexual encounter on this trip.

It was amazing how getting out of town gave one a temporary sense of freedom. It was as if every time you traveled, you had the opportunity to reinvent yourself. She welcomed this chance not to be the Everly Dalton who had tried so hard to make up for the humiliation and pain of being practically left at the altar. Instead, she could just be a woman reaching out to a man, a woman who was desired, who was free to choose, let go.

If Kirk didn't come to her room soon, she was going to lose her nerve.

She heard a quiet tapping on the door.

"Who's there?" she asked, just to be sure.

"Who do you think?" Kirk answered.

Everly opened the door and he rushed in saying, "Come on, we're not in New York where you have a lot of crazy nuts running around."

Even though she had lowered the lights, she could see that he had changed shirts. He was wearing a white silky-looking top open to midchest, which showed off his tanned, well-defined physique. A hint of sandalwood filled the room, and Everly smiled at the thought of his bothering to splash on some cologne before coming over—not that she was too surprised.

He put a small brown paper bag on the night table next to the bed, and then he sat down and smiled, patting the space next to him. "Hey, come here, you."

Everly went to him, suffused with fear, anticipation, and a vague sense of arousal. It had been such a long time since she'd even allowed herself to give in to these feelings. It was enough of a shock a year ago making the transition from a steady relationship—one that she had thought had a future—to absolutely nothing.

And now this.

She sat next to Kirk, and he put his arm around her, gently stroking her shoulder in tiny little circles. She'd previously taken off all her clothes and was only wearing a thin robe.

It felt as if he were burning a hole through the material.

He moved closer and, with his free hand, lifted her face to his. He leaned down to kiss her, and for a split second their eyes met. Everly quickly closed hers. She didn't want to think about anything; it was almost as if she were in a dream. She just wanted to let the evening happen.

His lips brushed gently against hers, and then he kissed the side of her neck and the little hollow behind her ear. She couldn't help but sigh, and he pulled away for a moment and gave her a knowing smile.

She knew she was an easy target, but she didn't care.

"Let's get comfortable, babe," he said, as he slipped off his shoes. "Take off my clothes," he whispered.

Everly could do nothing but obey. She was still a little nervous, but she wanted to appear sophisticated and relaxed. She was also curious about what he looked like naked. She unbuttoned his shirt and quickly pulled it off his shoulders. His jeans were next and it was a little awkward getting them off. He wore dark bikini briefs underneath and the sight of them made her lose her nerve for a moment. Jared wore the same kind.

Kirk threw her a questioning look.

"My hands are cold," Everly lied. "You better finish."

He laughed and said, "Your turn to be undressed." He untied her robe, edging it off her shoulders, clearly relishing what he saw in the dim light. He motioned for her to lie back on the pillows, and as he kissed her, she sensed him fumbling with his underpants.

"That's more like it," he said, as he pressed their naked bodies together.

The feel of flesh against flesh almost sent her into a swoon. This first taste of intimacy after such a barren period was almost overwhelming.

It was wonderful.

Kirk was kissing her again, very slowly. Every inch of her body responded to him. God, he was good. She could feel herself warm to his touch. She'd almost forgotten the pleasurable sense of surrender she felt when a man kissed her and caressed her a certain way.

His lips were so gentle and soft. He ran his hand slowly up and down her body. There was something so sweet about how he was treating her that she wanted to cry. His touch was comforting, yet quietly erotic.

Everly marveled at how perfect strangers could lock into each other's sexual rhythms. Kirk knew exactly what to do.

Her entire body ached for the feel of him. It felt as if she were sinking slowly into some delicious pool of sensations. She was floating, floating.

Amidst everything, the practical side of her brain had acknowledged that condoms would have to be mentioned soon, when suddenly, Kirk stopped what he was doing and reached for the paper bag he'd set down on her night table.

Maybe he'd brought his own protection.

"Come on, babe. Try some."

Everly didn't know what he was talking about because of the dim lighting. She couldn't see what he held out to her.

"What is it?"

"Amyl nitrate," he said.

"Are you serious? I mean, do I have to?" Everly suddenly felt scared. What the hell was she doing in bed with a guy who used drugs? "I'm just not into that sort of thing," she added. "You know—I'd rather have a natural high." That sounded pretty lame, but she didn't know what else to say.

"But this stuff is great, babe. Have you ever tried it?"

"What is it supposed to do?"

"Really get you going," he said.

"But you've already got me going. I don't need anything else." She was feeling more and more uncomfortable.

"This will make sex really special. It's a real kick."

"Plain old sex is enough of a kick for me."

He laughed, but continued to press the issue. "You should try it. Just break a capsule under your nose and inhale. It's simple."

"It's just not for me, Kirk."

"Come on. What's the big deal? This isn't dangerous stuff or anything. I promise you—the sex will be incredible. Trust me."

That did it.

She never trusted anyone who said, "Trust me."

"Look," she said, irritated. "I was having a fine time

without it. If you want to use it, go ahead. But you'll have to use one of these, too." She reached for the package of Trojans she'd placed in the night table drawer and held it up for him to see.

He squinted and flipped on the lamp next to the bed. The light hurt her eyes, and for a moment she felt embarrassed to be naked in the bright light.

"Forget it, babe. It's like doing it through a blanket."

"Kirk, what century are you living in? You don't know me that well; I can imagine *your* track record—"

"Hey—give me a break! I'm not exactly in a high risk group—I've never been with prostitutes or homosexuals—God forbid—or drug addicts. I take care of myself."

"Then you shouldn't mind using these."

"I can't believe this," he said, moving off the bed. He picked his jeans up from the floor.

Everly scrambled under the sheets and watched him, her heart pounding. Everything had stopped so suddenly.

She felt like a jerk.

"So that's it, then," she said, "despite all the come-ons today and last night."

"I don't use condoms."

"Fine. You want to be stupid about this—your loss."

He looked at her and shook his head as he zipped up his pants. "Sorry, babe. Those are just my rules."

There he was, standing there half-naked, his incredible body just a few feet away. He was so damned arrogant about his stupid rules and his obsession with amyl nitrate. Anger quelled any residual desires.

"You can stuff your rules," Everly said.

He quickly grabbed his paper bag and walked out of the room.

At least he didn't slam the door.

It was hard to believe that this stubborn idiot was the same man who just moments ago had made her feel so incredibly good.

It was going to be a long time before she went to bed with anyone again.

At least she had some good memories from Indianapolis to live on vicariously for a while.

"I love having you in my arms," Jared said as they lay nestled on a picnic blanket.

It was one of those crisp spring days that could have masqueraded for fall were it not for the delicate buds on tree branches and the wonderfully fresh fragrance in the air.

They were in a secluded part of Eagle Creek Park. It was a slow time at the television station, and they had impulsively decided to take the day off and spend it in the park. Not too many people were around—not even the ubiquitous sheriff. For some odd reason the Indianapolis town fathers had placed a sheriff's station smack in the middle of the park grounds, and when you least expected it—or wanted it for that matter—you were confronted with someone in uniform.

"You'll be going to Chicago soon," Everly said. "Not too many more of these opportunities to take advantage of—"

"That's short term, Everly. So we'll have a commuter marriage for a while. It's been done."

She looked up at him and caught that faraway look in his eyes that sometimes sent her into a mild panic. Even though part of Jared's appeal was the sense of mystery he carried with him, it posed problems as well.

She was always certain he knew her far better than she could ever know him.

"I've never had a long-distance relationship," she said. "Guess I should hurry up and get a phone company with good long-distance rates."

They'd known about his move for a month now. The thought of his being in another city scared Everly, but it didn't seem to bother him. When the subject had first come up, she tried to be excited. This was a big move for Jared—being promoted to a major television market like Chicago. It seemed selfish to worry about how it would affect their upcoming marriage. So what if the wedding had to be postponed a few months—the change of date was easier to arrange than she'd thought it would be.

Everly interpreted that as a good omen.

Whenever the move came up, she tried not to say anything negative about it. Jared seemed so right for her that she was afraid of saying or doing anything that might threaten their relationship.

"You're always so practical," he said, flashing a sly smile that cut through to her heart. He gave her hand a squeeze. "That's why we're such a good team. I know you're going to get that new talk show. After some solid live interview experience, you'll be ready for the Chicago market—I'm sure of it. Jane Pauley made the leap from this town to Chicago pretty quickly—you'll do the same. I'll bring you on board at WMPQ. And no one will put up a fuss about nepotism or lack of experience. God, it'll be great, Everly!"

Jared was always most animated when he talked about anything related to work. She ran her fingers through his thick mane of dark brown hair. It was surprisingly soft and fine, like baby hair.

"Bet you'll have to cut your hair more often when you're in Chicago around all those hotshot executives," Everly said.

"Not if I can help it. We'll see. It's no big sacrifice if that's all they care about there. Hey—it'll grow back."

It was starting to get dark and the wind had picked up a bit. Without warning, Jared reached over and pulled her closer to him. Before Everly could say another word, his lips pressed against hers and the sudden taste of him sent quiet shock waves through her body. It was as if she'd been in sexual limbo all day and this unexpected intimacy activated some kind of switch that had been patiently waiting to be turned on.

Their legs were entwined, and she pressed against him slowly, rhythmically, as they continued to kiss. He rolled on top of her, and the weight of his body only fueled her desire for him.

Jared suddenly reached down to her belt, and she could feel him struggling to get it undone.

Were they really going to do it here? In the park? Anyone could walk by.

He'd read Everly's mind. "It's okay," he whispered in her ear, his breathing heavy. "No one's around. It'll be all right. I know what you want, Everly. I know what you want."

In an instant their jeans and underwear were out of the way and he was inside of her, pushing into her, caught up in the spontaneity of the moment.

"I know what you want, I know what you want," he said, over and over, as if it were some private mantra that was theirs and theirs alone.

Part of Everly couldn't block out the park, the open space, the hard-packed ground beneath her, but she told herself to relax, relax. Her fiancé was making love to her—outside, under the trees, in the fresh cold air—because it was what she wanted. He was giving her what she wanted . . .

But he was taking something, too.

"I have all of your interviews lined up for you," Melanie Sorkin announced as Kirk and Eddie filed behind Everly into the hospital with their equipment.

"Thanks, Melanie. Your help is most appreciated," Everly said. Melanie Sorkin was the public relations coordinator for Stanford University Hospital.

As anyone who works in the media knows, public relations people can either be a blessing or a curse—and they're usually the latter. They are often the last people to know what a good story is—especially when it comes to network television—and they're the first ones to get in your way when you're on to something interesting.

Melanie set an example for her profession, and Everly wished she could have cloned her, because she was one of the most efficient PR people she'd ever met. Since this was a fairly straightforward human interest segment, Everly didn't expect any trouble from the hospital—certainly not from Melanie, at any rate. Kirk Peterson, however, was another story.

He'd been moody in the car on the way over from the hotel. It wasn't clear how much he'd told Eddie about last night, because his partner was in fairly chatty spirits for most of the ride, which made a potentially awkward situation bearable. She'd hoped that Kirk was enough of a professional that he wouldn't pull anything malicious, like purposely shooting tape that was slightly out of focus. There was plenty a vengeful cameraman could do to ruin a segment, and Everly didn't want to be on the receiving end of that kind of spite.

"Dr. Benson can see you this morning," Melanie said, glancing at a small stenographer's pad that she held in her hand. "He's not due in surgery until one o'clock. Risa Vyner, one of the staff psychologists, is available at four. Two of our successful transplant patients are going to have their monthly checkups this afternoon, so you can interview both of them if you like, and I've also arranged for you to take a lunch break at about twelve-thirty." She looked up from the pad. "Is that all satisfactory?"

"Do you do windows, ma'am?" Eddie asked.

Even Kirk had to laugh at that.

"Well, I'm just trying to be efficient," she said, blushing.

Everly was sure Melanie had never dealt with characters like these before.

"I know how valuable your time is and I just want to smooth the way for you," Melanie added, clearly embarrassed.

"Sounds like you've arranged our whole day for us pretty effectively," Everly said.

"We'll have to figure a way to show you our appreciation," Kirk said, flashing her one of his suggestive looks.

To Everly's amazement, she actually felt jealous.

"I beg your pardon," Melanie said.

"Don't mind him, ma'am," Eddie said. "He's just tryin' to be friendly."

Melanie giggled and blushed again. She looked to be in her late fifties and was a rather sophisticated, no-nonsense kind of woman. Everly sensed she wasn't used to being propositioned in this manner.

"Oh, nonsense," Melanie said. "You must have your hands

full with these two," she said quietly to Everly, a touch of envy in her voice.

"You could say that," Everly said. "But I think we better hustle on over to Dr. Benson before it gets too late."

"Of course," she said. "Please follow me."

"We'll follow you anywhere," Kirk said as he looked at Everly and winked.

It was as if last night was just a bad dream. Everly's apprehension dissolved. So this was how it was going to be—a lot of innocuous flirting. If it wasn't targeted at her, it would be directed toward any readily available female. No, Kirk wouldn't stoop to sabotaging her story. It wasn't worth it. He wasn't going to blow his reputation as one of the country's best cameramen because of some insignificant one-night stand that didn't happen.

What could she have been thinking? How could she forget that there was only one thing that counted in this business: it was what they all threw their creativity into, what they all fought for, did their best for. It was what culminated for a few brief moments into the ultimate high: a segment on the network's valuable airtime.

It was the only thing that really mattered.

EIGHT

Coming back from a field shoot always left Everly feeling slightly schizophrenic. While it was a relief to be home—and New York actually felt like home to her now—her return also meant she would once again have to deal with the realities of day-to-day life: handling office politics and the consequences of being in the doghouse with Nigel; reconciling her new attraction to Hank with his new attraction to another woman; Jared's impending visit; and the simple responsibility of the work she had to do. The hours of material she'd shot with the Limona family would have to be edited down to a five or six minute piece—with Reggie Graham and Nigel Elliot staring over her shoulder.

Everly would never deny how much she loved working in television news, but sometimes the demands seemed utterly overwhelming.

She checked the time—9:30. Not too late to call Beryl.

She glanced at her answering machine, grateful that there

were no calls. No more surprises from Jared . . . yet.

Beryl picked up right away.

"Hello?"

"I'm back."

"So how was it?" Beryl asked.

"I almost had a fling . . ."

"You're kidding! Isn't that a little dangerous?"

"Well, nothing happened. I'll tell you about it when I see you."

"How'd the shoot go?"

"We got a lot of good stuff," Everly said. "I hope you get to meet Kathleen Limona someday. She's quite special."

"Just watch out, Everly. You told me how involved you sometimes get with your stories—like when you started doing volunteer work after you did that 'homeless in hospitals' piece a couple years ago, or when you almost became a foster parent after a segment on child abuse."

"This is different. We spent a lot of time together on this shoot. I think I really got to know her, and I just have this feeling. *Someone's* story has to have a happy ending. Strange, now that I think about it, Kathleen reminds me of you in some ways. She *has* to get that operation."

"I think you already have enough on your mind to deal with, without worrying about her."

"Don't remind me," Everly said. "Maybe I should just expect everything I do to go down the drain. Then I wouldn't have to worry about it."

"Didn't you once tell me that you *majored* in worry?"

"Right. And I passed with flying colors. So did I miss much while I was away? I called in for messages, but there didn't seem to be anything earth shattering here."

"I hear Kerri Marks is on the rampage. Something is going on with her and Reggie."

"What do you mean?"

"Well, they seem to be spending an awful lot of time together in Reggie's office behind closed doors," Beryl said.

"Hear anything like jungle sounds through the walls?"

Beryl laughed. "You're something else, Everly."

"Well, maybe they're getting back together again," she said. "That should keep him out of *your* backyard for a while."

"I told Stephen your idea about Atlanta, and you know what? He might actually meet me there."

"Terrific. Have you seen Hank at all? How's he doing?"

"Fine, I guess. He always seems so down on everything. It's hard for me to picture you two together. Anyway, he did ask if I'd heard from you."

"When?"

"This morning. I told him no and that you were probably very busy, and that the time difference didn't make it any easier to call back east."

For a second Everly had a disturbing thought. "You didn't say anything about us, did you?"

"Come on—I can keep a promise. He told me you were going to bring back a souvenir for him. What is it?"

"Some candy. No big deal."

Hearing about Hank made Everly feel a lot better. She was glad he'd asked Beryl about her. Somehow that had a calming effect.

With Hank on her mind, maybe she'd be able to deal with the time bomb she knew awaited her with Jared's arrival . . . unless Hank's new girlfriend was still in the picture.

"This is great stuff, Everly."

She was sitting with Fred Keller in an editing room, looking over the material she had just shot in California. He was one of the few editors at EBC who knew what he was doing. Fred was in his early sixties and had made the switch years ago from film to tape—not a simple transition. And he was damned good. It didn't take too long, after people had worked with different editors, for his talent to stand out.

His opinion meant a lot to Everly.

"Thanks. Kirk Peterson and Eddie Lister were my crew."

"Peterson's hot stuff, I hear," Fred said, his face deadpan as he watched the screen. "Looks like you guys did a lot together."

"He's a great cameraman," she said nonchalantly, amused that Fred was trying to get some "dirt." Everyone in television devoured gossip, and Everly wasn't about to provide them with anything to chew on.

"Gorgeous kids," Fred said. "We should use as much of this stuff as we can."

They were looking at the playground material where Jonathan Limona was playing with his sister, Wendy, on the swings, out of earshot from their parents.

"When I grow up, I want to be just like Mommy," Wendy was saying, her clear voice spirited as she swung through the air. "I want to marry someone like Daddy and have a little boy and a little girl.

"Only I won't be sick all the time. And we'll never have to go to a hospital ever again."

"I want to be a doctor," Jonathan said, as he pushed his sister on the swing. "I want to help people. It's important."

Even though he was only six, the combination of his dark glasses and serious demeanor made it seem as if he were a little old man.

"What's it like taking care of your mommy?" Everly's voice cut in, off-camera.

"I know she's going to get better real soon," Wendy said, a smile on her face. "Daddy told me so."

Jonathan looked at his sister and said nothing. The camera lingered on his face just long enough to catch the sadness in his eyes.

Kirk had done some fine work.

Fred stopped the tape. "What do you think is going to happen?" he asked. "Seems tough."

"I don't know. It's hard to tell. Kathleen has a tougher problem than most people who need a heart/lung transplant, because she's so tiny. But I just have this feeling . . ."

"Woman's intuition, huh?"

"No, not that . . . I can't be sure. I want so badly for everything to go well for her, I can't tell if it's my instinct or just wishful thinking."

As they continued viewing the material, Everly was reminded how being in an editing room was like being in a time warp. There were no windows to the outside world; the clock on the wall might just as well have signified four o'clock in the morning as four o'clock in the afternoon—it didn't matter. The atmosphere was always the same.

For her, coming to an editing room was equivalent to a homing pigeon returning to the roost. There was something comforting about being in this private world—accompanied by just one other human being—where you could magically tell a story or explain a news event, create a mood or relive a precious moment.

You became completely absorbed by what you saw on a small television monitor; it was easy to lose track of everything but the story you were working on. Here was a world of picture and sound that you had captured, that only you would shape, and you became involved in the creative process with an intensity that was all-consuming; you were totally impervious to the outside world.

"Mommy and I have a special song," Wendy was saying as she played in the sandbox.

The camera pulled back to include Jonathan, who seemed absorbed in building the perfect sand castle.

"What is it?" Everly asked, off-camera.

"Is it okay if I tell her?" Wendy asked her brother.

He shrugged his shoulders. "I guess it's okay."

" 'Over the Rainbow,' " she said, with obvious delight.

"Would you like to sing it for me?" Everly asked.

Jonathan made a face, but said nothing.

"Sure!" Wendy said. She cleared her throat and looked straight into the camera. Her high, sweet voice filled the room.

"Somewhere over the rainbow, bluebirds fly. Birds fly over the rainbow, why then, oh why can't I?"

Everly looked over at Fred and couldn't help but notice that his eyes had teared up, as had hers.

"You did good, Everly. That's the closer," he said, his voice nearly breaking. "No matter how this story goes."

She nodded in agreement.

And hoped for a happy ending.

* * *

Everly was back in her office going over her notes when she sensed a presence. She looked up, half expecting it to be Kerri Marks, the consummate spy and busybody. No wonder Reggie had pushed for her to be in charge of Special Projects. It gave her a license to snoop around and do his dirty work for him.

But she was wrong—it was Hank Forrest.

"What a nice surprise," she said, genuinely happy to see him.

"Got my stuff?" he asked, sitting in the seat next to her desk.

"Whatever happened to 'Hi, Everly, welcome back. Have a good trip? Nice to see you. Oh, by the way, were you able to do that favor I asked?' Some greeting, Hank."

He looked a little embarrassed and glanced down at the floor. "You're right. Sorry. Guess I'm too much of a chocoholic to be a gentleman. But it is good to see you back."

"You're forgiven."

"So where's my stuff?" he asked, smiling broadly.

"I'll bring it tomorrow. I forgot to bring in my canvas bag. You know, they had some free samples and you were right—it was great."

Once again they were spending a rare moment together talking about the damned chocolates. Was he really glad to see her? Was he still seeing Miss Subways? He still had his beard.

"Food is probably the only thing I'm ever right about," he said.

"What do you mean?"

"You might have been on to something about Bernice—her old boyfriend is trying to get back in her life and she's not sure what she wants to do."

How ironic.

Perhaps there was something in the air.

"It's just another crazy situation I've gotten myself into," he added.

Even though Everly wanted to confide in Hank about her

own similar situation, something kept her from doing so. She just shrugged her shoulders and said nothing.

"It's pretty weird," he continued. "I don't really know her for that long, but the few times we've been together, this guy, Bert, occasionally came up in conversation, and all she talked about was what a shit he was. Now she's done a complete hundred-and-eighty-degree turnaround and is being real defensive about him."

Everly rather liked the fact that he was complaining about Bernice, but she hid her satisfaction and tried to be helpful. "Well, whenever my life seems to be getting out of hand—which seems to be happening a lot lately—I have this little game I play—just for the hell of it. I ask myself, 'If I could wave a magic wand, what would I want?' Sometimes it helps. Sometimes you don't really need a magic wand."

He looked skeptical. "That's just for kids," he said.

Everly tried to quell a sudden flash of anger. "Is that what *I* am?"

"In a way. No offense."

"Well, sometimes we 'kids' are smarter than you might think. You did say I was probably right about Miss Subways."

He laughed. The tension in the room dissipated slightly. "Miss Subways? That's a great monicker. I'm sure she'd like it."

"You're welcome to try it out on her. So what do you want from this lady?"

"I don't know. Chicks just drive me nuts."

"It's mutual," Everly muttered.

"What?"

"Nothing. Look—it's not like you're engaged. What if she does see this other guy? Did she say she didn't want to see you anymore?"

"No, but it sounded like they almost got married."

"So? Is that your game plan?"

"How the hell do I know? I just met her a month ago. Why does everything have to be so damned complicated! No wonder I've been in this business so long. News is cut and dried. You got fifteen seconds to write, you write it. You need twenty seconds—no problem. Every story with a beginning, a middle, and an end. Who, what, where, when—all that stuff they teach you in journalism school. Facts. No gray—strictly black and white."

Right, Everly thought. And sometimes just as dull and predictable. "I don't know how accurate *that* is," she said.

"Chocolate would make me feel better," Hank said solemnly.

She couldn't help but laugh. "Maybe we should send some of this stuff to the Soviet Union. World peace and all that," she said.

"Imagine what Nigel would do with that one. I can hear the fanfare now—and then the announcement: 'See's Sends Celestial Sweets to the Soviets!' Boy, I'd like to hear Glen Korbett say that real fast five times in a row."

Hank didn't care for their co-host's powers of enunciation and sometimes scripted real mouthfuls for Glen—when he could get away with it.

"How about, 'Kremlin Comrades Crave Candy Kisses'?" Everly said.

"Wrong company," Hank said.

"Just fudging it, I guess."

He groaned and gave her a pained look.

"Sorry," Everly said. "I just couldn't resist."

"You should try writing some of the teases once in a while. We could use some new blood there."

"Teases" were the phrases their hosts used to promote the next segment of the show before they went into a commercial break. Hank loved to throw in the occasional pun. It was a way to entice viewers to keep from switching channels—a routine part of viewing habits, thanks to remote control.

"No, thanks. That's your territory. Wouldn't want to take that away from you, good buddy—"

Her phone interrupted them.

"*Morning*," she said.

"Everly? We need a little favor."

It was Reggie. He was the kind of guy who never asked

for volunteers. You just did what you were asked. And if you didn't come through, it was remembered . . . and used accordingly.

Everly dreaded what kind of "favor" he had in mind.

"Sure, happy to help," she said. "What do you need?"

"Can you be set writer for tomorrow?"

"No problem. Who canceled?"

"Victoria Lenox—something came up and she had a conflict. Whatever. See you in the a.m."

He hung up.

It was frustrating how Victoria seemed to do the least amount of work compared to the rest of the staff, and she got away with it. The only thing Everly could figure was that she must have known where an awful lot of skeletons at EBC were buried.

"What was that all about?" Hank asked.

"Guess who the lucky set writer is for tomorrow?"

"Tough break, kid. Gee, I was all set to ask you out for a late night drink after work."

Everly looked at him, trying to guess whether or not he was telling the truth.

"Bullshit," she said.

"On second thought—you just got back from the Coast—I guess you need your rest so that you can be in at 5:30 tomorrow."

"You're really full of it, you know that? I should have gotten you a shovel."

"Just don't forget the candy."

"Right. First thing on my list."

He winked at her, got up, and walked out the door.

Everly shook her head, trying to sort out everything that was on her mind. She'd accomplished absolutely nothing with Hank. She was worried about Jared. Her editing schedule for the week was a great looming catastrophe. And now she had just enough time to head back home, grab something to eat, and get a few decent hours of sleep before getting up at four-thirty to make it back in time to handle Reggie's "little favor."

Some life.

As long as she didn't think about it too hard, everything was just terrific.

NINE

Everly shuddered as she got into the cab.

Venturing out into Manhattan at five o'clock in the morning was an otherworldly experience. You might as well have been on the moon.

Massive structures towered over craters of darkness. The absence of light at that hour robbed the usually strident buildings of their glitter, and everything looked gray and colorless. Sidewalks normally clogged with humanity were eerily stark, save the occasional homeless sprawled across recessed store entrances.

Everly's lone cab glided breezily through the dreary streets. EBC's brightly lit lobby offered a harsh welcome from the foreboding outside world.

She nodded at the security guard, who recognized her by now, so she didn't have to pull out an ID card. "Security" was a misnomer around EBC. She'd heard countless tales of crazed fans getting easy clearance into *Morning*'s offices while Glen Korbett or Corah Washington, two of the most public personalities in the country, were delayed by the guard until they produced their ID cards. One ex-con with a gun almost followed Corah into the ladies' room.

So much for protection.

Everly rushed into the control room. As set writer of the day, you never knew what to expect. Sometimes a late-breaking story had been set up by the overnight news staff, and script writing was required. Other times, a guest wouldn't show up, and updated introductory material would have to be written for one of the shelf tapes that would be substituted—a rare occurrence. Most of the time the set writer just stayed in the greenroom and watched the show, chatting with the guests before they went on the air.

Reggie was responsible for the set-writer concept. He'd gotten stuck once with hastily rewriting part of the show and, being the great shirker of responsibility, had put a mechanism in place that ensured this would never happen to him or any of the staff's other associate producers again.

"Good morning, people," Everly said as she walked in.

"People? You think the nuts around here are *people*?" Mel Stone, their director, asked, his dark eyes glittering.

Their assistant director, Ed Brown, turned to her and raised his eyebrows in mock bewilderment.

"Certainly not the director," Everly answered, smiling at Ed.

"Right. We're maniacs," Mel said. "Artistic maniacs. Only way to survive in this business." He tugged at his headset and pulled the microphone toward his mouth. "Listen up, gang," he announced to the studio crew. "The seven o'clock news has a live spot from the Mideast. If the satellite goes down, we gotta cover our asses here, so don't decide it's time to take a pee break after the open."

Mel was such a class act.

"The satellite's all set," Leon Posner, their production manager, intoned. "Nothing is going to go wrong, Mel."

"Yeah, yeah, you tell that to Markfield if the guys in transmission screw up," Mel said, his pudgy fingers striking out at a cockroach that crawled across the front deck. "Murdered!" he yelled.

Everly shook her head and walked over to Reggie, who

was sitting in the back deck. He was looking through the scripts one last time to make sure everything was in order.

"Got anything for me?"

As soon as she'd said it, she recognized the double entendre.

Reggie smiled and for a brief instant radiated the easy charm that had earned him his reputation as the office Lothario. "Plenty," he said. "And I know you can handle it." He gave her the folder with the day's scripts, his calculating eyes unabashedly raking her body.

Why don't you just take a picture? she thought. "Any surprises for today?"

"If the goddamned camera crew knows how to stay in focus, that'll be a surprise," Mel said.

Reggie ignored him. "No. Pretty routine," he said. "You might want to stay in here to watch the show, though."

Something in his tone of voice and the way he looked at her indicated that this was a command and not just a friendly suggestion. What was it with this guy? She thought Beryl had said that he and Kerri were back together.

Everly ignored the sudden twinge of panic that grabbed at her stomach and said casually, "Sure. Just let me get some coffee."

He winked at her and she turned away quickly. Reggie had never flirted with her so blatantly before. Did something happen while she was away that Beryl hadn't mentioned? Everly didn't like this kind of attention. But there was nothing she could do about it now.

"Anyone want something from the greenroom?" she asked in a loud voice.

"Yeah. Tell Maria to clean out the coffee pot for a change," Mel said.

"Nothing here," Leon said.

The assistant director said nothing and the rest of the control room crew were too busy getting ready for the show to answer.

" 'Allo, Ever*lee*!" Maria Hernandez shrieked as Everly entered the greenroom.

"Hello, Maria. Coffee ready?"

"I just plug it in," she said. "Few minutes—you just wait." She wiped her hands on a coffee-spattered apron that looked as if it hadn't been washed in ages. Maria examined her with her sharp brown eyes. Everly knew what was coming. "You gettin' too skinny," Maria said. "Need some meat on the bones."

"I'll keep that in mind," Everly said, toying with a paper cup.

"I put out doughnuts later," Maria said "But you want somethin' now, I get it—just for you."

"It's too early to eat, Maria. I'll come back at six-thirty."

"I pick out somethin' good for you, somethin' special."

"Great," Everly said, heading back to the control room.

Nigel had just arrived and taken his customary seat next to the wall.

"How's it going, Nigel?" Reggie said.

"Blasted driver forgot the morning papers," Nigel fumed. "Spent the whole ride chitchatting about his family. Bloody bore!"

"At least you have a driver," Reggie said.

Everly knew this was a sore spot for Reggie. Leon Posner was tight with the budget and only approved limousines for Nigel, the talent, and the guests. Everyone else who worked the early shift took cabs.

"Should've taken a cab," Nigel said. "What are *you* doing here?" he asked, acknowledging Everly's presence. "I thought this was Victoria's day."

"Something came up," Reggie explained. "Everly volunteered," he lied.

"Lovely," Nigel grumped, burying his head in the control room copy of the *New York Times*.

Reggie shrugged and edged his seat closer to Everly's. She caught a faint whiff of men's cologne, and her stomach churned.

She opened her folder and ignored Reggie's stare.

"Hi, group." Jenny Spiegel poked her head in. She had been assigned to the greenroom shift today. All of their support staff were part of a rotation that came in at six o'clock every day. Their most important responsibility was to make sure the show's guests arrived on time, so they were supplied with a list of overnight numbers. The rule was to call guests at their hotels or apartments if they hadn't shown up at least thirty minutes before their segment aired.

More than once, this call from one of the staff members had served as a wake-up alarm.

The person on the early shift also had the guests sign standard release forms, which confirmed that they were appearing on television of their own free will. Then they took the guests into the makeup room and brought them into the studio about five minutes before their segment began—just enough time for them to clip on a microphone and get as comfortable as one could get before appearing on live television in front of millions of viewers.

"Any sexy people on the show today?" Jenny asked.

"Just behind the scenes," Reggie said.

Jenny flashed him a lascivious smile. "Well, I already *know* that," she said. "Want some coffee, Nigel?"

"If you must," he said. "Asinine driver," he mumbled, returning to his paper.

"What?" Jenny asked.

"Just get him what he wants," Reggie said.

"Okay," she said, a touch of exasperation in her voice.

"Shit!" Mel said. "Check out monitor six. Satellite's down from Marquir." Marquir was one of the few Arab countries that had diplomatic relations with Israel. They had expected a live report that morning from EBC's Mideast correspondent about Marquir's newly reelected president.

Nigel looked up from his paper. "No big deal," he said. "We'll get it for the seven-thirty. Bloody Arabs know zip about technology."

"Arabs nothing," Mel snorted. "It's probably those bozos in transmission."

"Fifteen minutes to air," Ed Brown announced.

"I'll see what the problem is," Leon said, grabbing a phone.

"You're actually going to do your job?" Mel asked. "Some red-letter day. Ten to one it's our own rope-a-dopes in broadcast control."

Nigel shook his head and turned his attention to the scripts.

A news intern ran in, breathlessly distributing the first news scripts of the day, which would be read after the seven o'clock open.

"Slow down," Reggie said to him. "You're going to kill yourself."

"Can't," the young man panted. "Mr. Markfield says we have to run."

Before Reggie could protest, the young man was out the door.

"I think our news president has to learn to take it easy," Reggie said.

"Fat chance," Nigel said. "He loves making those poor youngsters tremble. Thinks it gets him respect, the fool."

"Five minutes!" Ed yelled.

Jenny Spiegel waltzed in, balancing a tray of doughnuts and Nigel's coffee. "Here you go, Boss," she said.

Nigel grunted and she left the room.

Nothing like the camaraderie of *Morning*'s control room.

"We got a few minutes to air, Leon," Mel said. "What's the story? We gonna get Marquir or what?"

Leon was still talking quietly into the phone. He lifted his head up. "It's not us—something on their end. Maybe for the seven-thirty. I got the whole two hours booked, so we'll get it for at least one of the newscasts."

"Told you it was the Arabs," Nigel said. "Probably some camel taking a leak on the cables."

"Disgusting," Ed said. Then he yelled, "One minute to air!"

Nigel picked up the red phone installed in his area of the back deck, which was connected to the phone between Glen and Corah on the set. "Tell Glen to pick up the phone," he said.

Mel spoke into his headset that was wired to the studio crew's earphones and to the tiny earpieces worn by the co-hosts. "Phone, Glen," he said.

Everly looked at one of the monitors and saw Glen lean over and pick up the brown phone that was next to him.

"Drop the Marquir story from the open," Nigel said. "Just say we'll have a report from Marquir on President Abu El-Halakeem later in the show."

"You got it, boss," Glen said cheerily, making a few notations on his script.

"Fifteen seconds!" Ed announced.

"Get ready, gang," Mel said. "Let's make Uncle Mel happy and not have any major screwups today."

"Five-four-three-two—"

"Take music, roll tape," Mel announced.

"*Morning*'s" new space-age theme flooded the room. EBC had hired the country's most prestigious movie soundtrack composer to write a theme for the networks' news programs. Thousands of dollars had been spent to create a new image, which was supposed to be enhanced by this original music.

Every time Everly heard the theme she expected their co-hosts to take off in a spaceship.

Announcer Milt Hoffman's sepulchral tones filled the air as he proclaimed the day's date and introduced Glen Korbett and Corah Washington to the viewers.

"Take one!" Mel shouted.

Glen's smiling face filled the screen as he said good morning and talked about the day's guests.

"Looks like a shaggy dog," Mel said. "Korbett needs a haircut. Take two."

"He thinks the long hair makes him look younger," Nigel said, crumpling up a used page of script and tossing it toward the front deck.

"Yvonne probably likes it that way," Reggie said.

Everly turned to him, surprised that he would so openly mention Glen's mistress.

"Nah, probably doesn't get it cut too often so that he can

save a few bucks," Mel said. "Ready for a two-shot, Ted. And we want it in focus."

Ed Brown chuckled. "Two minutes to commercial," he said.

"Take one," Mel said.

Corah was talking now, her photogenic face an animated contrast to Glen's smug expression.

Some team.

"Think she ever had a lift?" Ed asked.

"Close-up on Korbett, Camera Two," Mel said. "Watch the glare for Christ's sake!"

"Not Corah," Nigel said. "No need."

"You must have been a beautiful baby," Mel sang.

"That's why Harvey Markfield hired her," Reggie said.

"You must have been a wonderful child," Mel added. "Take two. Okay, Camera One, go over to the interview set and get ready for another two-shot."

"Think they ever had anything going?" Ed asked.

"Who? Corah and Harvey Markfield?" Nigel asked, incredulous. "Please, the mere thought of him even getting it on—positively nauseating."

"Maybe he's still a virgin," Reggie said.

"Screw that!" Mel said, laughing.

It was no surprise that people called their control room a zoo. Everly wondered how they could keep track of what was going on the air with so much chatter and gossip going on.

A phone rang on the back deck.

"5K control," Reggie said.

Nigel glanced at him as he threw another page of script over Mel's shoulder.

"Shit! You're kidding," Reggie said.

"What's wrong?" Nigel asked.

"It's Grabowski in Marquir. There's been some kind of military attack. It was in the middle of some welcoming parade. El-Halakeem's been shot."

Suddenly the news intern came running into the control room. "Marquir," he said, trying to catch his breath. "There's been—"

"An assassination?" Nigel asked, his eyes gleaming.

"Don't know," the intern wheezed.

"Wait . . . What? Was he killed?" Reggie asked.

More phones started ringing, and Nigel grabbed the receiver out of Reggie's hand. "Grabowski, we're putting you on live. Leon—get this phone line patched in! Somebody throw me a headset."

There was pandemonium in the control room.

Ed hopped out of his chair in the front deck and threw his headset to Nigel, who grabbed it and whispered loudly. "Glen—emergency—El-Halakeem's been shot. We're doing a live phoner with Grabowski—Sam Grabowski."

"Get the slide up of Marquir," Mel screamed.

"Don't argue with me," Leon shouted into the phone. "We have to patch this call into the network feed *now*! It's a news emergency!"

"Chyron group—type up the following: Sam Grabowski, Live—with a capital L—from Marquir," Ed said in a shaky voice.

Everly looked up at the monitor. While Nigel was hissing in his ear, Glen was asking his guest, an expert from the Environmental Protection Agency, about new radon test kits. He must have also heard the chaos in the control room in his earpiece, yet he looked totally unfazed as he finished the question and smoothly said, "But if you'll forgive me, Dr. Fraser, we just got some very bad news from Marquir. Here with the latest report, EBC News correspondent Sam Grabowski."

Miraculously, Sam's stilted voice came flooding into the control room.

"Uh, that's right, Glen. Just minutes ago, Abu El-Halakeem, Marquir's president—just reelected yesterday—was shot at while he and his family and palace dignitaries sat at a reviewing stand. We don't have details. We do not know how many people have been killed or injured, but there was bloodshed."

"Any word on who was responsible for this tragedy?" Glen asked.

"Where's the fucking slide of Marquir?" Mel shouted.

"Just stay on Glen until they find it!" Nigel said.

"Slide's up," Ed Brown said.

"Take the slide!" Mel shouted. "Throw in the live chyron."

The chyron with the words "Sam Grabowski, Live from Marquir" appeared on the screen super-imposed over a slide showing the outline of the country.

"No word on the full extent of the damage," Sam said.

Jenny came running in. "The guests want to know if they should stay or leave. What should I tell them?"

"Not a blessed thing," Nigel said. "We may need them to plug in a few holes. Is there anyone on the show today who knows about the Mideast?"

"No such luck," Reggie said.

Nigel whispered into the headset, "Glen—the whole show is up in the air, but we'll let you know who's coming on as soon as we can."

"Everly, the entire program has to be changed," Nigel continued. "I want you to get Secretary of State Wexler in the D.C. studio, and try for Nat Ambrose from the United Nations. Don't bother with scripts—Glen will be able to wing it."

Everly had been numbed by the morning's turn of events. It was a relief to have someone give orders. "No problem," she said. "I've got their home numbers," she added, about to run out the door.

Rolodex to the rescue.

"Just get to them before anyone else," Nigel said, his voice tense. "And don't give anyone to the competition," he added.

As if she needed to be reminded.

Twenty minutes had passed. Luck was definitely on her side that morning. Everly had been able to get both Wexler and Ambrose.

She ran back into the control room with the news.

"Got 'em both," she said, whispering into Nigel's ear. "Ambrose is on his way in a cab, and Washington is all set for Wexler."

"Good girl," Nigel said, beaming.

Everly felt as if she'd finally be forgiven for the Greenes. But she didn't want to press her luck. "Anything else?" she asked.

"Kerri called in from home," Reggie said, as if that had been the most astonishing event of the morning. "She was able to get that Professor Lufkind at Columbia—the hotshot on US-Marquir relations—and Hank's coming in early to help update the show for the West Coast. We also have some good stuff lined up at the State Department. So for now, everything's under control."

"Smashing," Nigel said. "We've got Sam back now from Marquir," he added.

"Has there been any kind of official reaction from the Marquir government?" Glen now asked, ad-libbing with easy authority.

"Not to my knowledge, Glen. Everything happened very fast—Oh, wait! Someone in our bureau just handed me a slip of paper."

"Ted, stay focused on our host, for Christ's sake!" Mel screamed to the cameraman. "Lose the slide. Ready, One—we want a reaction shot from our fabulous journalist host."

"What do you have there?" Glen asked, filling the uncustomary silence.

"This is unofficial, but there are reports that the president was rushed to a hospital. His wife and children were not hurt—but again, this is unofficial."

"No other information?" Glen asked.

"There's more here," Sam continued.

"Sam sure knows how to wing it," Reggie said, his voice thick with sarcasm.

"Get that slide up again," Mel said.

"People are going to get sick of that bloody slide," Nigel said. "Can't we come up with something better?"

"What, the *Mona Lisa*?" Mel asked. "Throw in the Grabowski chyron again."

"Apparently there were three military planes flying overhead with some colored smoke, and then the next thing that happened, some, uh, some militia men got out of a tank and just gunned down the stands," Sam said.

"How tragic," Glen said.

"Oh, Lord!" Nigel said. "You can do better than that."

"We got it!" Leon yelled.

Everyone stared at him. Leon had never raised his voice in his life.

"Look!" he continued. "The satellite—someone was rolling when it happened—look! There are the planes and the smoke—red and yellow—"

Nigel saw the satellite monitor and hissed into his headset. "Listen up, Glen, we are about to show pictures that are coming now on the satellite. Watch your monitor—it's what Grabowski just described."

"You want me to take this feed sight unseen?" Mel asked.

"Take it!" Nigel roared.

"Take the satellite," Mel said.

"Ladies and gentlemen, we just now have some pictures from Marquir," Glen said, looking at his monitor.

The screen was filled with the colorful smoke designs formed by the official air force of Marquir. Suddenly, the camera jerked down to show three men holding machine guns and getting out of a large tank.

"We haven't seen this footage before," Glen said. "There may be some unpleasant sights coming up."

Just as he spoke, scenes of carnage and screaming crowds poured onto the monitor. Luckily, the lighting for the camera hadn't been too good, or the pictures might have been even worse. As it was, the sight of bloodied limbs and lifeless bodies was shocking enough.

Everly was sure that subsequent airing of this footage would be heavily edited.

"Good God!" Reggie said, clearly horrified.

"Looks like the competition's stomachs are as strong as ours," Nigel remarked quietly, looking over to the side.

Everly followed his gaze to the monitors that displayed the network feeds from ABC, NBC, and CBS. One by one, they had followed EBC's example, and all four morning shows were airing the exact same satellite feed.

For a moment, Glen was silent as the pictures kept coming, one scene more gruesome than the next.

It was dreadful, Everly thought. And riveting.

As Nigel would put it, chalk one up for "good television."

TEN

"Good afternoon, Miss Dalton."

Phil Schutz, one of the building's more astute doormen, held the door open for her. "You're home early," he added with alacrity.

Everly was exhausted. The last thing she wanted to do was carry on a conversation.

"It was a tough day, Phil—day-and-a-half, actually. Came home to get some rest," she said, praying that he'd take the hint and forgo the opportunity to chatter.

There were basically two types of doormen in this town, she mused: semi-comatose or Hedda Hopper. Half the Christmas tips for these guys were really bribes in exchange for silence.

Doormen knew all.

"Big news day, Miss Dalton?" he asked. "Must have been exciting!"

Everly didn't recall ever having told him what she did for a living; it was just one more personal detail he'd apparently ferreted out from one of his sources.

"You'll hear about it tonight on the news," she said. "I really have to go."

"Sure thing."

She sensed his disappointment, but all she wanted to do was lie down. The physical and mental demands of the past few weeks had built up to such an extreme that she actually felt dizzy. It was a struggle to be coherent.

She leaned against the back of the elevator with a vague sense of unease, as if she'd left something important back at the office. Her mind was so jumbled, it was difficult to keep all of the tumultuous events of the day straight.

Thanks to an entertaining battle between Nigel Elliot and Harvey Markfield, *Morning* had stayed on the air until three in the afternoon—which was quite a coup for them. Nigel had insisted that *Morning*'s cast and crew stay put to cover the Marquir story, even though their venerable news president wanted his precious *Evening News Worldwide* team to take over.

Quite a shouting match had ensued, with Nigel finally threatening to pull the plug on the entire network if anyone dared to take his staff off the air.

Reggie Graham—bless his obsequious soul—had actually come up with a compromise: they'd relinquish the hot seat at three o'clock. By then *Morning* would have had enough time to establish its presence on the West Coast, and *Evening News Worldwide* would get on the air early enough to get sufficient input on this gem of a news story. This would also give the *Evening News* staff plenty of preparation time to gear up for what everyone knew would be an arduous evening of intense coverage and news specials.

Once the transition was completed, Nigel, in an uncharacteristic show of concern, had ordered Everly home. Other staff members would handle the next day's program. She was only too happy to comply. She had returned to her office and canceled an editing session, and then had gotten the hell out of there as quickly as she could.

As Everly thought it through, nothing seemed amiss, yet she couldn't shake the notion that something was wrong. Maybe it was just her imagination, but for now, the only thing that mattered was getting into bed. When the weight of sheer exhaustion interfered with one's senses, the basics in life took on monumental proportions. Everly only wanted one thing now, just one thing—sleep.

The apartment that she'd left almost twelve hours earlier appeared eerily unchanged. The black-out shades in her bedroom effectively blocked the bright afternoon sun, and the tousled sheets on the bed gave the impression that she'd only left for a few minutes.

Everly decided to play a little game. She would pretend it was really nighttime, time to go to bed.

She quickly shed her clothes, leaving them in a pile on the rocking chair in her bedroom. Then it occurred to her to unplug her phone. Everly didn't want to hear from anyone—even if the world was falling apart.

Someone else could cover that.

At last, her wonderful, welcoming cozy bed. If there was anything she'd forgotten to do at the office, she'd figure it out tomorrow. Nothing could be that important.

Her head hit the pillow, and that was the last thing she remembered.

Brrrrrring. Brrrrrring. Brrrrrring.

Everly jerked up, startled. Her head throbbed. The clock radio dial read seven o'clock. Was it night or morning? She picked up the phone, only to hear a dial tone.

Of course.

It was the doorman.

Brrrrrrring. Brrrrrrring.

She ran out to the foyer, grabbing a sweater that was hanging on a doorknob, and was peripherally aware as she passed the living room window that it was dark outside. Nighttime. She pressed the talk button near the door.

"Yes?"

"You've got a visitor, Miss D.," a disembodied voice announced.

"I'm not expecting anyone," she said.

A blast of static was the response.

"*What did you say?*" she yelled.

"He's on his way up."

"Who? I just said I wasn't expecting anyone!"

Great. This was one of the half-dead doormen whose mission in life was to hold the door open for burglars and rapists.

"Said he was from your hometown in Indianapolis, Miss D."

Oh, God. It was Jared.

Shit.

It was too late to do anything about it. He'd be there any minute. And Everly knew she must look like a wreck.

She raced into the bathroom, appalled at the pale apparition that stared frantically back. She splashed some cold water on her face, applied two near-symmetrical swipes of blush-on, brushed her hair, raced back to the bedroom, and scrambled into a pair of jeans and an oversized sweater.

If they had an Olympic category for Fastest Dresser in the World, she'd definitely win a medal, maybe even the gold.

Just as she slipped into a pair of sandals, she heard a knock at the door. Her heartbeat suddenly went into high gear, and she fought the heady rush of adrenaline as she calmly closed the door to her bedroom and walked to the foyer.

"Who's there?" she asked, hoping Jared couldn't hear the tension in her voice.

"Surprise!" his inimitable voice answered.

Everly slowly unlocked the door, trying to affect indifference. But the sight of Jared Kammer, standing a mere few inches away, was not something about which she could ever be nonchalant.

"God, Everly, it's good to see you."

His voice was husky, suggestive. It was as if nothing bad had ever occurred between them. There hadn't been much time to think about how she'd feel seeing him, but she wasn't prepared for the familiar sense of comfort and attraction that washed over her as she looked into his steady blue eyes.

He reached out to kiss her, and before she could push

him away, his lips were on hers, soft and warm, igniting desires she had thought were long extinguished.

Everly pulled back, stunned and embarrassed at the visceral response her body still had to his, despite their history, and—with what she hoped was a stinging reminder of what had actually happened between them—she asked, "Where's Pam?"

"Aren't you going to invite me in?"

Jared was an expert at avoidance.

"Oh, sure. Come on in."

Everly followed him as he looked around the foyer and walked into the living room.

"Nice place. I like what you've done here," he said, taking off his coat and draping it over a chair.

He was casually dressed in tan corduroy pants and a brown sweater. His hair was shorter now; the glasses were the same. Everly noticed that he'd put on some weight.

"Well, I know you didn't come all the way over here to talk about my decorating taste. What do you want?" She was determined to stay in control.

"Aren't you going to sit down?" Jared motioned to the place beside him on the couch.

She hesitated a moment, and chose to sit on the matching chair kitty-corner from him. She didn't want to encourage any physical contact.

"Oh, for God's sake, Everly, do I have the plague?" He looked at her with such longing that for a split second she didn't know what to say. But then he turned away and laughed. "Fine, have it your way."

"So where is Pam?" Everly wasn't going to make it easy for him.

"She'll be coming out in a few months. I thought I mentioned that on the phone. So how are you, Everly? You look terrific."

"I'm just great, Jared," she said brightly. Fine. She could dole out small talk just as well as he could. She'd find out soon enough what this visit was all about. "They like my work at *Morning*," she continued, "and I really think I'm going to make it there, and make it *big*."

"This is certainly the town to do it in."

"That's why you're here, I suppose." Everly was waiting for the favor. There must be something he wanted and he just assumed she'd help him—as if helping him was number one on her list of priorities.

"Let's face it, there's nothing like the Big Apple," Jared said. "Just walking down the street is exciting."

"If you know the right streets," Everly said, a hint of condescension in her voice.

"So how are you, *really*? I mean, what's happening with your love life? I just wondered—"

That was going too far.

"You've got a hell of a lot of nerve, Jared!" she said, raising her voice. "Who do you think you are? You practically left me at the goddamned altar, and now you come crashing back into my life with no real explanation, and you're asking me about my love life? What gives you that right? It's none of your business!" She stood up and was about to ask him to leave.

He got up and grabbed her by the arms. "I'm sorry. Really. I just—Please, Everly, don't get angry. I can't help it if I still care."

She looked into his eyes and felt a connection to him that she wanted to deny. Why was it so impossible to get Jared Kammer out of her system?

"If you cared that much, you wouldn't be here," she said calmly. "What good does it do either of us?"

He pulled her down to the couch and took her hands in his. "Maybe you don't want to hear this, but I've just got to be honest. I have this wall around me, Everly. You know that—you've always known it. And somehow, you slipped through. I was concerned about it when we were engaged, and believe it or not, it was part of the reason I couldn't go through with our marriage. You scared me."

She was confused. What was he getting at?

"Well, it's one thing to run away—but you married someone *else*," she said. "You're still married, aren't you?"

"For now." He gave her hands a squeeze. Again—that urgent look in his eyes.

"What's going on here, Jared? I mean, you're coming on to me; what is this?"

"I had to see you. I had to see if the old feelings were still there. Pam is . . . well . . . she's safe. She doesn't get to me like you did.

"You know, when I got the promotion to Chicago, I wanted everyone to think I was pretty hot stuff. But you and I both knew that I was scared, even though we never talked about it. And that's the whole point—one of the reasons you and I understand each other so well is because underneath all the bravado, we're both the same. We need each other, we're *good* for each other."

It was strange to hear Jared finally admit what she'd always known about their relationship. Of all the women he'd ever dated—and there were plenty—no one had gotten under his skin the way she had. Even though he'd kept a great deal from her, even though there was this "wall," as he put it, she knew that she had a unique perception of who he was.

And it worked both ways, which had made the breakup all the more devastating. Everly never thought she'd meet another man who would understand her the way Jared did—who would love her for who she truly was, insecurities and all.

But this confession was still puzzling.

"What exactly do you want, Jared?" she asked quietly.

"I'm not sure, but I don't want to lose you. I know this is kind of out of left field. You should *hate* me. But I know you don't. I want to have a second chance."

"But how? Does this mean you've filed for divorce?"

"Not exactly. But it's part of the reason Pam and I will be separated for several months."

"Does she know about me?"

"Not everything." He ran a hand through his hair and leaned back on the couch. "It's all kind of complicated—but let's just take this one step at a time. I didn't want to say anything to her about you, because I wasn't sure you'd even see me again. Hell—I didn't even risk calling tonight; I just came straight over."

"What if I was out, or with someone?"

"It was a risk worth taking," Jared said. "And I had a feeling that since it was such a crazy news day, you'd probably not have made any plans to go out."

"Yeah, and my top-notch doorman practically gave you the key."

Jared laughed, a dazzling smile flashing across his face.

And then he pulled Everly to him, and this time, she let herself be drawn into his warmth. The feel of his body against hers, the familiar smells and tastes to which she'd once grown so accustomed—the sensations all came flooding back as if they'd just been apart a few days, not a year. She allowed herself to let go of the pain and to revel in the special chemistry that existed between them.

How perfect their bodies were together; they were meant to be together, she thought dreamily, as she felt his hands glide to her breasts, stroking them gently, heightening her arousal. Oh, God, it had been such a long time . . .

"Do you have a bedroom?" Jared whispered.

Everly looked at him and smiled. Maybe she was crazy, but she wanted him, and she wouldn't let this opportunity pass her by. He still loved her, he wanted her back—isn't that what he had just said?

She pulled him into the bedroom, not caring about the pile of clothes on the chair or the messy sheets.

Jared quickly pulled off all of his clothes except a pair of dark bikini briefs.

"Shy?" Everly asked, as she watched him undress.

"A little," he said, getting in bed and pulling up the covers.

"I'll be back in a second," she said. Perhaps she was being foolish to hop into bed so easily with her former fiancé—a married man, now—but birth control was one area where she wouldn't be irresponsible.

She didn't want to think too much about what she was about to do; the sexual hunger she felt was almost overwhelming. There was so much anticipation building inside of her, she thought she was going to explode.

Everly rushed back into the bedroom and felt a little self-conscious as she crawled into the bed and got next to Jared. He turned to her, and she felt his now completely naked body against hers.

Again, the slow, easy, passionate kiss as he reached for her, his hand tenderly skimming the length of her body, finally coming to rest on the swell of her breast.

She groaned as he knowingly caressed her with a touch so delicate that it was almost unbearable. He moved slightly and whispered softly into her ear, "I want this to be special, Everly, very special."

He nibbled lightly on her earlobe and then moved again, placing his mouth gently on her right breast, stroking her nipple with his tongue ever so lightly. Everly didn't want to move; she could hardly breath.

His hand moved down as he continued to suckle, and he caressed the back of her knees and then her inner thighs. She thought she would die from the utter pleasure. She arched against him as she felt his fingers enveloped in the wet warmth inside of her. She shuddered slightly as he expertly stroked her, and suddenly she was gasping for breath as the tension built.

He moved her on her back, and the air felt suddenly cold as their bodies separated. He looked into her eyes as he straddled her.

"You want me, Everly, don't you? Tell me that you want me."

She looked at him in the semidarkness, vaguely seeing the passion in his eyes. She had never wanted anyone as much as she wanted him at this moment.

"Take me," she whispered. "Just take me . . ."

A slight motion awakened Everly. It was Jared, turning over on his side. She didn't move; she just watched him. He was still asleep.

How innocent, she thought, inching closer to him so that she could feel his body against her. She couldn't remember the last time they'd spent the night together. It had always embarrassed her that for all the time she'd been alone in Indianapolis and even when she moved to New York, she still slept on one side of the bed. She never wanted to get used to the fact that she had the entire double bed to herself. Now that she was with Jared, she reasoned that perhaps it hadn't been such a silly idea after all.

Jared must have awakened, because he groaned and reached out for her.

"Morning, Cupcake," he murmured.

" 'Cupcake'? What's that from?"

"Oh, I don't know. Does it bother you?"

"No, not really. You just never—We just never had names like that," Everly said, suspicious that it was something he called Pam.

"What can I say? You inspire me, that's all," Jared said, tweeking her nose. "Come here, woman," he said, pulling her closer.

Everly loved having him next to her. It felt so right. She didn't want to get out of bed.

The phone rang. She remembered turning it back on when she had gotten up once in the middle of the night.

"Tell them you can't come in," Jared said, sleepily, turning away from her.

"Hello," she said, grabbing the phone, giving him a little kick.

"Hi there, good buddy."

It was Beryl. For a moment Everly panicked and thought she was late for work, but then she remembered that it was Saturday morning.

"I didn't wake you, did I?" Beryl asked.

"No, but I, uh, I can't talk long . . ."

"You sound funny. Are you alone?"

Beryl must have had a sixth sense.

"Not exactly," Everly said.

"Is it Hank?"

"No . . . Listen, I can't really talk . . ."

"I know, I know. The suspense is killing me, but I guess I'll have to wait until you *can* talk. But there's something else. I'll be quick. I have some great news: I'm engaged!"

Everly sat up, wide awake now. "That's fantastic!" Jared moaned and she lowered her voice. "It's Stephen I assume, unless you've been hiding something from me."

"Of course it's Stephen, silly. We haven't set a date yet, but he proposed last night. It was so romantic."

"Well, I'd love to hear the details, but now is not the best of times."

"I'm dying to know who's there with you, but I'm almost afraid to find out."

Everly sighed. "Your instincts are usually pretty good. Listen, I'll get back to you later and we can have a good long talk—and a celebration! Congratulations. That's really terrific."

She hung up the phone and looked at Jared, who had managed to fall back asleep. She felt strange—elated for her friend, but also depressed at the state of her own personal life. Was it a mistake for her to have so readily taken him back? He wasn't really hers to have, not technically. But hadn't he said he wanted to give their relationship a chance? Even if the circumstances were a bit bizarre?

She'd just have to play this one out. If things were looking so great for Beryl, maybe some of what was in the air would rub off on Everly. It wasn't totally absurd to think that she and Jared might actually have a future. He wouldn't have come to her like this unless he sincerely wanted to test their future together.

What could she possibly have to lose?

ELEVEN

"I'm in big trouble, Everly."

Lester Kay was sitting in her office, speaking barely above a whisper. Since he often had a tendency to be dramatic, she didn't think anything was out of the ordinary.

"Some guest dropped out for tomorrow's show?" she asked as she checked the computer terminal at her desk for the day's wire stories.

"Lord, I wish it were that simple. No, this has nothing to do with our illustrious program." He grabbed the white handkerchief from his jacket pocket and nervously wiped his brow.

"Money trouble?"

"No, and I won't have you playing twenty questions . . . Just give me a moment, dear." He patted her knee and returned the handkerchief to his pocket.

Lester took a deep breath and settled back in the upholstered chair next to her desk. The former set chair was actually compensation for having an office with no windows. Though it was far more comfortable than the orange plastic monstrosity most of her colleagues had, Everly sometimes wondered if it was worth the trade-off. At least her predecessor had left behind a framed, beautifully photographed window view of Central Park on the wall, so she could pretend to have the best of both worlds.

Lester double-checked to make sure her office door was closed, and then he leaned toward her.

"You must swear that this conversation never leaves this room," he said.

Now her curiosity was piqued. She looked away from the computer and gave him her full attention. "You wouldn't be here if you didn't trust me, Lester," she said. "What is it?"

"Well, I don't really know how to say this without sounding—Oh, Lord! I suppose there's no other way to handle this matter than to just get on with it—I made a dreadful mistake."

He stopped a moment, giving Everly the impression that she should goad him on.

"Lots of people make mistakes," she said, quickly. "What did you do?"

"It's rather personal, you see, so I must absolutely insist on confidentiality . . ."

"I already *told* you I can be trusted."

"Well, it's more than that. I actually think you might be able to extricate me from this absurd situation."

"I'd be happy to help, but you're going to have to explain what this is all about *first*."

She was trying very hard to be patient.

"It's, well, it's this young woman—lady—girl, I'm afraid." He suddenly looked sheepish.

Uh-oh, Everly thought. Lester had a reputation for many things, most of them aboveboard. But she'd heard rumors that since his divorce several years ago, most of the women he squired around town were barely out of college. Everly often wondered how a thirty-year age difference impinged on a relationship. Perhaps now she was going to find out.

"Did you get someone pregnant?"

"What!" He was clearly offended. "Oh, goodness, no. Now *that* would really be awful! No, no. You see, I met this woman—well, this girl—at one of those infernal publishing functions I often have to attend. She approached me, actually, and she was an absolute delight, such a charming creature."

Everly winced at the description but smiled warmly so that he would continue.

"Well, it's just we—that is, I—offered to take her to dinner—perfectly harmless. Just dinner. True, it was a nicer place than usual, but then you know my tastes—only the finest."

As long as you have an expense account, Everly thought. "I see no problem there, Lester," she said.

"Of course not, no. Please bear with me, dear lady." Again, the light tap on her knee.

"Well, she was just *so* entertaining, *such* a breath of fresh air, that we saw each other a few times, and . . . well, one thing led to another. And—oh, dear—I just got a call from the girl's mother. She's a minor, for pity's sake—and she may want to press charges."

"Does she have any grounds for these charges?" Everly asked, trying to be delicate. It was hard to imagine the staid, professorial Lester Kay getting it on with some sixteen-year-old.

"My dear, this was most definitely a two-way street. Nothing was forced. And she lied to me—said she was about to graduate from college! She seemed quite knowledgeable about so many things; I had absolutely no idea she was so young."

So, some smart, hormone-crazed teenager intent on making it with a celebrity had fooled Lester into thinking she was older. For all of his worldly experience, he was incredibly vulnerable when it came to women, especially *young* women. Everly decided she had to believe him.

"Now, here's how I see it," he continued. "This is probably not the first time Jessica has been in a similar imbroglio, but I suspect that when her mother found out who I was—Well, I think she wants to use the situation in some way, or perhaps she has a vendetta of sorts against her daughter. It's a broken home, and even though the father is a major real estate mogul from the Midwest, life must be a bit dull out there, and she wants to spice things up."

"Shouldn't you be speaking to an attorney?"

"Yes, yes I suppose I should—but you see, I had to talk to you first."

"Why?"

"Because you might know them. They're from Indianapolis."

There was a look of enormous expectation in his eyes.

"Well?" she said.

"Her full name is Jessica Taft Everitt."

"As in *Charles* Everitt?" Everly's eyes widened.

"Yes. The very same. Do you know them?"

"You're in luck, Lester."

The Everitts were one of the wealthiest families in the country. Charles Everitt had expanded the family real estate empire by investing in securities and various venture capital enterprises that made him a formidable power on the American business scene. Everly knew his ex-wife, Gloria, and had grown up with the older two of the four Everitt daughters. The youngest, Jessica, was an art history buff, and Everly recalled hearing that she'd been sent to a private school in New York to be near her father. But since he traveled so much, Jessica had a great deal of independence.

Everly also remembered that there had been an ugly custody battle over the two underage girls several years ago, and the father had won. For the most part, the Everitts truly lived in another world—a world of privilege and great wealth, where money had a unique way of paving the road to opportunity. Now this rarified world was colliding with Everly's.

"Small world, Lester," Everly said. "But don't you think it would be more appropriate to work this out with an attorney?"

"That's the problem. When lawyers get involved—Well, it makes everything rather complicated, and public. I can't bear to think what this would do to my reputation. It's a veritable scandal! I am a respected individual on the air and in the world of letters, and I just fear that this sort of . . . involvement might be terribly detrimental to my future—particularly here at *Morning*. My credibility would be utterly *destroyed*.

"But it occurred to me that if *you* could personally prevail upon Mrs. Everitt not to press charges, I would make certain nothing like this would ever happen again—at least not with me. I can't control what dear Jessica does with her life—but I would stay out of it. I thought you could intervene and save us all a lot of trouble. Of course, I'm not quite sure what her mother is after—I mean, it's not as if she needs money."

That was true. Lester also was probably right about how this incident could ruin his career if word got out about it. Office gossip was one thing, blazing headlines quite another. Everly could imagine what a cutthroat like Kerri Marks would have done with this information. But then another thought leapt into her mind.

This problem of Lester's might actually work to her advantage.

"Gloria Everitt is a very difficult woman," she said, slowly. "Maybe she thinks this is a way to get back at Charles, because he has custody of Jessica. But the whole thing could backfire with all the publicity. I think I can explain the . . . delicacy of the situation, as well as the fact that little Jessica must bear some responsibility here. Gloria probably doesn't want this splashed across the tabloids any more than you do. I'm sure I can reason with her. I'll certainly try my best, Lester."

"I would be most grateful, most grateful." Again he clutched at his handkerchief and then looked at her earnestly. "There must be something I can do for you in return, now—if you can work this out—even just for the effort of going through it all."

Everly smiled to herself. She was taking a gamble, yet she couldn't have scripted the situation any better.

"There *might* be a way you can help me," she said. "It's rather simple, really, to borrow one of your expressions.

I haven't been here that long, but you should know that one of my goals is to get back on the air—here in New York."

Lester gave her a puzzled look. "Oh, really?" he said. "Certainly not in—well, just like that? Go on the air?"

"Most of the staff doesn't know that I was already on camera in Indianapolis. It's a long story—not worth going into right now. But it's something I want to do again. And I know how you can help me."

"Do you?" He appeared confused. "Go on," he said.

"There's no rush on this, but there will come a time over the next few weeks when you and Nigel are having lunch, or just a chat. I'd like you to mention to him that you think I'd be good on the air. You know—plant a little seed, to get him thinking. And then, when the moment is right, some project will come in for you—something that requires a little more than just the usual approach for a spot on publishing.

"And that's when you'll suggest that I do the story, and we'll both present it to Nigel. Now before I go any further, Lester, please understand something: I'm not after your job. You have your own specialty, and you're very good at it. All I want is a fair chance to show what I can do. Since you're tied to the publishing industry, you have access to more different kinds of program suggestions than anyone on the show. You're probably the best source for a segment that would be just right for me—for my network debut.

"I'll work with you on this Everitt situation. I'm only too happy to help. But I'll need your assistance in return."

He looked at her and frowned. "I see," he said. "Well, well, very interesting."

She knew she'd taken him by surprise—she'd even surprised herself. But this was one of those rare serendipitous situations, and she couldn't ignore it. "So do we have a deal here or what?"

"You *do* know the Everitts," Lester said quietly.

"I told you I know them. Gloria will certainly accept my call. I can't promise anything, but there's hope. I truly believe the odds are in our favor."

She gave him an encouraging smile, and for the first time that morning she saw his face brighten.

"So what gives?" Beryl asked.

"You're not going to believe this," Everly said, popping a piece of tuna sushi in her mouth.

She and Beryl were having lunch at a Japanese restaurant. The concept of raw fish, as well as its relative lack of availability in the Midwest, had kept Everly from sampling this delicacy for years, but shortly after her arrival in New York, Beryl had urged her to try it.

Now she had cravings for the stuff.

"Although I think I'd rather hear *your* news first," she continued.

"There's not much to add," Beryl said. "It was such a shock when Stephen said he wanted to take me out for a fancy dinner after the Marquir show. It had been such a crazy day in the office that at first the thought of going home and changing and everything seemed like a truly bad idea. But there was *something* in his voice that told me I better not turn him down."

"I *told* you you have terrific instincts," Everly said. "I envy that about you."

But that wasn't all she envied.

Everly was only too aware that most of the women on the staff of *Morning* were single. It seemed to be a prerequisite for their success in network television. The industry was so all-consuming that one had to truly struggle to build a private life. It was simply easier to handle a hectic career when your life outside the office had few demands or responsibilities. This created a certain camaraderie amongst the women on the staff—no matter how disparate their personalities. It was fun to bemoan the single state together and share horror stories of New York City dating.

Now Beryl would no longer be a part of the "being single" predicament, and Everly would be left behind.

Everly also realized that this marriage would inevitably have repercussions on their friendship. She and Beryl would always be close, but their relationship couldn't be the same with Stephen in the picture. Everly had been through this type of thing before, but somehow, her close friend's pending marriage juxtaposed with everything else that was going on in her life seemed a bit overwhelming—even unfair.

It wasn't easy for Everly to admit she had these feelings, but they were certainly there.

"Well, I guess instinct is just one of those things," Beryl said, her voice full of excitement. "Anyway, we were at this neat little Italian place in Murray Hill—Marchi's, where there's no menu, they just keep bringing out the food, one dish better than the next—and I noticed that he wasn't eating much."

"Guess he had a lot on his mind."

"No kidding. Well, all of a sudden, just as they were putting down one of the main courses, he asks me about spending the rest of our lives together—and the next thing I know, I'm saying, 'yes,' and crying—and then's he's eating up a storm and I've lost my appetite!"

Everly laughed. "I love it!" she said.

"Yeah, well, I'm just so happy! And if it can happen to me, it can happen to you, Everly. You just have to give guys a chance—the right guy. Which reminds me—since we didn't get a chance to talk this weekend, who was your mysterious visitor?"

Everly had stalled for as long as she could. Even though she'd been excited about Jared's coming back into her life, she wasn't sure if her friend would be supportive. She had her own doubts about what was happening.

"It was Jared."

"I thought so," Beryl said.

"You're not surprised? I sure was," Everly said.

"Be real! I mean, it's not as if there were a lot of possibilities, and I didn't think you'd suddenly have some stranger—whose name you couldn't mention—in your apartment on a Saturday morning. What did he want?"

Everly avoided looking into Beryl's eyes. She was afraid of what she might see there.

"I think he wants me back," she said quietly.

"You mean he got a divorce?"

"Not exactly." Everly toyed with her chopsticks. This was going to be difficult.

"Then *what* exactly?"

Everly took a deep breath. "He wants to give our relationship a chance. He's going to be out here alone for a few months before Pam moves here, and depending on what happens between the two of us, she may never come."

"Oh. Does she know about this arrangement?"

"No—not yet. He wasn't even sure I would see him. He didn't know what was going on in my life and he wanted to make sure it was an option before he told her anything—"

"Wait a minute, Everly," Beryl said, her face serious. "This doesn't sound right to me. If he's not happy with her, he should leave her. It shouldn't have anything to do with you. Either he's got a good marriage or he doesn't. What he had or wants with you should have nothing to do with it."

Everly realized that her friend was voicing the same thoughts she'd had about the situation, but a part of her didn't want to deal with what Jared might really be up to.

"I guess he's just not sure," Everly said, getting defensive.

"Well, that doesn't seem fair to you. I mean, what if after the next few months he decides he was wrong about you?"

"I know, I know—but something tells me I have to go through with this. I want him so badly, Beryl. It's crazy—I'll give you that. But we were so good together. I don't think I could live with myself if I let this opportunity go by."

Beryl shook her head, as she tried to maneuver some rice onto her chopsticks. "I don't know. It doesn't feel right. I guess I can understand how you want him so much, but I wish he were truly free and clear, if you know what I mean. Are you going to be able to handle it if it doesn't work out?"

"The way I see it, I don't have much of a choice. I've got to give this relationship one more chance—it's the only way I can deal with it."

"What about Hank?" Beryl asked. "You were making some progress there, weren't you?"

"I think 'Miss Subways' is making more progress than I am," Everly said. "He's a strange one, though. I just can't figure him out."

"I bet he says the same thing about you," Beryl said with a devious smile on her face.

Everly shook her head and sighed. "You're probably right," she said.

Suddenly the manager of the restaurant came up to their table.

"Miss Dalton?" he asked.

"Yes?"

"Urgent phone call. Come! You can take in my office."

The *Morning* staff was supposed to let the receptionist know where they could be reached at all times—during office hours and otherwise. Naturally, some people were more responsible about this than others. Since her run-in with Nigel, Everly had been particularly assiduous about leaving her numbers with the front desk. They even knew when she was in the ladies' room.

"Be right back," she said to Beryl.

Everly followed the manager as he walked swiftly to the back of the restaurant and up a narrow flight of stairs that she'd never noticed before. He reached for the battered knob on an old wooden door and opened it, revealing a spare office equipped with a small metal desk, one worn desk chair, and a low couch. Several tattered Japanese beer posters adorned the wall.

"Please, sit here," the manager said, motioning to the chair.

Everly saw the flashing light on the phone console and picked up the receiver just as the manager turned and left her alone.

"Everly here," she said.

" 'Bout time."

It was Jenny Spiegel.

"Does Nigel have something for me?" Everly asked. Even though the office was covered by a rotation of segment producers during lunch hour, she wouldn't have put it past Nigel or Reggie to want to interrupt whatever she was doing and assign her to handle the dirty work of the day.

"No, but I have terrific news! I'm covering the front desk and you just got an urgent message from Bill Limona. He said to find you no matter where you were to let you know that they got the call."

"*They got the call!*" Everly shrieked. "That's fantastic! When? Did the operation start? Can I go out there?"

"Whoa, girl. He just called a few minutes ago from the hospital. He said that they were still running some tests but that it looked good for Kathleen and he wanted to let you know."

This was fantastic! Everly was genuinely thrilled. The Limonas must be wildly happy, she thought.

Immediately, her producer mind went into gear. Given the dearth of editing facilities in New York, she'd have to place an order today for a substantial chunk of editing time. Or maybe she'd finish editing the piece in their San Francisco bureau—in which case special tape shipments of what she'd already laid down would have to be made.

She'd also need a crew, hotel and plane reservations. She'd try to get Peterson and Lister again since they knew all the players—surely Phoenix would hustle for her. And Nigel would certainly let her go back to California to shoot the rest of what had turned into a terrific story. Who cared about budget constraints—Kathleen was actually going to get her transplant!

Wait till she told Jared the great news!

Maybe Everly was right about happy endings after all.

TWELVE

"Okay, troops," Nigel said, pounding a gavel on the conference room table. "Who has some scintillating ideas for next week's show?"

Morning's weekly staff meetings were held every Tuesday morning in a harshly lit, white-walled conference room. A plastic, wood veneer rectangular table, surrounded by two tiers of folding chairs, took up most of the space. Several pitchers of water and stacks of paper cups dotted the table surface. There was a coffee urn on a small ledge in the back of the room. One of the fluorescent lights overhead gave off an annoying, high-pitched buzzing sound, and even though almost everyone complained about it, it never got fixed.

In one of his more amusing moments, Hank had suggested to Everly that this was merely one more example of Nigel Elliot's master plan to drive everyone on his staff just a little bit crazy.

There were times when she believed that this idea was not so farfetched.

The staff seating for these weekly gatherings had a definite protocol, which didn't take anyone long to learn. The "grown-ups"—what Nigel called his editorial and management people, his associate producers, segment producers, and field staff—were allowed the privilege of actually sitting at the table, while the "kids"—the researchers, production assistants, and other support personnel—were relegated to the second row of chairs. Nothing was ever formally stated about this; it was just the way the system worked. And no one ever dared to challenge the scheme.

Everly had originally thought it odd that these meetings weren't held first thing at the beginning of the week, until someone explained that Nigel had an enormous distaste for scheduling anything on Monday mornings, or Friday afternoons, for that matter. He wouldn't even take phone calls during those times, except, of course, from the press.

Nigel rarely had a planned agenda. Sometimes outsiders came in to make presentations on one bureaucratic item or another. These weekly meetings were primarily a forum for show ideas or, at the very least, an opportunity for their feisty executive producer to give feedback in public to his staff. One spoke up at great risk. Depending on the kind of mood Nigel was in, you could either be ridiculed or venerated—there was no way to foresee how he would react.

As Everly looked around the table this morning, she noticed that most of the staff were trying to avoid direct eye contact with their unpredictable boss. Even Corah and Glen, who often gave salient comments, weren't offering anything. They probably thought that their presence alone was enough of a commitment.

Everly watched Kerri Marks examine a scarlet fingernail and then look expectantly around the room. She hesitated for a fraction of a second and then said in a clear voice, "How about introducing a special series? A sort of 'where are they now' type of thing—people that have been in the news, people from sports, entertainment, that we haven't heard from for a while—"

"If we haven't heard from them for a while, there may be a good reason," Nigel said, whipping a softball from his jacket pocket.

That was another thing Everly had to get used to—Nigel was constantly in motion at these meetings. If he wasn't banging his gavel, he was tossing around a softball or Whiffle balls, or gliding paper airplanes across the room.

It wasn't enough to be a responsible staff member; you also had to be a coordinated athlete.

"And that means extra editing time," Leon Posner said in his typically weary voice. "You're going to have to screen stuff and then get edit time to set up the segment. It's gonna cost."

"Everything in this bloody business costs," Nigel said, throwing the ball toward Kerri.

"But if we come out to the guest live in the studio, we shouldn't need that much tape," Kerri said, catching the ball while trying hard not to ruin her manicure.

"Maybe," said Nigel. He motioned for her to return the ball to him. "Why don't you get a list together of some specific people you have in mind, and we'll see what we can do."

"But wc *do* have to watch the budget, Nigel," Leon said emphatically.

"You know, I'd love to see the day when the 'suits' on the eighteenth floor in business affairs learn what the hell a television production is all about," Nigel said, pitching the ball to Leon, who caught it and promptly threw it back. "We make thousands of dollars for this sagging network and they are still trying to stick it to us. They can bloody well go to hell for all I care." He smacked the ball against the sidewall, leaving a vague dent in it, and then he stared moodily around the room as he caught it on the rebound.

"What else do we have on our plate?" He turned around and looked at the large white scheduling board behind him, which had two weeks of *Morning*'s programming written on it segment-by-segment. There were several vacant spaces in the second week.

"I can always give you a few more author interviews," Beryl said.

"Anything hot?" Reggie asked from across the table.

The perpetual lech always had something brilliant to say,

Everly thought. She glanced at Kerri in time to see her glaring at Reggie, but when Miss Special Projects noticed Everly looking at her, her expression turned bland and she looked away.

"Isn't what's considered 'hot' rather subject to individual interpretation?" Nigel asked. "Actually, I'd rather not be any more of a flack for the publishing industry than I already am, but if nothing else is suitable, I may have to take you up on your offer, Beryl, my dear."

Nigel gave her a particularly sweet look, and Everly wondered if her friend had changed her mind about notifying all of her family about Stephen first, before filling in the staff. Had she already told Nigel her personal news? As if Beryl had read her mind, she looked at Everly and shook her head, mouthing the words, "Not yet."

Victoria Lennox raised a limp hand and Nigel nodded at her.

"The network is giving that new mystery series on Sunday nights a big plug," she said in a pinched, tinny voice. "We could always have one or more of the stars on with a clip—"

"Any big names?" Nigel asked, tossing her the ball.

She paused and just barely caught it, then shakily threw it back. "I don't think so, but we could always have them give us a guest star with one of the regulars—"

"Forgive me, Victoria," Glen Korbett broke in. He obviously felt it was time to show his authority. "It might be a terrific series, which I doubt, but do you have any idea how hard we have to work to get the entertainment division to give us some of their precious prime time to promote our news program? Why should we give them such easy access to our air?"

"I just thought—"

"Perhaps we shouldn't have that attitude," Corah Washington said in a sultry voice. Once Glen had broken the ice, it was now her turn to hold court.

"What do you mean?" Glen asked, crossing his arms in front of his chest as he addressed her from the front of the room.

Everly caught a look of glee on Nigel's face as he watched his co-hosts spar.

"Well, I don't think things have to be on an eye-for-an-eye, tooth-for-a-tooth level between the entertainment division and the news division," Corah said sweetly. "After all, their shows *are* rather expensive and they do need the airtime to promote all of their series."

"All the more reason to be selective with how we handle ours," Glen said.

"But we can't really afford to antagonize them," Corah said, her voice a shade haughty.

"Excuse me," Victoria said, clearly upset at what was going on. "But I was only trying to help—"

"And not launch World War III?" Hank said.

Victoria ignored him. "What I mean is," she continued, "if we're really clamoring for segments, this wouldn't be such a bad idea, would it?" She turned to Nigel, looking for support.

He threw the ball her way; she grimaced as she caught it and threw it back.

"All right. Fair is fair. If we are absolutely begging for ideas, we might take your suggestion," Nigel said. "See who they're pushing and whether or not we could do it live in New York. I hate those blasted remotes from California. Most of those star and starlet types are night people, and when we get them up at bloody three o'clock in the morning, they are positively monosyllabic. Half the time they're barely coherent."

"Sometimes they're better that way," Hank said sardonically.

A few people around him, including Everly, laughed.

"I beg your pardon?" Nigel said, glancing toward Hank.

"It wasn't worth it," Hank said.

"If you're going to go through with Victoria's idea, I'd prefer *not* having to do the interview," Glen said, eager to regain center stage.

"I have no problem with it," Corah said languidly.

"Splendid," Nigel said. "Of course, I understand your point of view, Glen—but that's why we have such a good mix here with you and Corah." Ever the politician, he flashed a delighted grin toward them both.

"I have an idea!" Andrea Dobbs, one of the production assistants in the back row, raised her hand. Nigel threw a wide ball her way and she caught it easily.

"Yes, An*drey*a," Nigel said, purposely distorting her name.

"It's *An*drea," she said, laughing as she whipped the ball back.

"Come, come, what is it from the back row, then?" he said.

"There was an article in the paper this weekend about clowns that go around to hospitals entertaining the kids. Might be a good tape piece."

"I saw that," Reggie said.

Of course you did, Everly thought.

"Just think of the great stuff we'd get with the kids interacting with these guys," Reggie continued, as if the idea had been solely his. "We could get someone to shoot it this weekend and have it ready to roll for next week."

"Quite," Nigel said. "Any volunteers?"

A smattering of hands went up, and Nigel pointed at Rutie Proctor. "It's yours," he said.

A few people groaned and Everly knew what they were thinking. Rutie would probably take eight hours to shoot a story that should take two or three, but she'd get the job done. And she loved working weekends.

"And Andrea can help with the research," Nigel added, throwing the ball back to her.

"As long as she still does her regular job," Mel Stone growled, ever protective of his staff.

"I can do both, Mel," Andrea said, easily returning the softball to Nigel. She was clearly pleased to have the chance to take on more responsibility.

"Well, that fills in *one* of these damned holes," Nigel said, getting up and writing the words "hospital clown" onto the schedule. "What about giving us a part of your marvelous transplant piece, Miss Dalton?" he asked, suddenly turning around and tossing the ball her way.

Everly deftly caught it and threw it back. It was not easy to turn Nigel down when he was desperate for stories, but she didn't want to ruin what she had so carefully put together. "We're still waiting to hear from the hospital in California," Everly said deliberately. "If you want me to split it into a two-parter, I suppose I could have something ready for next week, but I'd prefer to do one long segment."

"I could definitely use something for the close on Friday," Nigel said. "But then I don't like too much time to pass before we can air the second part. When can you get that ready?"

"I can't finish it until I shoot the rest of the story, and the doctor's don't want me to come out until Kathleen gets through the first week—"

"I don't think we should split it," Hank piped up.

Everly glanced at him, mildly surprised that he was once again bothering to stick up for her. Perhaps he did have some special feelings for her.

"Oh?" said Nigel, a wary expression on his face. He threw the ball at Hank, who swore lightly as he just barely managed to get his hands on the darned thing.

"I happened to see some of the stuff that Everly's already put together," Hank said, tossing the ball up in the air over his head and catching it.

I wonder when, Everly thought.

"It would ruin the impact of the piece to break it up," he continued. He turned slightly away from Nigel and started bouncing the ball lightly against the wall behind him. "The story already has a nice emotional build to it, and I think it would work better as one complete segment."

"Do you really?" Nigel asked with great sarcasm.

"Absolutely," Hank said, still playing with the ball.

"Are you thoroughly enjoying yourself?" Nigel asked, clearly irritated.

It was hard to tell what was more upsetting to their executive producer—the prospect of being challenged or the fact that Hank was hanging on to his precious softball.

Hank shifted his bulk in Nigel's direction but continued bouncing the ball against the wall. "As a matter of fact, this is *great* fun," he said. "You really have some balls, Nigel."

A few titters scattered through the room.

"I didn't know you were such an extraordinary sportsman," Nigel said. "Will you please throw back the blasted ball?"

"What's a man without balls?" Jenny Spiegel said.

"You should know," someone murmured.

"Hey, what is this crap!" Mel Stone suddenly came to life again. "Give the man the damned ball!"

"Be a sport, Hank," Reggie said. "Throw it back to Nigel."

"Here you go, Reggie, ol' *sport*," Hank said, throwing him a curve ball. "Your court."

Reggie missed, and the ball bounced against the wall behind him, nearly knocking down his water pitcher on the rebound.

"Nice shot," Reggie said between clenched teeth as he recovered the ball and sent it high in the air to the head of the table.

Nigel easily caught it and chuckled. Now that he had his toy, he was happy. "What a bloody group I have working for me," he said.

"So what about Everly's segment?" It was Kerri Marks. She held her hands aloft, waiting for Nigel to take aim.

It was all Everly could do to keep from strangling her. She tried to keep her face composed as she waited for Nigel's answer.

Everyone assumed he'd throw his precious ball to Kerri, but instead, he threw a fast one to Everly, who, thankfully, caught it with ease.

"Great catch," Nigel said. "It's decided, then. We'll wait to air it as one long segment."

Everly smiled and tossed the ball back, marveling at the way Nigel made decisions. Some meeting, she thought.

No one ever would have believed it.

It was difficult for Everly to concentrate on going through the stack of newspapers on her desk. Every time the phone rang, she hoped it was either Jared or someone from Stanford University Hospital calling about Kathleen.

The operation had taken place yesterday, but the hospital said they needed time to see whether or not Kathleen's body would reject the new organs. Although blood types matched and special medication had been given to Kathleen to increase the possibility of her body's accepting the transplant, there was still great risk involved. The first few days were crucial, and the doctors advised Everly that it might be a while before she would be allowed to make the trip back out there.

As for Jared, Everly had been warned that they probably wouldn't have a chance to see each other during the week. They'd spoken on the phone several times, but Jared had been pretty rushed. Now with a trip to California hanging over head, Everly wondered whether she'd be able to see him this weekend.

But the Limona story had to come first.

Someone knocked on her door.

"Come in," Everly said.

"Don't you ever ask, 'who's there?'" Reggie Graham asked as he walked in and took a seat.

"You mean it might be the big bad wolf?" Everly said.

"Not that I would ever huff and puff and blow your office down," Reggie said, settling down in the chair near her desk.

"Might do some good," she said. She had to admit that for all his shortcomings as a human being, he was still a fine specimen to look at. "So, to what do I owe this pleasure?" She hoped she wasn't sounding too sarcastic.

"Oh, there you both are!" Kerri Marks was suddenly at her door.

Great. Her two favorite people. "Come on in, Kerri," she said. "I'll get a few more folks in and we can throw a party."

"Very funny," Kerri said.

"Sure, some champagne, turn up the network audio feed, and we could have a real shindig!" Reggie said.

Kerri smirked and announced imperiously, "I'm afraid

there are more important things to do. Nigel wants to see the two of you in his office."

"That's the reason I'm here, Kerri," Reggie said.

"You mean you know already?" Kerri asked.

"Know what?" Everly said.

"Of course I know. You're not the only one around here who talks to Nigel," Reggie said.

"But I *am* the special projects coordinator, and *I'm* the one who is supposed to make the assignments."

"What assignment?" Everly asked.

"Look, we all know Nigel is the one who does the handpicking," Reggie said. "And he talks to whoever the hell he wants."

"He's not supposed to," Kerri said, pouting. "This was *my* baby."

"I'd like to see you tell him to keep his mouth shut," Reggie said, his brown eyes suddenly dark and menacing.

"Yeah, and you'd probably like to see me get fired, too," Kerri hissed.

"Oh, come on, just because he let me in on this—hell, you know my background. It's obvious why he'd speak to me on this one."

"Will someone please tell me what this is all about?" Everly asked, exasperated.

They both looked at her, then back at each other.

"The show's going on the road—" Reggie said.

"Now just wait a minute," Kerri interrupted, holding up a gold-braceleted arm. "You are both supposed to come into Nigel's office with me. Then we can discuss this as a group."

"Discuss *what*?" Everly said. This was getting ridiculous.

"Just come with us, Dalton," Reggie said, shaking his head as he stood up. "Play along."

"What's the big secret?" Everly asked. "Can I at least have a hint?"

"No," Kerri said. "It's not supposed to be done this way," she said as she turned and walked out of the office.

Everly shook her head, and she and Reggie followed

Kerri down the hall, past the reception area and into Nigel's office.

"Come, come, my little cherubs," Nigel said, ushering the three of them into his office. "So, what do you think of this marvelous idea of ours?" he asked, taking the seat behind his desk.

"I think it's great," Reggie said, pacing behind Kerri and Everly, who sat in the chairs across from Nigel's desk.

"It was actually my idea," Kerri said.

Everly lost her patience. "Excuse me," she said, "but will someone *please* tell me what is going on?"

At times like this she couldn't believe the utter lack of communications that existed in the communications business.

"You don't know?" Nigel said.

"How can I know when these two refuse to tell me anything?" Everly said.

"We didn't refuse!" Kerri said.

"You didn't give us a chance," Reggie said, disingenuously.

"I give up," Everly said, throwing her hands up.

"Now, now, children," Nigel said. "It's quite simple, dear ones. You know how we like to work in advance. Well, it's barely the end of the summer, and at the end of September, we're going to do a remote from one of the country's leading universities: the University of Michigan—"

"My alma mater!" Everly said.

"Mine, too," Reggie said.

"It was my idea," Kerri said. "Although I didn't go there—"

"Come, come, children. Stop bickering," Nigel said.

"Great choice," Everly said.

This was going to be fun. She hadn't been back in Ann Arbor since she'd graduated ten years ago. Maybe she could get Jared to join her there for a weekend. She'd always wanted him to see the place, and for some reason they'd never had the time to visit when they were in Indianapolis. It figured that an opportunity to go to Michigan together would occur when they both were out on the East Coast.

"College students have a lot to deal with these days," Kerri explained, glancing down at her legal pad. "We thought that if we spent an entire show on one campus, we'd give our audience the chance to get to know one particular school and at the same time learn about issues facing all places of higher education."

"How did you decide on Michigan?" Everly asked.

"Should we tell her?" Nigel asked.

"Please, no more secrets," Everly said. "It was bad enough with these two trying so hard not to tell me what this was all about in the first place."

"Do we have to?" Kerri said.

"You know Uncle Nigel always tries to be fair," Nigel said.

"We had one of the researchers draw up a list of popular colleges and universities; we cut it up into little pieces and then put them in an upside-down umbrella," Kerri said, sounding a bit sheepish.

"You're kidding," Reggie said. "That's not what you told me, Nigel. I thought you chose Michigan because you had some staff members who went there."

"I never said *how* we chose the blasted place. What difference does it make? Probably better that I didn't know beforehand about you and Everly and the University of Michigan. Worked out just splendidly."

Everly had heard legendary stories about the apparent absence of common sense when it came to special staff assignments. When the show was on location in Japan, and another time when it originated from Spain, Nigel had neglected to include the very staff members who were fluent in Japanese and Spanish. It shouldn't have been so surprising that interoffice politics were more critical than actual logic when it came to making assignments.

Given that she and Reggie knew Ann Arbor, it was almost a miracle they'd been given this story.

"I think this will be great, Nigel," Everly said. "Of course right now I'm devoting my energies to the Limona story, but that should be taken care of soon—"

"Any more news on that?" Nigel said.

"Just keeping my fingers crossed for now," Everly said.

"Excuse me for interrupting, but I just want you to know that I've been in touch with the university's public relations department," Kerri said. "They said they'd be willing to help us in any way they can."

"Oh, Lord! That can sometimes be the kiss of death," Nigel said.

"Not in this case, Nigel," Everly said. "They have some pretty on-the-ball folks out there."

"Remember, Ann Arbor is where JFK announced the formation of the Peace Corps," Reggie said.

"And it's the place where Tom Hayden got his start," Everly said.

"Lovely," Nigel said. "We could use a few campus radicals to stir things up around here."

"No, we couldn't," Everly said. "We have enough action around this place."

"I wouldn't know about that," Reggie said.

Everly saw Kerri blush, but Miss Special Projects said nothing.

"I just bet you don't," Nigel said, his voice a shade sarcastic.

Nigel probably knew more about what was going on behind the scenes than he let on, Everly thought. He had incredible sources. She wouldn't have been surprised if he knew the name of every woman Reggie had ever made a pass at. She even bet he already knew about Beryl and Stephen. Maybe even Jared.

Something told her she had better be careful. The television industry was a small world . . . sometimes *too* small.

THIRTEEN

Things happen so quickly around here, Everly thought as she headed toward her office. When you worked in a fast-paced industry, you never knew what to expect—which had its good and bad points. But no one could ever call the television news business boring—except Hank Forrest, perhaps, in one of his more "charitable" moments.

She'd intended to thank him for helping her out that morning at the staff meeting. Bailing her out was becoming a trend. She also wanted to find out if he'd told the truth about having screened her material, but between waiting to hear about the Limonas, getting the Ann Arbor assignment, and trying to complete her tape editing work, she'd just barely had time to go to the ladies' room—another hazard of her profession.

Everly had spent most of the afternoon carefully editing the Limona material she'd already shot, so that she could easily add new footage from the follow-up trip. Whether or not Hank had actually seen what she'd put together, he'd been right: there was a definite rhythm to the way she had edited the story, which would have been ruined by breaking it up into two parts.

Nearly bleary-eyed from her lengthy editing session, Everly returned to her office, only to find that Kerri or Reggie had dumped off a pile of folders bulging with articles relating to the U. of M. remote. They'd be counting on her to comb through the voluminous material and generate some programming ideas. Nuts-and-bolts work was beneath their lofty positions on the staff.

To hell with 'em, Everly thought. They'd have to wait. There were more important things for her to take care of now. Specifically, it was time to get in touch with Gloria Everitt.

Fortunately, Everly had saved the private Indianapolis telephone/address directory she'd had for years. The Everitts had an unlisted number, and although she could probably have wheedled it out of a local reporter or persuaded an operator to place a call to Gloria under the guise of a "news emergency," Everly preferred using the direct route.

After two rings, the phone was picked up.

"Everitt residence." Everly recognized the distinctive Southern voice that belonged to the Everitt's housekeeper, Deena Jackson.

"Deena? It's Everly Dalton. How are you?"

"Why, Miss Dalton, what a surprise! The missis will be so glad to hear from you. Shall I get her?"

"Yes, please."

Several moments later Gloria Everitt got on the phone.

"Everly, *dahling*. What a pleasant surprise! How *mahvelous* to hear from you."

Why was it that when some people fell into money, they felt obliged to speak with an affected accent? Everly suspected that Midwest born-and-bred Gloria never spoke that way before she married into the Everitt fortune. She wondered how long it took to cultivate. And who gave lessons.

"Hello, Mrs. Everitt."

"Please—call me Gloria. We're both adults now, *dahling*."

"All right, Gloria. It's been a while, I know, but I have to speak to you about something. Did you know I was working on the staff of *Morning*?"

After two beats of silence, Gloria responded. "Oh? Well, good for you, dear. How nice."

Everly could imagine what was going through Gloria Everitt's head. She was certain none of it was "nice."

"The reason I'm calling concerns a situation with someone on the staff here," Everly said.

"Are you referring to that positively horrid Lester Kay? Do you have any idea what he did to my Jessica?"

"But you may not have all the facts—which is why I'm calling," Everly said.

"What are you implying? Jessica is a mere *child*. And that old man had the temerity to force himself on my innocent daughter!"

"Is that what Jessica told you?"

"Are you saying that I'm making this up?"

Everly didn't want Gloria to be so defensive. She tried a more direct approach. "Gloria, is Jessica the one who wants to press charges, or was that your idea?"

"How would you expect a young, naive girl to know of such things? No, this was my call," Gloria said. "Your Mr. Kay has quite a surprise coming. Some role model he is. I want justice! And I want Charles to give Jessica back to me. What kind of custodian would let this happen? She has no right to be sashaying around New York City unchaperoned while he's traipsing all over the world with Lord knows what young tramp or another!"

Tramp? It had been ages since Everly had heard that word. Gloria Everitt was living in another era and probably couldn't accept the fact that her sixteen-year-old daughter might be more experienced than Gloria wanted to admit.

This was not going to be easy.

"Please let me explain something," Everly said. "I can understand why you're upset; it's only natural. There's quite an age difference between Lester and Jessica, and the thought of them together—well, I'm sure that's very disconcerting—"

"You don't know the half of it!" Gloria said.

"You're probably right," Everly said. "But from what Lester told me—and I do trust him—*she* went after him—being a television celebrity and all. She even lied about her age. Jessica has always looked older than her years, so why wouldn't he believe her? And I'm not surprised that Lester was attracted to her. What man wouldn't be?

"But he's not the person you should be angry with—*Charles* is the real culprit. I remember how horrible all the publicity was during the court battle for your children. But think of the coverage a celebrity trial would get. Can't you just imagine the headlines?"

"What exactly do you mean?" Gloria asked.

"Well, think about it. You'd probably end up reliving your divorce. Reporters will dig up those old stories and come up with new ones. You don't want to go through something like that with the press again—and I'm sure you don't want Jessica to, either. Think of *her*."

Gloria was quiet for a moment and then said, "Well, you may be right. It would be a pity to drag her through an experience like that. I suppose I hadn't really thought it through—but I must do *something*."

"You have every right to go after Charles about this. It could affect his custody rights. As for Lester, he swore to me he'd have nothing more to do with Jessica—and I believe him. Maybe his judgment isn't so great, but he's a man of his word. Ruining his career doesn't really serve any purpose. You can see that."

"Well, yes, dear, you may actually be right. Charles is the *real* scoundrel. Jessica never would have gotten into this situation if she had stayed in Indianapolis with me."

Everly didn't want to place bets on that, but she said nothing.

"All right," Gloria continued. "You've made your point. I'll have my attorney contact Charles's lawyers, and we'll deal with the matter more discreetly. Thank you, Everly dear. You always had *such* a good head on your shoulders."

Everly smiled. "Glad I could help," she said. "And I

know Lester will be most grateful."

And so will I, she thought.

It was a few minutes after nine o'clock when Everly arrived at the Berkshire Hotel. Jared had called only minutes after her conversation with Gloria Everitt. They had arranged to meet in the lobby of his hotel and have a late-night supper. She wasn't due back in editing until midnight, so she had some time to spend with him. She couldn't wait to tell him everything that had happened today, especially the details of her Everitt triumph.

She sank into a plush armchair and sighed, relishing the sensation of comfort that enveloped her as she sat down. It felt as if this was the first moment in the entire day when she could actually relax and not worry about anything.

Sometimes Everly wondered where she got the energy to handle what was more often than not a grueling schedule. Most of the time she tried not to think about it.

Life was more manageable that way.

Jared hadn't arrived yet, which wasn't such a bad thing. Since it was so rare to have the time to sit and actually do nothing, Everly enjoyed the change of pace.

It occurred to her that there weren't too many hotels in New York City that encouraged visitors to sit in the lobby. Even the Plaza had no seating in its main entrance. Life was too hectic and exciting for some thing as mundane as sitting down. But mostly, hotel owners didn't want to encourage vagrants or other unsavory types to mar their pristine surroundings. The Berkshire was an exception.

The entire lobby was a potpourri of comfortable love seats and couches, chairs and ottomans, all decorated in a pleasing array of matching pastel fabrics. Mirrored walls and enormous, strategically placed flower arrangements gave the room a bright, airy feeling.

At this hour, a string quartet played classical music and uniformed waiters hovered about, ready to serve drinks. Late afternoons found a harpist accompanying tea and tea cakes, and at either time of day it wasn't unusual to find someone sitting there simply to enjoy the atmosphere—although, depending on your proximity to the entertainment, there was often not-so-subtle pressure to purchase some kind of food or drink.

One of Everly's favorite pastimes was people watching. New York City had the largest and most eclectic selection of people to scrutinize. She turned her attention to the motley group gathered around the room.

Two attractive young couples in black tie and long, shimmering gowns drank champagne while perched on a couch near the musicians. Next to them, several dark-suited middle-aged businessmen huddled over a coffee table, occasional raucous laughter erupting as they gobbled peanuts and practically chugged down what appeared to be hard liquor. A lone elderly woman, elegantly attired in an old-fashioned lacy black dress, with several dilapidated shopping bags at her feet, sat in a straight-back chair across from the men, quietly sipping what looked like sherry. A tiny smile softened her face after each taste.

Everly wondered if she was a regular.

A cackling threesome of overweight women in their fifties, each wearing a garish polyester pantsuit—one worse than the next—sat to Everly's right, sharing a large carafe of white wine. Their harsh clothes and vibrant makeup were such a marked contrast to the lovely old woman nearby, they seemed like cartoon characters come to life.

As Everly glanced over to the main entrance, a coterie of Oriental businessmen wearing similar navy suits entered the lobby. They checked the front desk for messages and then were herded by their apparent leader toward the hotel's restaurant.

Everly prided herself on her ear for language, and she recognized several distinctive Japanese phrases as they passed by. She could have used one of those guys when she was trying to get through to the Harcrests several weeks ago.

Then Everly almost laughed aloud. Did anyone give a damn about the Harcrests *now*? But that was the ephemeral nature of the news business. The Harcrests were plastered all over the headlines one day; Tina Greene usurped them the next. Now that she was getting established in one of the major news capitals of the world, Everly felt that she played a significant part in whatever captured the public's attention for the day. She got the most satisfaction, however, when *she*, rather than breaking news events, controlled what the audience out there watched—as with the Limona story.

"Hi, gorgeous!" Jared whispered in her ear. He must have secretly entered the lobby and snuck up behind her. He came around in front of her chair and pulled her up toward him. "God, you look good," he said. "Do you know how truly beautiful you are?" He gave her a quick kiss on the lips, and Everly peripherally noticed how deeply this slight contact affected her.

She also smelled Scotch on his breath and wondered how long and with whom he'd been having drinks. Surely it was something to do with business.

She wouldn't mention it. An argument would only ruin their precious time together.

"Beautiful, huh? How am I supposed to respond to that?" she said.

"Just nod and agree," he said, steering her toward the hotel's restaurant. "I figured this was the most convenient place. How's the food here, by the way?"

"Adequate," Everly said. "Nothing spectacular, but good just the same."

A lot of local restaurants had similar menus—a combination of American and quasi-Continental cuisine, with a dash of Cajun and/or "Tex-Mex" thrown in. Everly didn't mind the lack of originality. Even mediocre establishments in this town had a distinctive New York ambience—something about the tense undercurrent in the room, the subdued lighting, the dress of the clientele, the pace set by the maître d' and his staff. She never tired of trying to define what made this city remarkable.

"I'm sure you'll find something you like," she added, knowing exactly what he'd say next.

"I already have," Jared said, giving her arm a squeeze.

It was disturbing that he was so predictable in some ways,

yet in other ways a total mystery.

As the maître d' led them to their table, they passed the large circular bar that dominated the front of the restaurant. Everly couldn't help but look at the crush of people swarming around the bartenders and immediately think of ants desperately feasting at a picnic.

She never wanted to end up like that.

They were about to be seated at a small table near the kitchen when Jared tapped the maître d' on the shoulder and spoke in a subdued but firm manner. "We'd like that table over there," he said, pointing across the room to a quiet table for two in a dimly lit corner. "It's more romantic," he added with a knowing smile.

"No problem," the maître d' responded, winking at Everly.

She tried to appear nonchalant, but hearing the word "romantic" set her mind off in a thousand different directions. Stay calm, she told herself, just stay calm. It was still too early to predict what the future would mean for the two of them.

"So, here we are," Jared said, grabbing her hand across the table and giving it a squeeze. "Just like old times," he added.

"Not quite," Everly said quietly. "We're not engaged anymore, remember?"

"But we're together," Jared said. "I have to tell you, though, my schedule here is totally crazy—one meeting after the next. I guess there's something about this place that makes it almost impossible to relax."

He was still trying to change the subject. If only she could have ignored his married status as easily as he seemed to. But she was determined to be pragmatic.

"That's part of this city's attraction," she said. "There are some terrific ways to cope with stress here. Maybe when you're more available, I'll share some trade secrets."

"I'm available right now," Jared said.

"No, you're not," Everly said, trying to quell the sudden flash of anger that enveloped her.

"Come on, Cupcake, you know what I mean. I can't tell

you what I had to go through to get sent to New York so quickly. I knew you were here and I knew we needed to have time to spend with each other. This is such a plum assignment as you know—station manager for one of our most important 'O and O's.' It was quite a battle to get them to send me here."

Her resolve not to fight had weakened. She had no other choice but to remind him that he was still married. Maybe Jared could pretend Pam didn't exist, but she couldn't.

"Really?" she said. "You came here for *me*? I suppose your father-in-law would think differently about assigning you to this particular owned-and-operated station if he knew your real motives."

"Give me a break, Everly. You don't think I've thought about you all this time?"

"It doesn't make sense, Jared. How much could I have been in your thoughts if you married someone else? Don't tell me you were thinking of me on your way to the altar."

"Look, I told you. I might have made a mistake marrying Pam. That's why I wanted to give us a chance. I thought you understood—what's gotten into you?"

"I'm just concerned. I mean, what about your career? You *do* have a powerful father-in-law. Who knows what kind of revenge he might take if you walk out on his daughter?"

"Let me worry about that. Come on, we don't want to argue now, do we? Tell me about this Lester Kay situation. I bet he's going to owe you big on this one."

Everly sighed. It was no use. For now, she decided to go along with the change of topics.

"You're right," she said. "And I intend to take full advantage of the situation."

"Atta girl!" Jared said. "What do you have in mind?"

"I haven't really thought about it," Everly lied. In the past, she'd never kept anything from Jared, especially when it concerned her career. This time she decided it would be wise to keep her plans to herself.

"I'm sure you'll come up with something," Jared said, clearly excited as their conversation turned to business. "That old adage, 'it's not *what* you know, but *who* you know,' is definitely true in *this* business. It's important to use everything and everyone you can, believe me."

Like the way you used me, Everly thought, and now your wife.

"If there's anything I can do for you once I get established in this town, I want you to call me," Jared said. "Hell, maybe I'll get you to jump ship and come over to my station. From the tapes I've seen and the people I've met, I have a feeling we just might need a new anchorwoman for the five o'clock news."

"I don't know if it would be such a stellar idea to have us working at the same station," Everly said. "And it's still too early for me to think about going on the air."

"I'll give you all the time you want," Jared said, giving her hand a squeeze.

"We don't really have that much time," Everly said, pulling her hand from his grasp.

"Then we should make up for lost time."

Everly looked into his enormous blue eyes and felt the familiar, irresistible pull of him that never failed to elicit a sense of surrender from her. Even after all this time, after all that had happened, she was still drawn to Jared in a visceral way that she'd never experienced with any other man. The phrase "soul mate" came to mind, and she wondered if she and Jared were truly meant for each other. She wanted him in her life so badly.

But at what price?

"Penny for your thoughts, Cupcake?" Jared asked.

Everly looked away and said, "With inflation, it's up to a dollar."

Jared pretended to reach for his wallet. "I'm prepared to pay, you know. Of course I gotta figure a good way to explain it on my expense report. Who knows what kind of secrets will be revealed?"

Everly smiled coyly. You only live once, she thought. What the hell? "I only give secrets in the bedroom," she said.

"Is that a promise or a threat?" Jared responded.

"You'll just have to find out," Everly said, conjuring up

romantic visions of the two of them together in his hotel room.

"I'm all for that," Jared said. Then he suddenly looked embarrassed. "But not tonight," he added.

"Why not? I'll be finished with editing by two, and I don't have to show up until noon tomorrow. That gives us just about enough time," she said.

"I'm afraid I'll have to take a rain check, hon," Jared said. "I'm expecting an important phone call later tonight."

"How *much* later?"

"It's, uh, well, Pam and I haven't had much time to talk since I left, and I told her to call me in my hotel room around 11:00. I also have a breakfast meeting at seven, which means I have to get up early to be extra sharp for it. So I guess we have to call it quits after we eat."

"Oh, really?" Everly said, fighting to stay in control. "So she's checking up on you. I guess I don't blame her."

"Look, Pam wasn't too happy that I was traveling to New York alone. Anyway, she was busy when I called her this afternoon. So I told her to call me tonight at the hotel. It's probably not the best idea for us to be together when she calls."

"She'd never know I was there," Everly said. "I know how to be discreet."

"I'm not doubting that, hon," Jared said. "But I just don't think it's a good idea. Trust me on this."

Trust him? Everly felt torn between throwing her glass of water at him or begging for some time to be alone with him. Why was she so drawn to Jared, even when she had misgivings about getting involved again with the very man who had done so much damage? She just couldn't get rid of that tiny kernel of hope that everything would work out between them. Maybe it was just as well if they weren't together tonight. The smart thing to do after her editing session would be to go home and get some sleep.

"Okay," she said. "You'll just have to owe me."

"With pleasure, my dear," Jared said. "Guess we'd better order or they'll be able to hear my stomach growling in

Times Square! Nothing like wall-to-wall meetings to build up an appetite."

She smiled at him and tried to pretend that everything was all right. There'd be other opportunities to be alone with Jared.

It was simple.

She'd just have to trust him, that's all.

Everly's head was throbbing. She had thirty more minutes to go before her edit time would be used up. It was sheer insanity to make *Morning* staff members sign up for editing rooms at midnight. But ever since a huge conglomerate had bought EBC, the "suits" had made drastic cuts in facilities and manpower. *Evening News Worldwide* still had free reign, but the documentary unit and the *Morning* staff had to juggle their schedules accordingly.

As it was, Everly was lucky to get an editor who knew what he was doing, even if it meant working horrendous hours. Some of the old-timers who were the best at their job had been bought out.

The worst result of the cutbacks was that once you started to edit something, you didn't necessarily continue to work on it with the same person. The bottom-line folks couldn't get it through their heads that a creative endeavor required consistency. In their tiny minds, one editor was interchangeable with another. That just wasn't true.

Everly learned early on to plan her editing sessions around a particular editor's schedule, rather than just go with potluck. Fred Keller had been with her at the start of the Limona story, and she was determined to use him no matter what hours he'd been assigned. The finished product was more than worth it.

She and Fred were finishing up a segment that showed Kathleen and Bill talking with their kids over a meal in their eat-in kitchen. It was one of the final sections of the story. Everly wanted to show how similar the Limonas were to other families. The more "normal" they appeared, the more extraordinary would be the realization that this family was anything but typical.

"It's a good thing the kitchen scenes were well lit," Fred said. "I've seen indoor footage that was totally unusable."

"Kirk Peterson is a real pro," Everly said.

"Yeah, in more ways than one, I hear," Fred said, ever persistent to get some juicy gossip.

"Beats me," Everly said innocently, secretly amused at his tactics. "How long is the tape that we've put down so far?" She was eager to change the topic.

"About three minutes. We can use another thirty seconds or so on this stuff. Then you'll have about another one or two minutes for the follow-up material, if they give you the time."

"More airtime? Now *that* would be a miracle," Everly said.

"Well, you gotta promise me you'll use me to finish this tape. I like doing stories that have a happy ending. That's why I like working with you guys. It's all crash and burn with the folks on the evening news—no time to be creative. The stuff I do with you is Emmy-award material, no doubt about it."

"You might be right," Everly said. She'd known from the start that this piece was significant. She'd definitely make sure Nigel would enter it when Emmy nomination time came around.

The phone rang, giving both of them a start. Who would be calling at one-thirty in the morning? Fred picked up the phone and in a shaky voice said, "Edit room seven. Keller speaking."

He paused to hear what the caller wanted, shook his head, and handed Everly the phone. He was clearly upset.

"What is it?" she asked, as she grabbed the receiver and put her hand over the mouthpiece.

Fred shook his head and pointed to the phone. "It's for you," he said, his voice breaking.

"This is Everly Dalton," she said.

"It's Melanie Sorkin, Miss Dalton. I'm afraid I have some bad news."

"Oh no," Everly said. She felt a wave of panic. Not bad news, I can't take any more bad news, she thought. "Didn't the transplant work? I was going to come out there in a few days. Is Kathleen all right?"

"I'm afraid she didn't make it," Melanie said.

"What do you mean? Bill was so ecstatic that you'd found a donor, I just thought—Is Kathleen going to be all right?"

"She didn't make it. She's dead, Miss Dalton. Her body just went to pieces after the operation. It had been too long a wait."

"On, no," Everly said. She was stunned for a few seconds and then her mind started racing. "Is Bill all right? How are the kids taking this?"

"Better than I thought. We had informed Bill that once Kathleen had passed the six month mark, chances were that her body couldn't sustain the kind of complicated operation involved for a heart/lung transplant."

"But everyone was so hopeful," Everly said, thinking of all the doctors she'd interviewed. "She seemed perfectly fine when I saw her—"

"This type of procedure demands a lot of stamina. And there's always a chance, despite many obstacles, that it will work. When a donor was found that fit Kathleen's needs, we had to try. We did the best we could, but her body just didn't hold up."

"Oh, God," Everly said. "This is awful." Suddenly she felt dizzy. She closed her eyes and tried to concentrate. "Is there anything I can do?"

"Not really," Melanie said. "There's going to be a short funeral service here tomorrow, and then Bill and the kids will go back to Michigan for a memorial service."

"Oh, this is so awful. Please give Bill my love. And the kids. And please make sure I get their address in Michigan. I'm so sorry."

"We all are, Miss Dalton. Kathleen was so excited about all the attention she was getting for organ donation. It was a good thing your show did, sending you out here and all. It meant a lot to her. I just wanted to be sure you knew that."

"Thanks, Miss Sorkin. I appreciate that."

"I'll be in touch with you again."

"Right. Good-bye," Everly said. She looked at Fred, who'd been watching her carefully. She didn't want her emotions to get the best of her. But it was hard. "Bad news," she said quietly.

"What a shame," Fred said. "Just hearing how that lady sounded when she asked for you was pretty telling. I'm sorry, Everly."

It was all she could do to stay in control. "We've got to finish this piece as soon as we can," she said.

Fred reached out and touched her arm. "I'm off in a few minutes, but I'm back in at nine this morning. I can pull a few strings to get you into the edit room with me."

"That would be great," Everly said, suddenly feeling exhausted.

"You could use some sleep, you know. And then you and I will come back and put together the best damned tribute anyone could ever create. I promise you that."

"I hope you're right, Fred. How can I thank you?"

"Just keep asking for me when you gotta edit, sweetheart. That's all I want. Now, come here." He stood up, gathered her in his arms, and held her for a moment.

"Sometimes we all just need a little hug," he said as he pulled away from her. "You can always come to Fred when you need one."

"Thanks," Everly said, her eyes tearing.

It was almost two A.M. She went back to her office to put away her notes and was about to head out the door when she thought about calling Jared. She would probably be waking him up, but he'd understand.

She dialed the hotel and asked for his room. After the phone rang twelve times, the operator got back on the line.

"There's no answer, ma'am. Care to leave a message?"

"No answer? And you were ringing Jared Kammer's room?"

"Yes, ma'am. No answer."

"All right," Everly said. "No message."

She was devastated. And furious.

He had lied to her.

It was bad enough to be upset over the news about

Kathleen; now she was in a virulent rage at Jared's absence. Where the hell was he? He'd damn well better have a good excuse, she thought.

She had never needed Jared more than she needed him now.

FOURTEEN

"Where do you think he was?" Beryl asked, handing Everly a fresh cup of coffee.

It was seven-fifteen. After an uneasy night, Everly had called Beryl as early as she dared and immediately been invited over for breakfast. They were seated on two wooden bar stools parked side-by-side in front of the small counter that overlooked Beryl's living room.

"I don't know. I can hardly think straight," Everly said. "He made such a big deal about not staying out too late and being alone when Pam called. It doesn't make sense. I can't believe he was with some other woman."

"Who knows? From what you've told me, this guy must really be something!" Beryl said.

"Jared is definitely not typical."

Everly shook her head and took another sip of coffee. Beryl owned one of those fantastic Japanese contraptions that not only ground the coffee beans, but brewed the coffee as well. It was one of the few small pleasures Everly could count on that morning.

"No offense," Beryl said, "but he sounds like a real jerk to me. I mean—he has an awful lot of nerve. And he's cruel. Look at what he did to you the first time he was in your life—abandoning you so he could move ahead in his career. If he hurt you once, he can do it again. One minute he's telling you how important you are to him—that he's even considering a *divorce* because of you—and then when you really need him, he's not around. What kind of a relationship is that?"

"He wasn't always that way," Everly said. It was hard not to sound defensive. Despite his unavailability last night, she felt she owed him the benefit of the doubt. "Maybe he turned his phone off," she added, suddenly hopeful. "He told me his schedule was pretty hectic here. It takes a lot to get used to this city."

"Maybe, but it's not as if he's some country bumpkin. He's been around.

"You know, I have to tell you, Everly, times like this I really don't understand you," Beryl said. "You're still sticking up for him, but he doesn't *deserve* you. Maybe he *was* terrific back in Indianapolis—until he dumped you. I think he's taking advantage of you. Can't you see that?"

"Well, this is a change—you giving *me* advice on relationships. It wasn't so long ago that you were bending my ear about your problems with our beloved Reggie Graham."

"Maybe he gave Jared a few lessons. You couldn't ask for two more inconsiderate, self-centered guys."

"Men can be that way," Everly said quietly. She nibbled at a piece of whole wheat toast, forcing herself to eat so that she'd have some energy to face the rest of the day.

"You're wrong. There are plenty of men around who are decent. You just don't want to give them a chance," Beryl said. "Look at Hank. I don't understand what's going on between you two, but he's probably one of the most reliable guys you could ever meet. He's there for you."

"When it's convenient," Everly said.

"That's not fair. Who knows how he'd act if you gave him the right encouragement," Beryl said. "Hank may not be the most sociable guy in the world, but he's a good person. He'd do anything for a friend."

"You're probably right. But I still don't think it's fair to automatically write Jared off. He may have a perfectly legitimate reason for not being in when I called. I can't turn my back on him just yet."

"Maybe," Beryl said. "It's funny, though. I'm just remembering that little phrase you practically drilled into my head right after we first met."

"What was that?"

"You don't remember? You kept saying, 'Don't believe what men *say*, Beryl. It's what they *do* that counts—their actions, not their words.' I've never forgotten that, Everly. Maybe you should try to follow your own advice."

"So when did you become Miss Know-It-All?" Everly asked.

"When I started listening to some of the things you told me."

"Touché," Everly said, smiling and raising her coffee mug in a mock toast.

"It's good to see you smile," Beryl said. "I was beginning to lose hope."

"Don't do that," Everly said. "Everything will work out." She glanced over at the antique grandfather clock that dominated Beryl's cozy living room. There was such a warm atmosphere in her friend's apartment, with its eclectic blend of needlepoint hangings, afghans, and antiques. It was hard to leave. Everly took a deep breath.

"I better get moving," she said. "Fred Keller is pulling some strings with the scheduling folks, so I better haul ass and show up on time."

"I'm really sorry about Kathleen," Beryl said, lightly touching her friend's arm.

"I know you are. I can't believe she's gone—there was so much hope in her life. And she had so much to look forward to. Those poor kids—it seems so unfair."

"Well, in a way, you're helping her do what she wanted—making a difference to all those people who need transplants. We both know how powerful our show can be. I can't tell you how many books have become bestsellers just because of one author appearance on *Morning*."

"This Limona segment has to be special," Everly said, grabbing her coat and an oversized leather bag that held the day's morning papers along with a multitude of belongings. "I'm lucky to have Fred in the editing room. He's truly a genius."

"Don't underestimate *your* talent, kiddo," Beryl said. "Hey, I better get in the shower or I'm really going to be late."

"See you in a bit," Everly said. "And thanks again, Beryl. I feel a hell of a lot better now than when I first got here. You're a good friend. I really am lucky."

"We both are," Beryl said.

"The future? I can only take one day at a time," Kathleen Limona said, looking head-on into the camera. "I've already extended my life—thanks to the special medication I'm on out here. It was pretty rough back in Michigan. Almost everything I did there was a challenge—just getting dressed seemed to take forever. And I'd be in and out of hospitals, going from one expert to the next.

"But now I'm constantly surrounded by my family, and I have a team of physicians helping me and rooting for my success. This will probably sound corny, but I really believe this entire experience has been a gift." Her voice broke and she paused a moment.

Everly spoke off camera. "Do you want us to stop tape? I don't want this to be difficult for you."

Kathleen shook her head as the camera pulled back to show Bill lightly caressing his wife's shoulder. They were sitting outside on a park bench.

"You don't have to do this," Bill said to his wife. "We can wait."

"No, I'm all right. Let's go on."

Fred stopped his machine a moment and looked at Everly. "You want to keep this stuff in?"

Everly bit her lip and nodded. She knew if she tried to speak, she'd start crying.

"Are you okay?" Fred asked.

Everly took a deep breath. "I'm fine," she said quietly. She didn't want Fred to know how vulnerable she felt that morning. "Let's keep going."

Kirk had pulled back to a wide two-shot. Bill Limona looked at Kathleen and then into the camera. "I don't believe any family in this situation thinks much beyond each day," he said. "It's funny. All our lives we hear about how important our health is, but none of us ever give it much thought until it's taken away."

"I've always loved my children and my husband," Kathleen said. "But when this happened, I cherished them in a way I never did before. Wendy and Jonathan are two terrific, beautiful kids." She paused a moment and smiled, adding, "I'm not saying they're *perfect*, but I don't think I ever thought much about how special they really were until all this happened to me."

"You've said you don't think too far ahead into the future," Everly said off-camera. "I'm sure anyone in your situation would say the same thing. But every parent has visions about their children's futures or what they'll be like as adults. Can you talk about any of that with us?"

Kathleen tilted her head to the side and looked away from the camera for a few seconds. "You're right about that. I do think about what they'll be like when they grow up. I just want to be around to see it.

"I picture Jonathan in some kind of responsible profession. He talks now about being a doctor. I'm sure he'll achieve whatever he wants. It's funny, he's always seemed more like a little man to me than a little boy—always so conscientious and reliable. Sometimes I feel guilty. I think if I were a different kind of mom—a healthier one—he'd allow himself to be more of a kid, and not be so serious at such an early age."

"But don't you think children are born with certain traits in them?" Everly asked. "A lot of professionals would say that no matter what you and your husband did, your children would be the same people they are today."

"Maybe," Kathleen said. "Now that I think about it, they were entirely different from birth—as if they were born with fully developed personalities."

"Both of them were beautiful babies," Bill said. "But you're right—Wendy always had to be entertained, almost from day one, while Jonathan was able to amuse himself for hours at a stretch."

"If Jonathan is going to become some kind of intellectual professional, what do you think Wendy will grow up to be?" Everly asked.

"She loves music," Kathleen said. "We kept an ancient record player in her room, and I used to play all kinds of musical comedy albums and movie soundtrack records to help put her to sleep when she was a baby."

"We never did that with Jonathan," Bill said. "We didn't need to. He'd rub his eyes to let us know he was tired, put his little head down on the pillow, and within minutes he'd be fast asleep."

"You were very lucky parents," Everly's voice cut in. "Did Jonathan sleep through the night right away?"

Kathleen and Bill laughed.

It was bittersweet to see them so happy, Everly thought as the tape kept rolling. "We need to keep that in," she said, turning to Fred. "Don't you think?"

"Good choice," he said.

"I want people to remember them as a happy family."

"Yeah, but you know it's also gonna be a real tearjerker the way it's going so far," Fred said.

"But *that*, my dear fellow, is what brings in bloody good ratings."

Everly and her editor turned around to see Nigel lurking in the doorway.

"How long have you been there?" Everly asked. She had truly been startled, but she kept her voice steady.

"You don't mind that I occasionally spy on my own troops now, do you?" Nigel said. "I haven't been here that long. But Hank was absolutely right the other day. It would have been horrible to cut up this precious story into two segments. I can tell it's going to be smashing! In fact, when it's ready, I'll make sure he plugs it before all of the commercial breaks so that our audience will stay tuned in for it. People love these kinds of stories."

"I just wish it had a happier ending," Everly said.

"Of course you do, dear. Don't think I'm heartless, I'm sure she was a lovely person, but—"

"Don't say it, Nigel," Everly said. "I don't want to hear that her death makes for good television."

"Of course not," Nigel said, looking guilty. "What I was going to say was that hard luck stories sometimes make our audience feel better about themselves. You know—counting one's blessings and all that?"

Fred shook his head. Everly said nothing.

"And another thing," Nigel continued. "You're a damn good interviewer, Everly—not that I'm surprised. In fact, Lester Kay, of all people, said something to me the other day about giving you a chance on-camera in the near future. At first I thought you'd bribed the dear boy, or triple spiked his already spiked coffee, but I can see now that you didn't have to stoop to that sort of thing. You're rather good, actually."

Everly couldn't tell whether Nigel was being sarcastic or genuine. She was hearing exactly what she'd dreamt about when she first made the decision to come to New York.

But she was afraid that if she opened her mouth, she'd say the wrong thing.

"She really *is* good," Fred added. "I've been in thousands of editing sessions, and Everly is one dame who knows exactly what to ask. She got a lot out of this story—not only with the adults, but with the kids, too. Not too many interviewers can do both."

"I know that, Freddie, dear. Well, your day in the sun will come, Everly. I don't know when—but soon. Keep up the good work, you two. Now, when do you think this little masterpiece of ours will be ready?"

"I'm not sure," Everly said.

"At the end of the day," Fred said, ignoring Everly's frantic look. "You can count on it."

"Lovely," Nigel said. "We'll give it the premier spot at 7:47. You can have an absolute eternity for this piece, Everly—an entire seven-and-a-half minutes."

"That would be wonderful—" Everly said.

"One thing, though," Fred interrupted. "I'm supposed to be with one of the *Evening News Worldwide* producers this afternoon. You better see about getting me a replacement, or someone will go running to Harvey Markfield and then I'll really get screwed."

"I thought your fabulous unions protected you from that sort of thing," Nigel said, a touch of sarcasm in his voice.

"Not from the wrath of Markfield," Fred said.

"Consider it done, my dear fellow. Oh yes, while I think of it, Hank Forrest came up with a lovely idea."

"Oh, really?" Everly asked, suddenly worried. Hank rarely got involved with major editorial decisions. He just wrote "intros" and "outros" for the script. This segment was hers and in a way Fred's, and she didn't want any additional outside advice—not even from Hank, no matter what kind of friend he was.

"What is it?" she asked.

"Well, it's against our news policy about raw footage, but he thought it would be a nice gesture to send the Limonas copies of all the cassettes you shot. Those kids aren't going to remember a great deal about their mum. This would give them a sort of video heirloom they could always see for themselves, show their own children, grandchildren—whatever."

Everly was stunned. The emotions she'd tried so hard to control welled up with a force that was nearly overwhelming. She fought for control.

"Neat idea," Fred said quickly, as if he were aware that Everly was speechless.

"I thought so, too," Nigel said. "Imagine—*me* agreeing with Hank Forrest. Anyway, if Leon Posner *dares* to get on our case about the extra expense to dub this material, we'll just remind him that he's always included in our travel budget—no matter what the cost. As I always say, 'fight fire with fire.' "

"Right," Everly said. "I'll remember that the next time I need approval for a travel voucher."

"Indeed," Nigel said, as he patted her on the shoulder.

"Enough of this drivel—back to editing, my dearies."

As soon as he left, Everly turned to Fred. "That really *is* a great idea," she said. "Has *Morning* ever done anything like that before with raw footage?"

"Not in the thirty-seven years *I've* been here," Fred said. "In fact, we better keep this to ourselves. Markfield would have a fit if he found out—on principle alone."

"Well, let's keep going, then," Everly said. She would have to remember to say something to Hank about his idea. He truly was special. "And we'll break for a 'green dot' in about forty-five minutes."

"Green dot" was union terminology for a fifteen-minute break. No one knew where the term originated, but a union employee could request a limited number of green dots during the day. Fred Keller was one of the few editors around who never took his full quota of breaks. The work came first.

"I just had a thought," Fred said. "You know how we have the footage of Wendy singing in the sandbox? I know we have some stuff on another tape with her mom singing, too. If they're in the same key, or near enough, maybe we could mix them together for the close."

"That would be perfect," Everly said. "And we can put it over one of the shots where the family is walking through the park—you know, where the tree branches look like a cathedral?"

"If that doesn't get 'em, nothing will," Fred said.

This piece was going to definitely "get them," Everly thought.

Her very future depended on it.

Fifteen

"Greetings all," Glen Korbett intoned in his majestic voice. "Coming up after this break, a remarkable story—but a sad one, as well."

"Stay tuned, now," Corah Washington added. "You won't want to miss this one. We'll be right back."

It was seven forty-five. Everly sat mere inches from the portable television that had been placed precariously on her small dining room table.

The Limona spot would air in exactly two more minutes. Even though it had been given one of *Morning*'s premier places in the schedule, Everly was afraid that something would go wrong.

The most crucial factor was time. Even though Nigel had arranged for her spot to air during the longest time slot in the show, it didn't mean that the scheduling was foolproof.

There were occasions when Corah or Glen ran overtime during an interview, so that sometimes—though this was rare—the piece scheduled to end the half hour would wind up either getting chopped off midstream or given only two or three minutes.

Despite the fact that the television industry had become more technically sophisticated, there was still plenty of room for human error. Even computers could be unreliable. Sure, they could be programmed for all kinds of tasks, but there wasn't much a computer could do if it had been set up to run a commercial at 7:58:30 and your segment still had fifteen more seconds to go.

You could only sit and watch it happen.

Everly didn't think of herself as a superstitious person, but right now she actually crossed her fingers, hoping that nothing would interfere with the Limona segment.

A flurry of ads filled the two-minute commercial break. Ever since advertising companies had gotten approval for fifteen-second commercials, the breaks seemed more interminable than ever.

"Hurry up," Everly said aloud. "Let's get on with it."

"Welcome back to *Morning*," Corah Washington announced. "Our next story is about one woman's courage and her desire to give the world an important message—that someone's life can actually be sustained by the death of our loved ones."

The story opened with a scene of the Limonas at their kitchen table, where the typical breakfast fare for an American family was juxtaposed with Kathleen's morning dosage of numerous pills and vitamins.

In the narration, Corah went on to describe Kathleen's illness, and after several soundbites from her doctors explaining the heart/lung transplant program, the focus of the story returned to the Limona family.

Everly watched, scarcely breathing. It was almost impossible to be objective. Though she and Fred had viewed the finished piece several times, there had been no way to tell if the segment worked within the context of the show. She was too close to this story; it was difficult to give it an accurate critique.

The closing shots of the Limona family now filled her television monitor as Corah's final narration began. More so than ever before, Everly noted that Nigel's decision to assign this story to the show's reigning actress had been a wise one.

"Kathleen Limona had many dreams. She knew she was at risk when she signed up for the heart/lung transplant program, but she never stopped hoping. She became a strong advocate of organ donation programs and she worked hard to spread the word. Tragically, her donor came on the scene too late. Kathleen's body just gave up. Her spirit, however, will never be forgotten."

Tears came to Everly's eyes as she watched Bill and Kathleen, hand in hand with their children, their backs to the camera, walk in the woods toward a bright patch of sunlight in the distance. Kathleen and Wendy's clear voices rang with a sense of promise that was devastating in its innocence.

" . . . birds fly over the rainbow, why then, oh why can't I?"

Everly raced into the office via the back door. She didn't want to break her mood, which had been so lovingly created by the Limona story. No doubt some of her more competitive colleagues would make nasty remarks. This assignment had become so personal that she didn't think she could handle any criticisms.

A tidy stack of pink telephone message sheets were pinned to her bulletin board, but it was Nigel's distinct blue memo paper on her desk that she grabbed first.

"*Come to my office at once*," it said. Or that's what it appeared to say. With handwriting like that, Nigel should have been a doctor, Everly thought. She threw down her belongings and headed towards Nigel's office. She hoped he'd been happy with her spot, but one could never be sure of his reactions—which was obviously the way he liked it.

"Bravo, my dear girl, bravo!" Nigel bellowed as she walked into his office. His eyes were gleaming. "Deserves a standing ovation," he said, standing to applaud her.

"Thanks. That story meant a lot to me, Nigel, and I'm glad we were able to give it so much airtime."

"Yes, well, Uncle Nigel knows a good piece when he sees one," he said as he plopped himself down and gestured toward one of the leather chairs across from him. "But unfortunately I have some bad news."

Everly immediately tensed up. *Now* what?

"Seems our beloved news president is getting pressure from the bloody 'mucky-mucks' that run this company. We have to put in another commercial break in the seven-thirty to eight half hour."

"You're kidding! I thought all those fifteen-second commercials were already bringing in more money because we were advertising more products."

"You're far too logical, my dear girl. Far too logical. Haven't you learned that those money-hungry bastards on high have only one motivating principle: greed. They know a good cash cow when they see one. They're probably going to milk the blasted thing to death. Then they'll be sorry—when it's too late."

"How is this going to destroy *Morning*?"

"Such innocence! My dear, they're trying to kill us in the name of the bloody dollar. But I won't let it happen. For the time being, their absurd machinations mean shorter segments—which translates into more talking heads and less taped pieces. We'll use less crews, less editing time. We'll end up with oodles of unspent money that won't be worth a damn when our ratings fall."

"I thought one of our strong points was that we had a good balance of live and taped pieces. People watch our show because they know there's a lot of variety. Don't the folks upstairs ever look at their own research?"

"Again—you are too logical. They only look at what can help them achieve their goal—which is more revenue. They're going to kill us—a slow death, mind you, but a death nevertheless."

"Isn't there anything we can do?"

"Well, to some extent, I'm afraid we have our hands tied. Since you're one of our best as far as taped pieces are concerned, I just wanted to let you in on what was happening. I still want you to do as much as you can in terms of production—but we have to cut down on the number of field pieces. I didn't want you to think this was any reflection of your work—but rather the disgusting politics around this place."

"I appreciate that, Nigel. But maybe it isn't such a bad thing after all," Everly said, immediately seeing a glimmer of opportunity.

"Oh? Would you mind explaining that?" he said as he rummaged through the debris on his desk to pull out some darts.

Not darts again, Everly thought. But she pressed on, hoping he wouldn't be too distracted by his little toys.

"If we have less tape on the show, maybe we could use more live reports from correspondents who have specialties. At least our audience would have some variety that way."

"Well, well," Nigel said, as he aimed toward the dart board. "Damn!" he said when the dart hit the bulletin board instead. "Tooting our own horn, are we?"

Everly smiled. "What would you expect when I've been taught by the master?"

"Ah, yes. Flattery will indeed get you everywhere—though you'd better be damn sure that's where you want to go. I haven't forgotten about our conniving friend, Lester Kay, and your wanting to get back on the air. But we have to take one step at a time.

"In the meantime, I just want you to be aware of the constraints we have here. Specifically, when we go to Ann Arbor, I want to have a show packed with exciting live segments."

"Why don't we just broadcast a three-ring circus? That's what they're turning us into," Everly said. "I'm sure we'd get fantastic ratings."

"Now, now. Sarcasm won't solve anything. You know Uncle Nigel has never let his troops down. We'll work around this somehow. But more important, would you care for a game of darts? You're always such a challenge for me."

"Another time, if you don't mind, Nigel. Can I take a rain check?"

"I suppose. But you owe me one. Uncle Nigel won't forget. Ta-ta."

Everly shook her head and walked out of Nigel's office, her mind flooded with details. First she'd have to rethink some of the pieces she'd planned on doing at the University of Michigan. And then she'd have to start coming up with a list of stories that would provide her with a spectacular network debut—which she hoped would occur when she was truly ready for it.

She was so oblivious to everything around her that she almost bumped into Hank, who pulled her toward the water cooler.

"A drink for a job well done," he said, hoisting a paper cup toward her. "I have stronger stuff in my office if you care to join me."

"That would be great. But I don't have much time—especially for a mental health break."

"Come on—let's celebrate. Forget your pressing responsibilities for a change. That Limona segment was spectacular! It's not every day that you get a chance to strut your stuff in our best time slot.

"Look," he continued, grabbing her arm for a moment and giving it a squeeze. "I know how much this story meant to you. The hard work and caring really showed."

"It's strange. I feel kind of numb," Everly said, taking a sip of the refreshing cold water. "I keep expecting to get a call saying that they were able to save Kathleen—that she made it and there'd been some kind of error—switched bodies, something like that."

"Come with me," Hank said, taking her hand and pulling her toward his office. "Even workaholics can stop the clock for a few minutes."

"Not *this* workaholic."

"Well, you don't have a choice. I'm a lot stronger than you are, kid."

"Okay, okay—just for a few minutes, though." Perhaps the diversion would be good, Everly thought. Her emotions were all jumbled—relief that the piece had worked, frustration at the new production restrictions, both coupled with an odd combination of fear and elation at the possibility that her on-air stint might be just around the corner.

And then there was Jared. She still was angry that he hadn't been around when she really needed him. Where the hell had he been?

And now Hank. He was truly a gem. Why couldn't they work something out between them?

She sighed. Maybe she and Jared just weren't meant to be together. She had always believed that if a relationship was was right, nothing would get in its way— it would happen almost effortlessly. But there was nothing effortless about her relationship with Jared. That was hard to accept. Yet she wasn't prepared to do anything about him now. She was too emotionally drained.

"Nice work," Jenny Spiegel called, interrupting Everly's thoughts as she and Hank passed Jenny on their way to "writer's row."

"Fine job," Reggie said, heading for Nigel's office. "We want the same top-notch tape stories in 'A squared.' "

Just great, Everly thought, cringing at the term "A squared" which was the vernacular for Ann Arbor used by locals and by graduates who had attended the University of Michigan. It was clear that Nigel had not told Reggie—supposedly one of his chief deputies— about the budget changes. She decided to let Reggie hang himself.

"Whatever you say," she said wearily. If this was the way Nigel communicated with his troops, fine. She wasn't going to be the one to tell one of his key producers about the new financial restrictions.

"Excuse me, Reggie," Hank said, his voice ringing with authority. "Everly and I have an appointment in my office. We're already late."

Hank could be such a lifesaver, Everly thought.

"That's right," she added, playing along. "We don't want to be rude, but there are some important production matters Nigel wants us to take care of."

"You two? I can imagine," Reggie smirked. "Well, okay, guys, but I want to see you in my office sometime this afternoon, Everly. There are a few items we have to discuss about our Ann Arbor remote."

"Sure thing," Everly said.

"Let's get out of this place," Hank said, curtly nodding to Reggie and dragging Everly along with him.

"Nice going," Everly whispered.

"What a jerk," Hank said. "It never ceases to amaze me how incompetent people end up in high places around here. Half of our associate producers don't know how to write a complete sentence, and the other half don't even try."

"Well, at least they're consistent," Everly said.

Hank laughed. "Leave it to you to put things into perspective. You're too nice to say what's really going on—that these guys are terrific ass kissers. They've turned it into an art form."

Before Everly could respond, Hank pulled open his office door and there was Beryl—arranging a plate of blueberry muffins.

"Surprise!" Beryl said, walking over to Everly and giving her a big hug. "What an incredible story. I bet the phones will be ringing off the hook today."

Everly smiled and tears came to her eyes.

"Oh, Lordie—are you going to cry?" Hank asked. "Come on now," he said, gently wiping away a tear on Everly's face with his forefinger. "I know you got close to Kathleen Limona, but you did her proud. There are so few examples of quality work around this dump that when we do come up with something worthwhile, it's time for recognition. Hats off to you, Ms. Dalton," he said, bowing deeply. "Now you better grab one of Beryl's stupendous muffins or I'll eat them all myself."

"You made these?" Everly asked her. "You guys are the greatest," she said, her voice wavering.

"You, too, chum," Beryl said.

"Enough of this mutual admiration stuff," Hank said, taking a large bite out of a muffin. "Damn, these are good! You're in the wrong business, sweetheart," he said to Beryl. "You should get out of this den of iniquity and open a bakery."

"Oh, sure," Beryl said. "Running a bakery in this city must be a real snap. Just imagine the hours I'd have to keep for *that*. I think I'm better off staying right where I am."

"Well, anytime you feel the urge to bake, just come on over to my place," Hank said, grabbing another muffin.

"Stephen would love that," Everly said, taking her first bite. "These *are* good. I didn't know you liked to cook—or that you were so good at it."

"Only baking," Beryl said. "It's sort of funny because I'm not really good at anything but breads, desserts, and hors d'oeuvres. I guess Stephen will have to cook all of the main courses when we get married."

"Main courses?" Hank said. "Hell, girl, you can make a meal out of baked goods for me anytime."

"You mean it's true what they say?" Everly asked.

"What's that?" Hank said.

"That the way to a man's heart is through his stomach?"

"Damn straight," Hank responded. "I'd fall for anyone who could cook even half this good!"

Beryl gave a conspiratorial wink to Everly, "If you think I'm good, you should try Everly's home cooking. *She*'s a real pro."

Oh, great, Everly thought. Talk about being subtle.

"I'm already hooked on her," Hank said. "Talent's a real turn on for me."

Everly felt herself blushing. She didn't know what to say. Did he really mean what he said, or was this all in the name of platonic camaraderie?

Hank's phone rang before Everly could think of an appropriate retort.

"Forrest here," Hank said. " . . . Who? Sure—hang on a minute. It's for you," he said, handing the phone to Everly, his face suddenly impassive.

She gave him a quizzical look and grabbed the receiver. "Everly Dalton," she said.

"I just had to call you."

Everly was stunned when she heard the voice.

It was Bill Limona.

"Oh, God, I'm just so sorry about Kathleen—"

"I know. We all are. She did her best. Everyone did. But what you put together this morning was really special. We all watched the show and I can't thank you enough for what you did.

"And all of your tapes came yesterday. I don't know when we'll be ready to look at them—" He stopped suddenly, as if he was trying to control his emotions. "But I know they'll mean a lot to Wendy and Jonathan, especially when they get older." His voice broke, and Everly could tell that he was crying.

"It's okay," she said. "You should cry. It'll probably make you feel better."

There were a few seconds of silence, and then Bill Limona continued in a shaky voice. "We're going to have a memorial service next week in Southfield. It would mean a lot to the kids and me if you could be there, but I know it might be hard for you to get away."

"I don't know," Everly said. Then it dawned on her. "You know, I just might be able to make it. We're doing a show from the University of Michigan this fall. I would just have to convince my boss that I need to go out there for a production survey next week."

"Well, see what you can work out. And let me know."

He gave Everly his phone number and address, and she put down the phone. "That was Bill Limona," she said.

"You okay?" Hank asked.

"I can't believe he called," Beryl said. "What did he say?"

Everly took a deep breath. "He invited me to Kathleen's memorial service. Next week."

"Think you can deal with it?" Hank said, putting a protective arm around her shoulder.

"I think so," Everly said. But she wasn't certain it was something she could handle right now. Before she could give it much thought, the phone rang again.

"I didn't know you were so popular, Hank," Beryl said.

"Oh, yeah. Real popular. Forrest here," he said. "Let me check." He pressed the mute button and looked at Everly. "Are you here for Jared Kammer?"

Her eyes widened, and she could feel a burning sensation

in the pit of her stomach. "I'll take it in my office," she said.

"Fine," Hank said, curtly. "I'll transfer you to her office in a moment," he said into the phone.

Beryl didn't say anything, but Everly knew what she was thinking. She should have refused to take the call, especially since Hank seemed to be giving her extra attention. But she still wasn't strong enough to let go of her dreams—far from it.

Despite all the misery Jared Kammer had caused her, she just wasn't ready to give him up.

SIXTEEN

Stay calm, just stay calm, Everly thought, taking a deep breath before she picked up the phone. She didn't want him to know she was angry.

Yet.

"Hello, Jared," she said.

"Hey, Cupcake, great show. Unbelievable! Too bad the missis didn't make it—but it was incredible television."

How she wished he hadn't said that.

"Hey—are you all right?" Jared asked. "You still there?"

"I'm here," Everly said.

"You're awfully quiet. You okay?"

"Just fine. A woman my age with a beautiful family dies; the most important man in my life gives me a big song and dance about getting back together—even though he's married—and then he mysteriously disappears when I need him most; I have a major assignment coming up where I'll be on location with one of the sleaziest associate producers on the staff; and in the middle of all this, my boss thinks I'm just about ready to go on the air; and—"

"Whoa, girl! Slow down. What's this about going on the air?"

"Is that all you care about?"

"No! Of course not. It just means we have something to celebrate," Jared said, sounding defensive.

"Where were you the other night?" Everly asked. She couldn't procrastinate any longer about confronting him.

"What do you mean?" Jared asked.

"After we met at the hotel—you know, you had to go back to your room, wait for a call? It had to be an 'early' evening for you."

"Yeah, and?"

"I was editing that night when I got the news about Kathleen Limona I was devastated. You were the first person I called, but you weren't there."

"Oh, hon, that's impossible. I was there all night. I don't know what you're talking about. The operator must have screwed up."

He sounded so contrite, Everly didn't know whether or not to believe him.

"You still there?" Jared asked.

"Why do you keep asking that?" Everly said, her anger rising.

"Look—we should discuss this in person. There's a lot I have to take care of today, but we can meet later, okay? How late will you be there?"

"I don't know," Everly said.

"Do you want to see me?"

"I guess," Everly said.

"You *guess*? Come on, Cupcake. I know what you're going through; I swear it. Let me make it better. Don't I know how to do that?"

"Yes," she said quietly. She couldn't deny that the very man who made her miserable was the same man who could make her feel wonderful.

"Come on, cheer up," Jared said. "We'll get together tonight—it'll be late, but I'll call you there when I know my schedule."

"Don't call me at the office," Everly said.

"Why not?"

"Because it's no one's business that you and I are seeing each other."

"That's bull!" he said. "We have every right to maintain a friendship. What's wrong with that? If anyone doesn't like it, screw 'em."

"You don't understand," Everly said. "It has nothing to do with impropriety. It's just no one's business. I like to keep my private life as private as I can."

"Oh. I get it," Jared said. "Whatever you say, Cupcake."

"Please stop calling me that," Everly said.

Jared sighed. "Look, I'll leave a message on your machine at home, and we can take it from there, okay? You going to be all right?"

"Probably," Everly said.

"That's my girl," Jared said. "Till next time."

She heard the phone click before she could say anything. With all he'd put her through, there was still a delicious sense of anticipation at the thought of being with him again. Yet she wondered if she was being a fool. Why did he have such a hold on her life?

Maybe when she could honestly answer that question, she'd be able to win back some of the ground she'd lost.

Everly was leafing through some material from the University of Michigan when Jenny Spiegel knocked on her door frame.

"Emergency staff meeting in reception—now," Jenny announced.

"What's up?" Everly said.

"Some interoffice memo Nigel got."

"From who?"

"Harvey Markfield," Jenny said, sounding smug.

"What's it about?" Everly was sure Jenny had read it.

"Top secret," Jenny answered, turning away quickly to hound the next writer.

"If it's so secret, why are we having a meeting?" Everly said to herself. Whatever it was, it had to be pretty serious for Nigel to have Jenny round up the staff in person. He knew that his people could easily duck phone calls, especially since automatic answering machines had been installed. There was nothing like a personal summons to get a full audience.

Everly hastily organized her U. of M. material into a neat pile, grabbed a steno pad, and walked quickly to the reception area.

Right away she noticed that Hank was already there, talking to some of the researchers. He must have been telling jokes or going on about some amusing story, because they all were laughing. Everly caught his eye for a moment. His expression remained unchanged and he turned back to the group.

Everly sought Beryl for refuge, hoping her friend wouldn't give her a hard time about Jared. Everly spotted her across the room talking to Victoria Lenox. She went over to join them.

"I don't know what Glen expects," Victoria was saying. "Hey, Everly, did you hear about what our wonderboy did in *Playboy* magazine?"

"No. Is that what this meeting is about?" Everly asked.

"Is Glen even here?" Beryl added.

"He's taping an interview," Victoria said. "Burt Reynolds—at the Waldorf Towers."

"So what did Glen do?" Everly asked.

"You know how he gets so 'name-droppy' whenever he has a few drinks. Well, *Playboy* must have really poured on the sauce wherever they interviewed him. We can definitely write off, oh, about six or seven major league celebrities.

"And it's a good thing he's not here, because if he was, I'd kill him," Victoria said, her fists poised for boxing.

"Was it really that bad?" Beryl said.

"It could have been worse," Victoria answered. "But not much."

"Just give it some time," Everly said. "We've been in the lead ever since that Tina Greene spot, so if any of those folks need a big television audience to promote something, nothing will keep their publicists from begging us for airtime."

"Maybe," Victoria said. "But they can always go to the competition first."

"Let's be real," Beryl said. "If any of them ever writes a book—which a lot of celebrities are doing these days—we'll still be the first show they'll go to. Even if we're not number one, we have too good a track record with book buyers to be ignored."

"You're probably right," Victoria said, resigned. "Compared to the other shows, we have the most book buyers in our audience. But you can bet they'll be clamoring for Corah to do their interviews."

"How does Nigel feel about that?" Beryl asked.

"What do you think?" Victoria said, clearly exasperated.

"I bet he'll purposely set them up with whichever host they don't want," Everly said.

"Ladies, I'm a bit smarter than that," Victoria said. "Whenever I ask Nigel to assign talent to one of my entertainment spots, I have a little scheme and it works like a charm. All I have to do is say that 'so-and-so doesn't want Corah to do this interview,' Nigel gets that wicked little gleam in his eye, makes some obvious comment about how 'so-and-so' has a lot of nerve telling him how to schedule his show, and then assigns the spot to Corah—which is exactly what I wanted in the first place."

"Are you serious?" Beryl asked. "You really do that?"

Once again, Everly was struck by her friend's naïveté.

"Listen up, people!" Nigel suddenly shouted, banging a wooden hammer on the reception desk. "Listen up!"

The room immediately grew quiet.

"Much better," he said. "I know you all have plenty to keep you occupied instead of attending another blasted staff meeting, but, as you know, we occasionally receive a missive from on high that requires our immediate attention.

"Sometimes I think our news executives expend all their energy writing horrifically boring memos. As I'm sure you can imagine, your leader generally ignores the damn things, and then they go directly into our venerable circular file."

Nigel paused a moment while everyone laughed.

He was such a master at timing, Everly thought.

"But once in a while," he continued, "something crosses my desk which demands our consideration."

"The suspense is killing us, Nigel," Hank said. Everly saw Reggie give him an annoyed look, which Hank ignored.

"Yes, well, you know how I love a little suspense, a little mystery. Keeps us all on our toes," Nigel said. "Nothing wrong with that.

"Here goes then. I have here an interoffice memo from our beloved news director, Harvey Markfield. It says:

All news personnel must follow specific rules when covering a news event for the radio and television divisions. You must call in to your respective assignment desks every hour to ensure that no major news story goes uncovered. And if you are working on a story that has no immediate deadline, you must forfeit your field crew time in the event of a major breaking story. You will then be placed on a special priority list to retrieve a crew as soon as possible to complete the piece you were working on.

The staff's reaction was immediate.

"Is he kidding?"

"This must be a joke."

"He can't be serious!"

"Is this guy on drugs or something?"

"This has got to be some kind of prank."

"Is Markfield prepping for some kind of April Fool's contest?"

"Now, now," Nigel said, hammering the desk again. "Settle down. I said this was something we should all be informed about. I did *not* say anything about taking his preposterous suggestion seriously."

"What are we supposed to do then?" Victoria asked.

Nigel paused a moment and then flashed a sinister smile. "We ignore it," he said. "Let the local news shows and *Evening News Worldwide* muck up the system by observing this ridiculous idea. The assignment desk is already hassled. Can you imagine what it will be like after this?"

"Won't we get in trouble?" Beryl asked. Some of the

staff glared at her. "I mean, well, they'll notice we're not calling in—"

"That's where your wrong, my little lovely," Nigel said. "They'll be too damned busy to notice. Anarchy—that's what they're asking for, and that's what they'll get.

"In the meantime, when the smoke clears, they'll be thankful that we put things into our own hands, out of the singular desire to make life easier for the assignment desk. We will, as the saying goes, come out smelling like roses."

"Is there anything else we should know?" Hank asked. "Looks like you have a pretty long memo there."

"Well, my dear boy, most of this is utter rubbish. There is one more item to discuss, however, so I'm glad you asked. It appears that our Mr. Markfield wants all sign-offs to be consistent throughout the news division."

"How progressive," Hank said.

"Well, he might have a point here, actually," Nigel said. "From now on, the correspondents in the field have to say, 'From Terre Haute, Indiana, this is Nigel Elliot for EBC News.' "

"Excellent idea," Reggie Graham said. "It used to really get me when some of our talent had corny sign-offs."

"I loved it," Hank said. "Especially Tammy Labunski. She'd say things like, oh, I don't know, 'You'd better believe that this is Tammy Labunski for your favorite network' or—and this one was the best—'Where seeing is believing, this is Tammy Labunski for your 20-20 vision network.' I loved that stuff."

"Perhaps," Nigel said. "But I can see why our fearless leader would prefer to have that kind of originality and creativity channeled elsewhere."

"They want creativity flushed down the toilet," Hank said, eliciting laughter from the group. He glanced over at Everly and she winked at him. He smiled back, and she felt as if a twenty-ton weight had been removed from her shoulders.

"I won't dignify that with a remark," Nigel said, though everyone knew he probably agreed. "Back to work, people. Chins up, chests out—especially you ladies."

Groans and laughter filled the room as the staff broke up into smaller groups and headed back to their desks.

Hank walked toward Everly, looking a little embarrassed. "How's it going?" he asked.

"I'll live," she said. "Thank God we don't have to call in every hour. Is Markfield nuts?"

"Probably. It's part of the job requirement."

"Excuse me, Everly." It was Reggie Graham.

"Yes?" She'd felt slightly uncomfortable with Hank and was actually glad that Reggie had interrupted them.

"We have to talk about a survey trip to Ann Arbor," he said. "You, me, Mel Stone, and Leon Posner."

"Sure," she said. "Is now a good time?"

"Yeah," Reggie answered. "I'll round up Mel and Leon and then we can coordinate our schedules."

"Make sure it's not on a breaking news day," Hank said, his voice caustic.

"Yeah, right," Reggie said. "If I could predict that, I sure as hell wouldn't be slaving away here."

"I beg your pardon?" It was Nigel. He'd been following them, but no one had noticed. "If you're unhappy here, I'm sure we could make arrangements."

Everly had to concentrate hard to keep from laughing.

"It's nothing," Reggie said. "You know—just griping like everyone else around here."

"Careful, dear boy. Mustn't bog down morale," Nigel said.

"We were just setting up a meeting about Ann Arbor," Everly said. "Any suggestions?"

Reggie gave her a grateful look. Good.

He owed her one.

"Of course not," Nigel said. "I'll wait until you all come up with the first draft of the rundown. Then I can tear it all apart," Nigel said. "But Hank's the one I need to see for the moment. Do you have time for me now, dear boy?"

"Do I have a choice?" Hank asked. "Of course I'm ready—anything you want, Boss." He touched Everly's arm before he left the group. "I'll catch up with you later," he said.

Reggie shook his head. "I don't know what it is with you two," he said.

"Nothing wrong with a little office camaraderie," Nigel said.

Talk about irony, Everly thought. Reggie had gone well beyond simple camaraderie in too many cases. Nigel must have known.

"You should try it sometime," Hank said, all innocence.

Reggie glared and motioned for Everly to follow him.

She smiled. The situation with Hank was not as bad as she'd imagined. If she could only get some perspective on how to handle Jared, her life would be much less complicated.

To the simple things, she thought with a touch of irony, following Reggie to his office.

Seventeen

"Sorry, hon, I'm at JFK and I can't make it tonight—gotta get back to Chicago. The 11:00 news co-anchor is threatening to quit, and even though I'm technically out of there, the big guns want me to iron things out. Guess I'm more indispensable than they thought.

"Anyway, I'm really sorry. We'll have to wait to get together until I'm here on a permanent basis. Love ya, Cupcake. Till next time."

It was the third time Everly had played back the message—just to make sure she had heard everything correctly.

Bastard.

But *she* had been the real jerk to even *think* of being with him again. Yet she wondered why Jared's message didn't have the kind of devastating effect that she would have expected.

Maybe some part of her finally accepted that their future together was nothing more than a fantasy. Why else would she feel more relieved than angered by his having to leave?

She took a deep breath.

It was time to move on.

She knew he'd call again. But the next time, she'd be emotionally prepared. It wasn't that she'd suddenly changed her mind about him, but rather that she had gained a sense of perspective about her priorities. No doubt Kathleen Limona's life—and death—had had a profound effect on Everly.

She still wanted to have a man in her life, but she would have to be more realistic about what was best for her. Going after a former fiancé who was married was not exactly conducive to reach her goals.

It was masochistic.

She deserved to have a healthy, normal relationship with a man—whatever "normal" meant. In this eclectic city, that gave her plenty of options.

She smiled, knowing how Beryl would react to this latest update in the Jared Kammer saga.

Hopefully, this would be the last installment.

"Well, don't you look like the cat who swallowed the canary," Hank Forrest said, interrupting Everly's thoughts as he stood in her doorway. "May I come in?"

"Make yourself at home," she said.

"The Cheshire cat look is most becoming," he said as he sat down in the chair by her desk. "What delectable bit of gossip have you unearthed?"

"*You* were the one who met with Nigel today," she said. "He's the best source."

"Sometimes. But it's our rotating group of receptionists who know the most about what goes on around this place. I used to wonder why they never made that a permanent job. But there was this one chicklette who had a crush on me—"

" 'Chicklette?' There you go again. Where was *your* feminist consciousness raised?"

"I'm just a born natural, I guess. Anyway, this chicklette who'd been on the job about two months had more dirt about the sordid lives around here than folks who'd been on staff for years. So then I realized that for a change, the top brass knew what they were doing when they set parameters for that position. Change receptionists every three months and the blackmail potential is greatly reduced."

"You can't be serious," Everly said. "Blackmail? I mean, are we running some kind of numbers racket? Drug schemes?"

"No, nothing like that. Use your imagination. I don't want to name names . . ."

"Bullshit," Everly said.

"No—really. There are lots of skeletons around here. We even have some married folks who swing both ways."

"And how is a receptionist going to know that?" Everly asked.

"Well, if you notice John Doe getting more calls about late night meetings from Roger than from the missis, you might put two and two together."

"I guess I've been too sheltered to come up with something like that," Everly said.

"My turn to say, 'bullshit' back to you," Hank said.

Everly laughed. She loved sparring with Hank. It was one of the best aspects of their friendship. "You win," she said. "Now don't keep changing the subject. Did you get any good gossip from Nigel?"

"No. He mentioned that you, Leon, and Reggie would be taking a survey trip soon for that Michigan remote. That's one party I don't mind missing. But he also said he wasn't sure whether I'd be going on location with the Ann Arbor show, thanks to the budget that Leon put together."

"And to fax machines," Everly said.

"Yeah, I know. Modems, too. The wonders of technology. How the hell did we ever manage without faxes and xeroxes and computers? Hell, I remember mimeograph machines! Of course our brilliant management keeps changing computer systems in pursuit of the best deal. Soon as you learn one piece of hardware or software, they come up with newer machines and more programs to plague us with. How long is it going to take those yo-yos to learn that as soon as you buy any of this computer shit it becomes obsolete?

"Even so, I still prefer my old Smith Corona—vintage 1965. Now *there's* a real classic."

"Contrary to what you may think, Hank, management is not out to get you."

"Sure. You just keep thinking that, Everly, and they'll be sending you to the funny farm real soon."

"I could use a good rest," she said.

"Not in a straitjacket."

"Such a lovely idea. Now why on earth do people think you're cynical?"

"Who knows? Anyway, back to the grind. And whenever this survey trip of yours comes up, I want you to take notes. I'll want details, woman. Especially about our office Lothario."

Everly thought a moment. She'd totally forgotten about how Reggie Graham notoriously strayed on field trips. She could imagine how he'd act around college coeds. What if he made a pass at *her*?

"I'll have reams," she said.

"Maybe we should enter him in the Guinness book," Hank said.

"For what—number of affairs?"

"No—for Consistently Making an Asshole Out of Himself," Hank announced, as if he were handing out awards.

I could hold that record, Everly thought.

"Of course the competition for that is pretty intense around here," Hank added.

"Present company excluded," she said.

"Of course. But we'd be here all day if we actually put a list together," Hank said, standing up. "Anyway, catch you later."

"Right," Everly said.

Great, she thought, now she'd have something else to worry about: being on the road with Reggie. Of course, there was always the possibility that he'd run into some old college buddies. Michigan was the kind of university where you were bound to find someone from your class still hanging around Ann Arbor—no matter what year you graduated.

Perhaps she'd find an ally in Leon Posner.

But she couldn't ignore the sudden sense of apprehension that clouded her thinking.

Ann Arbor was *not* going to be as much fun as she'd originally thought. She'd just have to make sure they went everywhere as a foursome.

"I can't believe it," Reggie said. "The Diag hasn't changed a bit."

The "Diag" was the main square around which the University of Michigan was built. Its name came from the two large diagonal paths that crisscrossed in the center of the cement-paved, tree-lined area, where the university's seal was inlaid.

Campus superstition had it that if you stepped on this symbol, you would fail all of your exams. Though some students probably thought that was a bunch of bull, most of them carefully avoided walking over this central spot.

"You're right," Everly said, amused by the machinations some students still went through to save their footing at the last split second. "It's as if time really stopped here."

"This place is huge," Leon said. "I wonder what kind of operating budget they have."

"You kidding?" Mel Stone asked. "Who cares?" he continued, hiking up his pants in a useless effort to hide his middle-aged paunch. "This spot is where we'll do the show. It's perfect! Lots of open space—my camera crew is going to have a field day here."

At that moment, carillon bells started chiming the half hour at nearby Burton Tower.

"We're gonna have to have 'em shut that off during the show," Mel said.

"No carillon?" Reggie said. "It's not going to be the same without hearing those bells every fifteen minutes."

"How much could it cost us to arrange for it to be dead for two hours?" Mel asked.

"We must stay on budget," Leon said.

"Leon, the reason you're here is to make up a budget," Reggie said patiently. "We don't have one signed and sealed yet, so be prepared for some contingencies."

"Let's just leave it alone," Everly said. "It would be great to have the show start with a shot of the Tower chiming seven times."

"Good point," Reggie said. "What do you think, Mel?"

"Not bad, but we need to find out what time sunrise is going to be on our air date. If we have to light the damn thing, it'll eat into Leon's precious budget."

"We could do it for the eight o'clock then," Everly said.

"You're right," Mel said. "We'll get one of our cameramen in a cherry picker so they can zoom from a tight close-up of the tower to a wide shot of the campus. It'll look spectacular!"

"Maybe we should discuss some of these details after we meet with the university officials," Leon said.

"You sure know how to get those creative juices flowing, Leon," Mel said.

"I wasn't hired to be creative," Leon retorted.

"You can say that again," Mel said.

"Guys, guys," Reggie said. "Let's loosen up here. This is supposed to be fun, remember?"

"Yeah—we'll just wrap those university bozos around our little finger," Mel said, a wicked gleam in his eye. "How often do they get this kind of free publicity, you know? They'll probably let us do whatever we want."

"If the price is right," Leon said, his face gloomy.

"Relax, Leon," Everly said. "This is a college campus. It's not like we're dealing with a foreign country."

"Yeah," Reggie said. "Remember that remote in Europe where all the locals had their hands out for things like showing us the way to get to the bathrooms?"

"Remember? How could we forget? First damn time the men had to pay to find out where it was safe to pee," Mel said.

Some class act we have here, Everly thought. She could imagine what the university people would think of *Morning*'s intrepid director.

"Cost a fortune," Leon said, shaking his head.

"But our ratings went through the roof," Reggie added.

"Let's not forget ratings," Mel said.

"How could we?" Everly asked.

Before anyone could answer, the Diag started to fill with students as classes changed.

"God! Look at 'em all," Mel said. "How many students are here?"

"The whole campus has something like forty-five thousand," Everly said. "But in this central part, I don't know—twenty, twenty-five thousand."

"These kids look too young to be college students," Leon said.

Everly had to agree. "You're right." She looked at the growing crowd—a profusion of blue jeans, sweatshirts, long-haired men and women, an occasional adult, probably a professor, hurrying along to get to a meeting or a class or back to the office. Most people were chattering away, a few walked alone; some were rushing to class, others meandered along. For the most part, this was a vibrant population that exuded the kind of unique energy only to be found on a thriving college campus.

For a moment, Everly was transported back to the late seventies, when she had been a student here. It was eerie. So much of what she saw was familiar. It had been years since she'd last been on campus, but it still felt like home. Yet there was something haunting about being there without the men and women who'd been such key players in her college life. She half expected to see one of her former sorority sisters gamboling across the Diag, bursting with news about a disastrous test or the latest boyfriend.

Such bittersweet memories. It hurt to accept that those days of innocence and limitless possibilities were gone forever. Maybe it was trite, but Everly couldn't avoid wondering how different her life might have turned out if she had only known then what she knew now. Some of the different relationships she'd had during her four years in Ann Arbor came to mind. A few men had seriously vied for her attention, but only one would always be especially cherished. Richard Haynes.

Her first lover.

It was freshman year. Everly had met Richard the first day she came to Ann Arbor. As a first-year student, she'd arrived the weekend before classes started, and Richard, a sophomore, just happened to be one of the students who helped her move into the dorm. He'd asked her out for dinner that night, and they began a relationship that would last a year and a half.

They had a lot in common—both from the Midwest, small families with old-fashioned values, and an intellectual curiosity that had put them in the top echelon of their respective high schools. Their differences were intriguing. Where Richard was methodical and almost painfully thorough in his approach to life, Everly was spontaneous and exuberant. He was pragmatic, carefully weighing pros and cons, while being generally open-minded. She was more apt to take risks, eager to seek different ways to express her creativity. But there were definite limits to their relationship—primarily when it came to sex.

Richard sometimes teased her about her virginity, but she never felt pressured. The physical aspect of their relationship was intense and special. Just holding hands gave her a thrill, but they would only go so far. After four months of dating, however, Everly realized that something was missing.

It was time to change the rules.

Coincidentally, Richard's roommate was going home the very weekend after Everly made her decision.

"Let's have dinner at my place," Richard whispered. They were in the study lounge on his side of the dorm. "We'll have the whole place to ourselves for two whole days."

"Are we really going to have dinner?" Everly asked. "Or just dessert?"

"Both," he said, pushing back the dark-framed glasses that were always sliding down his nose. "If you still want to, that is. I just want to be sure you're ready."

"I'm ready," she said.

She was scared, but she knew she could handle the responsibility of taking this next step.

"I love you, Richard. If I'm not ready now, I'll never be."

He leaned across the desk and gently tilted her face up to his. Their lips touched softly. The effect he had on her was uncanny. The slightest touch set off a marvelous sensation of warmth, of intense sensuality. Tonight she would finally cross the threshold that in the past had frightened her. Now, she could hardly bear to wait for the rite of passage.

True to his word, Richard prepared a picnic dinner. The dorm didn't allow hot plates, so he had bought French bread, cheese, salami, and, as he called it, "fine Rhine wine." They spread out an old gray army blanket on the floor between the two single beds that were against opposite sides of the room.

It wasn't dark yet, but he turned off the fluorescent light in the room and carefully lit two candles. "For atmosphere," he said.

Neither was particularly hungry, but they finished the wine. "All we need now is a fireplace," Richard said, pouring the last of the wine into their glasses.

They stared across the blanket at each other, each leaning back against one of the two beds. It was dark now, and the play of shadow and light in the candlelit room softened their features.

Suddenly, the atmosphere changed. The air felt heavy with a tension that was both oppressive and exciting.

Richard got up and silently cleared everything away. Everly watched his careful movements. She loved the way his red-blond hair curled over the back of his neck. She wanted to reach out and run her fingers through it, but instinct told her not to move.

He finished putting everything away. Then he reached for her hands and pulled her up. She felt a deep yearning, but she still held back, sensing that he was the one who had to orchestrate the evening.

He kissed her with a quiet ardor. Something different was happening between them. Everly felt an extraordinary rush of warmth diffusing through her body. She was amazed at this new sense of passion that seemed more intense at the knowledge that it would finally be fulfilled.

Richard paused a moment, then slowly unbuttoned her blouse, lifted it off her shoulders, and let it drop to the floor. Everly took her cue and gently tugged at the bottom of his V-neck sweater, slowly lifting it as he raised his arms to help her along.

She was nervous; her fingers trembled. He waited patiently for her to remove his undershirt, and then he unfastened her bra, letting it fall from his hands. He stared at her small, firm breasts, and then he pressed her body to his, moaning softly as he felt her breasts against his chest.

"God, you feel good," he whispered.

Everly groaned in response. She felt as if she were floating . . . so light and warm. She knew she was feeling the effects of the wine, but it didn't matter. She knew exactly what she was doing. And she never wanted to forget this moment. She felt so alive and aware, yet at the same time, calm and relaxed.

It was a delicious sensation.

Richard pulled away from her now and unzipped her pants. She stepped out of them and left them in a crumpled pile. Soon, his jeans joined hers on the floor. They stood staring at each other, clad only in their underpants—she in pink bikini pants, he in white briefs. Without a word, almost ritually, they slowly slipped off each other's final bit of clothing, and then stood apart from each other, their bodies illumined by the candlelight.

It was the first time they had been naked together.

"Gosh, you're beautiful," Richard said.

Everly didn't know what to say. She was preoccupied with her own feelings—surprised that she felt so comfortable naked in his presence; scared about losing her virginity; excited by the sight of Richard's body. She had never seen a naked man before, much less an aroused man. She stared at him with wonder. His skin looked so smooth—almost incandescent—in the room's dim light.

She ached to hold him close to her.

"I love you, Everly," he said.

He'd said those precious words to her before, but tonight they seemed to have more significance. He walked toward her and reached for her hand. He brought her over to his bed. They lay down on top of his comforter, their arms wrapped around each other.

Everly thrilled at the feeling of flesh against flesh. Their lips pressed together. Richard caressed her shoulders, her breasts, her arms, while seductively moving his tongue inside her mouth. Everly felt as if she were melting. She was aroused, yet powerless—every inch of her sensitive to his touch. She didn't want to move. She didn't want him to stop.

Richard continued to delicately stroke her body, but then he took her hand and placed it where it had never been placed before. He moaned at her touch, which gave her an odd sense of both power and pleasure.

She became aware that they were breathing in tandem. Suddenly, he touched her where no one had ever touched her. She felt an explosive rush throughout her body and found herself almost gasping. He was on top of her now, and suddenly he penetrated her. She felt a sharp painful sting and cried out.

Still inside of her, Richard stopped moving.

"Are you all right?" he whispered, propped up on his elbows.

"Yes. It just hurt a little," she whispered back. She didn't want to break the mood. "I'm okay. Don't stop."

Then, slowly, Richard regained his momentum, and Everly, amazingly—for it was her first time—got caught up in the rhythm of their desire, and their bodies pulsed together, wet and gleaming in the dying candlelight, until their precious passion was spent.

"Hey—Everly! What's the deal here? You out to lunch or what?"

Mel's shrill voice snapped her back to the present.

"Uh, sorry, Mel. I was distracted."

Understatement of the year, she thought.

"No kidding! Anyway—we gotta do something with the marching band—only where the hell can we put them? It's not like they have a football field on the Diag to march in—more like a postage stamp. Any bright ideas?"

She didn't answer right away; she had to force herself to focus on the present. "The university is famous for its marching band," she said. "It would be a pity not to use them."

Suddenly, she got an idea. "They have a lot of synchronized moves that they do in a stationary position. Why don't we just place them on the steps of the Graduate Library?"

"I was just about to say that myself," Reggie said.

"Of course," Everly said. You slime, she thought.

At least he was consistent.

"Well, let's get all this stuff down on paper before we have our meeting with the university folks," Reggie said. "Everly, why don't you jot down a few notes before we head over to the administration building?"

"Fine," she said. It would do no good to object. Why was it that whenever men and women got together to discuss ideas, the only people capable of taking notes were of the female gender? No matter how much women's lib had accomplished, this was one area untouched by progress. Maybe this next generation of supposedly liberated kids will make a difference, Everly thought, pulling out a small reporter's pad.

But she wouldn't bet on it.

EIGHTEEN

"Did he try anything?" Beryl asked.

"Of course," Everly said. "I would've been insulted if he hadn't."

It was Sunday. Everly had returned from Ann Arbor the night before, and they were having lunch at a local pizzeria in Beryl's neighborhood.

"You're kidding, aren't you? I mean, Reggie's good looking, but—"

"Calm down, Beryl," Everly said. "Obviously it's a situation I'd rather not have to deal with, but it didn't go as badly as I imagined."

"What do you mean?"

"Well, first of all, we were only there one night. Since there were four of us, I made sure we went everywhere together. And thanks to the university's PR folks, we didn't have much free time. I couldn't even get to the memorial service for Kathleen. Bill was understanding about it, but I still felt badly."

Everly paused a moment. She wasn't being completely

truthful. She could have made time to go to the service, but she didn't think she could have handled what would have been an emotionally draining experience. Just seeing those kids would have been heart-wrenching enough. And she couldn't bear the thought of hearing more tributes to Kathleen. She already knew how special she was, and how utterly unfair it had been for this courageous woman to be taken away from her family at such a young age—especially when she'd had so much hope about her future.

Perhaps Beryl would have understood, but Everly didn't want to confess that she'd actually been relieved when she came up with the excuse for Bill that her Ann Arbor schedule had been too hectic to get away.

Sometimes you just couldn't tell a friend everything.

"So it was wall-to-wall meetings the whole time we were there," Everly continued.

"So when did Reggie make a pass?"

"I have to give him credit—he was very discreet. After a late dinner, we all went back to the Campus Inn, where we were staying. About twenty minutes after we'd all said good night, my phone rang. I swear, Reggie must have X-ray vision, because he waited until the exact second that I got into bed to call. He wanted to know if he could come over for a little nightcap—to discuss the show, of course."

"What did you say?"

"What do you think I said? I told him to grab some condoms and come right over."

Beryl gasped, holding her slice of pizza in midair. "You didn't!" she said.

"Of course I didn't! You know, sometimes I really worry about you, Beryl."

Her friend blushed. "I knew you were kidding," Beryl said. "I, um, I was just playing along."

"Right," Everly said. "Anyway, I made up some bull about being flattered by the extra attention, but I said I had to make a personal call and I needed privacy. I expected him to suggest we get together after that, but he didn't. I guess he got the hint."

"He may try again when you're there for the show."

"Maybe. But Corah and Glen will be there, and Reggie likes to suck up to the talent whenever he has the opportunity. He won't have much time for any of his little forays then."

"Will Nigel be there, too?"

"I don't know," Everly said. "I can't imagine how he'd react to a Midwest college town—or vice-versa, for that matter. He can get so crazed if anything goes wrong—they probably wouldn't believe he was a functioning adult."

"I wonder what he was like in college," Beryl said. "Didn't he go to Oxford or some place like that?"

"Who knows," Everly said. "If we asked him, he'd probably say whatever suited him best at the time. I'm sure our press department has some kind of official bio on him in their files. Of course, that doesn't mean that what's written there is true."

"He's been in the States a long time," Beryl said.

"But not long enough to lose his accent."

"Do they have pizza in London?" Beryl asked, grabbing another slice from the platter in front of her.

"They must," Everly said.

"Gosh, I just remembered I'm getting my cholesterol level checked tomorrow. Hope all this cheese won't make a difference."

"Oh, Lord. Not you."

"Not me what?"

"I didn't think you were the type to obsess about that sort of thing."

"Well, people have been talking about cholesterol levels for ages," Beryl said, sounding defensive.

"I know, but as far as I'm concerned, moderation is the rule. Just about everything we eat could eventually kill us. No matter what we do, we're all going to die either of heart attacks or cancer."

"That's a lovely thought."

"Just being honest. Look, let's just enjoy our food while we're still alive, okay?" Everly said.

Beryl smiled. "Okay," she said. "You know I can't believe this place actually uses fresh mushrooms. Most places use canned."

"I think you say that every time we come here."

"Well, as you always say, at least I'm consistent," Beryl said. "You can always count on me."

"I know," Everly said, getting serious for a moment. "And I do," she added.

"All right, my lovelies," Nigel said. "Time for some ideas. Television eats 'em up, you know."

The staff meeting was coming to a close, and as was often the case, people were reluctant to talk about their program suggestions and risk public humiliation.

Everly felt uniquely justified in not saying anything, because she had too much to do for the Ann Arbor remote.

"Come, come," Nigel said. "I do hate having to wring it out of you like this every week. Perhaps we should have some kind of incentive program—beyond your bloated salaries and the sheer rapture of working with yours truly."

"I have something," Beryl said.

It seemed to Everly that ever since Beryl had been engaged, she'd become more confident and participated more in these open forums. Nigel must have noticed the difference. He treated Beryl more gently than he treated the consistently vociferous members of the staff.

"Another book?" he said. "I know authors are a sort of Rock of Gibraltar for us, my dear, but I really prefer something a bit more creative."

"It's not a book—just something that I thought we should look into: employment agencies."

Some staff members groaned; others hissed.

Such a supportive bunch, Everly thought.

"What about them?" Nigel asked.

"Well, I hear they're real rip-offs. They put these terrific ads in the classifieds, and then when the applicants show up, it turns out that no such job ever existed. It's just a sneaky way to get quality people to sign up with them. They're like factories—large, impersonal."

"She has a good point," Reggie said, ever ready to

take a good idea and make it his own. "Most of those job counselors are on commission, so they send people off on job interviews with no consideration for what the applicants are looking for or what their skills are—"

"It's pretty rough," Beryl said, delicately cutting Reggie off.

Nice work, Everly thought.

"People are pretty vulnerable when they're unemployed," Beryl continued. "So when they go for these interviews, they don't realize what they've gotten into until it's too late. And if you've just lost your job, you're not about to walk away from an offer, even if it's not what you really want."

"Interesting," Nigel said. "I do love exposing rip-offs, which are so prodigious in this country."

"What would the Big Apple be without 'em?" Hank Forrest said.

"True, true, my dear boy," Nigel said. "Now, how do you propose we do this, Beryl? A sort of *60 Minutes* confrontation or what?"

"Well, um, maybe we could rig up some kind of hidden camera and have one of our staff members go to a few different agencies."

"Oh, I love that," Mel Stone said. "Hidden cameras. That's one good thing we can thank the Japs for—all the state-of-the-art stuff we have now is small and portable. Used to be ridiculous—the outrageous ideas we had to come up with to conceal our cameras when we did undercover-type stories. Hell, we can rig up something that'll fit right into a lady's pocketbook—one of those large ones that women use as a self-defense tool. Ever get hit in the head with one of those damned things?"

"How much is it going to cost us?" Leon Posner said.

"Oh, please," Nigel said. "Use your head, man. This is a local piece with equipment that we already have. Any volunteers?"

"I think Everly should do it," Lester Kay said.

Everly's heartbeat suddenly escalated. She knew Lester was supposed to come up with an on-camera idea for her, but an investigative field piece wasn't what she had in mind.

She also assumed that someone on staff would object to the "new kid on the block" getting a plum assignment that would put her on the air.

"Great idea," Hank said. "She's new enough so that no one on the street would recognize her—"

"Who would recognize *any* of the staff?" Kerri Marks asked, her voice barely disguising her anger. "Shouldn't someone with more experience handle it?"

Like you, of course, Everly thought.

"Makes no difference," Nigel said. "We need someone who is articulate and aggressive, yet would conceivably be the type of person who'd go to one of these agencies. Someone like yourself, for example, would be far too sophisticated."

What a shrewd man. Someone else might have taken offense at his implication that only some hick like Everly would be appropriate for this kind of assignment. She knew this was just another example of one of Nigel's favorite ploys: flattering someone to achieve his goals.

"What a nice thing for you to say," Kerri said, a triumphant smile on her face. "I suppose you're right. Everly would be perfect."

Mission accomplished, Everly thought, struggling to keep from showing any emotion.

"Done," Nigel said. "We'll discuss details later."

"I know a few bona fide career counselors we might want to interview live in the studio," Beryl said.

"Maybe they could give all of us some career advice," Hank said.

"You're treading on some real thin ice, pal," Reggie Graham said.

"Come, come. No in-fighting," Nigel said. "Let's move on to something else."

Everly leaned close to Beryl and whispered, "Thanks. Did you and Lester cook this up, or what?"

"Nope—just happened. Guess it's your lucky day."

It better be, Everly thought.

She could use a little luck.

* * *

There must have been a sale on industrial gray carpeting when all these employment places started up, Everly thought, as she got off the elevator and walked into the reception area of her third agency.

She waited patiently while a young receptionist worked the phones.

"Which ad was that?" she was saying to someone on the other end. She kept cracking her gum as she talked. Wonder if she's got cavities, Everly thought. She had certainly earned them.

"Yeah, right," the receptionist continued. "Ya gotta make an appointment. I'll put ya through to Rebecca Danelen when she gets off her line. Please hold.

"Status Agency," she said, "please hold. Status Agency, one moment please." Another phone rang. "Status Agency, please hold."

It's just as bad for her as it is for Phoenix King on the assignment desk, Everly thought, suddenly sympathetic.

"Can I help you, ma'am?" The receptionist finally acknowledged Everly's presence. "Do you have an appointment?"

It always alarmed Everly momentarily when anyone called her "ma'am." "Yes, I'm Emily Gilbert," she said. It had been Nigel's idea that she use a fake name. No point in taking a chance that anyone would recognize her name from the weekly *Morning* credits that aired every Friday. "I have an appointment with Susan Margolick."

"Is this your first time here?"

"Yes," Everly said. Time to fill out one of the agency forms. After all the trouble she'd gone through to create a beautifully printed résumé, she was learning that it had been a waste of time. The damned agencies were rigid about their rules. They wanted everything written up on their little forms. You ended up rewriting the exact information that was on your résumé.

"Please fill this out," the receptionist said, handing Everly a clipboard.

"I have a résumé," Everly said, waiting to see what kind of reaction she'd get.

"You still gotta fill this out," the receptionist said, choosing that moment to blow a bubble with her bubble gum.

Everly hoped everything was being captured on the small videotape camera that was in her bag. She'd practiced for hours to get the position of the bag just right so that all the footage wouldn't exclusively be shots from the waist down.

It was not an easy thing to do.

"Fine," Everly said.

"And when you're done, you gotta take a typing test—in the room over there." The receptionist pointed toward a room to the side, where Everly heard the sound of frantic typists.

"Will do," Everly said, taking a seat. Maybe she could catch up with some of the applicants later and interview them on-camera to find out how they did.

She filled out the form and handed it back to the receptionist. "Time for the typing test," she said. "Ever time yourself before?"

"No," Everly lied. She'd already taken two tests that morning. Both came out at about sixty words a minute. Before that day, she hadn't taken a typing test since high school. It had actually been fun to see whether or not her skills still held up.

"Take this to practice with," the receptionist said, handing her a sheet of written material. "When you're ready, I'll start the clock."

"I'll let you know," Everly said. She noticed some of the other applicants eyeing her suspiciously. It was an eclectic group. Some young people, probably looking for their first job, and an equal number of older women, most of whom looked discouraged. It was difficult to imagine what it must be like to be over fifty looking for a job. Years of experience and wisdom meant nothing in a world that primarily valued nubile young things.

A few men were in the waiting room, too. By now Everly had learned that they were most likely applying for data entry positions. Although there were exceptions, most men were not in the secretarial market. They were computer specialists or bookkeepers.

Everly sat down at a vacant typewriter and put the writing sample she was supposed to copy on the metal stand next to her machine. Here goes, she thought.

Terrific. She was typing a story about looking for jobs. How original. It was the exact test that her first agency had given her. Who came up with these things? Then she paused a moment. She couldn't believe it. There was a typo on the test. Was this for real? She finished the practice session and called out to the receptionist. "Excuse me, miss, I'm ready," she said.

"On your mark, get set, *go*!" the receptionist said.

Suddenly, Everly felt her fingers trembling with an acute case of nerves. She tried to talk herself out of it. Slow down. Speed doesn't make up for mistakes. Just take it easy.

"Time!" the receptionist yelled. "Bring it over here."

Everly glanced at the sheet. There were three errors in the first sentence alone. Good grief! Maybe they wouldn't even send her out for interviews.

Everly paused a moment and almost laughed aloud. What was she thinking? She didn't need a job. She had become consumed by the role she was playing. It was a little unnerving, but it would probably translate well on-screen.

"Wow, not bad," the receptionist said. "Seventy-five words a minute and only five errors. You'll find a job real easy. Now who were you here to see?"

"Susan Margolick."

"Oh, right. That's not a real person."

"What?"

"It's just something we put on the ads so that we can tell which account is which," the receptionist said. "It ensures privacy. This business is a small one, and we don't want other agencies knowing who is handling which account." Clearly she'd given this little speech many times.

"So who is my appointment with?" Everly asked, trying not to sound impatient.

"I'll see who's ready," she said. "You can sit out here."

"Fine," Everly said. This was more of a scam than she thought. Not only were the ads fake, the people were, too.

It was going to be fun putting this baby together.

"Miss Gilbert?" Everly looked up. A twentyish woman stood in front of her, her face nearly obscured by a profusion of long, dark, unkempt curls. The messy hair was one thing, but Everly was even more stunned by what this creature was wearing. The charcoal-gray suit was acceptable, but the red halter top underneath, which exposed at least five inches of tanned midriff, definitely was not.

What am I doing here? Everly thought. This individual was going to counsel her on how to get a job? Everly wished she could tell what the other applicants in the room thought of this "fashion statement."

"I'm Angel Barton," the unkempt creature said.

It figures, Everly thought.

"Just follow me to my office."

They walked down a corridor and entered a brightly lit room crowded with ugly metal desks, computer terminals, rusted filing cabinets, and endless piles of paper. There must have been about fifteen or twenty placement experts in there, who were either talking to job candidates or on the phone. The noise level was just barely tolerable.

Everly wondered how these people could get anything accomplished in such cramped, noisy quarters.

"I'm right over there," Angel said, guiding Everly to her paper-strewn desk. Anticipating criticism, she added, "At least I have a window."

"I guess it's better than nothing," Everly said, trying to sound amiable as she looked at the dilapidated brick wall that dominated the view.

"It's still a window," Angel said.

Everly just smiled and said nothing more while this Angel character looked over her papers.

"Great typing," Angel said. "Do you mind a lot of typing? I've got lots of openings for good typists."

"I was here about the architect assistant job," Everly said. "The one that pays thirty-five."

"Oh, that," Angel said. "Sorry—we've already filled that."

"But this was in the classifieds yesterday," Everly said. "It's only Monday, and when I called this morning to make this appointment, I specifically mentioned that job. No one said anything to me about it no longer being available."

"Well, sometimes our receptionist doesn't know what she's talking about," Angel said.

She's not the only one, Everly thought.

"She shouldn't have said that," Angel continued. "But don't worry. With your skills, you'll find something soon."

She stopped a moment and started looking through a pile of five-by-seven index cards. "These are the openings I have," she explained. "Let's see—oh, how are you at steno?"

"Never took it," Everly said.

"How about fast longhand?"

"I guess I could manage."

She thought back to the days when she was an intern at the local cable news station in Indianapolis. There were many times—before fax machines were the norm—when a frantic writer would call in a script over the phone while Everly sat at a typewriter, her fingers flying over the keys as quickly as the words came. Then she'd run into the control room down the hall and hand the director the script while someone else ran into the studio and gave a copy of it to the newscaster. There'd been a lot of close calls, but Everly had never lost a story.

She wondered how little miss darling Angel would have handled the pressure. But then she'd probably have ended up sleeping with the producer, so it wouldn't have mattered.

"I can probably write fast enough," Everly said.

"Oh—I got two lawyers on Wall Street who need a secretary. They kind of prefer steno, but maybe you could fake it for a while. How do you feel about Wall Street? There's lots of men down there, you know."

Oh, sure, Everly thought. Lots of men—married men. "I don't think I could fake shorthand," she said.

"Think about it," Angel said. "In fact, there's a couple 900-type phone numbers you can call—twenty-four hours a day. They have dictation tapes with different speeds, and you can practice and build up your skills."

"Are they expensive? Some of those 900 numbers are a dollar a minute."

"I gotta tell you, I have no idea," Angel said, shrugging her shoulders. "But if you can build up some speed, the salaries are really terrific."

And since you get a percentage of my annual salary, you could give a flying leap whether I've got the right skills, Everly thought. "Maybe I should give it a try," she said.

Angel's phone rang and she picked it up. "Angel Barton," she said. "Connie? Yeah—just got back yesterday. Wait a second." She put her hand over the receiver. "This will take just a minute," she said to Everly. "I was on vacation last week—Club Med."

Perfect, Everly thought, careful to adjust the camera in her bag. Now we can really see what some of these so-called placement experts are all about. "No problem," she said.

"No, I didn't *do* anything," Angel said into the phone, laughing. "But I *could* have! It was so fantastic! What? How the hell do I know . . . I mean, I hope I'll see some of these guys again. A lot of 'em are from around here."

After about five minutes, Everly pointedly looked at her watch.

Angel got the hint, because she suddenly said, "Listen—let's meet for a drink after work. I got someone here . . . Yeah. Okay. See ya."

"I had so much fun last week," she said to Everly. "It's kinda hard to get back into job mode. Let's see now."

Again she flipped through her cards. "Can you work for more than one person?"

"It depends," Everly said. "How many?"

"It'll either be two or three. Maybe you should check them out and see what kind of vibes you get," Angel said.

"No, I'd really prefer working for just one person."

"You should be more flexible," Angel said, sounding pompous.

Everly wanted to strangle her. "Perhaps," she said, trying to keep her voice neutral. "But surely you understand how hectic it would be to have more than one boss—you have to deal with more than one deadline."

Just like *Morning*, she thought. She wondered how Angel would react when she saw herself on television. Most likely she'd love it, even if she came across on-camera as a sleazy jerk.

The beauty of it was that someone like Angel would probably never even notice.

NINETEEN

The studio lights were a lot hotter and brighter than Everly had remembered. Or maybe everything was more exaggerated in a New York City network studio compared to what she was used to in the Midwest.

"*Two minutes!*" Corry Haggerty, the floor manager, yelled.

Almost as soon as Everly sat in the guest chair, a technician carefully clipped a tiny microphone to the collar of her dress.

"Are you all right?" Corah Washington asked, leaning over and gently patting Everly's knee.

"I'm fine," Everly responded, grateful for what seemed like genuine concern. She felt surprisingly relaxed. She'd even had a decent night's sleep. "Thanks for asking," she added. "It's a little strange to be back on this side of the camera, but I feel okay."

"I didn't know until a few days ago that you used to be on the air," Corah said. "Why the career change?"

"Long story," Everly said. "But it was nothing like this

place. I've learned more about live television in the last six months than I ever learned in my first nine years in the business."

"*Minute thirty!*" Haggerty said.

"Quiet on the set!" Nigel's voice rumbled over the studio amplification system.

Everly was surprised to hear his voice, since she knew that it was rare for him to speak from the control booth like this.

"Now just remember, ladies, this is a quickie," Nigel said. "Corah intros, Everly sets up the tape, and if you behave and stay on schedule, there's time for some follow-up Q and A—about twenty seconds. A veritable lifetime! So let's not blow the timing on this, my lovelies."

"*One minute to air!*"

Everly sensed a slight jump in her pulse rate. Relax, just relax. She reminded herself that this was only a four-minute spot—not a half hour.

Television news was such a unique animal. For starters, you were in a relatively cozy setting. No matter how large the studio, the immediate broadcast area was always warmly drenched in light, surrounded by a small phalanx of equipment—each manned by an individual who had almost as much at stake in the outcome of what went on the air as the people on camera. And then there were the folks in the control room—the Greek chorus, who were often the toughest critics.

One of the nice things about *Morning* was that the staff and studio crews had a reputation for being family. Maybe it was something about the ungodly hours that brought people together; most of the time, it was as if you had your own little cheering section every time you did something challenging.

So here you were in what appeared to be intimate surroundings, yet the end product was going out to millions of strangers—some watching intensely, most half hearing the show as they got ready to face another day. You could be speaking to millions or to no one. Of course, nothing in a studio environment could ever give you an indication if what you were saying was hitting your intended target of viewers.

Ironically, whenever you looked directly into the camera, the sacred rule was to imagine that you were talking only to your best friend. You were supposed to ignore the potential millions out there.

Everly took a few deep breaths, careful to exhale slowly.

"Break a leg, Everly!"

Everly looked over to her left and saw Beryl leaning against the wall.

"You're going to be really great!" her friend added.

Everly managed to give her a confident smile. She'd known Beryl was going to come in early, but had assumed she'd watch the spot from the greenroom. She was grateful that Beryl had come into the studio.

"*Thirty seconds!*" Corry got into position next to one of the cameras. "We're going to open on Camera Two, Corah."

"Right," she answered. "This is going to be a great setup for the interview," she said to Everly. "You really did a terrific job with this story." Corah then looked at herself on-camera. "Oh, Lordie, Lord," she said. "Makeup!" she yelled. "*Now!*"

"Makeup!" Corry yelled into his headset.

Elizabeth Nelson, the show's makeup expert, came running in with a huge powder puff. She hurried over to Corah and patted her face lightly.

"Get rid of this damned shine," Corah said, watching herself in one of the studio monitors. "Much better."

"*Fifteen!*"

Everly clenched the sides of her chair. "Is this necklace all right?" she asked Corah. It was a long, thick gold chain that had been her trademark from the first day she went on the air in Indianapolis.

"It's fine," Corah said. "Now don't you worry. Everything will be fine."

"*Quiet on the set!*" Corry yelled. "Here we go, now. Five! Four! Three! Two!" and then he slashed the air with his arm and pointed at Corah.

"Good morning," she said. "We're back with an investigative piece on the job market. Unemployment is at an all-time high, and while many placement agencies do a good job, there are some unscrupulous companies out there taking advantage of people who are looking for full-time work.

"Joining us this morning is staff segment producer Everly Dalton who did some behind-the-scenes work for us. Good morning, Everly."

"Good morning, Corah. We decided to check out some of these agencies ourselves. Some of these places were downright scams. Untrained placement counselors are hustling to place as many people as possible in jobs—without any consideration of their skills. All that counts is their commission."

Was she making sense? Everly felt as if someone else was talking for her and that she was totally out of control. She had rehearsed everything in her mind again and again, but now that she was actually on the air, she had no idea if the words were coming out correctly. Corah was nodding encouragingly, so she must be all right. But it was hard for Everly to ignore the fact that Corry was behind her flashing time signals to the co-host. She hoped she wasn't running over.

"This is just one example of what we came across," Everly said, suddenly aware of the control room countdown to roll tape, which she could just barely hear from Corah's earpiece.

The tape started to roll. Everly looked over to the side and saw Beryl give her a thumbs-up sign. It was going well. She actually felt right at home.

This was where she belonged.

"Well done, Everly," Nigel said. "Much better than I expected, quite frankly. Much better."

The two of them were sitting in his office.

"But I don't want you to get your hopes up about more on-air work," Nigel continued. "I'm still battling with the damned 'suits' about our budget. The important thing is that we know what you can do. As Professor Higgins would say,

'By George, you've got it!' Right now, however, we have to focus our energies on the college remote coming up next week."

Everly felt a bit let down, but hid her feelings. "Of course," she said. "You have nothing to worry about—it's going to be a good remote. Are you going to be able to join us there?"

"Not sure. I'd *like* to be there, but we're in the penny-wise, pound-foolish state of things here at EBC, so who the hell knows? I've no doubt that the show will be in good hands with you and Reggie."

Everly was tempted to make a nasty remark about the associate producer, but she knew that in the long run, that would not be a good idea. Politics. No matter where you worked, you could never ignore politics. "Naturally," she replied. "I suppose we can manage without you, but it won't be the same."

"True, true," Nigel said. "Well, you did a fine job this morning. It was just smashing. Now before you start gloating, get back to work!"

Everly got up and walked out, just barely missing a head-on collision with Hank Forrest. "Sorry," she said.

"Yeah, you should be. We could've both ended up in traction, and I would have insisted on sharing hospital rooms. Then we could have spent weeks, maybe months, watching the soaps together. You really blew it, Everly."

"I'll make sure to crash into you the next time," she said.

"Hey, you know you were fabulous today."

"I expect the fan mail to be coming in in cartons," she said.

"Hey, no sarcasm. I mean it," Hank said. "Honest. Kerri Marks is probably pulling her hair out over this one."

"I don't know about that," Everly said. "Nigel made it sound as if only a neophyte would be right for this assignment."

"Yeah, but that was all a ploy to put Marks at ease. Everyone knows that. Come on now, she's one chicklette who doesn't have all her gears in place. I mean everyone has baggage, but she has steamer trunks!"

Everly laughed. "That's a great line. Can I steal it?"

"Sure. Everyone else does. I should charge for these brilliant *bon mots*. I could make a fortune!"

"And retire to Hawaii," she said.

"Nah—too many tourists. Some place remote."

"With no TVs?"

"You kidding? I'm going to become a professional couch potato. TV and movie videos—what a life."

"And if that won't make you go crazy, nothing will," Everly said.

"Nothing bad with that," Hank said. "Half the staff's already there. Especially with our fearless leader at the helm. Which reminds me—I have to see him about something."

"Having a problem?"

"Just a minor catastrophe. Some of the associate producers are messing up my segue stuff and it's driving me nuts. There's no quality control. You don't mess around with the script just because you want to get your ego out there. What bullshit!"

"But Corah and Glen do that all the time," Everly said.

"That's another pain in the ass, but this is different. I've been checking into the overnight script packets before they go to our beloved co-hosts, and there are certain particularly obnoxious staff members who consistently tamper with my stuff—and ruin it. I could care less about those wonderfully spontaneous on-air changes. There's nothing I can do about that. But when the scripts don't make sense to begin with, people are going to hold *me* responsible. I don't need that kind of horse manure. I've got enough of it to deal with—truckloads!"

"Well, good luck," Everly said.

"Yeah, well—now I got evidence. Luck has nothing to do with it." With that said, he shook his head and stormed into Nigel's office.

Everly passed the receptionist desk and noticed a huge gift basket. Probably payola for one of the associate producers, she thought. Curiosity compelled her to check and see who it was for. She gasped.

"It's for me!" she said.

"Must be somebody with a lot of bucks," the receptionist said, taking a break from filing her nails. "Those things start at around seventy-five. Who's it from?"

For someone who'd only been on the job for one day, this kid was awfully nosey.

"Excuse me, but I don't think we've ever been introduced," Everly said. "What's your name?"

"Katelyn. Katelyn Weston. And you?"

"Everly Dalton."

"Good name for a marquee," Katelyn said. "Anybody ever tell you that?"

Just about everyone in the world, Everly thought. "I've heard it before, Kate," she said.

"It's Kate*lyn*. I hate when people call me Kate. If I wanted to be called Kate, I'd tell you."

That was a quick change, Everly thought. What a shrew, she thought, immediately laughing when she recognized the connection with Shakespeare.

"What's so funny?" Katelyn asked.

"You know, if I were you I'd back off a little bit," Everly said. "Attitude is real important around here."

"Oh, really? Well, I'll just have to ask my dad about that. He happens to be a very important guy around this place."

Everly tried to place the name "Weston." Nothing came to mind. "And who might he be?"

"Harvey Markfield," Katelyn said.

Oh, no, Everly thought. Talk about opening your mouth to change feet.

"Weston is my stage name," Katelyn announced imperiously.

This was perfect, Everly thought, just what she needed. Maybe she could deflect the brat's anger by feigning an interest in her career. "You're an actress?" she asked.

"Yep. Got my union card and everything."

"So you're here to make some money for classes?"

"Right again. I figure this job is only for a couple of months and I can save some money—since I'm living at home. And then I can use it for some voice or movement classes. Dad set this up for me. There sure are a lot of nut cases around, huh?"

This was not a conversation Everly wanted any part of. "We have a good mixture," she said. She'd better warn Hank about who this girl was. She hoped he hadn't made any bad remarks about Markfield. This Katelyn character could really get him in trouble.

"So who sent this stuff?" Katelyn asked.

"Let's find out," Everly said. Nigel sometimes surprised the staff with gifts. She'd heard how he'd ordered a bottle of champagne for every staff member who'd worked around the clock when the Berlin Wall came down.

She struggled with the tightly sealed clear paper that surrounded the basket.

"Here—use these," Katelyn said, handing her a pair of scissors.

Everly cut back the paper and read the card.

"Oh, no," she said.

"Something wrong?"

"Ah—no. It's from one of my girlfriends," Everly said. She hurriedly grabbed the basket and ran toward her office, the note card clutched firmly in her hand.

"Great network debut," it said. "All my love forever, Jared."

TWENTY

"Mel Stone said you'd let me do anything I want."

"Excuse me?"

Everly looked up from the desk she'd borrowed from one of the classrooms and saw a rugged man wearing faded denim coveralls and a University of Michigan T-shirt.

She was so startled by his sudden presence and provocative greeting, that she was almost speechless—*almost*.

"What exactly are you talking about?" she asked.

"I always like a good opening line. I guess Mel Stone didn't tell you I was coming over. I'm Paul Slavin," he said, walking toward her and putting out his hand.

"Everly Dalton," she said as she shook it.

"I know," he said.

"Right," she said, embarrassed. Why did good-looking men unnerve her so? "Now what did Mel tell you? And why are you here?"

She was going to have a word with her dear director. How the hell was she supposed to coordinate this production if she didn't know what was going on?

"I'm building a scaffold for one of the cameras, and I'm also putting together the home-base platform. That Mel Stone is a real character, isn't he? Anyway, he said you'd know where everything is supposed to go and that you'd gotten clearance from the university for me to put up this stuff."

"Right—uh, did he really?"

It was hard to sound professional and at the same time appear unfazed by Slavin. She figured he was somewhere in his thirties; he was at least six feet tall and had what she assumed was prematurely gray hair. It gave a sophisticated touch to someone she knew was not an ordinary blue-collar laborer.

It was unfair to try to label him so quickly, but that was an inherent part of the TV news business. One usually didn't have time for anything but snap judgments about people.

And Everly's first impressions were usually correct, Jared Kammer being the one blatant exception.

"Um, Miss Dalton? Excuse me."

Alfred Foley, one of the volunteer students the university had rounded up for the show, ran over to her desk. Since their special on-location phone system hadn't been hooked up yet, the only way to communicate between the control room truck and this makeshift office was by using runners.

"Yes, Alfred."

"Um, well, Mr. Stone said he changed his mind. He doesn't want to go to band practice today. He wants them on the set at six-thirty tomorrow morning."

"But what does he want them to do when they get there? Square dance?"

"The *marching* band?" Paul asked.

"Yes—," she said.

"Where are they going to be marching at six-thirty in the morning?"

"Um, he's in kind of a rush, Miss Dalton," Alfred said. "Can I go back now?"

"Mel is always in a rush. Try not to let him get to you, Alfred. Remind him that the reason I arranged for him to go to the practice was because he needs to decide *ahead* of time what he'll want them to do for the camera rehearsal. Tell him he has to be there."

Alfred looked as if she'd told him to kick Mel in the pants. "You think *I* should tell him?" he said, registering sheer horror.

She'd forgotten what it must have been like for an inexperienced journalism student to be dealing with a network show—let alone a cantankerous, though brilliant, director. Mel had a knack for getting young people to do handstands and go through hoops for him.

The word "no" wasn't allowed in their vocabulary.

"I'll take care of it," she said. "But tell him I want his techies in here with the phone lines or we'll have no band and no show."

"Right, Miss Dalton," Alfred said, giving her a military salute before he ran out of the office.

"You're pretty important, Miss Dalton," Paul said.

She was about to make a sarcastic comment, but the amused look in his eyes stopped her. For a moment, Jared came to mind. He would have enjoyed a clever retort. But Paul was clearly a different kind of man. There was something gentle and warm about him. She wondered if he was being flirtatious. She cleared her throat nervously.

"And you're also just plain pretty," he added.

"I, uh, thank you," she said. She didn't need this now.

"Everly?" Reggie Graham walked in. He ignored Slavin and handed her a clipboard with a list of materials on it. "I need to have everything on that list by this afternoon. And then I'll need you in a half hour to go over the rundown."

Why did he have to sound so damned condescending? She wasn't one of his runners, for God's sake!

"I'm *sure* one of the interns can take care of this," she said, trying to keep the anger out of her voice. "This is Paul Slavin, by the way. He's helping us with the set. Reggie Graham is one of our associate producers."

Reggie gave Paul a quick nod and ignored his outstretched hand. "On this shoot, I'm the producer," he said.

And a supreme jerk, Everly thought.

"*I'm* building your set," Paul said.

"Then you better get to it," Reggie said.

"Only when I have the right stats. I don't do sloppy rush jobs."

"Neither do I," Reggie said.

Why was it that when certain men spoke to each other, it appeared that what they were *really* saying was "Mine's bigger than yours!" "No, *mine's* bigger." "*Mine's* bigger!"

Watching the two of them exchange words, Everly wouldn't have been surprised if Reggie had asked her to whip out a goddamned ruler!

"Hey! Slavin! Why isn't your butt out there on the Diag?" Mel Stone came gliding in. It always impressed Everly that someone of his girth could move so gracefully.

"I told him he should be getting to work," Reggie said.

Paul looked at him warily and turned to Mel. "This nice lady was going to show me where to set up," he said.

"Lady? Oh, you mean Everly," Mel said.

"Funny as a crutch, Mel," Everly said. "Why don't you take him out there? And by the way, I think you're making a mistake about the band."

"You get in touch with them yet?"

"With what? Smoke signals? Phones, Mel. We need some phones in here," Everly said.

"Those Telco guys still haven't shown up?" Mel said, all innocence. "I sent them over here hours ago."

"Don't lie to me, Mel," Everly said. "I'll bet you fifty bucks they're still in your little control truck."

"Be a sport, Everly. All right. I'll send 'em over," Mel said. "I promise. Let's go, Slavin. Good thing we're not paying you by the hour."

"I'll see you later, Miss Dalton," Paul said, giving her a salute.

"Of course," she said, playing along. "What time was that now?"

"Six o'clock. Lobby of the Campus Inn."

How did he know where they were staying? Or was that just a lucky guess.

"No can do," Reggie said. "We have a production meeting at six-thirty."

"We do?" said Mel. "I'm going to have to be late, good buddy."

"It's just for Everly and me," Reggie said.

This was the first she'd heard of it. "I see," she said. "How long will it last?"

"I'll meet you at eight-thirty," Paul said, before Reggie could respond. "In my book," he continued, "any meeting that lasts more than two hours is totally worthless."

"Perfect," Everly said. "Eight-thirty."

Reggie said nothing, but he glared at Everly.

It was going to be a long day.

"Oh, God. There are no limousines available tomorrow." Leon Posner looked as if he were about to cry.

It was four-thirty in the afternoon, and Leon had just learned that Glen Korbett was coming out a day early—with his girlfriend.

"Just send a decent car for him. Glen will understand," Everly said, trying to sound convincing.

"Not when he's with Yvonne."

"Loosen up, Leon," Mel said, in between bites of a roast beef sandwich. Dinner was only a few hours away, but food was a full-time habit with him. "Send over a red carpet, some cheerleaders, a brass band—he'll never know the difference."

"Right. And who's going to pay for that?"

"Use your head, man," Mel said. "This campus reeks with volunteers! Hell, just tell 'em they get to meet Korbett and his floozie of the week, and you'll have people crawling out of the woodwork."

"Not everyone has your gift of motivating people," Everly said.

"Gift, schmift," Mel said. "You just gotta give these kidlets incentive. Simple."

"Which reminds me," Leon said. "Is someone keeping track of the interns' hours? We have to make sure we're not overworking anyone."

"Overworking?" Mel said. "Give me a break, pal. These kids got more energy than you and I put together, which I guess isn't saying much. Anyway, they thrive on hard work. And think of all the glamour they're rubbing elbows with."

"Present company excepted," Everly said.

"Speak for yourself," Mel said.

"This still doesn't solve my car problem," Leon said.

"Will a Cadillac or Lincoln Town Car do?" Everly asked.

"Sure—you got one?" Leon said.

"No, but I'm sure one of the rental companies do. I'll have Alfred call around—"

"Hold it!" Mel shrieked. "Alfred is *mine*. Get one of your other runners for this."

Everly had forgotten how territorial Mel was with his staff, even when they were just temporary help. "Fine," she said.

"Does anyone know were Reggie is?" Leon asked.

"Not at the moment. You might want to check the sororities."

"Reggie going Greek on us?" Mel asked. "He's probably checking to see if he can find anyone who knows Latin."

He and Leon snickered. Everly suddenly caught on and shook her head.

"You guys don't have minds in the gutter—you have to step *up* to the gutter," she said.

"Yeah, but you love it," Mel said.

The phone rang.

"EBC," Everly said.

"Everly? It's Beryl."

"You sound awful. What's going on? Is Stephen all right?"

"He's fine—it's me. Markfield is on the rampage—cutting budgets and cutting people. We just had a staff meeting and Nigel said he was being forced to make some changes."

"He's always making changes. He hates status quo—"

"But this is really serious. He said he's going to have to fire some of us."

"If anyone's going to be out, it's me," Everly said, chilled by a sudden sense of doom. "I mean, I was the last one hired, you know? Last in, first out—"

"No, Everly. He said he'd fight to keep his segment producers but some of the specialty bookers would have to be let go."

"Does that include special projects?"

"Kerri? No chance. At least I don't *think* so."

"You're sure about this? What are you going to do?"

"I don't know. I mean, maybe in a way, with all the wedding plans I have to make, I'll be able to devote more time to it. Maybe it won't be so bad for me."

"What's going on, Dalton?" Mel asked, guzzling a can of diet soda while he tapped her arm. "World fall apart without us?"

Everly shooed him away with her free hand.

"Beryl, it's getting a little crazy around here, but I want to talk to you later. Are you going to be home tonight?"

"Probably at Stephen's."

"What did *he* say?"

"He said that maybe this was the best thing that could have happened,'cause I'll find something better. I don't know . . ."

"Well, don't start jumping to conclusions. And don't make any major decisions yet. How late can I call?"

"Midnight, I guess—either place."

"You can count on it," Everly said. "I'll talk to you later." She hung up the phone.

"What's the news, kid? What has our brilliant leader done now?" Mel asked.

"I heard you say something about staff cuts. What's going on?" Leon looked totally panic-stricken.

"Harvey Markfield is up to his cost-cutting tricks again. Sounds like there's going to be some pink slips going around."

"What the hell else do they want from us?" Mel asked. "Blood? They should start handing out razor blades instead of paychecks, so that we can die quick instead of this slow torture."

"You union guys are probably in the clear," Leon said.

"I wouldn't bet on it," Mel said. "Nothing's sacred in the news junk pile. It's the damned 'suits' again. They don't know shit about this business—"

"They're just full of it," Everly said.

"Touché, kid," Mel said.

"Oh, Lord, I just got a second mortgage, I have a kid in college—this is awful!" Leon said. "A nightmare."

"You don't know from nightmares, buddy," Mel said. "And what are you getting all pissy about? You're probably one of the few who's going to be sitting pretty when all the cuts are made. You're going to be under budget, for Chrissakes!"

Leon actually smiled. "You know, you're right. You're absolutely right!"

Everly was disgusted. "Can't you show a little compassion for some of the less fortunate on our staff?"

"Well, you won't be one of 'em. You're one of Nigel's pets," Mel said.

He couldn't be serious. Pet? "What makes you say that?"

"Oh, right—you don't see our fearless leader in the control room every day. Your spots are one of the few that he actually *watches*—even tells the control room to shut up so he can hear."

That was a nice surprise, but Everly's concern for Beryl evaporated her moment of triumph. "I didn't know that," she said. "But Beryl thinks she's going to be out—seems pretty sure of it."

"Who knows?" Mel said. "Maybe Nigel will keep folks on as vacation relief for a while. They might get screwed on benefits, but it's better than no paycheck at all. You gotta figure he'll do all he can. He may be loony tunes most of the time, but he *does* stick up for his people—you gotta give him that."

Reggie walked in, smiling about something. "Why so glum?" he said.

"You hear anything about pink slips?" Mel asked.

"*I'm* not getting fired," he said.

"How do you know?" Everly said.

"I just know," he said, clearly full of himself. "In fact,

Nigel wants my advice on who to cut." He looked pointedly at Everly. "Fancy that."

"I'm sure he's asking for advice from *all* of his associate producers," she said, struggling to control her emotions.

"Perhaps," Reggie said. "Anyway, I have to make a few calls and run some errands. See you back at the Campus Inn—my room—at six-thirty."

"Why don't we just meet here in the office?" Everly said. As soon as she'd spoken, she imagined Beryl saying, "Be real!"

"It's better for me if we meet in my room," Reggie said.

Not for her.

"Fine," she said, her voice full of resignation. "Just fine."

"It wasn't that bad now, was it?"

Paul Slavin was looking at her with such intense concern that she almost laughed.

They were sitting at a corner table in one of Ann Arbor's best restaurants, the Gandy Dancer. It was a renovated railroad station decorated by someone with a flair for turn-of-the-century. The place was replete with Tiffany lamps, copies of period mahogany tables and chairs, velvet wallpaper, and elaborate leaded windows.

Paul looked quite striking in a sports jacket and tie. It was as if he had taken on an entirely different persona from what Everly had seen in the office this afternoon. She liked the contrast but couldn't deny the attraction to both images.

"The meeting with Reggie? No, but I can't always expect him to keep his hands to himself," Everly said. "He has quite a reputation with the female portion of our staff—especially the younger ones."

"Want me to slug him for you? I despised him the minute he walked into the office."

"Reggie has a way of endearing himself to strangers," Everly said. "But at least he's harmless . . . and consistent."

"Yeah—always an idiot," Paul said. "So why did you make it so easy for me to get together with you tonight?"

She had to think a moment before she answered. She

wasn't ready to tell him about Jared, that she may have simply been looking for a diversion. She still hadn't made a definitive choice regarding her relationship with Jared. She'd chosen to ignore the gift basket he'd sent after the placement agency segment a few days ago, realizing that that was only a short-term solution. But that was all she'd been able to deal with at the time.

And now, here she was with Paul—a virtual stranger with whom she felt comfortable. Funny—if she'd met him in New York City, she probably would have launched a full-scale investigation before she'd have even considered sitting down in the same room with him. That was one of the nice things about Ann Arbor and the Midwest in general—people just seemed more grounded, more down to earth and trustworthy, more open.

"That's a good question," she said. "I guess for some reason I knew I could trust you—that you weren't some wierdo," she said. "And you didn't seem like another one of those glamour hounds I deal with in New York."

"You could probably write a book about *that*."

"No one would believe it. PR guys are the worst. They come on so sincere—quick with the expense account to wine and dine you, when you know perfectly well they're not spending time to get to know *you*, they're just interested in making a connection at a network show. And they all think they're so clever. It's a real joke. Of course I have to admit I was taken in a few times before I realized what was going on."

"I wouldn't think that would happen to you. You seem pretty street smart."

"Well, I wasn't really prepared for what New York had to offer. I mean, there was some of this stuff in Indianapolis—"

"Ah, but New York is the big leagues," Paul said.

"Right. There was this one PR guy who kept sending limos for me the first few times we met—usually for lunch. We went out to dinner only once—and that's when I finally realized what was going on. It was supposed to be an intimate dinner for just the two of us, and he ends up bringing his whole staff along because they all 'wanted to get to know me better.' What bullshit. I wanted to kill him. I should have."

"Did you ever book any of his clients?"

"Only one, because we were desperate. But he ended up being such a lousy guest that Nigel banned the entire agency from ever doing business with us again."

"Until they have a client you need."

"You don't know Nigel Elliot," Everly said. "Once he's made up his mind about something, he never budges."

"Is he really a genius like all the papers say?"

"Sometimes. He certainly is unique. But he's also very understanding."

"That's rare—especially in television."

"No kidding," Everly said. "I'd only been on staff for about a month when another PR guy pitched me a story about this computer service for home buyers. It could analyze a new home—you fed it all kinds of information—and it would let you know the most cost-effective, energy-efficient way to deal with the house's heating and electrical systems.

"Anyway, it sounded like a good consumer story, so I had this guy line up a couple of prospective home buyers for me. I pre-interviewed several couples, found the right one, and then we were all set to put something on tape.

"Since this was out in Seattle, I had our West Coast bureau chief oversee everything. Well, when he called me after it was in the can, he was having a fit! And this is usually a laid-back kind of guy.

"It turned out that not only was the PR guy there—with this somewhat shy, but articulate, couple—he'd dragged in a whole entourage—his staff, the client, their production people, *and* his own camera crew! Said they were going to make a 'news video' out of it. Can you imagine? Another crew? The sound men started fighting—almost broke some equipment. It's a miracle we got anything decent out of the spot. That poor couple. I was ready to strangle that guy."

"Would've done some good."

"Well, fortunately, the end product came out fine. But I

was worried about how Nigel would react when he heard from our West Coast guy. He finally heard the details—after the spot aired, of course—and he thought it was hilarious! He wanted to see the out-takes. Well, like I always say, if you want a little excitement, leave it to a company flunkie."

"Yeah, we can be a pretty lousy bunch."

For a moment, Everly was confused.

" '*We*?' What do you mean, '*we*?' "

Paul smiled. "You didn't think I'd only been a carpenter all my life, did you?"

"Oh, God—you're not serious!"

"It's the truth—public relations. Account exec extraordinaire. Scouts honor."

"And here I've been blathering away about how sleazy PR people are. Why did you let me go on so?"

"Because I happen to agree with you. Why do you think I'm plying the wood trade in Ann Arbor?"

"But still . . ."

Everly was horrified. Had she ever dealt with this guy over the phone? And told him where he could go?

"I used to work in Detroit—handled everything from Motown to pharmaceuticals and talking dolls. But forget it—I think it's funny. And I couldn't agree with you more."

"I feel so embarrassed."

"You shouldn't. You're not telling me anything I've never heard. I only made the change about two years ago. There are certain things I miss—the expense account, the incomparable high you get when you make a network placement or get one of the national magazines to do a good story. But the pressure, the deadlines—and the clients' demands—got to be too much.

"I've always liked doing things with my hands, so I decided it was time to change lifestyles. I got rid of the condominium I had in Southfield and I bought a house here in Ann Arbor—one of the old ones that needed fixing up. So here I am."

"Can we still be friends?" Everly asked.

Paul leaned over and patted her hand. "Maybe more than that," he said. "So, do you have any more great stories?"

"Your turn," she said. "Every time I open my mouth around you, it's just to change feet. Not a pretty sight."

"I didn't know you were a contortionist," he said. "But I'd like to find out."

"Let's order," Everly said.

"I'm not sure that what I want is on the menu," Paul said.

Oh, Lord. Not another smart ass like Jared Kammer.

"I don't see lobster anywhere," he added.

She looked up, sheepish. No, he was *not* another Jared Kammer.

This time, maybe she'd gotten lucky.

TWENTY-ONE

Rah-tah-tah-tah.

"Let's go blue!"

Rah-tah-tah-tah.

"Let's go blue!"

It was six forty-five in the morning. The wide steps of the Graduate Library were packed with the two hundred and twenty-three members of the renowned University of Michigan Marching Band.

"Is this fabulous, Mel, or what?" Everly shouted, even though *Morning*'s director was right next to her.

"Incredible!" he answered. "Hey, Winthrop!" he yelled into the headset that connected him to the Minicam operator. "You gotta haul ass if we're going to get the whole band in the opening pan shot!"

Winthrop Jones was from the network's Chicago bureau and was on loan to the show. He was known for his outstanding work with the hand held mini-camera. Not everyone had mastered the art of maintaining a steady camera shot without a tripod. Since Mel Stone was as much a choreographer as a director, he was especially demanding about who filled that particular slot.

Everly made a mental note to reward Phoenix King in some way the next time she was near the assignment desk.

"You guys are terrific!" Mel said to the band members when the song was over. "But you gotta promise me one thing. Ignore the camera. I know it's hard, but with all the televised games you guys play for, cameras should be old hat to you. Just pretend we're not here and do your thing. And you do it damn well, I gotta tell you."

Mel trundled over to Winthrop, a towering hulk of a guy who could have been a leading tackle in his college days.

Mel looked up at him and asked for his camera. "Let me show you what I want," he said.

"Right," Winthrop said. "You the boss, man."

"Everly! Cue the band!" Mel shouted.

She waited for him to get into position at one end of the steps. "Okay, people," she yelled through cupped hands. "At the count of three, 'The Victors,' " she said. "One, two . . . *three*!"

As the familiar college fight song filled the air, Mel ran down the line, focusing on the first row of band members. Everly looked at the portable television monitor hooked up to his camera and was impressed. The combination of camera angle and speed added an element of movement and excitement to the otherwise stationary band.

"That dude sure knows his stuff!" Winthrop yelled, watching along with her. "He's almost as good as Harry used to be!"

"Who's Harry?" Everly asked.

"You must be new," Winthrop said. "Harry S. Kowalsky—now *that* was talent—knew cameras inside and out. Pure genius! And an incredibly kind human being—not like most maniacs in that hot seat. I mean, like, we all know Mel means well, but he's sure one crazy character."

The two of them watched Mel running back and forth in front of the band, then up and down the steps as he focused in on individual instruments and faces. The television monitor was filled with brilliant combinations of movement and dramatic close-ups.

"Like I said, Winthrop, you gotta haul ass," Mel said when the song was over, breathing heavily as he approached them. "Guess I'm a little out of shape, huh?"

"That's putting it mildly," Everly said.

"You won't find no argument here," Winthrop said.

"Awright, awright. Don't rub it in. Anyway, you got the picture here, right, Winthrop? We gotta make this band look action-packed! They're so good, we're gonna kill our godforsaken outer-space theme music and use the band for all the music bridges."

"No theme music at all?" Everly asked. "Don't we have a legal obligation on that?"

"Screw 'em," Mel said. "This is a college show—so you need college music."

"Makes no difference to me," Winthrop said. "But this band sure will wake up your audience."

"Leon will have a fit if we get sued," Everly said.

"Yeah, but Nigel will love the attention," Mel said. "And Leon *loves* problems. If we didn't give him some bona fide disasters to work out, he'd invent 'em. He's that kinda guy. So now that that's settled, what can these guys give us for the ten to twenty second fillers?"

"I have a list of their songs here," Everly said, pulling out a file from the leather bag that held her portable office. "There's one song that's been around for ages—incredible drum arrangements—the kind you can feel in your gut. The percussion section has all these fantastic synchronized movements. Where the hell is it? Ah—here it is: 'Hawaiian War Chant.' "

"That's what Nigel does in the control room every morning," Mel said.

"How 'bout a run-through of that so that I can figure out some good camera shots?" Winthrop asked.

"Now you're talking," Mel said. "We'll be on the air in just forty-eight short hours, folks. No time to waste."

That was putting it mildly, Everly thought. Winthrop wasn't the only one who had to "haul ass."

* * *

"He's going to kill me," Leon said. "Absolute death."

"Very unlikely," Reggie said.

"Now what, Leon?" Everly asked.

She was exasperated. It was five o'clock, and she and Reggie were in the middle of figuring out how to close the show. He was going to book a discussion about outrageous college costs, while she wanted to focus on how more adults were going back to college, therefore ending the show on a note of hope, rather than on a financial downer. Reggie had said that if she could come up with enough solid proof about the new campus demographics, he'd let her use her idea.

This was not the best time to have to hold Leon Posner's hand, but there was no place to hide.

"I sent this student, Cameron Treister, to pick up Glen and Yvonne at the airport," Leon said, his voice shaky. "Rented a Lincoln Town Car, just like you suggested, Everly.

"Anyway, Glen just called from the hotel and said Cameron still hasn't brought their suitcases up and he should have been back an hour ago. Glen had sent Cameron off on some errand after dropping off Yvonne and him at the hotel. I guess they were in a real hurry to get up to their room—"

"I can imagine," Reggie said.

"Please—this isn't the time for your sordid mind to interfere here—"

Everly was tempted to make a snide remark about Reggie and all of his affairs, but she said nothing.

"Now, wait just one minute, Leon—," Reggie said.

"I'm sorry, I'm sorry! But you've got to hear this—I can't find Cameron! I've lost him!"

"What do you mean, you've lost him?" Reggie said. "He's probably looking for a place to park. Parking is as bad in Ann Arbor as it is in New York City."

"But you don't understand! He's been gone for over an hour and he has all of Yvonne and Glen's clothes—a fortune in wardrobe expenditures, and it's gone, all gone!"

"What do you think Cameron is going to do with Glen Korbett's clothes?" Everly said, trying to calm Reggie.

"Come on, now. He's a reliable kid. He's not going to go running off to some fence racket—"

"Who knows? Glen is scheduled to do a taped interview with the university president tonight, and he wants to change from his black suit to his navy cashmere sport jacket—*cashmere*!"

"Leon, get a hold of yourself," Reggie said. "It's just a jacket—it will turn up."

"My job—my whole life—on the line! All because of some stuck-up college kid! He's probably selling the clothes as souvenirs. Oh, God! What have I done!"

"Maybe he's doing something for Mel. Wasn't he working for Mel, too?"

"Oh, God—no! Don't tell Mel," Leon said. "He'll call Glen straightway and tell him."

Everly thought a moment. Leon had a point—Glen would be absolutely apoplectic if he knew that his wardrobe was missing. *Morning*'s co-host was something of a perfectionist when it came to his clothes. Only the best custom-made suits and shirts graced his body. He'd be so distracted about his damned clothes that he'd probably botch the interview, which she had to admit Reggie had gone through great pains to set up.

What to do?

"I'm sure Cameron will show up any minute," she said, stalling for time. If Leon had invested in some beepers for the runners, this never would have happened. She'd made the suggestion a few days ago, but he had quickly turned it down, blathering on about costs. It would have been cruel to remind him of her suggestion now, though it was tempting.

But then she remembered something.

"Leon, the first thing you should do is buy Glen a U. of M. sweatshirt. Tell him that the president is a no-suit, no-tie kind of guy and that we want to get right into the campus spirit, since the interview will run at the top of the show. Then call the president's office and let them know that we're going casual—that Glen likes to 'do as the Romans do.' And make sure to tell Glen that university sweatshirts are the latest fashion statement and that we know he'll fit right in with the young crowd."

"You think he'll believe that?" Leon asked.

"People usually believe whatever you tell them—if you say it confidently," Reggie said.

The king of B-S should know, Everly thought. "Right," she said. "And as for Cameron, there's no way that he could have gone very far."

"How do you know that?"

"Because he has to be back in time for a meeting at the hotel tonight. We're having Pizza Bob's delivered and we're going to talk through the rehearsal tomorrow. All the runners have to be there because that's the only time they can get their security credentials. No one's going to miss that meeting."

"Bless you, Everly. Bless you," Leon said, wiping his forehead with a handkerchief. "Let's just hope our man, Cameron, shows up."

"He'll definitely show up," she said.

"How can you be so certain?" he asked.

"Because I told all of our runners that anyone who works during airtime will get a *Morning* T-shirt and that they had to be picked up at the meeting."

"Did I authorize those shirts?"

She looked down at the papers in her hand and paused a moment. Even amidst a mini-disaster, one could always count on Leon to revert to his stubborn, parsimonious self. She wasn't sure which side of Leon was worse—the whining and puling complainer or the pompous penny-pincher.

"Of course you authorized them," she said with conviction, certain that she was lying.

"Uh, sure," Leon said. "That was a good idea I had," he added.

"Everything will work out just fine," Reggie said.

"Of course," Everly said.

"And I'm never wrong," Reggie said. "Right, folks?"

"Uh . . . Right," Leon said.

"Sure," Everly said.

If she or Leon had been Pinocchio, their noses would have extended at least a foot.

Six-thirty, and it was still light out. Everly took a deep breath and exhaled slowly. It was so peaceful at the Music School pond. Classes had ended about an hour ago and the grounds were deserted.

After all of the hubbub with Leon, not to mention Reggie's sickening ego, she needed to be alone. This was her first choice of escape.

She remembered what it was like to live up there on North Campus her freshman year. Most of the university's undergraduate housing was located on Central Campus. Everly had liked the idea of getting away from it all, preferring the vast wooded and, at the time, underdeveloped grounds of North Campus to the hustle and bustle that characterized the other, more conveniently located dorms.

Tonight's university bus ride had transported her back to her freshman year. It was hard to remember her exact feelings so long ago, but looking back, her four years in Ann Arbor seemed to have been filled with utter joy and exhilaration. It was difficult to believe that a good fourteen years had passed since that wonderfully innocent and hope-filled time.

Everly hugged her knees close as the evening chill pressed against her. She stared off in the distance, mesmerized by a family of ducks that had taken up residence at the far end of the pond.

"Don't move."

Everly looked up, startled.

It was Paul Slavin.

"I told you not to move," he said, joining her on the ground. "Don't look at me, look at the pond."

"Have you been following me or is this just a coincidence?" she asked, staring ahead but incredibly aware of his presence.

She was actually glad to see him there. She'd enjoyed their time together last night, but she had assumed that her tightly packed schedule would make it difficult to see him again.

"It's plain old serendipity," he said.

"I'm not buying," Everly said. "You followed me."

"The truth, my dear lady, is that you are trespassing on one of my most precious retreats."

He put his arm around her and, with his free hand, pulled her hair away from her face.

"There's something I've been wanting to do ever since I saw you in that classroom at Angell Hall," he whispered. He pulled her closer to him and gently kissed her on the soft spot behind her earlobe.

There had been no physical contact between them last night, so Everly had no idea what to expect.

She was astonished at the effect he had on her, yet she said nothing, afraid to break the mood and equally afraid to acknowledge the ache of passion stirring inside of her.

He kept kissing a small path on the side of her neck, his lips incredibly soft and pliant. She didn't move, but she was supremely aware of her own quickening pulse and shallow breathing. Time seemed to stop as she allowed herself to revel in the sheer intoxication of his lips, his touch.

Without a word, he tilted her face toward his and looked into her eyes. It was getting darker, but she could see a tender, almost protective, expression on his face. She wondered what he was thinking, and what he saw when he looked at her.

He inched closer to her and their lips finally met, at first tentative, gentle, as if they were delicately exploring each other's soul.

It felt so right to be with him here. She could feel herself relaxing, responding to the seductive pull of being kissed by someone who seemed to genuinely care about her. She didn't feel he was rushing her. He seemed to be saying with each exquisite kiss that there was plenty of time, that infinite pleasure could be gleaned from this simple yet passionate act.

What had begun as a faint stirring of emotions avalanched into a sudden rush of feelings. Everly stopped herself and pulled back. Not now, she thought, not now.

"What's wrong?" Paul said. "Is this news person watching the clock?"

"You're right. I have a meeting to get to."

"What time?"

"Uh, I have to be back at the Campus Inn by 7:45."

Paul took her left hand and glanced at her watch. "We have almost a whole hour," he said. "An eternity." He moved toward her again, and she pushed him away.

"What?" he said, clearly annoyed.

"I, you don't really know me that well. There's so much you don't—"

He touched her lips with his forefinger.

"Here's what I know," he said. "You're a very hard worker. You love what you do. Even though you're in a ridiculously high-pressured business, you haven't lost sight of your values—you know what's important. And you make people feel good. You calm them down when they need it, and you give them a good kick in the pants when they need that, too. Not only that, you know how to get the best out of them—whether they're a runner or a producer, or even a carpenter."

"But you don't—"

"I know there's more, even though we didn't get into much private life stuff last night. You know why I left PR and why I'm here. And I know you're heading back to an on-air career. But I don't know who your friends are or what kind of love life you have, or what it *really* feels like, inside, to be on the brink of making a huge success out of your professional life and yet still be able to handle a personal one.

"Just looking at you, I know you've been hurt. We all get hurt, but you're a survivor. I don't need to know anything else. All I care about is that you're one unique lady. There aren't too many of you around, and I'm not going to let you disappear. There's something special happening here, and I'll be damned if I'm going to stop it or ignore it and let it slip away. I know you're feeling some of the same things I feel. Am I right?"

Everly said nothing. Her mouth felt dry, and all she could

hear was the sound of her heart pounding. She turned away, startled by the quick tears that came to her eyes. She cleared her throat a few times, struggling to maintain control.

This was crazy. Why was she making this so difficult for herself? Hadn't she closed the door on Jared? That's what she'd thought, but he still must have had a hold on her. She didn't know what to say.

"Are you all right?" he asked. "This is not supposed to be Chinese torture or anything. But I have to know what you're thinking."

"You're a very special man, Paul. But there's a lot of, you know, baggage, that I'm trying to deal with, and I just don't know if this is the right time for me—I mean, we've only just met . . ."

"I can be patient," he said. "If you need to work things out, fine. I don't need to know the details. You have to understand that I'm not going away, but I'm not going to beat my head against a wall either. No mixed signals. Can you promise me that?"

"Yes," she said.

"Good." He stood up and offered her his hands to help her get up from the ground. "Slavin chauffeur at your service," he said. "Time to get you back to Main Campus and all those hotshots you work with."

"Are you going to be around tomorrow?" Everly asked as they walked toward his car.

"Most of my work is done. Are you going to have any free time?"

"Probably not," she said. "But I'll make sure you have a pass to sit in the audience when we go live."

"That's a date, lady," he said. "Come here, you," he added, pulling her to him before he opened the car door.

He lifted her face and gave her one last lingering kiss, a kiss resonant with possibility and significance.

Everly looked up at him as he pulled away and opened the door for her. For someone she'd only known for two days, he had an amazing effect on her. It was wonderful.

Why, then, did she still feel confused?

TWENTY-TWO

"Everly! I've lost them! I can't find them! What are we going to do? I have no idea where they went, they checked out of the hotel—this is impossible!"

It seemed that Leon had been having catastrophes ever since the moment he arrived in Ann Arbor, but Everly had to admit that right now, he truly looked deranged. He was sweating. His hair was disheveled, and he looked as if he'd been up for twenty-four hours, which was probably the case.

She'd never seen such utter panic before.

"Calm down, Leon," she said. "Just calm down. I have no idea what you're talking about. Get a grip on yourself."

They were in Mason Hall, in a ground floor classroom that had been transformed into a makeshift greenroom. Chairs and desks had been replaced by two worn sofas and a set of pathetic velvet loveseats. These were placed around a low coffee table, on the end of which sat a television monitor that carried the network feed.

There were also two long tables against the wall—one with several coffee urns and a tray of doughnuts on it, the other serving as a sign-in desk manned by the hapless Cameron.

Leon had banned him from the set, even though Glen and Yvonne's belongings had been retrieved. In Cameron's haste to do Glen's errands and then make it to the staff meeting on time, he'd simply forgotten that the precious suitcases were in his trunk.

"I can't find Glen! He's due here in fifteen minutes for a sound and light check!"

Everly glanced over at Cameron and then pulled Leon to the opposite side of the room.

"Keep it down," she said. "We don't want this to get around. Didn't you send a driver for him?"

"Of course. The driver just called. He said that Glen and Yvonne checked out of the hotel last night. I've called every hotel in the phone book—no Glen Korbett!"

Leon's panic was infectious, but Everly wanted no part of it. How could they have lost their co-host? It wasn't like Glen to be irresponsible. Maybe he'd just overslept. Whatever, they had to find him fast.

"What's Yvonne's last name?" she asked.

"What? How the hell should I know?" Leon said. "Who cares what her last name is?"

"Uh, it's Shamoon," Cameron said quietly from across the room.

Leon and Everly looked at him.

"Sorry, I could hear what you were saying," he said, turning bright red.

"How do you know that's her last name?" Everly asked.

"It was on her luggage tag," Cameron said, sounding more confident.

"Good work," Every said. "Call every major hotel in the area—there can't be more than five or six—and ask for Yvonne Shamoon."

"What should I say when I find her?" Cameron asked.

Ask her if Glen is any good in bed, Everly thought. "Just hand me the phone when you find her," she said. "I'll deal with it."

"I hope you're right, Everly," Leon said.

"Greetings, my lovelies!" Nigel Elliot came bounding in. "So here we are, all ripe and ready to go. Corah's already in the makeup trailer—no surprise. Oh, and thanks for the limo, Leon. Amazing that you actually acknowledge how important your executive producer is to this marvelous program. I did expect some cheerleaders, however."

"They were at practice," Leon said, giving Everly a look of terror.

She could imagine what he was thinking. It would not be a good idea to admit to Nigel that they had no idea where Glen was, with only thirty minutes to air.

"I was not serious, my dear boy," Nigel said, shaking his head. Then he discovered Cameron. "What have we here?" Nigel asked. "Some good cheap labor?"

"Just a student intern," Leon said, his voice shaky.

"Do you need to take another look at the rundown?" Everly asked, hoping to divert Nigel's attention from what Cameron was doing. "Mel has it in the control truck."

"I know," Nigel said. "Actually, I just wanted to get some coffee. How does this stuff compare to Maria's?"

"Nothing could compare to that," Everly said. "Here, I'll get you a cup— black, right?"

"Right-oh," Nigel said. "Oh—we do have a little problem, by the way."

Here it comes, Everly thought.

Leon glanced at her, looking like a frightened rabbit in the claws of a lion.

"The bloody promotion department ran a contest for families in the Michigan-Illinois-Ohio area. It was all sort of last minute—someone in Harvey Markfield's office had what they called a brilliant idea! I suppose they'll do anything to boost our Midwest ratings. Anyway, a set of winners from each state was flown in, and we've seated them in the audience. After the show, they are all going to get their pictures taken with Glen and Corah.

"Imagine—they *paid* for this privilege—cost twenty-five dollars to enter, proceeds to go to each state's college scholarship fund."

"So what is the problem?" Leon asked, his voice low but whiney.

"Well, it appears we have one set of bloody racists as winners. It's most appalling. Everyone was supposed to be in one photo together with our lovely co-hosts. One of the families is black, however, and one of the other families refuses to pose with them."

"You're kidding!" Everly said. "You mean they'll pose with Corah but not with a black family? That doesn't make sense."

"Come now, my pretty," Nigel said. "There you go trying to be logical again. When does racism ever make sense?"

"Well, why did they bother entering the contest?"

"I'm glad you asked," Nigel said. "That's exactly what *I* asked Bethany Chandler, the sycophant in Markfield's office who came up with this marvelous idea. She said that the wording of the contest rules and awards was a bit vague—something nonspecific about getting your picture taken with members of the *Morning* cast and crew. There was nothing written to indicate that it would be one big picture with everyone all together, though I can't imagine that would have made a difference to these people."

"So what are we going to do?" Leon asked.

"I will give them a choice. Either they agree to pose with everyone or they're on the next flight out of Detroit Metro." Nigel smiled wickedly. "I just wanted to warn you about this. I'm sure there will be some press here. If there is a major dispute, all requests for comments should be directed to me, of course. I almost want these bigots to put up a big fight, because I so look forward to kicking them the bloody hell off the set."

"Uh, Miss Dalton?" It was Cameron. "They're ringing the room."

"Well, don't let me interfere here," Nigel said. "I'll be in the truck if you need me."

Everly ran to Cameron and took the phone out of his hand. It was still ringing. Come on, she thought. Answer the damn phone.

"Hello? Who is this?"

Everly recognized Yvonne's voice. It sounded as if she were trying to catch her breath. Great, Everly thought. Maybe she'd interrupted them in the proverbial heat of passion—an amusing thought.

"It's Everly Dalton from *Morning*. Is Glen with you? He's supposed to be on the set in five minutes."

"What? Glen—it's for you."

Again, the sound of heavy breathing. For all Everly knew, he might have just climaxed.

"Who is this?" Glen said, nearly out of breath.

"It's Everly. Do you know what time it is?"

"Oh my God! We never got our wake-up call."

But *something* certainly got up, Everly thought.

"I'll be right there," Glen said.

"Preferably with clothes on," Everly said.

"Mind your own business," he growled. "I'll be there in a jiffy."

"Fine," Everly said. She turned to Leon as she put the phone down. "All set—he'll be here as quickly as he can get here—probably about ten minutes."

She looked over at Cameron, who was smirking. "This is just between us," she said. "Not a word anywhere. The three of us are the only ones who know about this. If I see it in print or hear it broadcast anywhere, you'll never get a media job the rest of your life."

Cameron's expression suddenly changed. It was doubtful that Everly could put any muscle behind her threat, but she figured there was nothing to lose by trying intimidation.

"Right, Miss Dalton," Cameron said, clearly afraid. "Whatever you say."

She nodded her head and walked out of the room. That was one skill she'd recently developed that she was not particularly proud of—knowing how to pinpoint someone's vulnerabilities and then take advantage of them.

But in the "big time," that was the only way to succeed.

Everly went out to survey the audience. She tried to convince herself that she just wanted to see what kind of crowd had bothered to get up at such an ungodly hour to get a good seat for the show. But she really wanted to see if Paul had shown up.

Sure enough, there he was in the middle of the second row, near the home-base set he had built. He was busy reading a paper and didn't see her. Amazing how her mood changed after seeing him—from her usual on-location jitters to a sudden sense of confidence and excitement.

No one outside of the business had ever seen her in action before. Family and friends had watched her on television back in Indianapolis, but this was different. She felt special and hoped that there would be no major gaffs when the show went on the air.

Although *Morning*'s format didn't change much when they went on the road, being on location presented myriad challenges not normally confronted back at Studio 5K. For one thing, there was a live audience. In the show's thirty-eight years, only once had there been any difficulties. They'd gone on location in Los Angeles, and some recently fired actor streaked buck naked across the set—live, of course—much to the horror of the news division.

Since then, security had been tightened—not only on the road, but also when occasional outsiders came to the studio in New York.

Another difference when the show traveled was the special camaraderie that developed between staff members. Everyone had to work together more closely and intensely because there were fewer people handling the full-scale details involved with getting the show on the air. Jobs overlapped, the hours were long, and sometimes you even had the chance to party together—something not usually done back at home base, where people had their own private lives to occupy their time.

There was also the chance to work closely with local people—everyone from runners to free-lance crews, support staff, drivers, and caterers.

And even carpenters.

Everly decided to greet her new friend. Paul looked up just as she was approaching.

"Good morning, Miss Dalton," he said. The people

around him seemed to look at him with new respect because he was talking to someone wearing official *Morning* credentials pinned to her coat.

This was not exactly going to be a private moment.

"Hello, Paul. You must have gotten up early to get such a good seat," she said, trying not to sound too eager.

"Yeah, well, I have connections in high places," he said. "It's important to know the right people."

That sounded like something Jared would have said. For a moment, Everly felt anxious.

" 'Course I usually never care about that stuff," Paul added, as if he'd known what she was thinking. "When you're a carpenter, all you need to know is who hired you, what the job is, and what you're getting paid. That's enough involvement for me."

"Right," Everly said. "Well, I hope you enjoy the show."

"Ma'am? Excuse me, ma'am? Can I have your autograph?"

Everly turned to see a young man in his twenties with deathly pale skin, wearing thick glasses, a shabby down jacket, and grungy jeans. He also was wearing a winter hat, despite the warm temperature, with the fur-lined earflaps down, tied neatly under his chin. He had a dazed look in his eyes, as if it were difficult for him to focus.

"I'm not anyone famous," she said.

"You work with *Morning*?" he asked.

"Yes, but—"

"Then that's enough for me," he said, thrusting a pad and pen into her hands.

One of the local security guards suddenly appeared at her side.

"You okay?" he asked her.

"Just fine," she said, quickly writing her name.

"Thanks, ma'am," the young man said, walking backward a few steps and then turning to find his seat.

"Everything under control?" the guard asked.

"No problems," Everly said.

Paul stood up and motioned to her. She leaned in toward him. "What?" she asked.

"That hat spoke volumes about that kid, don't you think?"

Everly laughed. "You're right," she said.

"I pride myself on keen observations," he said.

"Must come in handy in your line of work," Everly said, wishing she could spend more time with him. "I have to get over to the control room," she said.

"See you after the show?"

"Probably not," she said, wistful. "We're booked on a ten o'clock flight out of Detroit Metro—"

"Miss Dalton!"

Everly turned to see a frantic Alfred Foley running toward her.

"There's an emergency! One of the guests canceled!"

"Just great," she said. "I have to run. Sorry!"

Paul looked hurt, or did she just imagine that?

There was no time to give it another thought.

"Ah, here's the savior of the day," Reggie said.

Everly wanted to shoot Mr. Sarcasm, but she simply ignored him and squeezed past the audio board to get closer to Nigel.

"What happened?" she said.

"We just got a phone call from Wayde Taggert's agent," Nigel said.

Wayde Taggert was one of Hollywood's most glamorous actors. He'd graduated years ago from the University of Michigan and had promised to do a live interview that morning from Burbank for part of their "famous alumni" segment. That his appearance coincided with the opening of his latest movie was not lost on Everly, ever aware of the machinations studios and stars went to to publicize their projects—at their convenience, of course.

"What's the problem?" she asked. Had Taggert been hitting the bottle again?

"The damned fool simply canceled—a bloody ten minutes before we were to go on the air," Nigel hissed, his voice sounding so malevolent it sent shivers down Everly's spine.

"Why?" she asked, feeling small and insignificant, and

scared. It seemed that Nigel was about to burst into a full-scale rage. She'd rather he start yelling and ranting than allow his frustration to build up.

He looked as if he were on the verge of having a stroke.

"Lester Kay," Reggie piped up, ever quick to point a finger.

"He really lost it this time," Mel said from the front control deck.

"What are you talking about?" Everly asked.

"Wayde Taggert's new movie is a flop," Nigel said. "They've been in production for years, had three different directors, more rotating editors than you could count on both hands, and the end product is a travesty!"

"So he doesn't want to talk about it?"

"Use your head," Reggie said. "Didn't you see the show yesterday?"

"Some of us were busy rehearsing," she said.

She could fight fire with fire.

"Lester broke one of my cardinal rules," Nigel said. "Never review a movie or Broadway show before the stars appear on our show. I knew I should have paid more attention to the show—but with Markfield's recent dictum, I've had other things on my mind. So Lester gave his damned commentary yesterday—panned it, not surprisingly."

"I thought you appreciated his honesty," she said.

"Not before we get one of the hottest stars in the business on our air," Nigel said. "He could have waited a blasted day or two for his damned review."

"Didn't Lester know we were booking Taggert on the show?"

"He should have," Reggie said.

"So now what?" Everly asked, knowing she was not going to like the answer.

"You have to rewrite the eight o'clock and eight-thirty open. Reggie has come through with a segment we can substitute at the end of the show."

"Oh, really?" she asked, suddenly suspicious. "What's that?"

"Well, it doesn't have the glamour of Wayde Taggert, but

at least it's something to go live with, and something that Corah can handle easily enough. It's about rising college costs and how prohibitive it's becoming for students to go on to higher education."

"I see," Everly said, wondering how responsible Reggie might have been for the Taggert mix-up, just to get his own idea on the air.

"I'll be typing in the greenroom," she added. Then she turned to Reggie. "Just make sure Corah gets your background information pronto, or did she get it last night?"

Reggie's pompous expression quickly faded, as he realized he'd been caught.

Bastard, Everly thought, wondering if she could get any mileage out of this.

TWENTY-THREE

"And thank you for flying American Airlines," the stewardess said, just as the plane from Detroit touched the ground.

"Good landing," Mel said, popping the last of Everly's cheese and crackers into his mouth.

"I don't know which is worse," Everly said, "landings or takeoffs."

"Me, I don't give a damn. Either it's your time to go or it isn't. Nothing you can do about it." He took a swig of beer.

"Mel, how can you drink beer when it's only eleven o'clock in the morning?"

"Not for me it ain't. I've been up since God knows when. It's evening as far as *this* body is concerned."

The plane had reached the gate, and Everly collected her belongings. Exhaustion hit hard, and she was grateful that Nigel had given her the rest of the day off. With the long hours she'd kept during her week in Ann Arbor, she wouldn't have been very productive in the office anyway.

It was difficult to keep her eyes open as she walked out of the plane and down the corridor attached to the terminal. Crowds were waiting outside the gate. She noticed a small gathering of uniformed drivers holding signs up. There were several for EBC. Leon would probably have a fit that so many private cars had been ordered. She was about to look for Nigel and ask if his driver could drop her off on the way to the office when she heard an unmistakable voice.

"*Everly!* Over here."

It was Jared.

Despite her fatigue, a jumble of strong emotions assaulted her. How the hell had he known when she was coming in?

She was almost tempted to ignore him, but running away would accomplish nothing. She had to deal with him. *Now*. She mumbled to Mel that she had a ride into the city and then walked over to Jared.

"You look tired, babe," he said, as if everything was copacetic. He gave her a quick peck on the cheek. "Gosh, it's good to see you."

"Does your wife know you're here?"

"Knock it off, Everly. I haven't seen you in days. I came in special from Chicago to pick you up. Can we just try not fighting for a change?"

That did it.

"Not fighting? Why shouldn't we fight? You're still married, right? Still got the ring on your finger? I don't even know why you're here." Her anger had revived her energy.

Good. She'd need it.

"Keep your voice down, Cupcake," Jared said. "I know we have to talk, but simmer down first. Here, let me take your bags. Jeez! What have you got in here, rocks?"

She was too upset to respond.

"The show looked great. I could see why you used to talk so much about your alma mater. Too bad we never got there together. Maybe someday."

By now they were headed for the short-term parking area.

"Do you mind walking?" he asked.

"No," she said, her voice taut and controlled.

"Great," he said. "Just follow me."

Everly said nothing. The silence became a barrier between them, but she knew that if she opened her mouth, she'd lose control.

She wanted to gather her thoughts and speak rationally. She realized that this had to be the last time she'd see Jared—for a long time. He wasn't going to change.

She had to force herself to understand that.

With sudden clarity, she saw that Jared was the kind of person who needed to be the center of everyone's life. It was ironic. For all this time she'd thought he was basically confident and sure of himself. But what she'd taken as self-assurance was all an act. He was more needy than most people would ever know.

It should have been no surprise that he still wanted her in his life—but only on his terms. She was someone who understood him, who probably knew more about him than he'd ever allowed anyone to know. Yet he feared making a full commitment to her—because that would have somehow empowered *her*. It was curious that they'd even gotten engaged. Now she wondered if he'd known a lot earlier about having to move to Chicago. But that didn't change what existed between them now.

The recent arrangement he'd concocted was absurd—having a wife who worshipped him and a girlfriend he could manipulate. She could see the pattern. Whenever he felt Everly was getting too close to him, he would always run back to his wife.

How could she have allowed herself to be so swept away by him? It hurt to realize that the qualities that characterized the uniqueness of their relationship were the very things that scared Jared. He once had reveled in their closeness, at least that's what she'd thought. He had even talked about the incredible ability they had to read each other's mind.

Still, he never fully revealed his feelings to her, because somehow that would admit weakness. Everly understood now that she had broken down too many barriers, knew she had enormous empathy with him. When it came to making a definitive choice to have her permanently in his life, however, Jared wouldn't allow himself that kind of vulnerability.

He didn't want that kind of life partner. He didn't want an equal, he wanted a subordinate. The only way he could handle Everly was to have her off to the side—at his convenience.

And that had almost been enough for her. Why else had she agreed to see him when he came back to New York? Yet deep down she must have known that her fantasy of getting married to him was simply that—a fantasy.

In the end, she would never be able to accept the kind of warped arrangement Jared wanted.

For the first time in her life, Everly realized that she truly deserved better. How dare he try to deprive her of that—of a healthy relationship that was meaningful and worthwhile, that had a real future.

Her anger turned to sadness, and then she felt numb.

"You're not saying much," Jared said, as he put her bags into the backseat of his car.

"Not much to say," she said quietly.

"You know, I just can't get over how terrific the show was today. You did a fantastic job, though I have to tell you that the last segment about college costs ended everything on kind of a negative note."

Amazing how he could pretend that everything was fine between them. It was as if they were back in Indianapolis, talking about the station's programming.

At another time she would have enjoyed telling him about Reggie and how his segment idea had gotten on the air. Jared would have loved to hear about the behind-the-scene politics. Of all the conversation topics they'd ever had, their work had always been the most stimulating.

Of course, she thought. Talking about work was safe.

"It was just one of those things," Everly said. "Not my decision."

Jared seemed to be waiting for her to go on with the details, but she remained silent. This chitchat was not easy for her. She certainly wasn't going to make it easy for him.

As the silence continued, Jared flipped on the radio. It was one of those "light music" stations that had sprung up over the last decade. Some of the tension between them dissipated, but not all of it.

As they got closer to the city, she decided to break the ice.

"We have to talk, Jared. We can't go on like this. I can't live in limbo. You're still married, and no matter what you say, I don't think that's going to change."

"But don't you want to give us another chance? What changed?"

"This is not the way to do it. This arrangement is not fair to me or your wife. If you're not happy with her, then get out of your marriage. That should have nothing to do with me. So it's best if we just don't see each other until you get your act together."

"But I still need you in my life. Can't we just—"

"No! Why don't you stop thinking of yourself for a change? I've got to get on with my life. I can't wait around for you. There's too much going on right now—"

"Is there someone else?"

"That's none of your business."

"Damn straight it is."

"Whether I have someone in my life or not is not the issue. You are still married. You've got to deal with that yourself."

"There *is* someone else, isn't there?"

Everly didn't want to fight.

"You're not listening," she said. "I'm not going to have anything to do with you now. And if your circumstances change, well, we'll see. In the meantime, I have to concentrate on my career. I already gave up a big opportunity once because of you, and I'm not going to let that happen again."

"Your career? Your career! Is that what this is all about? I didn't think you were that kind of person."

Suddenly he accelerated the car. She knew he was angry, but so was she. Yet she was determined to stay in control.

"You have some nerve talking down to me about wanting to better my career," she said evenly. "What do you think your marriage was all about? And don't talk to me about love. I'm not sure you even know what real love is. As for my career, it's as important to me as yours is to you. That's how it should be. Maybe you're threatened by my success—"

"Give me a break."

"No, Jared. I've given you enough breaks."

They were in front of her building now. He stopped the car.

"Don't bother getting out," she said. She opened the back door to his car and pulled out her bags.

"Good-bye, Jared."

She slammed the door.

God, that felt good.

She told herself not to look back. The expected flood of emotions didn't come.

She felt nothing.

"Morning, Miss Dalton," Phil Schutz greeted her and took her bags from her hand. She went over to her mailbox, got the mail, and walked over to the elevator, where Phil had left her bags.

"Oh, this is for you," he said, handing her something from the local florist.

"Thanks, Phil. Put it on the floor in here, okay?"

He looked disappointed. He probably wanted to know who had sent it. Knowing Jared, she was certain they were from him, and she didn't think she could continue to keep her feelings in check when she opened the card. Phil would have to get his grist for the gossip mill someplace else.

She struggled to get everything to her door in one trip and opened the lock.

She felt more exhausted than ever.

Okay. Time to look at the flowers.

She ripped off the wrapping paper and set the glass vase which held a dozen anemones on her foyer table. With trembling hands she opened the card.

Surprise, it said. *For the lady I can't get out of my mind. Always, Paul.*

Her heart nearly burst with relief.

"Do you believe this stuff?" Hank Forrest walked into Everly's office, holding a stack of paper. "Markfield must have nothing better to do than write goddamned memos all day. He's crazy!"

He sat down and shoved the material in front of Everly's face.

She smiled and took the papers from his hand. It was refreshing to see a friendly face after what she'd been through yesterday.

"Hi, there," she said. Strange, she noticed that her feelings for Hank had returned to being platonic. It was more comfortable that way. "Is this a way to greet someone who's been on the road for a week?" she added.

"You bet it is," he said. "Especially since I was canceled from the trip last minute. 'Suits' again—getting involved in our budgets, for which I'm sure we can thank our dear news president. I didn't think it was possible for him to make this place worse."

"It's not *that* bad, is it? I mean, Nigel is doing his best—"

"You haven't read your copies of this stuff, yet, right?"

"No. They're probably buried under here somewhere," Everly said, looking at the array of papers on her desk.

"Don't bother," Hank said. "Here, let me do the honors."

He riffled through the pile he had just put on her desk and pulled out one sheet of paper. "Here, this is a great one. You thought we had bureaucracy before? Catch this."

He cleared his throat and began reading in a strong, authoritarian voice: " 'And further, I want to announce the formation of the following special committees.' "

He lowered his voice and said, "The drum roll goes in here." She laughed and he continued.

" 'First, A Daily News Council which will oversee all news coverage and programming throughout the division, including radio as well as television. The council will meet every day, promptly at 10:00 A.M., and will replace the

Executive News meeting that was previously in place.

" 'Next, an Editorial Committee which will establish policy and direction on a weekly basis. This group will include all of the network news talent as well as top production management.' "

Everly had to interrupt.

"Does that mean Corah and Glen will be part of this thing?" She could just imagine the battle of the network egos.

"You catch on quick, young lady," Hank said.

"Can you imagine the face-off between Glen and the people on *Evening News Worldwide*? Not to mention Nigel."

"They're going to charge for admission to these meetings. That's how they're *really* going to raise money for the news division."

"Is there more?" Everly asked. What were they turning this place into?

"Just one more committee," Hank said. He returned to his stentorian tone. " 'And finally, we are forming the Operations Services Group. This committee will coordinate all technical and news operations services and will meet on a weekly basis at a time to be determined.' "

"Great. They'll probably put Phoenix King in there so that once a week our crew requests will get screwed up," Everly said. "Why are they doing this?"

"This isn't all," Hank said. "There's more here about major changes—domestic restructuring, accounting and information service changes, revised personnel practices, cost reductions, new expense account formats, story management, correspondent hiring, corporate allocations—"

"*Stop!*" Everly yelled.

"It's just like Nigel said—they're trying to kill us," Hank said. He scratched his beard a moment. "I don't know, Everly, but our days might be numbered here."

"Don't say that," she said. "It's bad enough that we're going to lose Beryl."

"Yeah. Tough break for that kid. But she'll bounce back. She's too good not to find something."

Everly realized that she hadn't spoken to her friend yet. She'd gone through the rest of yesterday in a kind of dazed torpor and gone to sleep around six-thirty. She'd slept a full twelve-and-a-half-hours.

"Is she in today?" Everly asked.

"I think so. Why don't you give her a buzz?"

Everly picked up the phone and dialed Beryl's interoffice number.

"Beryl Sharpes."

"Come on over," Everly said. "Hank and I are having a memo burning party."

"Welcome back! I'm on my other line, but I'll be right there."

Within minutes Beryl was at the door.

"Hi, people," she said.

Hank stood up. "I'm going to leave you two ladies alone. Much as I'd like to be a fly on the wall while you dish the dirt, I've actually got to get some work done."

"A likely story," Everly said. "You're probably typing up your résumé."

"With my union seniority?"

"But you just said we might not be around here—" Everly stopped, feeling embarrassed that Beryl was there.

Hank quickly stepped in.

"No chance," he said. "How could I stop being a thorn in Nigel's side? What would he do without me?"

Both women laughed.

When he left, Beryl shut the door and sat down. "So, how was it?" she asked. "The show sure looked good."

"I broke it off with Jared," Everly said.

"That's fantastic news! Was he in Ann Arbor?"

"No, at LaGuardia when we got in."

"You're kidding!" Beryl said. "How'd he know what flight?"

"I was going to ask you that."

"Be real!" Beryl said. "I wouldn't give him information like that. If anything I'd send him to Newark."

"Maybe he called the switchboard—or Jenny Spiegel," Everly said. She'd felt awkward accusing Beryl, but she'd mentioned her friend often enough to Jared that she wouldn't have been surprised if he'd concocted some clever way to get the arrival information out of her.

Jared had a gift for such things.

But she should have thought it through first before accusing her friend of such collusion.

"So what happened?" Beryl asked.

"Well, the bottom line is that I told him it was over. And I told him not get in touch with me until he got his act together."

"Well, then that's the last you'll hear from him," Beryl said.

"I know," Everly said. "I thought I'd feel something when it was all over, you know? But I felt nothing. It was strange. But enough about me. How are you doing?"

"Better than I expected," Beryl said. "I've gone on some interviews, and just like Stephen said, there is life after *Morning*."

"Not for me, there isn't," Everly said. "But I'm worried about all this stuff Markfield is doing."

"It's not going to affect you," Beryl said.

"Why is it that everyone but me seems to think I have a secure place here? Mel Stone said the same thing the other day—something about my being Nigel's 'pet.' Can you imagine? Nigel doesn't have pets, he has playmates—the sandbox kind, not the *Playboy* bunny types."

"Reggie has *those*," Beryl said. "Rumor has it he might be kicked off the show."

"You're kidding! Why?"

"Too many affairs. Would you believe it? I guess Kerri Marks expected to be with him in Ann Arbor because that was one of her special projects. When he told her not to come, she assumed it was because he'd lined up some extracurricular activity at the university."

"We all figured as much," Everly said.

"Well, I think she blabbed about his other affairs to some of the higher-ups she knows—"

"I can imagine how she developed *those* contacts," Everly said.

"Whatever. He's supposed to be out of EBC in two months."

"Couldn't have happened to a nicer guy," Everly said. "Oh, and speaking of guys, I actually met a decent human being in Ann Arbor."

"Great! What does he do? Professor?"

"You'll never guess," Everly said.

"Dean? Graduate student? Lawyer? Come on, this isn't fair."

"He's a carpenter," Everly said.

"Oh. Really? Well, that's great. Maybe he can redo my cabinets."

"Can you see a carpenter living in New York City—especially one who used to be in PR and gave up the rat race to live in a college town?"

"Oh, well, sure. I mean, stranger things have happened," Beryl said. "Wow! It must be serious if he's thinking of moving here. He'd certainly find plenty to do. All the yuppies have bought up brownstones and *somebody's* got to do the renovation work. When can I meet him?"

"I don't know. I mean, it's all too new. I just met him a few days ago, but he seems kind of special."

"Trust your instincts," Beryl said. "That's what you always say to me."

Everly's phone rang. "Saved," she said, picking it up. "Everly Dalton."

"Is this the woman with the dulcet tones?"

It was Paul.

"Well, hello. Yes, it is," Everly said. "Hang on a sec, okay?"

"Should I call back later?"

"No—it's fine. Be back in a second." She put him on hold. "It's him," she said. She couldn't believe how terrific his call made her feel.

"That's great," Beryl said. "I'll let you have some privacy. But call me the minute you get off the phone."

"Yessir!" Everly said. She punched the hold button and got back on the line.

"Well, this is a nice surprise," she said.

"Is this a good time?" he asked.

"Absolutely." Everly smiled.

His timing was perfect.

Everly, Paul, Hank, and Beryl stepped off the elevator into a private lobby. The entire room was done in different marbles. The floor had intricate inlaid designs in pastel colors, and the walls were deep green. Four floor-to-ceiling alabaster columns completed the effect.

Paul whistled. "This room alone is worth a fortune," he said. "I don't know much about marble and semiprecious stone, but some contractor made a killing here, I'm sure."

"This cost a million bucks?" Hank asked.

"Keep it down," Everly said.

"Loosen up," Hank said. "Who cares?"

It seemed to Everly that Hank had become increasingly more dour ever since he'd met Paul in the bar downstairs.

"Quiet, you two," Beryl said. "Stephen arranged for us to come here under his company name. We don't need to have any extra attention brought to us."

"I know, I know," Hank said. "And if the poor guy didn't have to work, he'd be here in this monkey suit instead of me."

"You happen to look very good in it," Everly said.

"What guy doesn't?" Hank asked.

Everly sighed. It was no use trying to get him out of his negative, sarcastic mood. She was about to knock on a large mahogany door when it was opened by a uniformed maid.

"Good evening," she said. "You can leave coats here," she pointed to a small room off to the left, "and the bar is in there." She pointed straight back.

"This is some place," Paul said, as the four of them walked through to the bar.

"Stephen said Patrick Gaudin spent a million to buy it and another million to decorate it," Beryl said, equally awed by their surroundings.

Patrick Gaudin was the president of DeCormier Records, a label associated with the top jazz and rhythm-and-blues artists in the world. It was the night before the Grammy awards, and he always threw a party in his home then—either in Santa Monica or New York, depending on which coast the awards show originated from.

Everly had thought this would be a good event to invite Paul to. He'd been calling her every day—usually more than once—and this was the first chance they'd gotten to see each other since Ann Arbor.

It was hard to believe that only ten days had gone by, because it had seemed an eternity.

"Let's check this place out," she said.

Gaudin lived on the penthouse floor of a well-known midtown hotel. The entire place was one huge square built around the building's elevator shaft. The rooms were long and narrow, almost entirely built of glass on the exterior walls. There were no room dividers, and the only doors to be found were for restrooms and closets. One area simply flowed into the next.

The view from each was spectacular.

"What do you think of the decor?" Everly asked the group.

"Looks like there was a going-out-of-business sale in leather," Hank said as they walked around.

He had a point. Leather chairs and sofas were everywhere. One section even had an enormous leather-covered coffee table.

"This is real practical," Hank said, pointing to it.

"Don't you just love it?" asked a young man in a navy tuxedo, who happened to be next to him.

"It's interesting," Everly quickly said. For all they knew, this could have been one of the host's sons.

"I'm one of the decorators," he gushed. "My partner and I have been living here more than in our own apartments! I mean, isn't this just incredible? We were working under *enormous* pressure—you can imagine—so that everything would be ready for tonight's soiree."

He fluttered around, pointing out different objets d'art on the back walls and on the dark wood, custom-made bookshelves.

"Isn't this piece just marvelous?" he asked, pointing to an ivory mask. "Just about all the accessories here are on consignment. I mean we're just not sure *which* ones we'll keep, you know? Mr. Gaudin *never* makes a decision until he lives with it for a while. Sometimes they stay; sometimes, poof! Just gone—like that," he said, snapping his fingers.

Which explains why he's had six wives, Everly thought.

"I'm so glad that you like it. This is the first time it's been open to the public!"

"You gonna start charging admission?" Hank asked.

"What?" the decorator looked puzzled for a moment. "Oh! A jokester. You are funny," he said, patting Hank on the shoulder, and then making a quick exit.

"Yeah. A laugh a minute," Hank said.

"Why don't we all get a drink," Everly said.

"What for?" Paul asked.

"Who asked you?" Hank said.

Everly couldn't believe Hank's hostility. Why was he acting this way? He couldn't have been jealous; he and Bernice were still seeing each other. In fact, he probably would have asked her here if Beryl had been able to get another ticket. Maybe that was why he was acting this way.

"You don't have to get liquor," she said to Paul. "I'm sure they have a selection of designer water." Paul had had so many two- and three-drink business lunches and dinners that alcohol was anathema in his new lifestyle.

"What do we have here, Mr. Goodie Two-Shoes?" Hank said.

Paul turned to him. "I don't know what your problem is," he said quietly. "Maybe you got up on the wrong side of bed or something. But I know you're an important friend of Everly's and she's important to me and I think, out of respect to her, we should try to get along."

Hank looked at him silently for a few minutes.

"Maybe you two should have a shoot-out at high noon," Beryl said.

Everyone laughed, which broke the tension.

Everly wanted to give her a hug.

"How about water guns from Nigel's office?" she said, getting into the spirit of her friend's remark.

"Or darts," Beryl said.

"Or they could shoot baskets," Everly said. "Nigel has quite an office," she explained to Paul.

"Sounds real high tech," he said.

"More like a playpen," Hank said, clearly warming up to one of his favorite subjects. "You gotta figure that most execs in the news business are frustrated two-year-olds who like having the newest and shiniest toy on the block. It's all games and whistles and egos to them."

"You should see the public relations world," Paul said. "That's where the real screwed up egos end up. I sure as hell don't miss that."

Everly was pleased that they were finally making an effort to get along. Hank's friendship was very important to her. And Paul, well, it was too early to tell, but he was certainly special. She sensed this was not the kind of evening he enjoyed. But this kind of socializing was an important part of her world, and part of why she liked this city—its glamour and excitement, the accelerated pace, the challenges. All of which she knew Paul had purposely chosen to get away from.

This was not going to be easy.

TWENTY-FOUR

"I've been celibate for a long time, you know," Paul said, sitting on the edge of Everly's bed.

It must have been close to two o'clock in the morning. The Grammy party had still been going strong when they left, but Everly had been eager to get home. She was both scared and excited by the notion that she and Paul would be going to bed together.

"How long?" she asked.

"Long enough," he said. "You?"

"Same," she said. "I, uh, well, you have nothing to worry about."

"I didn't think I did," Paul said. "Amazing how the world has changed since AIDS. The sexual revolution in the sixties and seventies was one extreme. The eighties and nineties have brought another."

"I bet you get lots of offers with that rugged worker's body of yours," she said.

"Don't know where I'd be if flirting was hazardous to your health," he said. "But believe it or not, one does get a little impatient with coeds. Never thought I'd think that way. But a difference of fifteen or twenty years is a bit much when you're talking to kids just barely out of their teens. And I never went for the ivory tower types when it came to choosing women."

He got up and pulled her next to him on the bed.

"I'd much rather be with a worldly-wise lady who can teach me a few things, at least I hope."

Everly could tell she was blushing. "I doubt that," she said. She almost felt like an inexperienced schoolgirl.

"But if you don't like those types, why are you in a college town?" she asked.

"I knew you were going to ask that. Why don't you ask me about my hair instead," he said, running his fingers through it. "You're the first woman I've been with who hasn't said anything about my fabulous gray hair. It's usually a great conversation piece."

"Too obvious," Everly said. "I like to be different."

"That's clear. Except when it comes to climbing the ol' ladder of success. I mean, it seems like you're on the inside track."

Something in the way he said that bothered her. "Is that a bad thing?" she asked.

"Hell, no," Paul said. "I just think you and I are at different stages of our lives. I mean, well, you're kind of on the way up, I'm on a plateau."

"You must really hate being here."

"Here—in your bedroom? I'm never leaving," he said.

"You know what I mean—in this city. If you thought Detroit was bad—"

"Hey, wait. Don't put words in my mouth." He took her hands in his and focused on playing with her fingers.

There was something charming about that.

"When you're in PR, every city is the same," he said. "Same pressure, same deadlines, same demands. It doesn't matter where you are. Is it a little more laid back in the Midwest? Maybe, but not much. A rat race is a rat race. Yet it is possible to go through life and not go crazy.

"I wanted to make a real change. Ann Arbor had all the

right elements. You went to school there; you know what I mean. It's a college town; it's probably one of the most liberal places in the state, maybe even in the country. There's enough variety when it comes to sports, the arts, you name it, it's there. The main thing is that the lifestyle isn't crazed. The hassles there are nothing compared to what you put up with in most major cities, except if you want to get 50-yard line seats at football games."

Listening to him, Everly could only worry. What was she doing, getting involved with someone who had left behind the kind of environment that she was thriving in? She'd come too far now in her career to turn back. She'd just left Indianapolis—he'd probably love it there. But for her, New York City was where she had to be. Especially now.

"Hey, why so sad, pretty lady?" he said. "We've talked enough, don't you think?"

She felt ridiculously shy. She nodded her head.

"Are you really ready for this, Everly?"

For a moment, she hesitated. She didn't want him to know how she'd been fantasizing about this moment since that time at the Music School Pond. And everything he'd just told her should have set off a warning bell. What kind of future could they have? Still, her desire for him was so fierce it was almost frightening.

"I'm ready," she said quietly.

He leaned over and whispered softly in her ear. "I'm going to take your clothes off," he said. "Will you let me do that?"

"Yes," she said, as wave upon wave of desire welled up within her.

"I'll be gentle," he said as he slowly unzipped the back of her dress.

He proceeded to remove every bit of clothing she wore, very methodically and carefully. It was as if he were moving in slow motion. Everly was about to speak when he shook his head and silenced her. "Just lie back and relax," he whispered.

With almost the same care he removed his own clothes.

Finally he was naked and he joined her on the bed.

He pulled her to him and kissed her, slowly, his lips lingering; then he gently thrust his tongue into her mouth, taking infinite care not to rush anything.

Everly sighed as her whole being was suffused with incredible heat. She couldn't believe the feelings he aroused.

And they were only kissing.

He moved his hand away from her shoulder and began stroking her body, stopping near her breasts, just barely having contact. With the faintest touch he was bringing her to realms of pleasure that she'd never before experienced.

God, she wanted him.

As if he read her mind, he pulled away from her and she looked into his eyes. There was such tenderness there, but also passion.

"We have plenty of time," he said. "I've been waiting for you for a long time, you know. I don't like rushing things. Everyone is like a microwave oven these days, you know. Rush here, rush there, get this now, hurry up, don't waste time. Well, I'm not a microwave. I'm more like an old-fashioned convection oven."

Everly smiled. "And you're a master chef, besides," she said.

He chuckled. "No, you are," he said.

This was one time in her life when she had to surrender to her emotions.

At least just this once.

"Coming back in a minute thirty!" Corry Haggerty yelled. Everly adjusted her notes and smiled at her guest, Dr. Michael Slater.

He was a pleasant-looking man, early fifties. He had that kind of sophisticated air one associated with a learned scholar—complete with trim beard and wire-rimmed glasses. Everly almost expected him to pull out a pipe to complete the collegiate image.

Slater was a trauma specialist who'd written a book about conditions in hospital emergency rooms across the country. Lester Kay had insisted Everly do the interview, and particularly after all the press her Limona story had gotten and the good job she'd done in Ann Arbor, Nigel was ready to give her a tryout on the show.

"I'm a little nervous," Dr. Slater said. "I've never done live TV before."

"Just talk to me and forget everything else," Everly said.

She wasn't going to tell him that she was probably ten times more anxious than he. She'd hardly slept the night before. In fact, for the entire two weeks prior to today, she'd had trouble getting to sleep.

Her guest's confession actually made her feel a bit better.

She wondered if Paul would be watching. He'd told her he would. They hadn't talked much since his visit three weeks ago. She'd told him she needed some time to think about any future they might have. A commuter relationship just didn't seem to be the right thing for her—especially now.

"In forty-five!" Corry yelled. "We're going to open on Camera Two, Everly."

"As long as you have my best angle."

In her earpiece, she heard some laughter from the control room. Then she heard Mel Stone. "All your angles are good, kiddo."

"I can't believe people really do this for a living," Dr. Slater said, gesturing around him.

"That's what everyone says about your profession, too," Everly said.

He laughed.

Good. She'd gotten him to loosen up a little.

"Ask the doc what turns him on," Mel said in her ear.

"Sure, that will be the first question," she said.

"What?" Dr. Slater asked.

"Oh, sorry." Everly felt the color rise in her cheeks. "My director's talking to me through this little earpiece. I was just answering him."

"Any problems?"

"None. Now, stop worrying. Try to have a good time," she said, hoping that she sounded convincing. "Why don't we both take a deep breath," she added.

They did and immediately burst out laughing when they exhaled at the exact same time.

"Fifteen!" Corry yelled.

"Do I look all right? Any spinach in my teeth?" Everly said.

Dr. Slater chuckled. "You certainly know how to make someone feel at home."

"And five, four, three, two—"

Everly watched Corry point to her. And then she heard herself talking, reading the TelePrompTer script as it rolled by on Camera Two.

She was on automatic pilot.

"Good morning. I'm Everly Dalton, special correspondent for *Morning*, and we have a very unusual guest with us today. Dr. Michael Slater is assigned to the trauma unit at Boston General Hospital, and like so many surgeons assigned to emergency care, he faces life-and-death decisions every day.

"We're going to show you some tape of a typical day for Dr. Slater so that you can get a sample of how emergency rooms are run."

As she spoke, she could faintly hear the assistant director's voice in her earpiece, giving time cues for the tape to roll.

Everything seemed to be on time and running smoothly.

Still, she felt on edge.

On a nearby monitor, she watched the tape to make sure there were no mistakes.

"Is that really me?" Dr. Slater asked, pointing to his image on the screen. "Looks like I gained ten pounds!"

"Cameras can do that sometimes," Everly said.

"Well, *you* certainly don't have a problem," he said, with an admiring glint in his eye.

"Ten seconds!" Corry yelled.

"Thanks," she said.

She'd forgotten how the men she'd interviewed back in Indianapolis sometimes came on to her. Part of the territory, she surmised. Flirtation was more prevalent for her male counterparts, and she was certain more of *them* took advantage of the situation than the women hosts did.

Perhaps that would change.

Progress.

"And five, four, three, two—" Again the sharp gesture to cue her in.

"Tell me, Dr. Slater, what is it like to be in this position every minute of the day?"

For a split second, he froze and just stared at her.

"I can imagine how intense it must be," she said, giving him an encouraging smile. She leaned forward and tapped his knee gently. "Please tell us about it," she said.

And prayed.

"You try not to think about it too much," he said, finally. But then he stopped, appearing to be stunned.

"Could you elaborate on that?" she said, giving him her brightest smile.

Come on, she thought. You were a veritable magpie when we talked on the phone. Don't freeze on me now.

"Well, you, uh, you learn pretty quickly what your priorities are," he said.

And then something must have clicked, because he kept talking.

"The bottom line is that you're trying to save people's lives. Since the crack epidemic, we've seen a lot more drug overdoses and a lot more violence on the streets, so it's real tough work. You know, if you want to understand what's happening in a city as far as its drug situation is concerned, visit any public hospital and you'll see a real nightmare."

Corry motioned that she had one minute left.

In television, sixty seconds could seem like either a finger snap or a lifetime.

She hoped Dr. Slater would keep his focus.

"Don't you sometimes feel overwhelmed?" she asked.

"It depends. When you work in a trauma center, you get used to the pace. I mean, well, there's actually something exciting about it. Your day is filled with what I call 'peak experiences.' That's when you know exactly what your priorities are, who needs attention first—and you know precisely what to do. It's a high, in some respects."

Corry gave her the sign for thirty seconds. Time to ask the last and best question—the one significant enough to raise the issue viewers would remember about the interview.

"Tell me this, Dr. Slater." She leaned in, as if to emphasize the intensity of what she was about to ask him. "A lot of people look upon doctors almost as gods, which isn't surprising, since it's one of the few professions that involves making life versus death decisions. How do you handle those times when you really have to make that decision?"

There was a split second of silence.

Don't stall on me now, she thought.

"There's only one thing to do then," Dr. Slater said.

"And what's that?"

"I pray. I simply pray."

A doctor praying. That was a notion that people would remember.

Corry gave her the wrap-up sign. Everly was right on schedule.

Success.

"Nice job," Glen said, "for a first time out."

Up yours, Everly thought. You try doing a compassionate interview.

"Thank you, Glen," she said, as she and her guest walked out of the studio. "It's always nice to get encouragement from a colleague. This is Dr. Slater—"

"Not now, Everly, I'm on the air in another minute," Glen said as he rushed past Dr. Slater into the studio.

"No ego problem there," she said to Dr. Slater. "Sorry about his being rude."

Dr. Slater laughed. "That's okay. I'm used to that. You don't know what large egos are until you get a few practicing members of the American Medical Association together."

"I can imagine," she said. "Thanks for coming. I appreciate your traveling to New York."

"Yes, well, I'm off to the shuttle. But what's the quickest way out of the studio area."

"That back exit." She pointed to a door down the hall. "Just take the elevator down to the first floor."

They said good-bye, and Everly walked in the other direction, down the corridor past the control room.

Nigel must have known she was coming, because he stuck his head out from the control room door.

"Well done, my lovely! Thought you were at the gates of hell when you got started, yes? Quite a nightmare, having a guest freeze up on you. But you were able to charm him out of it, my dear. Good show!"

"Thanks, Nigel. Your opinion means a lot to me."

Everly heard herself talking, but she felt strange. Where was the deep sense of fulfillment she expected? She knew she'd done a decent job. She expected to feel better about the whole thing.

"Way to go, Everly!"

Beryl came running out of the greenroom.

This was a real surprise.

"Beryl! What are you doing here! I thought you were going to tape it from home."

"Are you kidding? Not come in for this? I was biting my nails in the greenroom. Some scare at the beginning. Gosh, I don't know what I would have done."

"Once we got him jump-started, he was fine—thank goodness!"

"I never had any doubts. I knew you'd pull him out of it."

"I'm not sure what did it. I knew he hadn't done much live television before, but he'd been so articulate on the phone. I just assumed he'd be all right."

"Now you know how I feel when I book an author on the show and they clam up. Sometimes Nigel doesn't understand that people can be brilliant on the written page but real dolts when it comes to talking about something."

"He understands," Everly said. "He just likes giving you a hard time."

"Well, he won't be able to do that too much longer."

"Did you get a job?"

"Well, I've had two interviews—and it looks good. Of course, I'm superstitious, so I can't tell you anything about it."

"Truth?" Everly wasn't terribly fond of Beryl's superstitions, but she tried to go along with them.

"I don't want to jinx it, you know?"

"Okay."

"Why don't we get some coffee in the greenroom?" Beryl said.

"Why? Time for a little food poisoning? I'm racing so much from the interview, I don't think I need any coffee."

"Well, I do," Beryl said.

"Fine. I'll watch."

They walked around the corner into the greenroom.

Everly was stunned.

"Congratulations, pretty lady."

It was Paul.

"I don't believe this! When did you get in?"

"Last night," he said.

"Where did you stay?"

"He stayed at my place," Beryl said. "And don't get any ideas. I stayed at Stephen's."

"This is—I mean, I—I'm overwhelmed!" Everly said. Looking into their faces, she suddenly was suffused with utter joy.

It felt so right to have them both there with her. That they had made a special effort to be with her on such an important day meant more than she could ever tell them. As they walked down the corridor back to the office, Everly couldn't help but wonder what the future held for the three of them.

Beryl was off to a new job, and to marriage. Paul, well, there was a great deal to work out. It was not going to be easy, but she had to give it a chance.

They walked into the front part of the office, and Katelyn handed Everly a stack of messages.

"The ratings must have shot up because of you," Katelyn said. "The phone hasn't stopped ringing for you since you got off the air!"

Everly couldn't tell whether or not she was complaining.

"Let's get Hank and go out for breakfast," Beryl said.

"It's on me," Paul said, "unless we can convince Hank to treat."

"Not likely," Everly said.

The phone rang.

"*Morning*," Katelyn said. "Can I help you?" She stopped a moment and held her hand over the phone.

"It's for you, Everly," she called out. "A Jared Kammer—at least that's what it sounded like."

Paul looked at her quizzically. He had been told all about Jared. This call was as puzzling to her as it must have been to him.

"Tell him I'm not available," she said in a loud voice, certain that Jared could hear.

"And it's unlikely that I ever will be," she added.

She motioned to Paul and Beryl to follow her, and they headed down writer's row to Hank's office.

"Let's celebrate," Everly said.

It was about time.

About the Author

Hilary S. Kayle lives in Manhattan. *Players,* her second novel, was inspired by the experiences she had working on NBC's *Today* program. She is currently at work on her next novel.